# PETER TUFFREY

CW01497199

# THE FALL OF
# THE HOUSE OF
# GREASBY

SCELUS

Thanks to David Burrill for his support.

Back cover picture: *Welcoming the New Cemetarian: Johnny Champagne*

*The Fall of the House of Greasby* by Peter Tuffrey

First published in Great Britain in 2024 by Scelus

A CIP catalogue record for this title is available from the British Library

ISBN: 978-1-914227-78-3

Design by David Burrill

Scelus,
PO Box 1380, Bradford,
West Yorkshire, BD5 5FB

*For Tristram*

# Chapter 1

Walking towards Greasby Fine Art Gallery on Askworth High Street, I notice Nicola Greasby outside. In her early 30s, she's chatting with a scruffy-looking man.

'This is my new car.' She points excitedly at a gleaming red Ferrari. 'I paid thousands for the plate. ART 1. It took ages to find.'

Parked nearby is a Rolls-Royce belonging to her father, Frankie Greasby. Although married, Nicola has retained her maiden name.

'I've nicked some top designer clothes for you,' Scruffy states. He holds up a bulky black bin liner.

'Brilliant, I'll try them on inside.'

She twists and says sniffily to me: 'Dad's upstairs, if you want to see him.'

'Thanks.' I force a smile.

Shouldering open a stiff glass door, I stroll into the spacious gallery. A long front window provides a natural light source. Furniture in the room is minimal. There are two desks, chairs, and three low-level cushioned seats. A double-door in a back wall leads upstairs. Immediately captivating me is a fine display of 20th century paintings. About thirty hang on the walls.

Greasby Fine Art deals in Victorian, Pre-Raphaelite and Modern British Art in various media – oil paintings, watercolours, drawings, prints and sculptures. The company operates galleries on an upmarket street in London, as well as sites in other parts of the UK. Their client base stretches across the world. Established by Frankie Greasby during the late 1970s, the company is jointly run with daughter Nicola. Frankie is the managing director.

The Askworth Gallery is housed in a spacious Victorian building. I wend my way up a marble staircase to Frankie's office on the first floor. Moving along a corridor, I pass studios populated by picture restorers and technicians. Besides selling top quality art, the company offers a complete restoration service for oil paintings and works on paper.

In a studio are two restorers, Dick and Paul. Both in their early 70s, one is sipping a goblet of red wine, the other, a tumbler of whisky. Well-trained, brilliant artists and restorers, they're having a game of darts. An extremely rude pen-and-ink caricature of Nicola Greasby is used as the target.

Frankie's office door is ajar. With trousers and underpants down, he masturbates whilst peering out of the front window. A noted expert and art collector, Frankie is in his late 50s with short, greying blonde hair. He's extremely successful, wealthy and a little effeminate. We met five years ago when he invited me to an exhibition preview. I reciprocated by asking him to shows I organised as Keeper of Art at Askworth's City Museum & Art Gallery.

Frankie's excited cries swell but he's noticed me. 'Enter, Al. Don't mind me pulling one off. I like a wank after dinner. Always been fond of pleasuring myself. Ever since I was a kid. I'll not be too long.' The words slip out with a rounded and educated accent.

'What's the stimulation?' I throw a glance towards the window.

'Nothing in particular. A male or a female. My imagination runs wild. I drop a Viagra each day. I'm highly sexed. Join me if you like.'

'No, I'll sit this one out.'

'Do you wank, Al?'

'Now and then,' I lie.

'Pleased to hear it.'

I'm amused and think he must feel comfortable in my presence to discuss the merits of male masturbation. Over the years, we've discussed a whole range of subjects.

Frankie has a warm, friendly manner. 'It's good to wank. Something men rarely confess. One of my pals said he experienced bad luck after wanking. Stupid bastard.'

I manage a laugh.

Frankie ruminates: 'I always maintain that if a man has empty bollocks, he can cope much better with life's problems. Wanking allows you to fuck who you want in your hand. In the past, I've fucked Royalty and countless pop, film and TV stars.'

The bookshelves fixed round the room hold copies of *Art International*, *The Artist* and *Royal Academy Illustrated*. There are dozens of books on individual artists and boxes filled with exhibition catalogues. As a specialist, Frankie has often guested on art and antiques television programmes. He's served on national art committees, written articles for art magazines and lectured to a wide range of academic institutions. Besides that, he paints and draws competently.

I drop into a chair. Moments later, Frankie emits a loud groan. After grabbing tissues from a box, his clothes are readjusted. He's wearing a blue pinstripe suit, white shirt and a gold tie.

'It's good to see you, Al. I can't remember when you last popped in.'

'I was at your Christmas party.'

'Yes, that's right. You witnessed another outrageous spectacle by my wife.'

'I did.'

Frankie always offers limp handshakes. I hate men with that habit. In my opinion, a firm handshake imbues a feeling of true friendship and trust. Thankfully, after holding his dick, he doesn't offer to shake my hand.

'Have you seen Nicola on the way in?'

'Yes.'

'She's taken delivery of a new Ferrari today. To her, it's like having another fanny.'

'Has she bought it outright?'

'No, it's on lease. The company pays monthly.'

'I'm here to ask you a question.'

'Go ahead.'

'You once offered me a job here. Does that still stand?'

'Yes, of course,' he responds enthusiastically. 'There's always a job for somebody of your calibre. I don't know why it's taken you so long. The timing is perfect and fortuitous. Johnnie, our top researcher, has left us. Hoovering up too much cocaine. Even first thing in a morning. Johnnie's boyfriend made him leave before he lost it totally. In debt up to their ears. Probably still are.'

'Although I didn't know him well, he was always friendly.'

'What's happened with your job at the city's Museum & Art Gallery?'

'I've taken redundancy. Very soon, the Museum & Art Gallery building is closing down.'

Frankie stuffs a hand down his trousers. 'Excuse me rearranging my tackle. The Viagra tablet I took earlier is a bit more potent than usual. Isn't Viagra wonderful?'

I offer a blank expression.

'Are you a regular user?'

'No.'

'I acquire a number of tablets on prescription. Even more from a bent doctor. I ought to have shares in the local chemist.' He stands to expose himself. 'Look at this gentleman. Hard as a ramrod. I'm proud at raising a member like him. Sorry, Al, I interrupted your story. Please continue.'

'Very soon the Museum & Art Gallery building will be used to store the city's archives as well as the collections. A number of pictures are to be shoe-horned into Askworth's former Boys' School. Art was once displayed in five galleries. Now it'll be in two of the old classrooms. Building work has already started on the school's conversion. It's a joke.'

'That's madness. Absolute madness.' Frankie pulls out a small bag of cocaine and rolls up a fifty-pound note. After laying out a line, he soon makes it vanish. 'I like a little pick-me-up,' he sniffs. 'Want a toot?'

'No thanks.'

'Why the reduction in the Museum & Art Gallery's activities?'

'Local authority budgets have been squeezed for years. Councils are much-reduced organisations compared to 20 years ago. Over the last 12 months, Askworth Museum & Art Gallery was only open two days a week – and with few curatorial staff. My exhibition and purchase funds were non-existent.'

'What a major blow for the city.'

'When I first started, there was a staff of 30. This included natural history people, taxidermists, geologists, antiquity historians and archaeologists. The new building is to be run by four teachers. To most councillors, art is too self-indulgent. They hate Modern Art and say they want to cater for a wider and non-elitist audience.'

'Imbeciles. That's a great pity.'

'Councillors can't justify maintaining a museum and art gallery. Finances are required in other areas. To preserve my self-respect, I had no other option than leave. In the present climate, local authorities shouldn't be in control of museums and art galleries...'

'Enough. Enough. Don't upset yourself. Please. I understand your frustration and sadness. Put it behind you. You'll have much more job satisfaction working for us.'

Our conversation is interrupted by Frankie's mobile springing to life. 'I must take this call. It's from one of our London galleries. Hello? Oh, fuck, no. I'm not accepting that offer. Where today would you unearth another William Henry Hunt bird's nest picture? No, fuck off. Bye.'

He peers out of the window. 'It's only early Spring, but the good weather is already bringing out lots of scantily clad men and women. I'm almost ready for another wank. Remind me, Al, are you married? We've been friends for a while, only I don't know much about you.'

'I'm divorced. My six-year-old son, Alex, was killed in a road accident by a drunk and drugged-up driver. My wife went crazy and for no reason blamed me. She would attack me when I was asleep. There was no future for us. I've not been in a relationship since our divorce over 15 years ago.'

Frankie snorts more coke. 'I'm sure better days are ahead. What raises a stiffy for you?'

'Art.'

'Why the obsession?'

'It fascinates me. Jeff Nuttall, an art critic and performance artist, once said something profound: "Art stands outside society and prods it." I believe that's true. I don't drink, smoke, take drugs or gamble. I live frugally. What role will I have here?'

'You can be the company's principal officer or area manager, third in line to Nicola and myself. Moving between the galleries and helping wherever and whenever you can. How does that sound?'

'Brilliant.'

I'm relieved and pleased Frankie has faith in me. Otherwise, I don't know what I would've done. Comfortable financially, I have a pension, my own home and a car. But a job is necessary to keep my mind active. Leaving my old position a month ago, it's taken a while to pluck up courage to approach Frankie.

'Whatever salary you were on previously, I'll double it, and give you a bonus every month.'

'Thanks, Frankie.'

'There's a spare office along the corridor. We can fit you up with a desk and a computer.'

'Is the art market buoyant?'

'Yes, particularly with British weirdo artists like L.S. Lowry, Stanley Spencer and Edward Burra. We sold a dingy industrial scene by Lowry six months ago for five million. Poor old bastard living up there in the stinking north west. You know, he hardly ever sold anything during his lifetime. Have you seen the erotic work that emerged after he snuffed it?'

'Yes.'

'That's much more exciting than mucky-brown and grey mill scenes. Not forgetting those fucking matchstalk men and matchstalk cats and dogs. Lesbian art is bursting out of the woodwork now. Paintings I've seen are absolutely pornographic.

In fact, I had a wank after viewing one of them. Nicola sold a painting to a wealthy dyke collector not long ago. We hope to do more business with her. I saw your series of articles on lesbian art in one of the art magazines.'

'It took months to undertake the research.'

'Today, collectors demand to know more and more about a picture's provenance before they buy it. This is besides information on the artist, their technique and lifestyle.'

'Isn't that reasonable if large amounts of cash are involved?'

'Yes, though often it's tiresome. After buying a painting, one old bag asked why I thought the artist had employed more considered and controlled brush strokes than in previous works. She was shocked when I said he was much more relaxed at that period. He was regularly tying up a very young strumpet and fucking her up the arse.'

Standing, then moving to the door, Frankie suggests I meet a number of the Greasby staff. On entering Dick and Paul's studio, they look at me warily. Dick is slim, stands six feet tall, has a shock of grey hair and two days' stubble. He's wearing blue jeans and an open-neck blue denim shirt. Paul is short, plump, with a shaved head and white goatee beard. Dressed in brown corduroy trousers, he has a cream shirt with the sleeves rolled up.

'I've finally persuaded Al to jump aboard the Greasby ship,' Frankie proudly announces. But, he suddenly holds a hand across his mouth. 'Excuse me. I'm feeling nauseous.' He exits to a washroom along the corridor.

Dick and Paul's studio is stuffed with books. In their youth, the pair rejected a contemporary art school training, opting to be taught traditional painting and drawing techniques by their fathers. Both were Royal Academicians. Dick and Paul's figurative paintings are stunningly beautiful. Their restoration work is outstanding. I notice Paul is occupied removing foxing from a Henry Moore pen-and-wash drawing. Dick is repairing damage on a small Stanley Spencer oil painting. Other works by noted artists are awaiting restoration.

'You must be crazy coming to work here,' Dick snaps.

Paul, the quieter of the two, agrees. 'You'll find a hell of a difference from working for the local Council.'

'Do you know what really goes on with this company?' questions Dick.

I shrug.

'Criminality,' Paul states forcefully.

'You'll be nothing more than a buffer between Frankie and Nicola,' Dick adds. 'She's leading Greasby Fine Art down the wrong path. A money obsessed bitch. Frankie can't control her and only has himself to blame. Always spoiled her. On Nicola's 18th birthday, he bought her a Lamborghini. When stopped for speeding, the police asked how she could afford the car. "Easy," she said, "I'm not a policeman." The cunt was strip-searched. They thought she was a drug dealer. Nicola's rotten to the core.'

Paul joins in. 'She couldn't give a toss about art. No interest. It's only a vehicle for generating money.'

Dick picks up one of the darts and throws it at the cartoon of Nicola. It finds her crotch.

'Bullseye.'

'Nicola rides roughshod over Frankie every day,' starts Dick. 'That's why he snorts cocaine and wanks at every opportunity. He's unsure whether he's straight or gay and doesn't care. Regularly pissed or drugged-up, he wears weird clothes. Last week, one of the office girls saw him dressed as a nun and wanking. A freak and constantly throwing-up. Hasn't written any articles or done any lectures for months. Paulene, his wife, is left alone for days on end. Frankie's not been near her for years. It's a crazy family.'

'Various individuals show up in the afternoon for his pleasure,' states Paul.

'But no animals,' I laugh.

'Not yet.' They both grin, joining in the fun.

An uneasy pause hangs in the air before Dick breaks the silence.

'Besides being the Council's Keeper of Art, weren't you a

trade union officer?'

I nod.

'Frankie causes problems with staff and customers in the other Greasby galleries. He'll rely on your experience to dig him out of tricky situations. Recently, there was a heated argument with a buyer in London. To resolve the matter, Frankie wanted to fight him in the street.'

'Nicola is certain to resent your appointment,' Paul remarks. 'Personally, I think it's a good move and sensible. You can bring stability to the company and take it forwards, otherwise we're on course for a major disaster.'

'Be careful,' Dick interrupts. 'Nicola knows no boundaries. She's no conscience and is completely oblivious of the law. Doesn't care about anybody. Every hour of the day she looks for easy money.'

'How does she spend it?'

'On designer clothes, though not very often. Sports cars are the main passion, only never drives them. Nicola's last Ferrari had a mere 2,000 miles on the clock after three years. A nutcase. Everyone loathes her. When the London staff make her a coffee, they piss a little in it. It's a small act of revenge. You must be strong and stand up to the bitch, otherwise this company is doomed. All the experience in the world is needed to cope with Frankie *and* her.'

Paul shows agreement, then looks seriously at me. 'Has Frankie told you about our involvement with a shady character called Y?'

'No.'

'Have you ever met him?'

'What's his proper name?'

'He's only referred to as Y.' They both smirk, and exchange knowing glances.

'Who is he?'

'An art dealer, entrepreneur. Sure you've never met him?' Dick prods.

'Yes.'

'You will, sooner or later,' states Paul.

'Good luck,' they both chorus.

'Thanks for your support.' I toss them a smile as Frankie returns. He suggests I meet the technicians and company admin staff.

A little later, we venture downstairs. I notice the back entrance is open. An old Transit van is parked outside. From the vehicle, two casually dressed, thick-set men carry pictures into the loading bay. Wrapped in black bin liners and tape, they have no proper protection against damage. I'm shocked most are being placed on top of each other.

I gaze suspiciously at both men who are in their 40s. They don't acknowledge me.

'We are trusted art advisers and confidants,' begins Frankie. 'Greasby's client base stretches back over years. We offer discreet services. Our vaults can be used by collectors to store valuable paintings. Or, held there for short periods when owners are on holiday.'

'Won't these pictures suffer damage, dumped here?'

'No. Very soon they'll be transferred to the vaults. Have I taken you down there before?'

'Yes.'

## Chapter 2

When Frankie and I appear in the gallery, Nicola hurls a hardback book in our direction. To avoid being hit, I dodge out of the way. Without an apology, she screams at Frankie: 'We've had a good offer for that crappy William Henry Hunt. It's been in your collection fucking ages.'

'The painting is so pretty and worth much more.'

'We need cash flow.'

'Not by accepting a low offer.'

'It's fucking sentimental Victorian shit.'

'I'm *not* tossing it off.'

Picking up the book, I walk over to Nicola and thrust it slightly below her small but pert breasts.

'Throw anything at me again and I'll take you to an industrial tribunal.'

'Fuck off. You don't work for us.'

'Good news, Nicola,' Frankie beams. 'Al is finally joining the company.'

'Bollocks. He's a Council worker. What can he do for us?' Her face contorts in disdain.

'Plenty,' Frankie answers. 'His knowledge of art is second to none.'

'How will that translate into sales? He's got no retail experience.'

'He's joining us. That's final.'

'Well, you can pay him. I'm not.'

Nicola began studying art at university, but left after a year because she was needed in the family business. Sales were booming. During her teens, Nicola was force-fed art reference books. Not even allowed to go out, or have a television. Her understanding of art techniques is minimal. Once, we had an argument over a print. Nicola said it was a mezzotint, but that was bravado. She had no idea.

Nicola is pretty, has fine features, and gleaming capped teeth. Shiny brown hair brushes her shoulders. Her skirts and dresses invariably hover just above the knee. Husband Nigel is a vicar. Brother Tony is an engineer. Tony lives in Australia and has nothing to do with Greasby Fine Art. Nicola doesn't like anyone befriending Frankie. She wants total control over him and be the sole focus of his attention.

A stout woman bangs on the front door of the gallery. For some reason, it's been locked.

'Open up, Nicola! I'm going to fucking kill you.'

Chewing on her top lip, Nicola flashes looks of surprise and fear. She's unable to decide what to do. Immediately, I recognise the woman as Brenda Fitch. Fortyish, she stands six feet tall, has cropped, dyed-blonde hair and is heavily made-up. She's wearing a well-cut, blue-and-white pinstripe trouser suit, light-blue silk blouse and dark-blue dickie bow. Only in her presence once before, she's even larger than I recall.

Brenda's father, Arnold Fitch, died recently. He was a billionaire property tycoon. Her mother passed away ten years ago. Brenda was their only child. She inherited everything. Graduating with an Art History degree, she's now a well-respected art connoisseur and collector. Brenda is with four other women, who are younger than her. Each one is her height and weight. They're grasping aerosol cans of black paint. One of them crudely sprays FAKE HOUSE in large letters across the gallery's front window.

Nicola is still hesitating to allow them entry. When the four are ready to deface her new Ferrari, she moves speedily. Tearing into the gallery, Brenda hurls a gilt-framed painting at Nicola. It measures four feet by three feet and almost knocks her over.

'This painting is a fake. A fucking fake.' The word FAKE defaces the picture in black capital letters. Narrowing her eyes,

Brenda has a blow-torch gaze.

'If I took this matter to court, you'd do a prison stretch. A pretty thing like you wouldn't last five minutes inside.'

Brenda confronts a shocked old couple. 'This gallery is closed for the day.'

They hastily make an escape to the safety of the street. The door is locked behind them. Brenda's ferocious expression suggests she might eat Nicola alive. Theatrically, Brenda's chums spray FAKE above each one of the paintings displayed in the gallery. Nicola stands petrified.

One woman, Deb, is Brenda's partner. Prettier than the others, and a touch slimmer, she's wearing denim jeans, short-sleeve open-neck check shirt, heavy boots and a jacket. The other three are also recognisable to me. Ellen is an artist who paints large sado-masochistic lesbian scenes. Her other works depict women humiliating and torturing men. She can demand as much as twenty grand for each picture. Jen fronts an extreme Punk band. Barb, with slicked-back hair, shaved on both sides, is the editor of a widely-read lesbian magazine. It's funded by Brenda. The four women surround Nicola and savagely rip off her clothes.

'I'm being raped!' she screams. 'Stop. You're raping me!'

Nicola is dragged naked to one of the low-level cushioned seats. Two of the women sit on her.

Brenda, high on adrenaline, is without pity.

'Wrong Nicola. Wrong. You're not being raped, sweetie. This is payback. If Greasby Fine Art fucks me over for ninety grand with a fake painting, we're going to fuck you and your dad. Ellen will take photographs. She can use them in her paintings.'

Brenda's accomplices eagerly anticipate sex. From two bags, five strap-on dildos are pulled out. I'm in a dilemma. It's hard to accept that someone, defrauded of ninety grand, has a legitimate right to rape the alleged perpetrator. Any judge would insist that fraud should be dealt with by the criminal courts. I can't watch Nicola brutally raped. She could argue I was part of the attack.

Or did nothing to rescue her.

'A gang bang. What a lovely experience, Nicola,' exclaims Frankie smiling easily. He then sings a snippet from The Sensational Alex Harvey Band's song, *Gang Bang*. 'How exciting, Al, for you to witness this on your first day with us.' Frankie starts undressing. 'After selling paintings for years, I'll now be in one.'

'No, please. No.' Nicola's face is white with fear. 'I'll refund you, Brenda. I can do it now. And give you something extra. I have your bank details.'

'Too late, sweetie. You'll do more than refund me. You and Frankie must have it long and hard.' Her words are spat with pure malice.

'I'm on my period,' Nicola protests.

A quick and intimate examination by Deb reveals she's lying. This is not lost on Brenda. 'You scheming little bitch.'

'Stop struggling, whore,' demands Deb, producing a handgun. 'Or I'll blow away your kneecaps.'

'Please don't do this. Please.' Nicola screeches loudly. Tears roll down her face.

I hope Brenda doesn't consider there was any involvement from me with the fake painting. Producing forgeries is totally unacceptable. It's against every principle of creativity. For Nicola to assume she wouldn't be caught out was arrogant and naïve.

'Better comply, Nicola. Enjoy yourself. Pain and pleasure are close cousins,' states Frankie.

Brenda glares at Nicola. 'Don't do the fake if you can't take the pain.' Casting off her clothes, Brenda then wriggles from a thong. A heady fragrance of body cream and perfume swirl round her.

'Before we start, Nicola, I want to be in the mood.'

Having heard Nicola's screams, two of the female admin staff appear. They're eager to discover what's happening, though hastily withdraw back upstairs.

Down below, Brenda is as smooth as a billiard ball. She's no unwanted body hair. Nicola does not reflect the same habit.

'What's happening down there, sweetie?' Brenda laughs. 'Is that a tar brush stuck between your legs?'

With force, Jen and Barb get hold of Nicola and press her down to her knees. They direct her face into Brenda.

'No. I can't. I'll be sick.'

Brenda ignores the protest. 'Show enthusiasm, sweetie. Go deep. Put lots of effort into it. That's good. Roll your tongue. Faster. Faster.'

Deb moves to caress Brenda's firm breasts before kissing her passionately. Their tongues intertwine with delight.

'I can't breathe. Do you hear? I can't breathe,' pleads Nicola, though Jen and Barb take no notice.

'Dad. Help.' Nicola looks like she's in a nightmare running in slow motion.

'Stop whining. Enjoy yourself. Have fun,' Frankie chuckles.

Nicola bends in my direction. 'Help me, Council Prick. Help me.'

'Keep going, Nicola. Don't stop,' urges Brenda. 'Don't stop. Yes. That's so good…so good.'

This is like a scene from a Martin van Maële engraving.

'Can I choose which lady will shag me?' Frankie appeals to anyone who might listen. 'I'm excited about being in a painting.' He picks up, fondles and licks one of the dildos.

With a full-frame camera, Ellen captures close-up shots of Nicola.

'Faster, I'm nearly there. Faster.' Brenda's face glistens with perspiration.

'I'm going to be sick,' gulps Nicola.

'Yes. Yes. Oh, yes. I'm there. It was so, so good.'

Brenda's cohorts applaud.

'Well done, Nicola,' comments Deb brightly. 'You've done well. Brenda's a hard woman to please.'

That's no consolation for Nicola, who retches yellow bile.

I perch myself on a chair. I ought to resign and leave as soon as possible. In the past, I've heard rumours about Greasby Fine

Art malpractices. But nothing was certain. Should I escape via the back door? Would any of these women pursue me? Fortunately, my presence seems to be unnoticed. As a trade union officer, I've handled tricky situations and wait patiently for an opportunity to assert influence.

'Is it my time for nookie?' yelps Frankie.

'We're fucking Nicola first. Then you,' Brenda answers. 'We enjoy inflicting pain on women and men.'

'And watching them scream,' laughs Deb.

Frankie licks his lips. 'Don't mind if I participate do you, Al?'

'No. Enjoy yourself.'

'Fancy joining in?'

'Not in submissive role-play.'

Adopting her Punk persona, Jen prances over to Frankie and delivers a few lines of a song, in a fast, monotonous staccato rhythm.

*I hate posh men. I hate posh men.*

*I'm gonna fuck you. I'm gonna fuck you.*

*Up your jacksie. Up your jacksie.*

*You'll not like it. You'll not like it. Da, da da, da da.*

Dancing round the gallery repeating the words, she plays air guitar.

'Those words are brilliant. Make sure you jot them down,' encourages Brenda.

People have tried to gain access to the gallery, including Nicola's assistant, Jess Jones. Through the front window, smeared with the spray paint, uniformed school kids strain to view the events inside. Highly amused, they're moved away by a shocked teacher.

With fiery eyes, Deb fastens a dildo on to Brenda. Anticipating what is to happen, Nicola wails again. She's tightly gripped by the three others and her legs are held back.

Taking a deep breath, I stand up. 'Excuse me. We can discuss this.'

'Who are you, honey?' asks Brenda.

'Al was Keeper of Art at the local Museum & Art Gallery,' informs Frankie. 'He's now working for us.'

'This bitch has sold me a fake,' spits Brenda, curling her lip. 'I was warned of the shenanigans here. But took a chance.'

'How do you know it's a fake?' I query.

Brenda picks up the painting. The dildo waggles comically in front of her. 'I bought this as an original Lady Dora Butler. The painter of erotic lesbian scenes. I've been to see her. She's 92, but still fully in charge of her faculties. This isn't an original work.'

'Why?'

'Lady Dora never included strapless dildos in lesbian orgies. The women in the painting have them and they're yellow. She's never painted yellow dildos, the colour is too difficult to control in a composition. I was convinced my picture is a blatant forgery.' Brenda looks at Nicola. 'You're so stupid, sweetie, assuming the picture's authenticity wouldn't be checked. I wanted to spend five million with this gallery. Not now.'

'I can help you,' I say confidently.

Nicola's husband, Nigel, peers through the front window. Resplendent in dog collar and cassock, he has a group of pensioners alongside. Presumably, they're here to look round the gallery. On seeing Nicola, he anxiously rattles the door.

'What's going on?' Nigel stands helplessly, watching tears stream down her face.

'Nigel has a black eye,' I point out to Frankie. 'Has he been in a fight?'

'No. Nicola beat him up. They fight like cat and dog. Then, fuck each other senseless. It's a game they enjoy regularly.'

Stepping over to Brenda, Frankie fondles the dildo.

'Fuck off, pervert,' she barks. 'With a father like you, no wonder Nicola is a criminal.'

'I had no idea she sold you a fake painting. I'm puzzled why she needed to do that.'

'Liar. Fuck him now,' Brenda instructs Jen. 'Make sure you take good pictures, Ellen.'

Frankie's face lights up and he runs away. 'You can't catch me. You can't catch me.'

Jen and Ellen chase him out of the gallery.

Dick and Paul have made their way downstairs. Seeing Nicola's predicament, they snigger, but vanish after a few minutes.

Still naked, Brenda approaches me. 'What's your name?'

'Al Cooper.'

We look at each for a few seconds until a smile brightens her face.

'I don't believe it. You wrote an absolutely brilliant six-part *Lesbian Art* series in *Art Happening Today*.'

'Yes.'

'It was a major piece of work.'

We lock eyes and shake hands. The other women view me with suspicion.

'You're a brilliant writer. The articles inspired me to start collecting erotic lesbian art. That's why I asked this whore to locate works by Lady Dora. How do you know so much about the subject?' Her voice is more controlled now.

'I enjoy researching controversial art subjects. In *Art Happening Today*, I've featured homosexuality and eroticism in art.'

'I've always read your pieces. It's a real pleasure to meet you. A real pleasure. Isn't it, ladies?'

'Yes,' Barb and Deb agree.

Nigel still peers in. 'Somebody, listen. I want to see my wife. What's going on?'

'Take no notice,' Brenda instructs. 'We're not ready to open the door.'

She unfastens the dildo, drags over a chair and sits near to me. 'This conversation is very interesting, Al. How did you locate the lesbian works illustrated in the series?'

'One discovery led to another. It often does. *Art Happening Today* has a worldwide distribution. That helped enormously.'

It's easy to relax and converse with her.

'I want to open a gallery or museum. The Brenda Fitch Foundation for Lesbian Art. I have the cash. And wealthy friends to support the project. Funding won't be a problem. I need someone with your impeccable knowledge to help.'

'Lesbian art,' I begin, 'is the new vogue in Europe and America. Over the last year, I've made good contacts and can liaise with collectors and artists on a global scale. They know and trust me. I'd like to produce an impressive coffee-table book documenting and illustrating lesbian art.'

'I've called the police,' Nigel screams. He's animated outside and a crowd has gathered.

'I can finance the book,' Brenda continues. 'No problem. This is fantastic. I habitually hate men and don't trust them. But, I like you. We must work together. As long as you're involved at Greasby Fine Art, I'll be happy to continue my association with the company.'

Rising, Brenda snarls at Nicola: 'Don't refund the ninety grand. Put it towards finding genuine lesbian art. I'm happy to transfer another hundred grand. Al can start buying immediately. Email or phone when more funds are required. In fact, Al, why don't you visit me? There might be pictures in my father's collection to offload.'

'Thanks, I will.'

Nicola throws a hateful look. But she realises I'm her only chance of avoiding more pain and humiliation.

'Have you enjoyed yourself yet, Nicola?' pants Frankie, bouncing back in with Jen and Ellen. 'We've had a great time taking pictures for Ellen's paintings.' He looks exhausted.

Blue flashing lights are seen outside as two police cars arrive. They disgorge four uniformed officers – three females and a male. After conversing with Nigel, they glance through the window. One of them bangs on the front door.

'Better unlock the door, Deb,' Brenda orders.

The larger of the three female officers, a sergeant, marches into the gallery.

'Hello, Brenda. I've not seen you for a while.'

'Hi, Nancy. We're taking pictures for one of Ellen's paintings. Frankie kindly handed over the gallery for a couple of hours. Nicola volunteered to play a role.'

'Everything is fine,' confirms Frankie.

'I guessed this might be a silly misunderstanding,' Nancy quips.

# Chapter 3

One Friday afternoon, weeks later, Frankie is in the Askworth Gallery with two smackhead shoplifters, Carl and his girlfriend Di. Both have horrible teeth and some are missing. In their late 20s, the couple look like they've fallen through a pile of jumble sale clothes.

Sweating and bone-thin, Carl has a number of stolen designer shirts, pullovers and trousers. These are for Frankie to try on. He's been missing for the previous week and only showed up today. Nobody wanted to divulge where he was or what he might be doing.

At a guess, Di is seven months pregnant. Her belly button protrudes vulgarly below a skimpy T-shirt. Greasy hair brushes her shoulders. She moves unevenly as one of her high heels is hanging loose. Pulling a new glistening tenor saxophone from a black bin liner, Di asks excitedly: 'Want to buy this, Frankie? It's gorgeous!'

'No, I'm a piano player.' Standing in only bright-pink underpants, he's ready to pull on a pair of red slacks. This is done in the presence of gallery visitors, including children. 'Perhaps Al might be interested.'

'Where's it from?' I stare at Carl warily.

'A massive music shop three streets away. We nicked it this morning.'

'How much?'

'New, they're selling for over twelve hundred quid. It's yours for a grand. Cash.'

'Far too expensive.' I've often considered learning to play an instrument might be a good idea. The saxophone sound is uplifting.

'Eight hundred and fifty,' Di suggests.

'I'll lend you the cash if necessary,' Frankie offers. 'There's plenty down here in one of the desk drawers.'

Carl and Di's eyes sparkle, believing they've struck gold for a drug-fuelled extravaganza over the weekend.

Trying to keep my voice down, I comment: 'No, I don't want to pay that amount.'

A known American collector is in the gallery. I hope he's not caught any of the conversation between Frankie and the two rogues.

The gallery is staging an exhibition of Arthur Rackham and Edmund Dulac illustrations from the collection of Brenda's dad. It has caused a wealth of interest with British, European and American collectors. Articles reviewing the exhibition have appeared in the art press.

Brenda has decided to sell the works on paper her father had kept in folders for years. The proceeds will go towards financing the Lesbian Art Museum. Already, she's acquired a large plot of land. An architect's design for the building has been accepted. Work is now progressing at a rapid pace. I understand one company walked away from the job as she refused to budge on the main entrance. It's in the shape of a vagina. She's persuaded other collectors to sell works through Greasby Fine Art to help fund the ambitious project. The commission we've earned is a welcome cash injection for the company.

'The sax is beautiful.' Frankie takes it from Di and plays a few notes. The noise startles everyone in the gallery.

'Can you play, Frankie?' asks Di.

'I took lessons in my teens but stuck with the piano instead.'

'Treat yourself, mate,' coaxes Carl, looking at me. 'Five hundred notes and it's yours. I'll nick one or two instruction books. They'll help you learn.'

'I'll take these three pairs of trousers, both pullovers and shoes,' Frankie interrupts, handing over a bundle of cash to Carl.

'Three hundred and fifty notes for a quick sale on the sax,' Di presses me.

A telephone sounds on a desk and I pick it up. It's Dick from upstairs.

'Is smackhead Carl in the gallery?'

'Yes.'

'Kick him out. The police have launched a big purge on known shoplifters. Details were given in the local paper. He must go.'

'Okay.'

'Fuck what Dick says,' fires Frankie, shrugging aside any worries. 'Carl has real bargains.'

'Are you having the sax, mate?' Di asks. 'Two hundred and fifty. That's our last offer.'

'No. I'm not bothered.'

'A mistake, Al. You'll regret it,' chides Frankie. 'I'll buy the sax. Is two hundred okay, Carl?'

'Yes.' Carl stuffs the cash into his grubby pockets.

Frankie carefully puts on his shirt, gold tie, and blue suit.

'We're in for a great weekend,' gushes Di. 'Thanks Frankie.'

'Ring Sonny, he's got brilliant white and brown,' Carl instructs his girlfriend. He can hardly breathe for excitement.

I point to Di's loose heel. 'Won't you buy new shoes instead of drugs?'

'Fuck off. We'll be out of it now, all weekend.' She eyeballs me. 'You need a good fuck, mate. Start enjoying yourself. I've not seen your miserable face alter once while we've been here. Want me to fix you up with somebody?'

I ignore her.

She kisses Frankie, almost knocking him over with the baby bulge.

Next to breeze into the gallery is Frankie's coke dealer.

'I hope you have Columbia's finest, Abe.'

'You know I only supply the best,' he smirks, handing over a package. It contains numerous small plastic bags of coke. Frankie can't resist having a taster. Putting a little amount on a desk, he takes out a credit card and arranges the powder into a long line. Via a rolled up twenty-pound note, the coke is vacuumed into his left nostril.

'Wow, that's good.' His head rolls in delight.

Once Abe has counted the bundle of notes Frankie handed over, he departs in a flash. Soon afterwards, the restaurant owner from next door shows, along with a pub landlord from further down the road. They've seen Abe leave and want to buy coke. This has occurred previously. More local businesspeople appear until Frankie's stock of coke runs low. A batch for personal use is stashed in his pockets and into one of the gallery desks.

'Isn't this a bit risky, Frankie?'

'Stop worrying. It's bohemian, Al.'

'Not if there's a police raid and everyone says you're a drug dealer.'

'It's harmless fun. Artists have used stimulants to produce masterpieces. Surely you know that? You can have this sax. It's a present. Learning to play an instrument will help you lighten up. Don't take this job too seriously. I know you're working tirelessly with Brenda. Enjoy life as well.'

For the past hour, the American collector, an obese man in a light-coloured suit, has been studying the works on display. He's viewed them from a distance, then moved in closer to examine details, changing his spectacles constantly. Leaning over the display cases, he perused the first edition books illustrating the artists' work. I watch as he approaches with confidence.

'This is a wonderful exhibition. You've done remarkably well to unearth this collection. I'd like to make a bid for the works and the books.'

'We've received a number of bids already,' Frankie interjects. 'A decision will be made when the exhibition closes.'

'Tell me the highest bid and I'll add fifty percent.'

'I can't disclose other people's bids. It wouldn't be fair,' Frankie says briskly.

'I'll leave my card. If there's a change of mind, phone me. By the way sir, I don't think you know how to run a gallery. Or talk to customers.' He throws Frankie a snide look. 'I think you're an asshole.'

For the exhibition, we've produced a catalogue and he buys a dozen copies. I process his credit card and hand over a receipt. Before leaving, he gives Frankie a final dig: 'I know Brenda Fitch and will be contacting her personally with a bid. I saw the drug dealing earlier. Clean up your act or go down the pan. Good day to you.'

As the American closes the gallery door, three people emerge from a police car. One of them is in uniform, the second is a plain clothes detective. The third man is much older than the other two. In his late 50s, he's of medium build, and looks dapper in a brown suit.

Bursting into the gallery, the older man moves ahead of the two officers and thrusts a painting in a gilt swept frame at Frankie. It falls to the floor and a corner of the frame is smashed.

'I'm Tom Brody,' he shouts, looking ready to explode with anger. 'Two months ago, I bought this picture for twenty five grand from your daughter. I've discovered it was stolen from a collection in Europe several months back. You're a bunch of crooks.'

'Do you want to step outside and repeat that?' Frankie displays a sickly smile and begins to remove his jacket.

'Certainly,' snarls Brody.

'You'll regret it. I went to public school and was in my house's boxing club. We were always winning competitions.'

'You might regret it too,' Brody swipes. 'I only went to a Comprehensive school, but my dad was a professional wrestler. He taught me everything I know.'

This is outrageous behaviour from Frankie. I stand in front of him and must take the heat out of the situation. I don't want it known he had a physical confrontation with a customer. Noticing Frankie has white powder on his left nostril, I furtively signal for him to wipe it away. Thankfully, he does.

The plain clothes officer introduces himself: 'I'm Detective Constable John Shires. This is PC Paul Scott. We need to investigate this in a proper manner.'

Brody glares at Frankie. 'I've been tricked by your company.

After the picture was stolen, a figure was added to the main group. An expert has confirmed the original work was done in the mid-19th century. The additional figure was painted recently. Perhaps your daughter never expected a forensic examination.'

Animosity ricochets across the gallery. Shires' eyes flit from Frankie to Brody, then settle on the black bin liner partially concealing the saxophone.

'This is a very serious allegation,' I intervene. 'You're questioning our integrity, Mr Brody. How can you confirm the supposed additional figure was created whilst in our possession?'

'I can't. But it's highly likely. You're a well-known bunch of forgers. I've seen photographs of the painting before it was stolen. There's no additional figure.'

'I strongly dispute your claim,' I reply. 'And, with the greatest respect, your evidence is flimsy. It'll be very difficult to substantiate.'

Brody tries to grab Frankie. 'The figure was added by you bastards. I want my money back now.'

The two police officers restrain him. 'Steady, sir,' they chorus. 'We must insist on keeping this matter civilised.'

Losing his earlier aggression, Frankie switches to peacemaker mode. 'I'm terribly sorry to hear of your disappointment after paying out such a substantial sum. However, like Al, I dispute we tampered with the work.'

'How did you obtain the picture, Mr Greasby?' interjects Shires.

'Officer, I can't give you an immediate answer, though I promise to give this problem my undivided attention early next week. I see hundreds of pictures each year. Stolen items and fakes are the bane of my life. They're an occupational hazard. We've been the victim of scams ourselves.'

The two policemen are lost. Unsure who to believe or what to do. The incident is very depressing.

Brody attacks: 'You're a fucking con artist, Greasby.'

'I'll pretend I didn't hear your silly accusation, Mr Brody. I'm an honest man trying to make a decent living.'

'That's the biggest load of bullshit I've ever heard.'

Frankie puts up his fists, theatrically shadow boxing and taunting Brody. He then dances in between the display cases. The police watch in amazement. Brody seethes, convinced Frankie is ridiculing him. Crazily, he launches an ambitious flying headscissors at Frankie. He fails miserably. Obviously, his wrestler father didn't impart correct instructions. The two officers spring into action, grappling with Brody until Scott tries to cuff him. Undeterred, Brody breaks free and rushes at Frankie with a headbutt. Ducking out of the way, Frankie crashes into the desk where the saxophone is resting. Falling out of the bin liner, it clatters on to the floor. I hold Frankie to thwart any further involvement in the fracas.

The two policemen restrain Brody. 'We're charging you with assault.'

'No. Let's be sensible. No need for any of that. Release him,' insists Frankie diplomatically.

Both officers view the saxophone suspiciously.

'What's that doing here?' quizzes Scott, his eyes not wavering from Frankie.

'I'm not sure.' Frankie doesn't hold eye contact with anyone. 'I haven't been in the gallery much today. Do you know anything, Al?'

'No,' I respond shakily, my heartbeat rising.

Frankie waffles: 'A patron must have visited earlier, placed it on the desk and forgotten to take it away as they left.'

Shires and Scott are baffled.

'Could this be the saxophone reported stolen earlier today?' asks Scott.

His colleague responds thoughtfully: 'We'll take it with us and make further enquiries.'

'Don't worry about the picture, Mr Brody,' Frankie announces. 'If one of our customers is not satisfied, we offer a no quibble refund. With interest. No problem. My office staff are still here and can refund your money.'

Frankie and Brody glare stubbornly at each other. I pick up

the offending picture and lean it against a wall. The additional figure is noticeable.

Frankie looks my way. 'I'll sort this out, Al. Go and pick up Nicola, Nigel and Annabel. Take my Rolls. Here are the keys. Go straight to the seafood restaurant. Are you okay to have a bite to eat with us tonight?'

'Yes.'

'Y is coming,' he whispers. 'I'd like you to meet him.'

'Okay.' I groan inwardly.

'I'll take a taxi to the restaurant with Y.'

# Chapter 4

Over the last few weeks, I've driven Frankie's Rolls-Royce on a number of occasions, making me reasonably comfortable behind the wheel. Initially, it was difficult to judge the speed, so smooth the ride. I can't help but be impressed with the interior details. They include natural grain leather seating, lambswool floor rugs and automatic climate control.

I've also driven Nicola's Ferrari. A real head-turner. Not many vehicles of that calibre are seen in Askworth. It's a fantastic perk of my job to use these two luxury cars. There's always a full tank of fuel in the Rolls. The same can't be said about the Ferrari. Whenever I slip into that vehicle the fuel gauge is on red. Clearly, Nicola believes a high-performance car runs on fresh air.

Gliding away from the gallery, I merge with busy teatime traffic. People admire the powder-blue Rolls as it purrs past them. Noticing the speed limit will soon drop from 50 to 30, I press hard on the brake. This stretch of road is obviously a speed trap and a money-earner for the authorities. A short distance away a female officer points a speed gun.

You'll not catch me, lady.

She waves in a friendly manner, indicating I'm obeying the law.

The Greasby admin staff said Nicola is diverting funds away from the company's bank account and into one of her own. Most likely, this includes cash we've earned from selling Brenda's pictures. Nicola has bought a piece of land and is financing the building of a new church for Nigel.

One of the admin lads, Roger – a quiet man who lives with his mother – told Frankie what Nicola was doing. Frankie promised to investigate. Days later, he rejected the accusation. There was a heated confrontation between Roger and Nicola. Roger's 68-year-old mother, Sue, heard about the incident, marched into the gallery and gave Nicola a good hiding. The police were called, though Sue wasn't charged. After taking legal advice on the matter, I staged a disciplinary, attended by Frankie and myself. I put it to Roger, he must apologise on behalf of his mother or be sacked. Launching into a fierce verbal tirade, he strongly criticised Nicola and Frankie. Afterwards, Roger resigned.

Nicola worked at home today. She lives with Nigel and their daughter Annabel on an exclusive new estate 12 miles from the Askworth Gallery. The double-gabled house has a central entrance and the front garden is immaculately well-kept. Stepping inside the house, the downstairs layout comprises, to the left, a lounge, a study, a washroom and toilet. There's an open-plan central staircase and beyond is a kitchen diner. To the right is a utility room and dining room. Upstairs there are five bedrooms. The house is full of crappy kitsch items bought from department stores. It's devoid of character. There isn't a single painting of note hanging on the walls.

Nicola is in the hallway area. 'You okay, Al? You okay, though?' That's how she greets me whenever we meet. It's monotonous and insincere. I'm surprised she's wearing a silk dressing gown and not ready to go out. Yet, her make-up is complete. Begrudgingly, she's pleased I'm working good deals with Brenda and her associates. These have given Greasby's finances a massive boost. People want to sell their paintings through us more than ever before. Our profile in America is very healthy. Brenda is encouraging us to set up a gallery there and for me to be involved.

Nicola's eight-year-old daughter, Annabel, appears from the study.

'My mum hates you. She says you're a Council Prick.'

Ignoring her, I slightly stoop forward and offer to shake hands. She spits in my face and tries to kick my shins.

'She thinks spitting is a sport,' Nicola almost boasts.

I grab Annabel and spit back. Looking like she's ready to

burst into tears, I swivel her round so we stare into a tall hallway mirror. My phlegm is trickling down her face.

'See, it's not very nice when a person spits at you. Is it, Annabel?'

'I'll have to do the same when she spits at me,' Nicola comments.

'Yes, you must.'

'It's her birthday tomorrow,' Nicola laughs. 'She loves fireworks and we've bought her loads to have a brilliant display in the back garden.'

Blubbering, Annabel moves into the washroom.

'How's business been today?' Nicola inquires anxiously.

'Brenda wants paying for one of her dad's paintings we sold a couple of weeks ago.'

'I've sent her a payment.' Nicola's face colours red.

'If not paid by the end of next week, she's coming to see you again.'

'Fucking bitch. Do you think she's actually got any cash?'

'Yes. I've been to her house, Banton Hall, and it reeks of wealth. Brenda's partner, Deb, drives her in either a Bentley or Range Rover. Both cars have a personal registration plate worth as much as the vehicles.'

'Why is she always chasing cash?'

'One of her friends hasn't been paid either.'

'Tell Brenda to fuck off.'

'I promised to make enquiries for her.'

'For fuck's sake. I'm dealing with nutcases every day.'

'We can't afford to have a reputation as poor payers. Or, people won't sell their pictures through us. We've been busy recently. Brenda is a good ambassador for Greasby.'

Nicola's dressing gown peeps open and it's noticeable she's nude underneath. But has taken Brenda's advice on removing unsightly hair.

'Frankie's back today. Everybody's been wondering where he went. He didn't even tell me.'

Nicola looks away. 'No idea.'

'He didn't say anything?'

'I'm not interested. Probably been on one of his pervy trips. Who knows? I don't give a shit. Any sales in the gallery today?'

'An American collector wanted to buy every picture we have on display. Your dad told him to wait until after the show.'

'What?' She fidgets uncomfortably.

'Before I left, a customer, Tom Brody, stormed in with the police. He claimed the picture you sold him has an extra figure. Said before it was altered, the picture had been stolen in Europe.'

Nicola phones Frankie and waits impatiently for him to answer.

She immediately attacks: 'Tom Brody's painting hasn't been altered. Don't refund him. You already have? Stupid old cunt. How can we pay bills this week? Fuck off. Just, fuck off.'

Each day, staff from the Greasby galleries telephone Nicola to report on daily sales. Still with the mobile in her hand, she takes a call from one of our London galleries and interrogates a member of staff.

'Done any business today? Nothing? Nothing at all? How much have you taken this week? Pathetic. I won't be eating steak tonight, will I? Or buying sexy knickers to excite my husband. Take money over the weekend or I'll shut the gallery and sack the lot of you on Monday.'

Closing galleries and making staff redundant could open a can of worms. I sincerely hope that doesn't happen.

Nigel enters the house looking glum. His hair is greasy and there's stubble on his chin. He's five years older than Nicola.

'Hi, Nigel. How are things?'

'Not very good, Al.' Swallowing deeply, he glances sheepishly at Nicola.

Annabel appears from the washroom and annoyingly keeps opening and closing the door.

Nicola hits Nigel with a volley: 'What the fuck is wrong with you?'

'Problems. Big problems.'

'Why?'

'There's been a mix-up at the Land Registry. We're building

the church on a section of land that isn't ours.'

'How did that happen?' Her eyes almost drill holes into him.

'I'm not sure.'

'You're so fucking useless.'

I suggest to Nicola: 'I can look into the problem if you want.'

Ignoring me, she glares at her husband. 'How much will it cost to buy the land?'

'Two hundred grand.'

Nicola is ready to combust.

'There's another issue,' Nigel mutters, fiddling with a cross dangling from his neck.

Before he continues, Nicola shouts at Annabel to stop messing with the door. She takes no notice. Nicola looks back at Nigel. 'What's the other problem?'

'The builder hasn't dug the foundations deep enough for a small section of the church. It'll have to be demolished.'

'Isn't that the builder's problem?'

'I'm not sure. We owe him a payment. It has to be settled by the end of the month or he's threatening to pull off site.'

'How much is the payment?'

'Fifty grand.'

'Aren't you watching what they're doing? Why didn't you know anything about this?'

'I'm a vicar not a builder.'

'I knew this would happen with you in charge.'

'I've done my best. I can't be in two places at once.'

'Fucking useless cunt. Why do I always have to solve your problems?'

'Useless, useless,' Annabel choruses. 'Mummy, what's a cunt?'

Nigel fumes. 'Parish work absorbs all the hours in my day.'

'Why we need to build such a big fuck off fancy church is beyond belief.'

'We've been through that before, Nicola.'

'Every fucker takes the piss out of you.'

'Not long ago, little miss perfect, I saved you from being brutally raped.'

'No, you didn't.'

'Yes, I did.'

'How do you think I'll raise the cash to pull you out of the shit?'

'I'm sure it won't be a problem.'

'Greasby Fine Art needs to be clearing over one hundred grand a week. Just to stand still. We've hardly taken any money over the last five days. The cost of building this fucking church is crippling. Our mortgage isn't cheap.'

'You can deal with these problems, Nicola.'

'Can't you raise more funds?'

'No. That's up to you.'

'Stop fiddling with that fucking cross or I'll ram it up your arse.'

Incensed, Nigel moves forwards and slaps her. Not to be outdone, she rains a flurry of punches on him. Nigel responds by rubbing a hand over her face, ruining the carefully applied make-up.

'You fucking dick. Now, I'll have to do my face again.'

Further insults, slaps and punches are thrown at each other as they climb the stairs.

Annabel spits at me from a distance and disappears into the study, slamming the door. Shouts, squeals and screams are heard from upstairs. They're punctuated by the smashing of glass and loud crashes. Ignoring the mayhem, I wander into the kitchen and gaze outside at the splendid back garden.

After a few minutes, the din upstairs subsides. I walk to the foot of the stairs, trying to guess what the pair are doing. There's an eerie silence and I fear the worst. Before I can muse further, strange noises steal from the study. Annabel opens the door and flings a firework at me. Deafeningly loud bangs assault my ears as smoke fills the hallway. An alarm emits high-pitched beeps.

Annabel follows up by throwing more fireworks, setting off another two alarms. Bright colours and sparks shower everywhere. For a moment, I believe I'm in hell, which is strange considering the head of this household is a vicar.

Thankfully, Nigel and Nicola hasten downstairs. She hugs

Annabel. 'Sorry darling, for leaving you alone with Al.'

Nigel opens the front door, allowing the smoke to escape. Standing on a chair, he silences the alarms. Then, he throws the dead fireworks outside. This is my first encounter with Annabel. Now I know why Dick and Paul refer to her as 'the kid from hell'.

'Come upstairs, Annabel. Help mummy get ready. We won't be long, Al. Obviously, you're not used to looking after kids.'

My eyes wander over the back garden once again. Memories of my dead son, Alex, fill my head. I struggle to drive away tears. Although this job is challenging, I don't want to endure hours and days alone. Grief might conquer me. Alex's tragic death isn't easily forgotten. I'll put more flowers on his grave next week. That, at least, is small comfort. Some parents have to cope with the loss of a child whose body has never been found.

Before long, Nicola, Nigel and Annabel are ready for the seafood restaurant. Nicola has put on a figure-hugging, short red dress and stepped into red high heels. She's enlivened her make-up to such an extent that it looks tarty. Nigel still wears a dog collar, matched with boring casual attire. Annabel is resplendent in a pretty white party frock. Nicola and Nigel climb into the rear of the Rolls. This is odd. Annabel settles in the front passenger seat.

'Don't one of you two want to sit with me?'

Nicola is smug. 'No. We want to amuse ourselves in the back.'

Easing away smoothly, I'm looking forwards to enjoying the meal. Not having eaten during the day has made me very hungry. Before Annabel can think about spitting again, I grasp her hand and squeeze it. 'You're not going to misbehave again, are you, Annabel?'

'No, Council Prick.'

'That's not my proper name. It's Al.'

'You're hurting me.'

'I can't hear you, Annabel.'

'Mummy, Council Prick is hurting me.'

Her hand is gripped tighter. 'I'll ask you again. We're not going to cause trouble are we, Annabel?'

'No, Al. No.'

I glance in the rear mirror. Nigel and Nicola have stripped off. Nicola is on all fours, allowing a diamond-encrusted, gold butt plug to be removed. I keep my eyes on the road. I'd forgotten what Frankie divulged: 'They fight like cat and dog. Then, fuck each other senseless.'

'Harder, Nigel. Faster. Get it right in, you useless prick.'

Annabel mimics her mother's cries. Then, she begins spitting at the windscreen. Up ahead there are queuing vehicles. A bus driver has misjudged the height of a bridge and the roof has been torn off. In attendance are police cars, fire engines and three ambulances. Don't bus drivers familiarise themselves with a route before travelling along it? Performing a three-point turn, the car is steered in another direction to the restaurant.

My mobile rings. It's Frankie.

'Where are you, Al? I'm at the restaurant with Y. Is everything okay? Is Nicola with you?'

'Yes. We won't be long,' I shout with the mobile on my lap. I don't want to be caught driving with it held to my ear.

On the opposite side of the road, a man in his 20s is texting while on a scooter. Unfortunately, he's not quick enough to avoid a van that brakes suddenly. He crashes into the rear. Normally, I would stop and see if he's okay though the incident has alerted people walking past. The van driver has also emerged from his vehicle to investigate.

# Chapter 5

I easily find a parking space near the entrance to the seafood restaurant. The building is long and single-storey. To the rear are offices, kitchens and a delivery area. For years, the company has been owned and run by the Braithwaite family. Sally Braithwaite, granddaughter of the founder, Syd, now manages the business. Her Mercedes, with a personalised registration plate, is parked nearby.

Online, I've read customers' comments about the food and they're very favourable. It must be a dilemma for a restaurant owner to decide whether opinions should be left. There's a great risk adverse criticism might seriously affect business or even close it down. Is it necessary? Unsure.

Although never sampling the delights of the establishment previously, I'm eagerly anticipating the experience tonight. The food is expensive and mainly attracts Askworth's more affluent residents. An online menu reveals the main courses are adventurous. Options are available for vegetarians and vegans.

Immediately on walking inside, there's a cacophony of voices. We're welcomed by Sally Braithwaite. The interior displays reproductions of Victorian fishing scenes. Nigel and Nicola are fully clothed again and flounce along hand in hand. They ignore Annabel who tries to thump me in the groin, while chanting: 'You're a Council Prick. You're a Council Prick.'

I grab her hand. She shouts in pain as I drag her along to a bar area. This attracts the attention of most people enjoying their meal. Frankie's with a man I presume is Y. Before introductions are made, Annabel kicks Y on the shin. Without hesitation, he slaps her hard across the face. Crying out, she almost loses her balance. Y bends down to her. 'Shut up or I'll slap you harder.'

He tackles Nigel and Nicola: 'I've told you both before. This young girl's behaviour is very bad. Do something about it.'

A similar comment is heard from a man in his 50s standing nearby. 'If I'd acted like that at her age, my dad would've killed me. Kids today want disciplining now and again. It never hurt people before.'

Nicola ignores the man's comment, slips her hand out of Nigel's sticky palm, and launches into a verbal assault on Frankie. 'Don't ever refund money for a painting I've sold. Don't poke your fucking nose in my problems.'

She smiles saccharinely at Y, gives him a tender hug and visibly preens. Frankie takes no notice of her and doesn't even acknowledge his son-in-law.

In the restaurant there are 30 or 40 tables. Most extend down each side of the room, with larger ones in the middle. Couples, old and young, as well as small families, are seated at them. There's a lively and happy end-of-the-week atmosphere. Waiting staff move about in a quick and efficient manner, offering a smiling and attentive service. Customers want to enjoy themselves with good food and wine. They're eager to kick-off the weekend on a high. The weather is predicted to be fine and warm.

Rudely, Frankie doesn't introduce Y. Instead, Y offers his hand and presents himself: 'I'm Yaroslav, but call me Y.'

'Hi, I'm Al.'

Looking a cold iceberg of a man, his steely eyes bore through me. Initially, he gives an impression that smiling is painful. As we shake hands, my fingers are almost crushed. I squeeze harder and we both exchange contrived friendly glances. Y says he's Russian. Immediately, I detect he speaks very good English. Forty five years old, stocky and bull-necked, his blonde hair is cut short. Wearing a black leather jacket, black shirt, trousers and heavy boots, Y soaks up the surroundings with a laser-eyed gaze that jumps about.

The conversation in our group is stilted and awkward. I'm pleased when a waiter materialises and leads us to a table which is set for six. A dozen or more heads track us in a silent pan.

Taking seats on one side are Frankie, Y and Annabel. On the other are Nigel, myself and Nicola. The waiter hands everyone but Annabel a menu. A table nearby is occupied by eight teenage girls. Several red balloons emblazoned with 18 are tied to the backs of their chairs. The girls appear to have soft drinks until I notice them produce spirit bottles from handbags, then top-up their glasses.

Frankie calls over the wine waiter and orders two bottles of Champagne and bottles of an expensive white wine. When the drinks arrive, most people look over in our direction as a Champagne cork pops. Frankie samples the drink and indicates his approval. Everyone's glass is filled, except mine. Y takes a sip and expresses delight. Annabel and me are served soft drinks. Frankie rises and invites everyone to share a toast.

'To Greasby Fine Art. Long may we trade.'

'Hear, hear,' is everyone's response. Even Annabel joins in. Summoning a waiter back to the table, Frankie states he would like seared tuna for his main course. But, he wants to be assured it is fresh.

'No problem, sir. Be patient and I'll consult our chefs.'

Y and Nicola regularly exchange friendly glances. This hasn't gone unnoticed by Nigel. Y and Nigel haven't acknowledged each other. No handshake. Nothing. Annabel's face shows a distinctive red mark from Y's slap. Thankfully, she's remained silent.

Frankie looks in my direction. 'Y's men are delivering a fantastic batch of pictures in the morning.'

'Do they have proper provenance?' I probe.

'Of course,' Y responds with alacrity. 'You'll have all the details as soon as they're gathered together.'

'We still have a few pictures supplied by you without any documentation. May I send you a list? Then, you can forward whatever is available.'

'Yes.' Blinking rapidly, he's clearly ruffled.

'I'm sure we'll have no problem selling these new pictures across the world,' Frankie assures Y.

I try to dredge up enthusiasm.

'Al, you must tell Y the type of pictures Brenda would like to buy for her new museum. He has a fantastic knowledge of art and many, many contacts. I'm sure he could be useful.'

'I will.'

Y tries to hold my attention, though I move my line of vision.

Access to the kitchen is through two doors in the middle of the restaurant's back wall. Most people pause from chatting as two chefs stride forwards with blank expressions. They're struggling to carry a tuna. One of them glares at Frankie. 'Does this look fresh enough for you, sir?'

Frankie is impressed. 'Yes, I think it does. Fine.'

'A photo of you with the fish would be brill, dad,' laughs Nicola, forgetting her earlier anger towards him.

'Okay, if necessary.'

Nicola pulls out her mobile and instructs the chefs to hold the fish near Frankie's face. In public, she has adopted a plummy voice.

'We want pictures too,' say the teenagers adjacent. They have pelmet skirts, tight tops and high heels. Their make-up is way over-the-top.

Struggling to hold the tuna, the chefs place a napkin on Frankie's shoulder and rest the fish on it. Three teens huddle round laughing and taking pictures. Flashes bounce across the room. The two chefs have taken an instant dislike to Frankie. One of them is muscular and Frankie flirts with him.

'Take my picture with this good-looking boy,' Frankie asks Nicola. He puts a hand firmly on the chef's arm. The young man is clearly uncomfortable as his face contorts in anger. Reluctantly, he poses with Frankie. One of the teens says 'hello' to Annabel and takes a picture of her. Annabel welcomes the attention.

For the main course, I order a fish pie. Y, has a seafood platter; Nigel, cuttle fish; Nicola, Dover sole; and Frankie, the tuna. Meanwhile, the behaviour of the birthday-partying teens is becoming rowdy.

My main course is delicious, if not small and over-priced. But, it's good fresh food. Initially sulking, Annabel doesn't eat much of her child's portion of fish cakes and fries. Now and then, she theatrically allows the food to slip out of her mouth and drop on the table. Y tackles his food with a healthy appetite. Every so often, he looks at Annabel. I'm sure he's keen on slapping her again. Whenever he's noticed, she retains the food in her mouth and chews rapidly. She's eventually hand-fed by Nicola.

'Is the tuna cooked to your liking, sir?' The waiter interrupts with a smirk.

'It could've been seared slightly longer. But otherwise it's fine.'

Nigel is still morose and I ask if he's okay.

'No. I've lost my appetite,' he offers in a whisper. 'I've not eaten properly for weeks.' Lazily, he plays with food on his plate.

'What's wrong?' I enquire.

'I hate that man.'

'Who?' I look over the restaurant.

'Y. He's a murderer.'

I listen intently as it's difficult to hear above the teenagers' loud chatter. This is besides the noise from the rest of the room.

'What's his background?'

'Nicola once said he's been in the Russian Army. Do you know how Frankie and Nicola met him?' Nigel leans closer, licking his lips nervously.

'Nobody has mentioned any details.' I slightly recoil from him as his breath stinks like a fishmonger's drain in summer.

We're handed dessert menus and I decide what to order. Y's mobile rings and he leaves the table. Nicola follows closely behind. This provides Nigel with an opportunity to continue our conversation.

'Three years ago, Frankie and Nicola attended an international art show. Y was staying at their hotel. He offered them pictures and Frankie immediately handed over cash. Y has a team of ex-soldiers working for him. They were going to murder Frankie and Nicola, then snatch the pictures back.'

I find this difficult to assess, though keen to hear more. 'Who told you this information?'

'An art dealer they know.' Nigel's mouth is barely moving. He wants to be anywhere but here.

'Y changed his mind. He believed the pair of them could be very useful. He thinks Frankie is a fool and can be easily manipulated. Frankie and Nicola were very lucky to escape alive.'

'What happened to the pictures?'

'They were sold, though I believe each one had been stolen.'

I don't comment. I feel sick.

'Since then, Y has sold them numerous paintings. He doesn't ask how many pictures they want to buy. He tells them the number they're having. Both are too scared to say no.'

'How are the paintings acquired?'

'Through robberies in Europe.'

'Are the pictures being altered?' I recall the Tom Brody incident earlier.

'Yes. Dick, Paul, and another competent artist and restorer, remove or add figures, animals or small buildings. This is an attempt to disguise the original.'

'Outrageous.'

'I agree,' he answers.

'Are Dick and Paul happy about this situation?'

'They don't care. After all, it's not them claiming the work is original. That's down to Nicola. She always takes ages to pay for their work.'

I remain silent.

Nigel adds further information: 'The publicity to sell the stolen and altered pictures is done by Nicola's assistant, Jess. Nicola has little knowledge of computers.'

'I've gathered as much.'

'Nicola's under enormous pressure to keep the business afloat. It's causing havoc with her mental health. She's on anti-depressants.'

Like a fool, I've stepped into someone else's nightmare. Art is my life. It's what I live for and hearing all these details is appalling.

'I ought to confront Y.'

'Don't. He's always armed.'

'He can't carry a gun in this country.'

'That doesn't bother him. I don't want my daughter in the same room.'

The little bitch seems to be in good company. Thankfully, two of the teenagers are keeping her amused.

'Does Frankie know Nicola is selling doctored stolen pictures?'

'He doesn't care. Profits fund his lavish lifestyle.'

'Isn't cash from stolen pictures underpinning your church project?'

Nigel doesn't hold eye contact when he answers: 'It makes me very uneasy.'

His face is pale, reflecting the turmoil within. The bizarre relationship he has with Nicola must also be taking its toll.

'If discovered the church was being financed by fraud, the press would have a field day. It's a disaster waiting to happen,' I state. 'How will the cash be raised to smooth over the church problems?'

'A massive robbery. A big job, worth millions, is going to happen. That will provide finance. My wife may have given the impression earlier that the company is struggling. But, she's very confident this deal can make a fortune.'

'Where, and how?'

'I'm not saying any more. I want this church project to happen.'

'Why not abandon the church for the sake of her health?'

'It's too late now.'

Frankie's wine glass seems like it's glued to his hand, but he makes a confession: 'I'm not feeling well. The tuna hasn't agreed with me.'

He releases a loud stink-bomb fart. This grabs attention from a family of four, two parents and two young daughters, seated behind him. The man twists round. 'You filthy disgusting animal.'

Frankie takes no notice.

'Urgh, what a dirty bastard,' one daughter shouts. The man's wife holds her nose and attracts a waiter's attention. I hear him promise that if there's another outrage, he'll alert Sally Braithwaite.

Annabel catches a waft of the offensive odour. 'That's disgusting, granddad.' She attempts to escape the stink by standing on her chair.

'What are you doing, Annabel? Get down,' Nigel rebukes.

A number of people stop eating to glance at her. Waiters mutter to each other. They're undecided how to handle the situation.

'My mum's a criminal,' Annabel suddenly yells across the restaurant. 'My dad says she's a prostitute. She says he's got a tiny willy.'

Gales of laughter howl through the room.

Frankie almost chokes on his wine, then laughs at Nigel along with everybody else.

Annabel doesn't want to stop. 'My granddad's a coke head and a pervert. He says my grandma's sex mad.'

The birthday party teens applaud Annabel's performance and take pictures. A few individuals stop eating and tell her to shut up and sit down. When a waiter approaches, Annabel spits at him.

'Please stop, Annabel, that's not nice,' says Nigel feebly. She responds by throwing leftover fries at him.

I leave the table to use the bathroom.

Whilst standing at a urinal, I hear a woman's gasps. They intensify until reaching a crescendo. Investigating further, I notice one of the cubicle doors is slightly open. Y and Nicola emerge. Adjusting a thong and pulling down her dress, Nicola smirks and heads for the exit. Y zips up, replaces a shoulder holster and gun, then slips into his jacket.

Nicola proves my theory that not every prostitute stands on a street corner to earn cash. What have I done to deserve being with this team of weirdo criminals?

After washing my hands, I head back to the table. Annabel is throwing food at everyone. Unimpressed, people lob it back. Y strides over to Nigel and slaps him hard.

'You're a wimp. Control her behaviour.'

People shout at Nicola: 'Your kid wants a good hiding.'

'Shut up, you fucking morons. Don't say that about my daughter!'

Nigel begins chasing Annabel. He's thwarted as the teenage girls block his way. Standing defiant with her new mates, Annabel hurls more food about. Rapidly, the restaurant is a battleground. People dash for the exit. One woman gets to her feet and gives Nicola a clout. The pair end up fighting on the floor. Two waiters bravely attempt to separate them.

'I feel unwell,' confesses Frankie. 'My tuna wasn't as fresh as they claimed.'

Sally Braithwaite commands us to leave.

'We haven't had a dessert,' I protest.

'Please, would you all leave?' she repeats, raking an unsteady hand through her hair.

I was looking forwards to a piece of New York cheesecake and a coffee. That would've finished off the meal nicely. I loathe Nicola. I'm feeling the same way towards Frankie. Why doesn't he assert himself more and stamp his authority on the company? He's such a coward.

Frankie releases more loud farts. Immediately, they bring a strong reaction. 'You dirty filthy bastard. Fuck off out of here.' Diners waft the air with menus trying escape the stink.

Sally's had enough. 'Leave now,' she shouts. 'You won't be charged for the meals.'

The waiters jostle us to the exit. When one of them touches Y, he's easily brushed aside. Other waiters are not allowing any new customers inside.

'Get out, fucking yobs,' people chorus.

Sally is insistent. 'Out. Get out now.'

Food and empty bottles are aimed us. I've never been so embarrassed in all my life.

Frankie confronts Sally. 'I'll pay for everybody. Sorry for the trouble. Take two grand off my credit card.'

'No. Fuck off, dad. Don't pay.'

'Shut up, Nicola, for goodness sake.'

Once the transaction is completed, the teenagers hug and kiss Frankie. They do the same with Annabel before leaving. Their birthday balloons are left bobbing about freely in the restaurant.

Nigel has Annabel in a headlock and they hurry to the exit. His fragile mental state is crumbling by the minute. Y and Nicola are in deep conversation and follow behind. Outside, Nicola orders a taxi for her, Nigel and Annabel to go home. Y and myself shall travel in the Rolls and drop Frankie off at his house.

'See you soon, Y,' Nicola winks.

'I'll have this restaurant firebombed in the morning,' he mutters under his breath. Then, he climbs into the front of the Rolls with me. Frankie looks washed out. He slouches in the back, farting frequently. Easing away with all the windows down, I glance in the rear-view mirror. Nicola and Nigel are fighting. Annabel, her white dress splattered with food, kicks out at people walking past.

# Chapter 6

Before leaving the restaurant, Frankie acquired six bottles of wine. Taking large gulps from one of them, he gives a new meaning to the word excess.

'Why are the windows down, Al?'

'Because it stinks in here. It's overpowering. I should have brought a gas mask.'

'Stop farting, Frankie,' Y demands, gazing straight ahead.

'Have you two heard these farting jokes?' he smirks as his arse sounds again.

'You're a one-man sewage farm,' I comment.

'A fart is a turd honking for a right of way. It's only a rumble in the backside jungle. I like playing my trouser trumpet. I'm in the brown horn brass choir.'

'Shut up, Frankie,' Y swipes.

He takes no notice. 'Behind every great fart there's a great behind. Wait a second. Here comes another one. Sorry, that could strip wallpaper. I'm conducting a methane production experiment. Oh dear. That was 7.4 on the rectum scale. I'm fond of singing the Anal Anthem. Performing the one-cheek sneak. Now I've had a big accident and done a wet poo.'

'Why not say you wanted a shit?'

'Oh, be quiet Al. I've not had a great night out until my pants are full of shit. Fuck, I've pissed myself as well, now.' Frankie looks dreadful but is still managing to be cheerful.

'This is disgusting.' Y's head is in his hands. 'You're an animal, Frankie.'

'Keep still, Frankie,' I urge. 'You'll soon be home.'

'Don't worry, Al. I'm enjoying myself.'

'You're losing it, Frankie,' admonishes Y. 'Excess will kill you. Have more self-control.'

'Don't talk nonsense. I'm a bohemian artist.'

'Can I use another vehicle to drop Y off, Frankie? Then, drive myself home.'

'Yes. Take Paulene's Porsche. This vehicle shall be valeted in the morning.' Attempting to take a drink, he misses his mouth, douses himself and drops the bottle. 'Oh fuck. Never mind, I have more bottles.'

'How will you open them?' I question.

'One of the wine waiters gave me a fancy bottle opener.'

Y and myself are bored.

'No, I won't have a drink. I'll have a snort instead.' From an inside jacket pocket, Frankie produces small bags of coke. Putting powder on the back of his hand, it's inhaled deeply. 'Ah, much better.'

Outside, people watch and marvel as the Rolls glides past. Some look like they might clap at the spectacle. One man stops, placing hands on his hips. Then, points out the car to his young son. Onlookers dream of wealth and having a vehicle like this one. Peering through the rear-view mirror at Frankie's pitiful state, I would advise them, don't wish too hard, wealth might not suit you.

The Rolls has been built by highly-skilled workers. They've served long apprenticeships. With this car, their talents have gone to waste. Shitting and pissing over the back seat of a Rolls is sacrilege. The car cost over two hundred and fifty grand, and Frankie paid two grand for his suit. After tonight, it will be dumped.

'Stop at the off-licence further along the road. I must buy wine for Paulene.'

'Have you none in the house?'

'No.'

Frankie climbs out of the Rolls and enters the store. Walking back to the car, he has four carrier bags with three wine bottles in each one. People passing by observe him, unable to believe his appearance. Clutching a big packet of crisps, he struggles to eat them whilst holding the wine.

Two yobs are loitering nearby. One shouts at Frankie: 'Hey, dirty bastard. You've shit yourself.'

'Fuck off,' Frankie replies. 'Or, I'll fuck you both.'

'Bet you wouldn't get it up in your state. You'd need a Viagra.'

'Don't worry, I've got plenty in my pocket.'

'Come on, Frankie,' I open the car door and shout. He moves away from the yobs and drops back into the rear seat.

I don't want to be present for very long when Frankie's wife, Paulene, sees him. She's prone to violence. Last December at the Greasby Christmas party – a lavish affair at a top Askworth hotel – she created an awful scene. One of the Greasby technicians is married to Carly, a stripogram girl. She has more than an ample cleavage. Frankie was transfixed, unable to divert his eyes. Seething with jealousy, Paulene pulled down Carly's top. Then, a fight started. The two women scratched, kicked and bit, though Paulene was easily beaten. She suffered a split lip, two black eyes and torn clothing. This didn't stop her attempting to save face by punching and kicking Frankie. Both of them had to be separated and were taken home by Nicola and Nigel. Carly basked in her victory and carried on partying.

Recently, when Frankie was abroad, Paulene asked me to pop over one afternoon with a few bottles of wine. Alone and craving company, when I arrived she was scantily dressed, with seduction in mind. I politely rejected her advances but ever since, we've remained good friends. Whenever she feels lonely, which is almost every day, she calls me for a chat. We talk like we're old friends. Previously, I'd merely danced with her at Christmas parties.

I fear for Paulene's sanity. She's a candidate for a suicide attempt. I would not be surprised to receive a phone call one day announcing she'd jumped in front of an express train.

Several months ago, Frankie brought Y to their house. Paulene overheard the Russian offering to make her disappear. She chased Y out. The reaction if she spots him tonight is perhaps predictable.

Opening another bottle of wine, Frankie spills it and drenches himself. He throws the half-empty bottle out of the window. A police car is behind, though some distance away.

'That chef was a real cutie,' Frankie begins, 'I should've got his number.'

'He spiked your tuna,' Y states.

'I wouldn't be so sure.'

'Is there a time when you're not pissed or coked-up?' Y asks.

'Each day, I try to drink and take more drugs than anyone.'

'You're a mess, Frankie,' Y scolds.

I can't resist speaking my mind: 'Frankie, you're out of control. You could overdose.'

He laughs.

Y changes the subject. 'Nigel is a pain in the arse. Poor Nicola. He's blackmailing her to finance his church.'

'How?' I ask.

'He's threatening to tell the police how Greasby operates.'

Yes, I thought Nigel wasn't telling me the full story.

'A prick like Nigel hasn't got the bollocks to open his mouth,' swipes Frankie.

'The church project is a ridiculous waste of money,' Y insists.

I nod in agreement. Frankie remains silent, taking swigs of wine.

'I've a plan to get rid of Nigel,' Y states.

'Shut up. Shut up, now. Planning a murder could make Frankie and me accessories to the crime.'

'Al, I like you,' Y admits calmly. 'I hope we can be friends and work together. I know you're keeping the Greasby ship afloat.'

He's carrying a gun. Will he use it?

Y leans over to me. 'Al, it would be good for you to have Nigel out of the way. He spends money you've earned on a fucking church. Nobody goes these days. Nobody.'

He continues in a lowered voice: 'I'm losing patience with Frankie, Nicola, and Nigel. I can easily have the three of them disappear. Then, we could run our own gallery. Your knowledge is great. I hear you know many collectors. We should talk about this.'

'No.'

'It could earn us plenty.'

Thoughts are overwhelming me. I must plan an escape route out of this rotten company. There's deep regret about putting my hopes in Frankie and Greasby Fine Art. I'm continuing to dodge away from grief. I've been doing it for the past 15 years. Something else is desperately needed in my life. A new project. Meet new people. But I'm not trawling the internet, demeaning myself by enrolling on dating sites to find an exclusive new partner. That's for sad, lonely people.

In the rear-view mirror, I see Frankie perk up and warn him: 'I don't want to be involved in criminality.'

'No need to, Al. Y is working with Nicola.'

'You've been missing for the last week. Where did you go?'

'Working out lucrative deals. You'll see the fruits of my labours very soon and, as you'd expect, I've been over-indulging myself.'

'Nigel tells me there's to be a big job soon. What did he mean?'

'No idea.'

I look sideways at Y. 'Burglary should not be a way of earning easy money and murder achieves nothing.'

'Al, there's no need for you to be involved with Y.'

'I'm happy to work with Nicola.'

'Half-an-hour ago Frankie, Y had sex with your daughter.'

'Where?'

'In the Gents' lavatory.'

Frankie is tickled. 'Well done, Y. I'm glad you could oblige. Nigel's definitely not satisfying her. Even Annabel said he's not endowed with a big chopper.'

'I didn't join Greasby to be mixed up in criminality. This is a real disappointment for me, Frankie. I'm thinking of handing in my notice.'

'Entirely up to you, Al. Personally, I'd be very sad if you left.

Very sad. Always regarded you as a true friend. Now, you're almost a business partner. Don't be so puritanical about life and art. I enjoy art giving me a good life. I live every day as if it's my last.'

Y laughs. 'Well said, Frankie. I couldn't put it better myself.'

'Don't be on a crusade to convince the masses about how great art is,' Frankie reasons. 'They couldn't give a fuck.'

I don't answer.

Frankie hasn't finished: 'For most people, Modern Art makes them recall the old tale of the Emperor being sold invisible clothes. They think it's one big con. I say, fuck them. Buy the fakes we produce. I couldn't give a toss. Stand back, Al. Look at art from a different perspective. The fake Lowrys we created sold faster than hotcakes. At one of the northern cunt's retrospective exhibitions, a number of the works were fake.'

'How do you know that?'

'A well-known forger told me so. I respect your stance, Al, only it's not relevant. Focus on organising our staff, the day-to-day running of the galleries, and your work with Brenda. Don't fuss. At Greasby, business is tough. We must make a living by whatever means we can.'

'Frankie, handling stolen goods and churning out fakes is a sure way to get us arrested.'

Disinterested, Frankie snorts another line of coke. Annoyed with him, I head down another route. 'Nicola should be made to leave.'

Frankie shows no reaction.

I switch to Y. 'What's the attraction of crime? Are you addicted to danger? The thrill of chancing your luck?'

He doesn't respond.

'I know what's happening. We're running two businesses. I'm attempting to operate legitimate art galleries. The rest of you are involved in nefarious illegal activity.' I'm half shouting the words. The police car still follows behind.

'Calm down, Al,' Frankie pleads.

'Cash earned from burgled art and fakes has made you too

comfortable, Frankie. It'll blow up in your face. Would you like to spend a few years cooped up in prison with no sex, drink or drugs.'

He cackles. 'The sex might be exciting. And, I'm sure there are ways and means to acquire drugs.'

Y is disgusted.

I lash out at Y: 'What are you doing carrying a gun? I ought to drive to a police station and hand you over.'

This job is a bigger nightmare than working for Askworth Council.

'Can't we try and work together, Al?' Y asks.

'No.'

'I need to talk about something touched upon in one of your articles. I've made an important discovery. We need to pool our resources. This is the big job you mentioned earlier.'

'No chance.'

Frankie sighs. 'Please Al, calm down. Why not take a holiday? See a psychologist. I'll pay. Don't lose yourself.'

'Greasby is falling apart,' I argue.

Any second, I expect Y to pull out the gun and threaten me. However, he remains calm.

'Al, don't concern yourself with Y.'

I never fail to be amazed at the amount of drugs and alcohol Frankie can consume, yet still be chirpy and reasonably coherent.

Unexpectedly, Y has a go at Frankie: 'You've lost it and incapable of running Greasby any longer.'

'I don't care,' he responds, gulping wine like there's no tomorrow. 'Do you guys want a drink?'

'No,' we both answer.

'Al is the best member of staff you have,' states Y.

'The only honest one,' I add.

Y offers a rare smile, then continues: 'Nicola needs cash. Fast. I want to help her...'

'Don't worry about Nicola,' Frankie interrupts. 'She's capable of looking after herself.'

'Is there a reason for building a church?' Y asks.

'Especially using cash earned from stolen art.' I flash Y a hateful glare.

'Don't quarrel, boys,' begins Frankie. 'Life and art are fun.'

'If you say so, Frankie.'

'Lighten your mood, Al. I'd no idea this job would wind you up so much. Live a little.' He uses more coke, leaving white powder traces under his nose.

I put questions to Y: 'How do you spend money earned from art robberies? Are you building a church too?'

'No. I look after my family. I want to give them the good things in life...I hear you're still deeply upset by your son's death.'

'Mind your own business.'

'Al doesn't drink, take drugs or fuck either sex,' Frankie tells Y.

'Don't mourn forever,' the Russian replies.

'Shut up.' I glare at him. 'I shall never stop mourning my son.'

'Have you painted grief, Al?' Frankie cuts in. 'You're an ex art student. Why not attempt to represent the subject figuratively? Or, in symbolic shapes and colours? It might help you.'

'Don't be sick, Frankie.'

'I'm being serious. It's surprising this hasn't occurred to you before. Use your trauma to produce paintings. Think of Edvard Munch's two pictures *The Sick Child* and *The Dead Mother*. He coped with grief marvellously. Translated it into great art. You must follow his example. A parent mourning a child might create something spectacular. Pick up the brushes again. You're a competent artist. You can paint and draw. I've seen your work.'

'No, Frankie. No.'

'You can have an exhibition in one of the London galleries. I'm sure paintings are ready to burst out. I should paint more often myself. If I could stay sober.'

'I'm not doing it, Frankie.'

'Have a few lines of coke, Al. I can hire two or three delicious escorts to pleasure you.'

'Never. The young bloke who mowed down my son was full of drink and drugs. He'd been to a brothel.'

Y tries to offer comfort: 'Don't suffer. Your son's death was a terrible accident. He wouldn't want you to live like this.'

'I'm not listening to a criminal.' Tears for Alex rise but they're swallowed down.

Y asks: 'Is your wife mourning the same way?'

'Shut up.'

'You can't stay in a state of perpetual mourning,' argues Frankie.

'I can.'

Frankie is dismissive. 'No, Al.'

'My son's body was a mangled mess. Hardly recognisable. My wife blamed me.' Tears trickle down my cheeks. My vision is blurred. 'Only a few hours before Alex died, I'd seen him play football and score an incredible individual goal. He was only a young boy.'

'Don't torture yourself,' Y insists.

'I'll do what I like.' My driving is erratic and the car wanders across the road. 'Clear off back to your own country.'

'Men shouldn't show emotion. Pull yourself together.'

'If I was given a pound whenever someone said that to me, I'd be very rich by now. Men feel deep emotions too.'

'You and your wife should've tried for another child.'

'Don't be so insensitive.'

'Leave grief behind.'

We look at each other face-to-face.

'You have to move on,' he's insistent.

I continue to weep and meander across the road in a built-up area.

'I've tiddled my pants again,' Frankie declares.

The police car behind flashes the blues.

'We're being stopped,' I shout to Frankie.

'Drive on, Al. I want a car chase. Drive on. I love the thrill of speed.'

'Put the coke in your pockets, Frankie.'

'Why?' He laughs. 'The officers might want a snort to help their night along.'

'Do it,' I insist, wiping away tears. Looking at Y, I dig: 'Make one wrong move and I'll grass you up. For carrying a gun. Organising art robberies. Selling stolen goods over here.'

Stoney-faced, he hurls a deadly look.

Rage has built up inside me and I glare back at him.

'I want to work in a healthy, normal environment at Greasby. You're spoiling it.'

Am I so desperate to remain involved with art? Can I continue to work at Greasby and endure any more criminality? A batch of stolen paintings will arrive in the morning.

'Do you want more money, Al? I'll pay whatever is necessary.'

'I ought to be as far away as possible from Nicola and this Russian idiot. I'm not risking my reputation or my freedom.'

'We'll sort something out, Al. I promise. Don't grass up Y.'

'My son is dead. This dickhead is alive. Life is unfair.'

# Chapter 7

Frankie stuffs the coke in his pockets. I hope the police don't search him. They may be put off by his appearance. Y is troubled. I pull up and jump out of the car, ready to confront both officers.

Members of the public are visible in this affluent area on the city's outskirts. One bloke is walking a small dog. Two joggers, a middle-aged man and woman, pause to admire the Rolls. They're probably trying to fathom how much it cost. How many miles it does to the gallon. The type of bullshit people run through their heads.

Two female officers, a blonde and the other with a ginger mane, step from their vehicle.

'Do you know why we pulled you over?' asks Blondie.

Frankie has opened his door. 'You were bored and wanted company?'

Both stare at me.

'Couldn't stop sneezing,' I explain, holding their attention. 'Might have a touch of hay fever. I'm okay now.' I blow my nose and wipe my eyes.

Frankie leaps from the Rolls and vomits. The two officers dodge out of the way.

'Are you celebrating?' Ginger questions Frankie.

'Yes,' he boasts. 'I'm championing art and being alive. *Ars longa, vita brevis.*'

Ginger faces me. 'As a matter of routine we need to breathalyse you.'

'And, give you a drug test,' says the other.

'Cool, which drugs are we testing?' jokes Frankie.

'How high are you?' Blondie asks him.

'No, officer, it's "Hi, how are you?".'

The two women assess Frankie's deplorable condition in his expensively tailored suit. I often pity the police. They never know what might be stumbled upon. It's a difficult job. A lousy one, in fact.

'How I would love to romp with you lovelies in those sexy, sexy uniforms,' Frankie admits. 'Permit me to touch the material. I like to pleasure myself wearing a police uniform. Could I borrow one?'

The two women roll their eyes and don't answer any of his pathetic questions.

Predictably, the results of my alcohol and drug tests are negative. They ask Y for his details and he gets out of the car. When he betrays a Russian accent, Blondie is curious: 'We want to have a look at your passport.'

I hold my breath. Both women scrutinise the document, though find nothing amiss.

'Are you here on a spying mission?' they joke.

'Yes, that's right.' He's reluctant to acknowledge the humour.

Frankie sprawls out on the rear seat and swigs the wine. Unfortunately, the officers notice small bags of coke he's failed to hide.

'These are for personal use,' he splutters.

The pair glance at each other.

'Are you Frank Greasby, the owner of that city art gallery?' asks Ginger.

'Yes.'

'I bought a picture recently. It's on my mobile. Would you have a look?'

After a while, Frankie sighs. 'It's by a competent amateur. No more.'

Ginger takes offence. 'It's better than the crap you were showing a couple of months ago.'

A wave of nausea washes over me.

Blondie is unable to resist joining in: 'I hate Modern Art. Those paintings were full of splodges and splashes. Nothing made sense. The colours were garish. What was the artist thinking? On night duty, we often peek through your gallery window.'

'I find all art stimulating,' spouts Frankie.

Blondie adds: 'I like paintings which look real. Like a photograph.'

I can't help but voice annoyance: 'Why are you and the rest of the public so obsessed with figurative art? Can't you appreciate anything else?' I try hard to control myself but fail. 'You're a bunch of morons.'

Ginger glares at me warily.

'Calm down,' pleads Y.

'Good job we tested you before hearing your rant,' says Ginger snarkily.

I'm wound up. 'Before the Renaissance, paintings looked crude and figures floated in the air. Medieval people thought they looked real.'

Both women believe I'm talking a different language.

I snatch the mobile. 'Your painting is shit.'

'At least you can see what it is,' they both argue.

Sensing I might lob the mobile away, both of them grab hold of me.

I rein in my anger. 'Sorry. Here's your mobile.'

'Al's under a lot of pressure,' Frankie speaks up for me.

I break down in front of the officers.

'Are you okay?' Ginger is concerned.

'Yes, I'll be fine.'

I move into the passenger seat. 'You drive the rest of the way, Y.' He nods.

Both officers eyeball him. 'We'd like to do more checks on your passport.'

'Why?'

'Only routine. Step over to our car.'

Another police vehicle arrives. Its two male occupants emerge and stand with Y.

The man who was walking the small dog has been lingering nearby for a while. In his 40s, he drops the dog lead, ambles round the Rolls and runs a hand along the bodywork. Half closing one eye, he bends down to admire the contours. Leaning into the driver's side, he smiles and says: 'I once worked for Rolls-Royce. May I sit behind the wheel?'

'Be my guest,' answers Frankie, coaxing the dog inside. It sits on the back seat, yelps and licks his face.

To my surprise, the car sparks into life.

'What are you doing?' I ask with alarm.

'Al, can't you see this guy wants to enjoy himself? Will you tell us your name, sir?'

'Derek. Could I take the car for a spin?'

'Do what you like.' Frankie is excited.

'What about Y?'

'Don't worry, Al.'

Frankie runs his hands slowly across the man's shoulders. 'What a physique you have.'

'Enjoy the ride,' says Derek menacingly.

'Take it easy. This is a 30 limit.' I point to a sign.

'Quiet, Al. This is unexpected. I like it. Away from normality.'

The police have sensed something is amiss and both cars prepare to follow. I notice Blondie ushering Y into a back seat.

'Slow down,' I shout.

'Speed is exhilarating,' Frankie crows.

'He's driving too fast. Much too fast. Slow down. Now!'

I want to go home. I'm depressed and can't take much more tonight.

Frankie zips down the rear windows. Air whistles through the car making the dog bark.

I gaze at Derek. 'Have you driven a Rolls before?'

'Of course.'

'Al, chill out. Embrace new experiences. Open your senses. You're too insular.'

'Frankie, we're doing 85 in a 30 limit.'

He belches loudly, then matches it with a noisy fart.

'Close your eyes, Al. A painting called *Speed* should be coming to mind. What images, colours, or shapes do you see? How will the paint be applied? Will it be on a large or small canvas? Maybe a wash drawing? Focus, Al. Your imagination must run riot.'

'Tell this joyrider to stop, Frankie. He'll crash the car. We might be killed.'

'Rubbish, Al.'

Derek howls with glee.

What's this about? Is there a grudge against the car company? What will he do next? Are we to be part of a ritual suicide?

'Don't mourn forever, Al. Put the experience to good artistic use.'

Derek laughs. Louder and louder.

Desperately, I try to take control of the wheel, only I'm forcefully brushed aside.

'My eyes are closed, Al,' begins Frankie. 'I see colliding orange and green rectangles. Large blue circular spots are attacking them. Surely, speed must be inspiring you?'

'Slow down,' I scream. We're rapidly approaching a man walking over a zebra crossing. 'Stop. You'll kill him!' Luckily, the man is mindful of the situation and escapes unharmed.

Both police cars are close behind. The blues are flashing.

'Frankie. He's driving on the wrong side of the road. We're going to die.'

Zooming into a Council estate, Derek brakes sharply. The car bounces over speed bumps.

I feel sick.

'Stop!' I scream again in Derek's ear.

'Only when I'm ready.'

Flying through a crossroads, fortunately we don't meet any traffic. Ahead, a car transporter slowly pulls out and stops. Joyriding Derek screeches to a halt. The police cars pull alongside. Manhandled out of the Rolls, Derek is handcuffed and led away.

'Leave him,' says Frankie. 'I've had the drive of my life.' He then allows the dog to jump outside. It yaps, and dutifully follows its master.

# Chapter 8

Frankie's three-storey, Gothic-style Victorian house is hugely impressive. The garden features a fishpond, water fountain, large urns and classical figures. It's well-kept and ought to be. Frankie employs two gardeners. The time is 8.45 pm. Both the house and garden are floodlit.

We move through electrically-operated gates before pulling on to a flagged courtyard at the rear of the house. I park adjacent to Paulene's Racing Yellow Porsche. Curiously, a battered Ford Mondeo is present.

'Who owns that scrapheap?' I ask.

'No idea.' Frankie walks towards the house, the mess in his trousers not bothering him. 'Don't go home straight away, Al. Take Y for a drink.'

Y raises a hand in protest. 'No. I'm feeling tired. You ought to remove your trousers out here, Frankie.'

The advice is ignored.

'I'll get Paulene's car keys, Al. Then, you and Y can be on your way.'

'Okay.'

Y rests on a white wrought iron seat, raises his mobile, and says: 'I'll speak with my family.'

'I won't be long,' I assure him.

Moving through the kitchen, I notice a half-eaten Indian takeaway on a table. Paulene never bothers to cook herself a proper meal. In kitchen wall storage holes, expensive bottles of wine and Champagne are evident. One night, when Frankie was paralytic, he gave me a thousand quid bottle of Champagne. We pass by a life-size, suit of armour. One hand clasps a fearsome pike.

Along the hallway, leading to the lounge, are six Pre-Raphaelite drawings. I often admire them and do the same briefly on this occasion. It's an enviable collection.

Paulene can be heard in the lounge. She's conversing with some males. A curious whirring sound is discernible. The room is sumptuous. It's adorned with heavy furniture and expensive antiques. Everything dates appropriately from the Victorian period. Nothing is out of place. Victorian oil paintings and drawings decorate the walls. Four of the paintings are by Henry Scott Tuke, one of Frankie's favourite artists. A deep-pile cream carpet smothers the floor. Air fresheners dispense fragrances that easily find their way to my nostrils. On a small table, lines of coke can be seen. Alongside, sit bottles of spirits and beers.

Paulene has black hair, dyed but stylishly cut to her shoulders. It glistens. She stands five and a half feet tall and is out of shape at 16 stones. Usually, she wears minimum make-up, only tonight she's gone over-the-top. It's a surprise to see her wearing just black patent high heels, stockings and suspenders. Clearly visible are rolls of fat and varicose veins.

Three naked studs – two white and one black – perform sex with her. In their 20s, they stand six feet tall and have well-honed bodies. All are Adonises. Designer clothing is flung over furniture. A fan wafts cool air on to perspiring bodies. Various sex toys are evident. I've easily identified the whirring sound. It's from a vibrator which one of the studs holds. The trio exude an assured, cocky air.

'Oh, hello, Frankie. Nice to see you,' Paulene scoffs, then, without flickering an eyelid, continues having sex. 'Where have you been for the last week?'

'Buying and selling pictures.'

'Whilst you've been away, I've been thinking. I'm taking a new lease on life. Waving goodbye to loneliness. And making my own friends and amusement.'

For Paulene, the days leading up to this must have been tortuous. She ought to be more involved with Greasby. She's intelligent and well qualified.

The studs remain aloof, their attention flitting between Frankie and Paulene.

'This is my husband,' Paulene announces aggressively to the trio. 'Take no notice of him.' She's pissed and slurring her words. 'The other man is Al. He's my only friend. Hi, Al. I'm having an orgy.'

Without doubt, Paulene is long overdue pleasure and excitement. I always thought of her as a Frankie Greasby junkie. Adoring him, never questioning his behaviour. She's finally snapped. Well done, Paulene. You've been roused at last. I want to give her a warm hug.

Frankie's eyes sparkle. 'This looks very exciting.' He claps his hands. 'May I join in?'

I never expected Frankie to react violently to this situation. He's such a wimp. I've frequently said: 'If you're so unhappy in the marriage why not get a divorce?' The question hasn't been answered coherently.

The black male offers an introduction: 'Hi, I'm Tyrone. My two mates are Troy and Ross.' He looks at Paulene. 'We can work out rates to include your husband.'

Frankie chuckles.

'Fuck off. That's not happening, Tyrone.'

Frankie is disappointed.

Paulene faces him. 'I spoke to Annabel earlier. You took everybody out for a meal tonight. Why wasn't I invited?'

Frankie doesn't react.

'I can't remember when we last went out together. I live on takeaways. I'm always ignored. It's not going on any longer. I've tried hard to support you and the business. No more, Frankie Greasby. No more.'

'I didn't think you'd be interested,' Frankie answers coyly. 'You're fed up with Nicola and Nigel always arguing. Tonight was no exception.'

Paulene continues: 'Fuck you, Frankie. These three are from Renta Stud. Men can easily hire women. Now, I'm hiring men. They can charge Greasby for tonight's session.'

Paulene has never spoken to Frankie in such a blunt way before. The studs don't look at us.

Like a marathon runner about to win a race, Paulene has joy pasted across her face. 'I'm not missing out on sex anymore. I've used countless batteries in my vibrator and never been satisfied. To have regular sex, I'll spend, spend, spend. Even if it bankrupts Greasby.'

Frankie has waited patiently to respond: 'Spend as much as you like, Paulene. It would be a delight to join in. These guys are so well hung. They're like donkeys.' His eyes linger on the men. 'Let's not fall out. I enjoy orgies. We'll organise many.'

'Fuck off. This is for me. I'm not sharing pleasure with you. No way. These three have made me feel alive again.' Paulene's words bounce with authority.

'No need to shout. I can hear you loud and clear.'

Paulene's studs aren't phased by our presence and continue to fuck her. A large television plays a porno film.

'Faster, faster,' she begs. 'Oh yes. Oh yes. More. You lads can do even better.' Her re-awakened sexual appetite bursts through. Hair and boobs bounce up and down in unison. Occasionally, her features are lost. She's sweating like a pig.

Frankie leans towards me. 'This is another subject for you, Al. The title can be *Woman in an Orgy*. For maximum impact, a scene like this demands a large canvas and must be depicted realistically. You might be applauded as *the* painter of orgies. Tonight, picture subjects are coming from all angles. Take snaps on your mobile. Use them like sketches. Awake from your mourning. Art cannot mourn. Rekindle the spirit of creativity inside you.'

I think deeply.

Frankie is on a roll. 'Before you die, Al, you must realise your talents and produce great paintings.'

Fishing out his mobile, Frankie takes pictures of Paulene and the three studs. 'Open your legs wider. Go on lads, give it to her, hard and rough.'

Paulene is suspicious. 'What the fuck are you doing, Frankie?'

'Al is ready to resurrect his artistic career. These photographs will help him create a painting he has in mind.'

'Brilliant. Take as many as you want. I'd love to be in one of Al's creations.'

'Very soon, I'm hoping to appear in a painting myself,' announces Frankie.

Something inside is stirring. Maybe I can relieve my grief by creating art again. If Paulene can break free, I will follow her example.

Frankie occasionally pats Tyrone's arse as it moves backwards and forwards.

'What a lovely dish,' he comments, then takes close-up shots of Paulene.

'Stand back, Frankie: I can't concentrate.'

Her attention transfers to the studs. 'Keep focused, boys. Don't stop. Please. Don't stop. Keep swapping over. It's Troy's go now, Tyrone, to stick it up my bum. Come on. Hurry up. I'm nearly there. Yes! Yes!'

Her cries become strident until there's an ear-splitting shriek.

'Oh! My first orgasm in years. In years.'

She takes deep breaths but is insatiable. 'Come on, fuck me again and again. I haven't enjoyed myself so much in ages.'

The scene is much different to our Sunday night business meetings between Frankie and myself. Paulene always tried to participate. Frankie constantly shut her out. Repeatedly, she's thrown wine in his face. One night there was a tense moment in the kitchen. Quarrelling like cat and dog, both eyed a collection of expensive knives sheathed in a block of wood. I was convinced each one would grab a knife and attack the other. Thankfully, they didn't. Nicola was expected to attend these weekly meetings though could never be bothered to show her horrible face.

Pausing, Paulene looks over at Frankie.

'I don't give a shit that you're watching three gorgeous blokes fucking me. Behind my back you've done the same with men and women. I'm not hiding anything and doing it in this house. Whenever I want to.'

Frankie smiles sympathetically.

Paulene continues her attack: 'I've helped with the business and got fuck all out of it. You've never wanted me to be involved. I'm more qualified. You've got a poor art degree. A pathetic 2.2. I have a First. I want more from this company.'

Paulene is controlling the situation like never before, drawing oxygen out of the room.

'You're already on the payroll, Paulene,' states Frankie.

'I'm paid no better than a cleaner. If I don't get more, I'll divorce you. Ruin you. There's only been indescribable loneliness for me. You've had everything.'

I'm trying to find an opportunity to ask Paulene for the Porsche keys. It's not forthcoming.

Frankie farts and bows his head. 'Sorry, I've had another accident.'

'What a stink,' Ross announces.

Paulene raises her head. 'You filthy bastard. You've shit yourself. Outside! Now!'

'Seems like he shit himself earlier,' says Troy with revulsion. 'Look at the carpet.'

Frankie makes for the door. Paulene follows, snatches a long-handled brush from the kitchen and hits him. 'Take your clothes off. Take them off. Trust you to spoil my enjoyment.'

Frankie obeys like a naughty child.

Clattering in high heels to the courtyard, Paulene spots Y.

'What's this cunt doing here?' Her face is wild.

Y expresses surprise on seeing her almost naked.

Before Paulene can launch an attack, I intervene. 'We're not staying Paulene. Frankie's messed up the Rolls. He said I can take the Porsche. I need the keys.'

Ignoring me, she glares at, Y. 'Fuck off, Russian dickhead. I told you never to shuffle your arse here again. Never.' Paulene throws a punch at him. 'Fuck off back to Russia. What would Lenin and Trotsky think of your poxy country now?'

I was praying they wouldn't meet. She slaps and punches

him. Y pulls out the gun. Fear runs down my back. Unimpressed, Paulene cleanly knocks the weapon out of his hand and picks it up.

'Shoot me, would you? Well, I'll fucking show you. Fucking scum.'

'No, Paulene, stop. You've started to enjoy yourself. Don't throw it all away. Give the gun to me.'

'Get him out of my sight, Al.'

'We're not staying, Paulene. I'm taking him to a hotel.'

'Call a taxi,' Y says, glancing at me as I pass the gun back to him.

Paulene bites at Frankie: 'Take your clothes off. You've ruined another carpet. We've only just replaced it.'

Frankie lies naked on the ground. Paulene hurls his clothes into a wheelie bin, grabs a high-pressure jet hose and aims the jet at him.

Pathetic.

# Chapter 9

Paulene is distracted when two police officers appear – a male and a female.

'What the fuck do you want?'

Noticing her appearance, the officers look at each other with unspoken questions.

'Show me your IDs,' Paulene attacks. Her face grows red with annoyance. 'I don't trust the police. Never have done.'

She throws down the jet wash and it bounces off the flags. Everyone ducks out of the way to avoid being drenched.

'I'm PC Atkinson and my colleague is PC Wormley,' the female reveals.

Paulene scrutinises their IDs with authority.

Frankie lays back, not bothered by the intrusion. Y and myself remain silent.

'Why are you here?' demands Paulene.

Atkinson speaks first: 'This afternoon, an individual filled a Ferrari with over a hundred pounds' worth of fuel. They drove off without paying. The vehicle is registered to this address.'

'Yes,' admits Frankie. 'It belongs to our daughter, Nicola.'

'This is irresponsible,' Atkinson continues. 'Driving a car which must have cost hundreds of thousands. It also has a personal registration plate. Yet, the driver won't pay for fuel. Disgraceful. As parents, you should be more responsible.'

'Fuck off, sanctimonious bitch.' Paulene points the jet wash at the pair.

'Stop, Paulene,' I intervene. 'The police have a difficult job. Don't drench them and add to their problems.'

'Are you drunk, Mrs Greasby?'

'What the fuck has that to do with you?'

Wormley confronts Paulene: 'There have been a number of incidents today involving the police and the Greasby family.'

Y swallows hard, finding this situation threatening.

'I know nothing of any other trouble,' Paulene answers truthfully, then fires the water jet on Frankie.

'Are things out of hand with the company?' interrogates Wormley.

'Not in the least,' splutters Frankie.

The police quiz Y and myself about our identities and we give satisfactory replies.

'Where is the Ferrari now?' Wormley queries.

'At Nicola's house,' I answer.

'Does she have the relevant insurance documents?' Atkinson asks Paulene.

'Of course. Don't be stupid.' The water jet is then shot towards Y.

'Stop, Paulene,' I plead as he moves nippily to avoid being soaked.

'I adore police uniforms,' Frankie enthuses. 'Could I touch them? I love having sex with someone in uniform.'

The officers are incredulous.

'What's actually going on here?' Wormley demands.

Ignoring the question, Paulene firmly holds the jet wash and continues to douse Frankie. 'Lie on your belly. Your filthy arse wants a good soaking. Part those arse cheeks, messy bastard.'

'Are you okay, sir?' The officers chorus.

'Stop interfering,' bawls Paulene. 'My husband enjoys a late-night shower. Al, fetch the washing-up liquid from the kitchen.'

After generously squirting Frankie, she drenches him again. He's lost under a sea of soap suds. Not phased, he turns to lie on his back, spreads his legs and laughs. 'Ah, beautiful, Paulene. Concentrate on my bollocks...Oh yes, lovely.'

Glancing at the police, Frankie has a big smile on his face. 'I'm okay. The water is cooling me down. It's not a problem.'

Atkinson and Wormley are lost for words. Y doesn't look at them. He remains detached, his eyes not settling on anyone.

'Al, there's cash in my wallet,' Frankie instructs. 'Pay the officers for Nicola's petrol, will you?'

I feel ashamed to be part of this scenario but retrieve the soiled jacket from the wheelie bin. Locating the wallet, I count out the required notes and hand them to Wormley. Y heaves a deep sigh of frustration. Like me, he's eager to leave.

Still naked, Tyrone, Troy and Ross step outside. Atkinson and Wormley exchange knowing looks. The studs dart back into the house. Clutching extendable batons, the two officers chase after them. We all watch in stunned silence.

A struggle is heard inside and voices are raised. Eventually, Troy is brought out in cuffs.

'What's happening?' I ask.

'There's a warrant out for his arrest,' replies Wormley.

'He ties up, tortures and robs old women,' sniffs Atkinson.

'Earlier, he wanted to know if I enjoyed bondage,' admits Paulene, grimacing.

'We noticed the cocaine in the house, Mr and Mrs Greasby,' comments Wormley. 'The drugs squad has to be informed.'

Troy is taken away still minus his clothes.

Tyrone and Ross appear and dress.

'We're off, Paulene,' says Tyrone.

'Okay. Thank you for coming. I've enjoyed myself. I love sex. You took me to dreamland.'

'We've left a card. Call us whenever you fancy mad sex,' Ross replies.

'Definitely. I want to be gang-banged and have multi-orgasms. Greasby Fine Art can pay. No problem.'

Everyone observes the pair drive off in their Mondeo, the exhaust noisily kicking out fumes.

'Why didn't Nicola pay for the petrol herself?' asks Paulene. We're still in the courtyard and she looks first at me, then Y, and finally Frankie.

'She's no cash,' Y volunteers. 'She's building a church for Nigel.'

'What? No cash? Building a fucking church? A fucking

church? Is this true, Frankie?'

Before he can answer, Paulene attacks Y: 'Instead of planning to murder me, Russian cunt, why not bump off Nigel instead? Have you thought about that?'

'Yes. I suggested it earlier.'

'Good.'

I can't believe I'm hearing this conversation again.

'The church design is quite pleasing,' Frankie reveals.

Y continues smugly: 'Nigel's blackmailing Nicola. Building the church is draining the company's funds.'

'I'll cut off the righteous twat's bollocks,' Paulene rages. 'Who goes to fucking church these days? Karl Marx said "religion is the opium of the people." It's still true today. Trouble throughout the world is caused by fucking religion.'

'The church building will make a pleasant addition to the area,' Frankie submits.

'Fuck off. You've always hated religious paintings. Thank fuck art is no longer dominated by the Church.' She stands over him. 'How much cash has been thrown at this fucking church?'

'I'm not entirely sure.'

Paulene slaps him. 'How much? Tell me.'

He doesn't want to speak.

'Can you answer my question, Al?'

'I understand it might be approaching half a million.'

'What? Half a million? For fuck's sake. How much have you earned the company since joining?'

'A similar amount.'

Using my mobile, Paulene contacts Nicola. 'What the fuck is going on? We've had the police here. You drove off without paying for petrol. Y says you're building a fucking church. It's going to stop. Right now…fuck off, Nicola…Nigel won't grass you up…I'll fucking kill the dog-collared wanker first. Building a church is not happening. No way. Not in a million years.'

Y holds his head in frustration.

Will tonight never end?

Paulene tackles Frankie: 'You're funding a fucking church

when I've wanted a new kitchen for the past ten years. What do I have to do to get one? Answer me.'

Frankie doesn't lift his head.

'I'll fucking show you. Watch.' Marching into a shed, she finds a long-handled axe.

Attempting to calm her down is fruitless. 'Stop, Al. I know you mean well. You've worked hard to earn cash for Greasby. We're not handing it over for wanker Nigel to build a poxy church. I should've been told about this before now.'

Having discovered sexual freedom, Paulene is now on a high. There's no going back. Disappearing into the house, she attacks the kitchen with the axe.

From a doorway, Y and myself watch glass and splintered wood fly across the room.

'Stop Paulene,' I implore. 'This is madness.'

'You could injure yourself,' warns Y.

'Don't anybody try to stop me, or I'll chop your fucking dick and bollocks off.'

'We need to talk, Paulene,' I suggest.

'Fuck talking. Greasby money isn't funding a fucking church. I want to spend cash being fucked every day. In fact, I'll buy Renta Stud.'

Dripping, Frankie stands with us. The kitchen is unrecognisable. Pots, pans and smashed crockery lie in a heap on the floor. Wall units, a ceramic hob and a glass-fronted oven are wasted. Paulene has done a good job.

'Now, Frankie Greasby, you'll have to buy a new kitchen.' She throws down the axe and strides over to him. 'Buy me one. Buy me one. Now!'

'You're on a coke come-down, Paulene. Snort more,' Frankie advises.

'Fucking arrogant bastard.'

'Not used to coke, Paulene. Are you?'

'I'll fucking kill you.'

Terrified, Frankie escapes to the courtyard and jumps into the Rolls. Snatching the pike from the suit of armour, Paulene follows. Frankie activates the central locking system.

Paulene isn't deterred. Smashing the windows with the pike, she attempts to impale him.

'The church isn't happening Frankie, is it?'

'No, Paulene, no.'

'You're going to stop it. Right?'

'Yes, Paulene.'

'I want the cash. I want to be fucked senseless. Every day.'

# Chapter 10

At 9.30 the next morning, I pick up Y and we drive to the Askworth Gallery. He's only managed a change of shirt from yesterday. Having a set of keys, I open up and we wait for Jess. She took a van to Germany on Thursday to collect the pictures Y is dumping on us. Within half-an-hour, she arrives.

In her late 20s, Jess is a Goth. She has tattoos, piercings and is always dressed in the customary black. Standing five feet eight, she's curvy and has a rounded pretty face. Her eyes are accentuated with heavy black eye shadow.

When Jess opens the van's back doors, I'm shocked. Pictures are stacked on top of each other with no thought of proper packing or transportation. Some are in bin liners. Others look like they've been literally ripped from walls. Frames are smashed and much of the glazing is shattered. Six pictures don't even have frames and show canvas abrasions.

This is scandalous.

I count 35 pictures in total, and the sizes vary from four feet by three feet, down to approximately 18 inches by nine inches. There's a mixture of well-executed 19th century landscapes and still lifes. Carrying each one from the van, we lean them up against the gallery walls.

'All the pictures are fantastic,' proclaims Jess.

She's right. The artists are well-known, and the entire collection must be worth well into six figures.

'A lot are damaged,' I sigh.

Y is unconcerned. 'They can be restored. Dick and Paul will sort it out.'

'Stop fussing, Al. They're only pictures.'

'Have you no pride in your job or respect for works of art?'

'Fuck off, Al. You're a pain.'

'Why weren't they packed properly?'

'It was awkward.'

'How?'

She smirks. 'Two of Y's men wanted a fuck so I had to oblige.'

'What?'

'Yeah, Al. To me, fucking is more important than neatly packing pictures.'

'They're worth tens of thousands.'

'Both men were animals. I thought they'd fuck fuck forever.'

I've not finished. 'There's significant damage to the frames.'

'If Dick and Paul can restore pictures, I'm sure they can do the same with frames,' Y answers.

'Of course they can,' Jess agrees. 'Easily.'

I glance at Jess and then Y. 'The pictures without frames may have lost exhibition labels and other vital information.'

Jess is dismissive. 'Fuck off. I can create any information required.'

'Fake it, or make it up.' Y is aggressive.

'In the past, we've regularly forged old exhibition labels,' Jess confesses, giving Y a tight hug.

He responds by squeezing her bum. 'You're so sexy, Jess.'

In response, she rubs his crotch.

'Where are the pictures from?' I glower at Y.

'Fuck off, Al,' Jess dismisses. 'Don't be so nosy. Who gives a fuck where they're from? I know loads of collectors that'll snap them up. Let's take money. Cash is king.'

Frankie pulls up outside in the Rolls. People stop and gaze at the vehicle's condition. After I unlock the door, he slips inside.

'Keep the door shut, Al, for now.'

'Okay.'

Although Frankie has a sepulchral complexion, he is dapper in another light-blue striped suit. A new day of drugs and debauchery has dawned.

'How are you?' I ask.

Nodding, whilst on his mobile, I instantly gather a conversation is taking place with a firm of kitchen fitters. In the other hand he's carrying an enormous holdall.

Ending the call, he hugs Jess. 'Have a good trip? Did you pick up everything I wanted?'

'Yes.'

'How was your night?' I ask him.

'Spent part of it in the Rolls. Paulene locked the back door before going to bed. Fortunately, she'd left the front door open. I sneaked inside for a few hours' sleep. Then, I showered, shaved and dressed before being chased out. She attacked me again with the pike. I bet it'd been in bed with her.'

Bruises are visible on him and an eye is swollen.

'Poor, poor Frankie.' Jess frets. 'What's happened to you?'

'I'm okay.' He pecks her cheek.

'You need to see what I've brought back.'

'Brilliant.'

I catch Frankie's attention. 'These pictures and frames are damaged. There's little provenance.'

Y moves towards me. 'Why don't you leave the company, Al? You're a pain in the arse and a liability.'

'I'm not going anywhere. I want to earn the company honest money.'

'Why not go to the cemetery and mope round mourning your son?'

'You scumbag.' I want to punch him but hold back. He's not winding me up.

Y draws his gun.

'Put that away,' orders Frankie. 'For goodness sake, there's no need for any of this. All of us should pull together.'

My mobile rings. It's Brenda.

'Are you in the gallery today, Al?'

'Yes.'

'I need you to sort out some business.'

'Okay. I'll do whatever I can.'

'We'll be there very soon.'

Frankie hands Y the holdall. 'There's eighty grand in there.'

I gulp, as Frankie appeals: 'Don't tell Paulene about any of this.'

I shake my head.

Y sits at a desk and begins to count the cash. It's in fifty-pound notes. I've never seen as much money.

'You're not counting it,' I comment.

'Why? I want to be sure it's all here.'

My eyebrows raise.

Y stresses to Frankie: 'This is only the down payment. I must have more.'

I've pricked up my ears. 'What's that for?'

Y pretends to not hear the question.

'Al, stop being nosy,' bites Jess.

'No need for you to be involved, Al,' sniffs Frankie.

I'm worried. Where's this leading? How will it end? Last night, I couldn't sleep, so found an old sketchbook and worked on ideas. It helped relieve the tension that had built up over the very stressful day. Strangely, my subjects mixed death with humour. I imagined skeletons stray from graves and involve themselves in various activities. The ideas made me laugh. I plan to continue.

'Here's the coke, Frankie.' Jess hands over a large package. 'It was ridiculously expensive.'

'Not an issue. Thanks for bringing it.'

'My pleasure.'

'I need to be sky-high after last night.'

Lines of cocaine are chopped on one of the desks. Frankie soon hoovers them up.

'Amazing,' he gasps.

I'm startled. 'Was coke sneaked through Customs?'

'Of course,' Jess boasts.

'This is a brilliant way to start the day.' Frankie punches the air. 'I'll have more.'

'I want a go,' insists Jess, laying out lines.

Frankie moves aside from the desk.

'Wow. It's very potent, Frankie.'

'I'm sure it's eighty or ninety per cent pure. Maybe even a hundred.'

'I agree,' says Jess confidently.

'This is a very rare batch. I've not had anything like it for ages.'

'Better be careful, Frankie.'

'Die happy is what I say.'

I look at Jess. 'Is this collection the big one I've heard about?'

'Nobody has said anything to me. Who gave you that information?'

'Nigel.'

She's amused. 'Get real, Al. Nobody listens to what that prick spouts. Surely, you've worked that out by now?'

'Cool it, Al,' states Frankie, who switches attention to Y. 'Was the hotel okay?'

'Yes, I sleep fine.'

'Did you collect the uniforms, Jess?' Frankie is excited.

'You're going to love them.'

'Oh Jess, what a darling.'

Carefully, she carries a number of cardboard boxes from the van. Removing the lids, she produces police uniforms, a Beefeater's attire and an archbishop's costume. Two St Trinians' school outfits complete the collection. They're neatly housed in transparent plastic bags. Frankie's eyes light up when he sees everything.

I'm curious. 'How did you get these?'

'Y's sister lives in Germany and makes items for a costume hire company,' Jess explains. 'She happily created them for Frankie.'

'They're beautiful aren't they, Al?' Frankie is ecstatic.

I'm not impressed. The weird clothing people want to wear for sexual excitement is astonishing.

'These costumes cost a fortune, Frankie,' Jess states.

'No matter. Anything to feed my ravenous perversity. Thanks for bringing them.'

'A pleasure.'

Y ignores everybody. He's counting the cash and doesn't give a toss about anything else.

Frankie strips, revealing a gold thong. It only just makes him respectable. Proudly putting on the archbishop costume, he's joyful the mitre fits comfortably.

This is madness.

'Can I wear one of the St Trinians' uniforms, Frankie?'

'Yes, by all means.'

She soon becomes a schoolgirl.

'Does it fit okay?' asks Frankie.

'Yes, fine.'

Frankie farts. Jess wrinkles her nose, pulls a can of air freshener from a desk drawer and sprays over him.

Two other boxes contain transgender porn magazines and a collection of sex toys. Jess picks up a strap-on dildo and fastens it to herself.

'Want to have fun, Frankie?'

'Oh yes, please.' His words are slightly slurred.

She nuzzles up against him playfully. Then, there's a chase in the gallery. The mitre falls from his head and both howl with laughter.

'I'm not feeling well,' Frankie admits. 'I need a little snort again.'

Y ignores the shenanigans.

Outside, people are queuing to enter the gallery. The Rackham and Dulac exhibition is proving to be one of the best shows staged since I joined Greasby. Carl and Di peer through the front window. Two youths, aged 17 or 18, stand with them.

'Open up the door for Carl, Di, and the two cuties,' Frankie instructs me. 'Tell everybody else we're closed today.'

'We could be losing business.'

'I need to enjoy myself.'

'Hi Frankie, are you okay?' Carl and Di enquire. 'We've brought entertainment for you.'

'Tell me more.'

Carl introduces the two youths. 'Meet Connor and Brady. They go to Askworth Public School.'

'Hello, nice to meet you both,' Frankie salivates.

'Can you help them with a Saturday job?' Carl continues.

'Yes. Put on these police uniforms. See if they suit you.'

Connor and Brady strip off.

'The lads want a hundred pounds each for the day,' Di announces. 'Of course, we'd like a fee too. Say, a hundred quid as well?'

'No problem.' Frankie produces a bundle of notes.

Public school rent boys. I groan inwardly whilst continuing to examine the pictures Jess has delivered.

Carl and Di spy the coke and beg a few lines.

'Be my guests,' invites Frankie.

Carl nearly falls over on hoovering up the coke. 'Fuck, Frankie. That's pure. A hundred per cent.'

'Exactly what I thought,' agrees Jess standing nearby.

'It's beautiful,' says Frankie snorting more.

'Me next.' Di steps forwards and makes the necessary preparations. 'Shit that's strong. Best I've ever had.'

'It must have cost a fortune,' guesses Carl.

'My face is numb,' admits Frankie.

'Take it easy,' urges Jess.

Di strolls over to me with a swagger. 'Still frustrated? Want me to bring you a Lolita? You look like a paedo. I thought so yesterday.'

I'm insulted and fire back: 'What sort of life will your child have?'

'Don't care. It's getting dumped after I drop.'

'Why not use contraception?'

'Punters pay good money to fuck pregnant lasses. The heavier the better. It floats their boat. I'm doing two blokes in a bit. Me and Carl can have a real crack-fuelled weekend.'

'You're throwing away a life. My son was killed in a car accident.'

'So what? I'm sure you're a perv.' She spits at me, though I dodge out of the way.

Alex enjoyed watching me draw cartoon characters. He showed early artistic ability himself. I must produce art. It's my way out of Greasby.

'Brenda's here,' I announce. She's with her team. They spray-paint the windows with the words FAKE HOUSE once more. It took us ages to clean from the previous occasion. Tagging along with them is a bloke I don't recognise.

'Our deputy headmaster is with those women,' reveals Connor now dressed as a policeman.

'He's a right perv,' adds Brady, also in plod uniform. 'Canes lads for cash. But, doesn't know when to stop. Everyone calls him Whacko.'

'Sounds exciting,' says Frankie expectantly.

'We'd rather not see him,' admits Connor.

'Go through those doors and find your way up to my office. I'll be along shortly.'

'Don't be too long,' they answer, fondling him.

'I've been looking forwards to meeting this bitch.' Y stands up, bristling with bravado.

'Don't cause trouble, Y. Go,' Jess begs. 'Brenda is one of our best customers.'

'Nicola has told me about her.'

'Stay out of it. We can't afford to lose you at this stage.' Jess looks at him knowingly.

'I'll teach her a lesson.'

'Please, take the cash and go.' Jess points Y towards the door.

Brenda and Y meet in the middle of the gallery and stand toe to toe. Whacko, carrying a snooker cue case, dodges aside. Jess and I are anxious to discover the outcome.

Will Y use the gun? I hope not and hold my breath.

Brenda is taller than Y and even heavier. He's intimidated, perhaps wondering if losing a fight to her might injure his ego more than his body. Y glances to see if I'm watching.

Jen, Barb, Deb and Ellen gather close to him. Deftly reaching over his shoulder, Deb grabs the gun. Without much resistance,

Y's wrestled to the floor and pinned down. The women are determined to humiliate him.

Brenda kneels and produces a felt-tip pen. Very slowly, she neatly writes MALE SCUM on his forehead.

Opening the holdall, she's pleasantly surprised. 'Money, money, money. This is mine. Nicola owes me thousands. Now, fuck off, Russian cunt.'

Brenda's women throw Y out of the gallery. Sensing more trouble, Carl and Di make for the door. Deb kicks Carl up the arse as he walks past. Di does not flinch. Her eyes are firmly fixed on the exit.

'Hi, Brenda,' I walk towards her. 'Is there a problem?'

She shakes my hand. The other women nod a hello.

Frankie distances himself from the melee, sits down and sniffs more coke. Jess waits waits patiently for a toot. Occasionally, she flicks through one of the transgender porn mags and shows Frankie the illustrations.

'This is my cousin, Jim Bennett,' Brenda begins and lowers herself on to one of the gallery seats. 'Nicola's ripped him off.'

'How?' I ask.

Jim collects paintings by Ralph Finnegan who died in 1952. Finnegan is well-known for his male flagellation subjects.

'Yes, I know his work.'

'Alarm bells rang when Jim said Nicola Greasby had sold him Finnegan pictures.'

Jim adds to the story: 'I don't have any sense of smell. I bought five pictures, each one dated in the 1930s. When Brenda examined them, she could smell fresh paint. A scientific analysis revealed they've been done within the last few months. Another discovery was the fake exhibition labels on the reverse.'

'I did those,' Jess confesses. 'I'm sorry, Brenda, I didn't know Jim was your cousin. I'll do anything to make it up.'

'I'm sure you will, sweetie.'

This is ridiculous. People are regularly bringing back fake pictures.

Brenda and her team gaze hungrily at Jess. Provocatively,

she fingers her crotch.

'Jim wants reimbursing,' insists Brenda. 'With twenty per cent interest.'

'How much has he spent?' Frankie questions.

'Sixty grand,' Jim answers.

'He wants extra cash for the inconvenience suffered,' hassles Brenda.

'I'll be happy to consider any request,' Frankie concedes.

'Good. He's going to thrash you, Mr Greasby, and your daughter.'

Jim removes his jacket and opens the snooker cue case which contains canes. Taking one out, he swishes it excitedly.

'This has whacked over a hundred bottoms. Both male and female. I keep detailed records.'

Brenda's women guffaw.

'Nicola's not here, today. I'll take any punishment for both of us. May I change into the Beefeater's costume?'

Brenda's women laugh even louder.

Jen moves towards him and sings in her Punk voice.

*We're gonna whack you.*

*We're gonna whack you.*

*I bet you'll like it.*

*I bet you'll like it.*

She plays air guitar and jumps up and down.

'I'll take the caning for Nicola,' Jess volunteers.

'No, sweetie,' says Brenda. 'You and I will enjoy ourselves soon.'

Frankie tries to speak but his words are jumbled. Attempting to remove the archbishop garb proves impossible. He can't coordinate properly. One side of his face has dropped. He slumps down on a chair and loses consciousness.

'What's wrong, Frankie?' Jess yells. 'Oh no. Frankie, I love you.'

A 999 call is vital. After a few seconds I'm connected.

'I think it's a stroke,' I blurt out.

Instructions are given to loosen clothing and make sure he

can breathe easily.

'We must save him,' Jess screams.

'Sit tight. Help is on its way.'

Brenda picks up the holdall and advances to the door. Her entourage follows.

Sex, pain and fun are the main areas of interest today. Should I make paintings showing these subjects? I'll give it thought.

# Chapter 11

At 6.00 on a Sunday morning, I park my car outside Nicola's house. We are travelling to the Liverpool Art Show. Thankfully, she's ready and waiting on the driveway. Working at the company's other galleries, I've not seen her for a week. I'm dreading spending an entire day together. For the show, I decided to wear a suit and collar and tie.

Nicola is dismissive. 'You're looking smart, Al. Is it necessary?'

'I think so.'

By contrast, she's dressed casually, though still looks attractive in trainers, jeans and a jumper. She possesses a strange beauty that punctures her horrible personality.

'Take Annabel with you,' Nigel shouts to his wife, pushing their daughter through the front door. The young girl looks like someone's dragged her out of bed. Still in a nightie, there's nothing on her feet.

'Oh no. She's staying with you.'

Nicola has no interest in Annabel. No motherly rapport or compassion.

'I'm taking three services today,' Nigel claims. 'She causes mayhem in church.'

'She's not coming with us.' Nicola shakes with anxiety.

Annabel wipes sleep from her eyes.

'Go inside.' Nicola shoves her.

Nigel attempts to close the door, only Annabel wedges it open.

'Stop it, both of you. This is cruel. You're hurting her.'

'Open the fucking door, you prick.' Nicola attempts to slap Nigel.

'She's not staying with me,' he protests.

Annabel cries. 'I want to go with you, mummy.'

'You're staying here with your dickhead dad.'

'No, mummy, no.'

This is a good start. I hope Nicola wins. A day with both her and the kid from hell will drive me crazy.

'Open the fucking door, Nigel.'

'She's not staying. That's final.'

Nicola punches Nigel in the face and he falls back. This provides Nicola with the chance to ram Annabel inside and close the door.

Thank goodness.

Annabel can be heard protesting. 'Mummy, I want to be with you. Please, mummy. I'm not staying with dickhead dad.'

Nigel responds by forcing her out, then locks the door.

Nicola is full of rage. 'Nigel, she's not dressed.'

There's no response.

Nicola bangs on the door. 'Did you hear, Nigel?'

Still no action.

'Don't leave me, mummy.'

'You're staying here.'

'No, mummy.' Annabel is crying.

Nigel shouts from inside: 'Have you transferred money to the builder?'

'Fuck your church. We've no money.'

'He's ready to put the roof on.'

'Offer him pictures instead of cash. Be resourceful for once.'

'That's ridiculous.'

Nicola is insistent. 'Annabel has got to stay with you. I must take money today.'

'To give your Russian lover?'

'He's a better fuck than you. Open this fucking door.'

A neighbour has been roused. 'What's going on? Do you know what time it is?'

'Fuck off,' Nicola volleys. 'Mind your own business…Nigel, you're holding us up. We'll be late for the show.'

He unlatches the front bedroom window. 'She's not staying with me. No way.'

Annabel tugs at Nicola. 'Please mummy, I want to be with you.'

'Nigel, your daughter is still in a nightie.'

He retreats out of sight.

How and why the pair came together is a mystery. I've never probed for details. They're repulsive. The less I have to do with them the better. Painting and drawing are helping to numb my grief. It's certainly less painful now.

One neighbour, standing outside her house, attracts Nicola's attention. 'You're not fit to look after that child. I've a good mind to inform Social Services.'

'Fuck off, nosy bitch.'

Nigel can't be seen.

Now full of energy, Annabel jumps up and down on the front lawn. Then, she kicks the heads off flowers along the borders. This is a shame, as the garden is lovingly tended by a local man who does a great job keeping everything neat and tidy.

'Where the fuck are you, Nigel? Let her back in.'

Frustrated, Nicola picks up a stone from a rockery and hurls it at the bedroom window. A pane is shattered. Annabel throws another stone and smashes a downstairs window.

Nigel reappears.

'Open the fucking door,' Nicola thunders. 'We'll be late.'

Flushed with success at breaking a window, Annabel is cackling.

Nigel throws down one of his daughter's dresses, underclothes and a pair of shoes. Once out of her nightie, Annabel flings it across the garden strewn with flower heads.

'You're fucking dead when I get back,' promises Nicola.

The three of us climb into a hire van which is parked nearby. I will drive. Annabel sits between Nicola and me on a bench seat. In the back are pictures we're taking to the show.

'Why couldn't Jess drive the van and we travel in a car?' I complain, setting off.

'She's gone to an orgy with a gang of bikers.'

Dick and Paul are meeting us in Liverpool. They have the display boards and will hang the pictures before going to look behind the scenes at the Walker Art Gallery. I arranged this for them. They'll be back later to load the boards.

Nicola scowls. 'You grassed me up to mum about Nigel's church.'

'Y told her. Not me.'

'I don't believe you. Mum now wants to run the company.'

'Perhaps she'll do a better job.'

'Fuck off.'

'I hope she doesn't spend the profits on studs.'

'She's sex mad.'

'Like most Greasby family members,' I poke.

'Fuck off. If it was up to me, I'd sack you.'

Annabel grabs hold of the steering wheel and we career across the road. I swerve to avoid a head-on collision.

'Stop it!' I shout at her. 'Don't ever do that again. We could have crashed, stupid little girl.'

Annabel giggles. Her mother says nothing.

The conversation is almost non-existent. There are long painful stretches of silence. With Nicola, there's no small talk. No friendliness. Nothing. She rarely smiles, and only after a customer's been swindled.

I break the monotony. 'The pictures I chose to bring today could have a good impact at the show.'

'I don't agree.'

'What?'

'I've loaded those we got from Y last weekend.'

'That's incredibly risky.'

'We need sales.'

'This is crazy. We could be arrested.'

'Whilst dad is in hospital, I'll say what's happening. Not you.'

Today, with these two, it'll be unbearable, I'm sure.

Movement can be heard in the back. 'Are the pictures properly packed?'

'Fuck off. Who's bothered? They need to be sold.'

During the week, Dick and Paul said Y's pictures were stolen in a burglary involving a Swiss collector.

I face Nicola. 'Brenda phoned last night. She wants paying.'

'We've no money.'

'She needs to finance her Lesbian Art Museum.'

'Who'll visit the place? There can't be that many dykes.'

'She's becoming impatient.'

Fear is evident in Nicola's voice: 'I hate dykes. I'll call the police if she attacks me again.'

'I wouldn't. She'll tell them about your fake paintings.'

'We've no money.'

'You're playing a dangerous game.'

Nicola shrugs.

Annoyingly, Annabel keeps kicking the dash panel.

'You should persuade Brenda to be more involved with Greasby.'

'I hate dykes.'

'That's stupid prejudice. Brenda wants us to continue handling her father's pictures. She knows other collectors keen to offload works. I've put her in contact with people willing to sell their lesbian paintings. Deals can be brokered. This is a marvellous opportunity. We can't upset her. There's a chance to earn honest money.'

'I'll have revenge for what she made me do. Y was pissed off at the way she treated him. We'll both have the last laugh on her.'

Annabel keeps yawning and pulling faces. She's bored with the conversation.

'I think we should work closely with Brenda.'

'There are lots of art collectors. She's not the only one. All of them can be of use.'

'I'm not convinced.'

'Why not fuck off and work for your beloved Brenda? I never wanted you to join us.'

'I'll leave when I'm ready.'

'Your matey relationship with her could be fatal.'

I don't rise to the bait.

Nicola's thoughts move in another direction. 'We owe one of the London landlords for maintenance charges on two galleries. If we don't cough-up soon, he'll bring in the bailiffs.'

This is unbelievable.

'Do you know how much we took last week?' Her cheeks flush.

'I've not seen any figures.'

'Fuck all.'

I'd like to believe you, Nicola, but you tell lies.

'Fuck all,' parrots Annabel springing to life. 'Fuck all. Fuck all.'

'How much have you and Frankie taken out of the company over the last few weeks?'

Nicola is furious. 'Greasby finances are none of your fucking business.'

'They are when you're robbing the company.'

'Shut up.'

'How much are you paying to cope with the problems Nigel mentioned last week?'

'Fuck off.' Her voice rises. 'If Greasby doesn't take more cash, we'll go bust.'

'How much has Frankie spent on coke and public school rent boys?'

She ignores the questions. 'We need cash. Or, galleries must close. You and everybody else might not be paid this month.'

'What about the big job? Will that help with cash flow?'

'What?'

I don't speak.

'How do you know about that?'

'Nigel told me.'

'I'll fucking kill him.'

'You were going to do that anyway. Will you kill him twice?'

'Fuck off, smart arse.'

There's no more conversation for mile after mile. The motorway traffic is heavy. Nicola falls asleep for an hour until Annabel thumps her.

'I want a drink mummy, and something to eat.'

From a bag, Nicola hands over a can of pop and a breakfast bar. Annabel deliberately shakes the can and pulls the tab, showering me.

Nicola and Annabel laugh.

'You're not used to having children, are you, Al?'

An arrow has pierced my heart.

'I bet you were a useless parent. Or would have been if your son had lived.'

Looking at her with revulsion, I want to go home.

Annabel takes a bite from the breakfast bar, chews, then spits it out over my trousers.

Nicola is amused.

I'd love to tie Annabel up and dump her in the back. That ought to have done before we set off.

At 7.30, Nicola phones one of the Greasby gallery managers.

'Fuck being in bed,' she begins. 'Get up. There's a job. Find your customers' credit card details. Remember, I told you to store them? Account numbers and passwords. Everything. Take two grand off each one...'

'That's illegal,' I interrupt.

'Fuck off.'

Continually trying to make a mark in the company, Nicola hates living in Frankie's shadow and being nothing more than his employee. She loathes people older than herself. They're intimidating and make her feel inadequate. A reminder Frankie is in control. Nicola's wayward ambitions are becoming ever more outrageous. They'll lead us down a road to ruin. Phoning more managers, Nicola gives the same instructions.

'Take as much as you can off each card.'

'What good will this do?' I exclaim. 'We'll have to pay it back.'

'No. Y's pictures will be offered instead.'

'How can that work? These pictures are worth more than two grand each.'

'I've done it before. This is how we earn cash in private

business. This isn't the fucking Council. We have to *earn* our living.'

'Staff have joined a trade union. There'll be trouble. Big trouble. You can't ask them to act in a criminal way. They'll take you to an industrial tribunal and win hands down.'

'Shut the fuck up. You really drive me crazy with your bullshit. I'll sack anyone who disobeys me.'

I grimace. 'You're not clever enough to be a criminal.'

Wrenching off the seat belt, she leaps up and hits me.

'No mummy, we'll crash.'

'Sit down, stupid cow.'

'Why not retaliate?'

'Will you want mad sex afterwards?'

'Yes. I'm ready. Do you fancy me, Al?'

What a nutcase.

'No.'

Annabel looks at me. 'Mummy says she's seen you wanking.'

Nicola cackles.

I glare at her.

'You told my dad you wank.'

Thanks, Frankie, for grassing me up.

Annabel sings: 'Al is a wanker. A wanker, a wanker. Pulls his plonker, plonker, plonker. What a wanker, wanker. We sing it every day. Dad doesn't, though.'

She fists me hard in the groin. I pull over to the side of the motorway and insist Nicola changes places with Annabel.

This does not silence Annabel. 'Al is a wanker, a wanker, a wanker, pulls his plonker pulls his…'

Nicola elbows her in the face. Annabel howls.

I'm annoyed. 'Give her proper attention.'

'What do you know about raising kids? You've got none.'

It's unbelievable how nasty and insensitive people can be.

'Bitchy today, aren't you? Had a tiring night shagging Nigel?'

'Mind your own fucking business.'

'When did last throw yourself at Y?'

She glares at me.

'Don't you feel any guilt shagging two men? Especially when one of them is a vicar.'

'You think we can't sack you.' Her eyes widen.

'That's right.'

There's more silence for miles. It's an easy though boring drive. The weather is dull, but the temperature is comfortable. I reflect on my skeleton pictures. One I completed recently shows two skeletons playing table tennis across the top of a tomb. I've done a pen-and-ink drawing of two skeletons copulating. Another depicts a male skeleton caning a female. My artwork owes a lot to English satirists like Hogarth, Rowlandson and Scarfe. It also nods to the work of Belgian artist, James Ensor.

# Chapter 12

The Liverpool Art Show is being staged at a large venue on the city's outskirts. Dick and Paul have already arrived with the display boards. Both are casually dressed on most days and today is no exception. Dick is letting his grey hair grow long. Paul's neat goatee beard has been allowed to extend across his face. They perfectly resemble Victorian artists, the type once captured in sepia photographs. The 19th century was an era when artists showed great technical ability and one in which Dick and Paul rightly belong.

Slipping out of the van, Nicola doesn't acknowledge them and they ignore her.

'When you've set up the pictures, bring my bag into the hall, Al.'

Leaving Annabel, she wanders off to chat with exhibitors. It's too mundane for her to help with setting up the display. She'll look at what the other exhibitors have to offer, then try to broker a deal using our pictures. I've heard it's done at every show.

Paul can't resist a comment when Nicola is out of earshot. 'After all the scams, I can't believe she's still alive. It's a wonder a bullet hasn't found the back of her head and the corpse dumped in a ditch.'

'I pray for that to happen,' Dick swipes.

Forty UK commercial galleries are exhibiting at the show. For a town or city to stage such an event is a coup. Prestigious pictures worth thousands are displayed. Annually, Greasby attends half a dozen of these art shows. I notice a security company is employed and their burly staff prowl bullyingly. This type of art event usually attracts a good, largely middle-class crowd. I've attended a number of them previously but only as a visitor. Often, there's a competition to select the best picture displayed. Throughout the day, four art historians will visit stands and agree a judgement. The winner is usually announced in the middle of the afternoon and an impressive cup presented.

Into an alcove, Dick, Paul and I arrange the freestanding display boards. Then, we pull the pictures from the van. Annabel follows and keeps lifting up her dress and flashing anyone who takes notice.

The two restorers are shocked to learn we're exhibiting the nicked Swiss pictures.

'After we spoke to you on the phone during the week,' starts Paul, 'we carefully bubble-wrapped the pictures you'd requested. We've been too busy to start work on this latest batch.'

During the journey here, a few works have suffered even more damage.

'This is unbelievable,' comments Paul. 'It shows a lack of respect for art by Queen Bitch.'

When I bring Nicola's bag to our stand, the pair eagerly look through the contents. They're overjoyed at what they find.

'There's twenty grand in here,' says Paul, his face lighting up. 'A bank receipt confirms it. We're taking it all.'

'Yes,' Dick agrees. 'The bitch hasn't paid us yet for those pervy Ralph Finnegan paintings. We put hours of work into those. Payment has been due for ages. Finding this cash is a godsend. I'll nip the bag to our van.'

'Are you being paid for working today, Al?' Paul asks. 'Nobody in the company wants to do art shows anymore. Nicola won't pay them. She takes the piss.'

I shrug my shoulders.

Paul continues: 'A year ago, staff agreed to work over the weekend at a show. Nicola booked three blokes and a young woman into one room. A cunt's trick. Today, she won't even offer to buy you a cup of coffee. Tight bitch.'

Annabel tags along as I buy food from a van in the car park.

Bacon sandwiches and coffees for Dick, Paul and myself. A cheeseburger and a can of pop for her. Back at our stand, I lay the pictures out. They'll be fastened to the boards with mirror plates.

Annabel shakes the can of pop and can't resist pulling the tab. The three of us and a couple of pictures are sprayed.

'Stop, you naughty girl,' shouts Dick.

'My mum says you three are Council house pricks.'

We make no comment.

'Urgh, this tastes awful. I don't want it.'

'You said you were hungry,' I submit.

She takes the cheeseburger apart and throws the contents at Dick.

Unable to control himself, he strides over and sharply slaps her face. Yelling, her eyes fill with tears.

Earlier in the week, we had a bundle of flyers printed. They give a brief history of the company and the services we offer. Annabel starts tearing them up.

'Stop it, Annabel,' I demand. 'We need those.'

Taking no notice she scatters the remnants everywhere, then thumps me in the goolies.

'If you don't pack it in, you'll have another slap,' promises Dick, stepping near to her.

From Dick's large toolbox, Annabel takes a hammer and hurls it at him. After he lands another smack, she runs away.

'I've been wanting to give the little bitch a good clout for a long time.'

Whilst hanging the pictures, we chat easily.

'Have you two heard anything about a big job?'

Both of them glance at each other. 'We've heard rumours,' begins Paul, 'but nothing else.'

Dick is eager to add more: 'I overheard Nicola talking to somebody on the mobile and she mentioned a big job. I'm certain Y was at the other end. A promise was made to raise loads of cash. I couldn't make out any other details.'

With quick eye movement, Paul looks at me with concern.

'Nicola mentioned there were interesting details in your past articles. She's latched on to details of a collection.'

I'm puzzled.

'She's planning something with Y,' Paul continues.

Dick joins in: 'Watch your back. Those two will stop at nothing.'

'This big job is hush hush,' I state. 'Jess is usually a good source of information but she deflects any questions.'

Our display looks pathetic. There are pictures without frames. Others still show significant damage.

Nicola storms back. 'Who slapped Annabel? Tell me.' She blinks rapidly looking uncomfortable.

Dick and Paul remain calm. This is a one-sided power struggle. Her position in the company carries no weight with them. Both are intent on making her explode. They hope she'll shout and scream, making a fool of herself. Nicola's a hate figure and knows it. They're talented, she isn't. They're worldly, she's naïve.

With penetrating eyes, Dick sticks his chest out. 'We all gave the horrible little cunt a slap. She deserved it.'

'What are you going to do? Sack us?' asks Paul coldly, tugging on his beard.

'Yes, I am.' She drops her head, afraid to look at us.

'We're your most important staff,' Dick answers back with a frown.

'You're all sacked.'

'Okay,' Dick continues, his face serious but with an undertone of malice. 'When we return to Askworth, I'll enjoy nipping to the police station and telling them all about you.'

Paul smirks. 'We're keeping your twenty grand. It's payment for the Finnegan pictures.'

Nicola desperately scans the area for her bag.

Dick stands closer. 'We didn't do the paintings on sale-or-return. Never will.'

'Give it back to me. Please,' Nicola begs, her eyes widening.

'No,' says Dick confidently.

Supporting her mother, Annabel throws more tools at the pair. I restrain her, only she struggles and kicks out.

'Why have you brought these pictures?' complains Dick.

'You didn't allow us to work on them,' Paul adds. 'This display is terrible and reflects badly on Greasby. How do you expect to sell pictures in this condition?'

Nicola boils with anger, though is at a loss for words.

'This display won't do our reputation any good,' says Dick. 'It's on the floor already. You're out of control. You don't deserve to be part of this company.'

Throughout any day, Nicola makes valiant attempts to speak quietly, politely, even jokingly. But she finds this difficult to sustain.

With a skinny fist, she throws a punch at Dick, though Paul thwarts her. He holds Nicola tightly while his mate swipes her hard across the face. People gaze in shock at what's happening. They're horrified, witnessing a man hitting a woman. What if he hadn't defended himself? What if he he'd gone to the police and complained of an assault? How seriously would it have been taken?

Nicola hurries away in tears, pulling Annabel along with her.

'Fuck off, bitch,' volleys Paul.

# Chapter 13

Nicola reappeared once Dick and Paul had left. Our display is attracting attention for the wrong reasons. Posing po-faced art connoisseurs in cravats and dicky bows sneeringly ask why the pictures are in such a state. Nicola snaps at them, saying they were in a road accident the previous day and there wasn't time to select any others. Of course, nobody believes her. On the other hand, some people linger and admire them. I hope our reputation isn't tainted any further, otherwise we're in trouble.

Thankfully, Nicola keeps wandering about the show. She's desperately trying to offload our pictures but always reappears frustrated. I'm pleased Annabel tags along at her side, though disappointed at not being able to leave the stand and enjoy what others are displaying.

My mobile rings. It's Brenda. When I answer, the line goes dead. The reception in the exhibition hall is poor. Seconds later, she sends a text. 'I'm on my way to Liverpool. Don't tell that whore.'

Good. I wonder what she has in store for Nicola.

Local authority Keepers of Art, who I once knew, are here at the show. They tell the same sorry stories about their galleries – severe budget and staff cuts and reduced opening hours. It's plain to see, with few exceptions, the future for art collections is not with local authorities.

Several individuals ask why I'm working for Greasby, stating it has an unsavoury reputation in the art world. Three even question if I'm desperate for cash or mentally unstable, or both.

It's warm in the hall, making me feel flustered. I don't want to sell any of our pictures. Nicola can do that. Then, if anything happens, I won't be accused of knowingly selling stolen items.

I hope nobody comes here wanting to shout and scream about a lashed-up picture we've sold them. The day's been eventful already.

One stolen painting causes more anxiety than any of the others. Created in the late 1920s, it's by noted Belgian Surrealist Louis Maes. He once worked with the movement's main protagonist, André Breton. The only Surrealist work in the batch, it could be worth a fortune. Maes has painted, very realistically, a massive unsliced loaf of bread in a wheat field. The idea and connection I suppose are obvious. It's humorous. I fear this distinctive work will arouse suspicion and set alarm bells ringing. Someone could have seen it illustrated in a magazine or book. Yet, I've discovered the artist's work isn't well documented. This may be our saving grace.

My unease jumps up a couple of notches when I recognise a Liverpool-based Detective Inspector. About 50, he's slim and stands six feet tall. Just a while ago, after lecturing at a police course held in Askworth, he popped into the gallery. Interested in one of Y's stolen paintings, it was eventually bought for nearly eight grand. Has he discovered the picture was stolen? Does he know the works we have here came from a robbery? Or, intent on catching us selling him another nicked picture? This is a nightmare scenario.

In the middle of the afternoon, I notice two black Range Rovers stop outside. Brenda and her four chums are here. They surge forwards excitedly into the hall. Wearing grim Elizabethan executioner costumes, their faces are partly concealed by hoods. Chatter in the hall subsides. Surprisingly, the security guards are amused and watch intently.

Playing loud raunchy riffs on a guitar with a built-in amplifier, Jen sings in a menacingly slow voice.

*We're looking for Nicola the whore.*
*The whore, the whore.*
*We're looking for Nicola the whore…*

Fear overwhelms Nicola and her face fills with terror.

With arms raised in a dramatic pose, Brenda storms into

the middle of the hall. 'This an art event,' she declares with outrageous self-confidence. 'There's no cause for concern.' She points to Ellen. 'This lady is a performance artist. Feel privileged to be in her presence. Today she's making a film, *Women Captive in Society*. That's the title.'

I don't mind happenings or street theatre. They're exciting, though I believe Brenda is spouting guff. Nonetheless, I'm eager to discover the role chosen for Nicola.

Enjoying being the centre of attention, Brenda continues: 'The police know we are filming today, so do the show's organisers. Please. Don't stand in the way.'

Annabel looks on with astonishment and claps whenever Brenda pauses. At first, Nicola seems perplexed but is soon chased screaming and crying by Deb and Barb. Make-up courses down her face. Ellen is filming with an impressive camera.

Jen jumps about energetically and pumps out another tune with a faster beat.

*We're gonna get you, Nicola Greasby.*
*We're gonna get you. You'll not like it.*
*You'll not like it, Nicola Greasby.*

'I'll pay in the morning, Brenda. I'll pay. I promise,' Nicola shrieks and searches for an exit. Annabel is entertained.

'Yes, you will pay, sweetie,' Brenda taunts. 'Yes, you will. You owe me money. You've had many opportunities and taken the piss. You're going to suffer.'

Deb and Barb deliver Nicola in a head-lock to Brenda.

The five women firmly hold her down in our display area, tearing off her jeans and top. Nicola bites, punches and kicks, trying to escape. She's overwhelmed. I hope Brenda doesn't force her to perform cunnilingus again. It wouldn't go down well here.

Brenda laughs when realising Nicola is wearing open-crotch knickers. 'Hoping someone might make an unrestricted entry, sweetie?'

A man strides forwards and leans over Nicola. 'This is what you deserve. Fucking bitch. You're always making fake pictures.'

Nicola's eyes are wild. 'How did these dykes know I was here? You told them. Fucking wanker.'

I don't respond.

Annabel skips and sings: 'Al is a wanker, wanker, wanker. Al is a wanker. Pulls his plonker all day long.' Occasionally, she lifts up her dress and flashes.

Brenda looks at me and sneers: 'That's why I've never wanted kids. They can be absolute monsters.'

'Stop. Get off. Let me go.' Terror saturates Nicola's voice. 'Call the police. I'm being kidnapped. Call them. Please. I'm not going down on you again, Brenda. I'll throw-up. Please, no. Not again.'

'Despicable is the only word to describe Nicola Greasby,' one female exhibitor volunteers.

'I'm loving seeing this happen to her,' adds another. 'Take the bitch away and dump her in a big hole.'

Dick and Paul should have stayed to witness this event. A number of people have their mobiles out, capturing the scene. Clips must be obtained to show them. The pair will split their sides laughing.

Posing again into the middle of the hall, Brenda, full of energy and purpose, holds out her arms to dispense further information.

'Don't worry, people. This is an Art Event. Women are captured by society and can't break free.'

The snotty arty types are not impressed. They've listened to Brenda with contempt.

'First, we had artists riding bicycles over canvases,' one starts, 'now happenings. What a load of pretentious drivel. How can these women take themselves seriously?'

A man agrees. 'Happenings are a cop-out. Nobody can draw or paint competently any more.'

A woman feels the need to pose a question: 'Why can't art slip back to the gentile watercolour landscapes of the late eighteenth century?'

Exhibitors have left their stands to observe what's happening.

But neither they, nor the general public, want to step too close to the action. The executioner costumes have the desired effect. They're intimidating.

Exhibitors mutter amongst themselves.

'Nasty bitch, Nicola Greasby,' one says. 'She's got her comeuppance at last,' another adds.

People display bewildered expressions. Several can't understand why the security staff haven't stepped in to rescue Nicola. Two women urge them to investigate. After a quick peek, staff laugh and walk away.

One of them even manages a comment: 'We've been told everything's okay and not to interfere.'

My mobile rings. It's Paulene.

'Where's Frankie?'

'Isn't he in the hospital?'

'No.'

'Is there a problem?'

'I want five studs. My credit card has been declined. The monthly minimum payment has been missed. I'll kill Frankie.'

'If he rings, Paulene, I'll tell him what's happened.'

'Is Nicola with you? She could pay with her card.'

'She's being kidnapped.'

'By who?

'Brenda.'

'Nicola's irresponsible. Like her father.'

Four pompous show judges have stopped at the Greasby stand and assess the pictures. I'm anxious. Please, don't select any of ours to win a prize.

Leading her team with ruthless precision, Brenda kneels down and booms out instructions. 'Hold her legs. Quick, don't let her escape. Hurry. We're out of here.'

Brenda's four accomplices move with alacrity. On the floor, Nicola struggles desperately but is tightly wrapped with strong tape.

'You fucking wanker,' she yells. 'I'll get you back. You're dead.'

'Al played no part,' spits Brenda. 'You've brought this upon yourself, sweetie.'

I lean over Nicola. 'Don't ever taunt me again about my dead son. I hope you get what you deserve.'

'You're sacked! You're sacked,' she cries, before Brenda straps a rubber ball gag to her mouth. She still wriggles pathetically on the floor, trying to break free.

Brenda is unimpressed. 'Feisty aren't you, sweetie?' Then, with a black felt-tip, she writes WHORE across Nicola's forehead.

Deb and Barb snatch five pictures from our display and take them to one of the Range Rovers.

'They can be sold to raise more funds,' Brenda declares.

Video camera in hand, Ellen captures everything. Nicola's facial expressions. Brenda's glee. People's reactions. Security staff look on with both disinterest and amusement.

Annabel is unsure how to react.

'Your mummy is going to be a film star,' Deb tells her.

'Smile, mummy. You'll be famous.'

'How much does Nicola owe you?' I ask Brenda.

With hands on her hips, she sighs: 'Two hundred grand. That's for pictures sold from my dad's collection. The debt is much more. She's sold paintings that were donated by other collectors. All the cash is to fund my Lesbian Art Museum.'

'Astonishing.'

'She takes the piss.'

'I know.'

Brenda looks at me seriously. 'Where's the money going?'

'On a big job. But nobody wants to talk.'

'No more details?'

'Not yet.'

'Is she using my cash?'

'Maybe.'

'I'll prise more information out of her.'

'Good. I'm sick of this company.'

Brenda surprises me with a comment. 'Re-reading your

lesbian articles, I've made a major discovery. I'll explain very soon. You can be involved.'

'Okay. Keep me updated.'

'Put the whore in one of the cars,' Brenda instructs. Nicola is picked up and carried out horizontally.

'Where are you taking her?' I ask.

'To Banton Hall,' Brenda replies. 'I have a torture chamber. Ellen is making gruesome videos. Nicola will star in them.'

Annabel skips to the door with the women. 'Bye, Mummy. Bye. I'll stay with Al. He's a wanker, a wanker. Pulls his plonker all day long.'

Jen cranks up the volume on the guitar's amplifier, bends down and sings to Nicola.

*Now we've got you. Now we've got you.*

*You'll not like it. You'll not like it.*

*Nicola Greasby, Nicola Greasby.*

'Please take Annabel,' I beg Brenda while we're walking to the exit.

'Sorry, Al.'

'Don't leave without this kid from hell. Please.'

'I'll give you a generous bonus,' assures Brenda.

'How long will you keep Nicola?'

'Until the two hundred grand debt is paid.'

Leaving the building, Brenda exchanges high fives with two hefty female security staff.

With the commotion at an end, everyone carries on as normal, studying and admiring the displays.

I'm furious when I notice that three of our pictures have been stolen during the fracas.

My mobile sounds. Frankie is on the line.

'Hi, Frankie. How are you?'

'Much better, Al. Much, much better. I'm at Jess's house. She's treated me to a blow job and we've done lines of coke.'

'You're joking.' I'm staggered at his stupidity.

'Ten per cent of those who have a stroke,' he begins, 'can recover almost immediately. I'm amongst the lucky ones. Alive and well.'

'I'm pleased you're okay.'

'Jess and I are enjoying ourselves. She's a port in a storm in many ways. You ought to fuck her. Or at least, have a blowie. Her blow jobs are sublime. We're going dogging later.'

Words fail me.

'Have you picked up the brushes again, Al?'

'I've done a painting of skeletons playing table tennis.'

He laughs. 'Brilliant. That Friday night car ride reawakened your artistic spirit.'

'Yes,' I confess. 'It has. Thanks, Frankie, for your encouragement.'

'I want to see everything you create,' he bubbles.

'The results are pleasing.'

'Al, the reason for my call is because I need your help.'

'In what way?'

'Those pictures we bought from Y last week.'

'Yes.'

'They're on a stolen art website.'

'We have them here in Liverpool.'

'Where's Nicola? She's not answering her mobile.'

'Brenda's kidnapped her.'

'Remove the pictures from display immediately. Leave the show. Go home now. Take them to your house. I'll sort things later.'

'Ten minutes ago, Nicola sacked me.'

'Ignore her. She tries to sack me every day. Give her a good hiding. Tan her arse.'

'That may be happening as we speak.'

'It will do her good.'

'Frankie. What is this big job I keep hearing about?'

'I don't know, Al,' he tries to answer sincerely. 'I was in the hospital most of last week. Jess and I are going away for a few days.'

'Abroad?'

'Yes.'

'Where?'

'Look after yourself, Al. Keep painting. Bye.'

Five irate exhibitors besiege our stand. They hold oil paintings defaced with graffiti. Annabel has been at work. This occurred when exhibitors left their stands. All were eager to see her mother taken away.

Two women hold Annabel, who kicks out while trying to escape them.

'Is this horrible child Nicola Greasby's?' they ask.

'Yes,' I admit.

Behind my back, Annabel had picked up Brenda's black felt-tip pen and scrawled *AL IS A WANKER* on each unglazed oil painting.

'Al is a wanker, wanker, wanker. Pulls his plonker,' Annabel chants until I whack her.

Clearly the response to her chaotic life is to create more chaos.

One aggrieved woman poses a question: 'Are you Nicola Greasby's husband or partner?'

'Neither, I'm Greasby Fine Art's area manager.'

'How does this girl know about masturbation?'

I look at her blankly.

The woman continues: 'She's not very old. I don't know how she understands what it means. Have you or her mother spoken about the subject in front of her?'

'I certainly haven't. But I can't speak for her mother.'

The woman hasn't finished: 'This girl's boundless energy ought to be channelled into a positive activity. Does she attend any drama or music classes? Or participate in any sports?'

'I haven't a clue.'

Three exhibitors pick up the rolls of tape Brenda's chums have left behind. Annabel is fastened to a chair so that she can't move or cause any further damage. One woman uses the offending felt-tip pen to write on a small board. *A WOMAN STRUGGLES TO BREAK FREE ALL HER LIFE.* It's then placed in front of Annabel.

After protracted negotiations, I assure everyone they'll be compensated for the damage. Nobody is impressed. The total value of the paintings affected is sixty grand.

'Until we're adequately paid, we're taking some of your pictures,' they voice together and remove items from the screens.

'You produce fake works of art on a regular basis,' a man comments. 'Now you deface them. Scandalous.'

In total, a dozen pictures are now absent from our original display of 35.

Although fastened to a chair, Annabel screams and cries until more tape is stretched across her mouth. I telephone Dick and Paul to relay Frankie's instructions. Details are also given of Nicola's kidnapping. They howl with derisive laughter.

'Was she yelping and in pain?' Dick chuckles.

'Yes.'

We agree that I will immediately load what is left of our display into the van, leaving them to collect the boards later.

My mobile rings. I don't recognise the number.

'Hello.'

'Hi, Al. It's Nigel.'

'Hi, how can I help?'

'Nicola's not answering her mobile.'

'She's gone off with people.'

'When she returns, tell her the builder has decided to accept paintings in lieu of being paid. '

I groan inwardly.

'The building work can now progress,' Nigel adds.

After I end the conversation, the hall goes quiet. An announcement is to be made. Our Louis Maes painting has won the award for best picture in the show.

I can't believe this is happening. It means I have to stay a little longer for the trophy presentation and be photographed holding it with Maes' picture.

Several exhibitors offer congratulations. One of them looks at Annabel and sniffs. 'Nicola Greasby behaved the same when she was a kid. Frankie always left her to run riot at art shows.'

One man annoys me when he mistakenly refers to one of our oil paintings as a watercolour. I don't bother to put him right. There are so many know-alls in art.

Another woman is intent on buying a painting for the wrong reason, saying: 'It will match perfectly with the curtains we have in our dining room.'

Her lapdog husband nods loyally.

'I'll give it a little more thought and pop back later,' she advises.

I've heard those comments often. Invariably, nobody ever buys a picture .

The Liverpool-based DI approaches. 'Hi. You will recall we've met before.'

'Yes,' I answer slowly.

'I want to buy the painting that's won the award.'

My heart pounds.

# Chapter 14

Jess and I are embarking on a ferry trip to Germany. We're picking up pictures for Brenda. They're owned by a female collector, Kirstin, who I've known for a while. Brenda has made friends with her. I'm pleased to have introduced them.

It's 1 pm and I'm meeting Jess at the Askworth Gallery. Jane Goldrick is here. In her 50s, she's smartly dressed, wearing a neatly cut charcoal-grey suit and a red silk blouse. Stout but attractive, Jane is furtively unconventional. A vibrant perfume floats from her. It's a fragrance that exudes a relaxed state which is appropriate for Jane. She has grace.

Dealing in 20th century British, European and American art, Jane has an international reputation and is well respected. She's intensely competitive. A former local authority Keeper of Art like myself, she left that job over ten years ago. Jane was often accused of running a private business during Council hours. Once her operation became very successful, she moved on. Jane's partner, Ron, is a gold dealer.

We tightly embrace each other.

'Are you okay, Al?' she whispers.

Our grip slackens.

'I miss my son every day,' I confess, bowing my head.

'I know how you feel.' Beneath sad eyes, Jane gives me one of her rare smiles. 'It doesn't get any easier, does it, love?'

Twenty years ago, Jane's husband went berserk and murdered their twin daughters. He's now in a mental hospital. Over the years, Jane and I have talked at length about how we cope with grief and the help-groups we've attended. We keep in touch, though not on a regular basis.

She also has twin boys, Jeddy and Juddy. They're in their late

20s and with her today. The trio arrived in a black Range Rover with tinted windows. Both men have cropped hair, and sport tattoos on their necks. Scars mark their faces. Wearing dark-blue sharkskin suits and white T-shirts, rings adorn nearly every finger. Caricature villains, they've been in and out of prison for much of their adult lives. This has put an additional burden on Jane.

A couple of years ago, they were accused of breaking into a well-known art gallery and stealing paintings worth thousands. Curiously, the case never came to court. I've not discussed the incident with Jane and the pictures have never been found. Only months after the robbery, Jane opened her new London gallery to critical acclaim. Was this connected? Who knows? Jane has since mentioned the twins run a very successful company supplying bouncers.

To her credit, Jane has coped well with everything. She's achieved success through hard work and determination. Although that can't erase grief, it's made her comfortable.

She once said: 'I want to make my own money so I'm not indebted to local authorities.' I admire those sentiments very much.

Jeddy carries an impressive easel. Juddy holds a framed and glazed drawing, measuring four feet square. Jane suggests a prominent viewing spot in the gallery, and the easel and drawing are placed in that position.

The pair nearly crush my fingers on shaking my hand, though no harm is intended. They acknowledge I'm good friends with their mother. I've known them from a young age.

Jane sits down on a chair near one of the desks. She has a bulky designer-label handbag. Taking out her mobile, she switches it off and places the handbag on the desk. The twins hold small bottles of water and occasionally sip from them.

With shrewd insight, Jane has amassed her own collection of Surrealist art and it must be worth a fortune. The drawing put on display resembles a Salvador Dali. It has the characteristic dream-like subject matter and looks to be from the artist's 1930s golden period. Exquisite. Dick and Paul drop into the gallery and both agree the work is a very masterly piece of draughtsmanship. They acknowledge Jane and me before walking away.

'Is this drawing an original, Jane?'

'No. Of course not. It's by an artist I'm promoting.'

'Why have you brought it here?'

'Nicola wanted to see it.'

'She's never mentioned anything to me.'

'I spoke to her last night and said I'd bring it today.'

What's this about? Nicola must have a cunning criminal plan. Anticipating Jane will divulge more details, she is reluctant to do so.

'The drawing is done on the right paper,' I comment taking a closer look.

'I want twenty thousand for it. Of course, if it were real, we'd be looking at a few mil.'

'There's much talk here at Greasby of something major, a big job taking place. Is this part of it?'

Jane furrows her brow. 'I can assure you, nobody has said anything about the Dali drawing being part of a larger project.'

'Why is a fake here today?'

Jane twitches her shoulders. 'I'd tell you if there was anything to say.'

The twins fold their arms defiantly.

'Don't know any more, Jane?'

She moves her head from side-to-side.

'Nicola wants to go for lunch. I said we'd be here today at one. I'll ask her about this big job then ring and tell you later. I'll find out as much as I can. Providing the twins don't upset her too much.'

'Are they going with you?'

'Yes. She wants to talk to them as well.'

Frankie once commented that Nicola and Jane were alike. They're both involved in dodgy dealings and try to outdo each other. I disagreed, saying Jane can easily run rings round his daughter. There are similarities I conceded. Achievement is measured in financial terms. That's how both believe they're judged and respected.

The twins are fascinated by an exhibition we're staging of Thomas Rowlandson's bawdy watercolour drawings. They're from the collection of Brenda's dad. The two lads occasionally pause and roar with laughter.

Jess enters the gallery, costumed in her Goth best. With dyed black hair, she has the same colour eyeliner and nail polish applied. Goths are often considered to have a morbid personality. Jess is different and always lively, being full of enthusiasm, particularly for sex. The twins have noticed her arrival and lick their lips.

'Have you seen that estate car, Al?' Jess asks with a troubled look. 'It's parked on double yellow lines down the street. Been there for a few days. Dick and Paul say a bloke drives it away at 6.30 every night. But they haven't had a good view of them.'

I'm curious. 'We should take a look.'

The twins dash forwards, scooping Jess up and smacking her arse. She squeals with delight.

'Hello lads, great to see you. Hope your dicks are hard.'

'Put her down, for God's sake,' grumbles Jane.

They take no notice, and throw Jess on one of the low-level seats. Both yank down their trousers ready to have sex.

'Stop it,' Jane implores. 'Stop it now. You're like a couple of walking dildos.' She frowns at the twins and Jess. 'Is sex the only thing you lot think about?'

'Yes,' they shout, punching the air triumphantly.

People in the gallery head for the door.

'You're such a spoilsport, Jane,' sniggers Jess.

The twins zip up.

'Text me when you're both here again,' Jess begins. 'We'll have brilliant sex. Like we did before, when I wore you both out.'

Juddy laughs. 'Fuck off. It was you who gave up first.'

'But there's two of you and only one of me. I'll be the winner next time.'

Outside, Jess and I scrutinise the estate car. The paint on the bodywork is fading and has been patched up. The tyres are barely legal. Looking at the registration plate, the vehicle is ten years old. There's nothing of interest inside.

But, I notice a black curtain fixed between the back seat and boot. All the rear windows are blacked out. This is puzzling. A hole is in the curtain and to my amazement a camera is peeping through. It's fixed on a tripod.

Uneasy thoughts run through my head. Is this a police surveillance vehicle? Is the gallery being watched?

'This is iffy,' says Jess. 'I can break in and see what it's all about.'

'No way.'

As a teenager, Jess was involved in car theft and joyriding. So, breaking into a car isn't unfamiliar.

Tugging at every door, she finds each one locked. People passing by are shocked at what's going on.

'Do you think we're being watched?' Staring at her, I'm eager for an opinion.

'Who knows?' She diverts her attention from me.

'Could this be connected with the big one?'

'You're obsessed with that. Forget it.'

'Try and guess where the camera is pointing. Do you know any other dodgy people besides ourselves along this street?'

'No. How would I know?'

My eyes examine both sides of the street and can only identify offices belonging to accountants, solicitors and an estate agent. There are also bars and two restaurants. In the distance is a T-junction and a line of properties on the opposite side of the road. I'm not sure who occupies those.

Jess takes out her mobile and enters the estate car's registration into the DVLA website. Seconds later, she divulges information: 'It's taxed, insured and has an MOT certificate.'

A male traffic warden comes into view. Tall with a smug face, the latter's a perquisite no doubt for the job.

'Is this vehicle parked illegally?' I quiz.

He stops and hesitates to answer.

Jess confronts him. 'It's on double yellow lines. No parking ticket has been issued. We know it's been here for a few days. Aren't you going to do anything?'

He lifts his hands idly.

'Is it a police vehicle?' Jess moves closer to him.

'Surely, you must know?' I add.

'It's okay.' He walks away with head down.

'This is very suspicious,' I sigh.

Jess rings Frankie. After explaining the situation, she switches her mobile to loudspeaker.

'Yes, you must break into the vehicle,' I hear him say and the call is ended.

'No,' I interject. 'This might be a police car. We don't want to cause criminal damage. It could have gone by the time we get back from Germany.'

Not long after Jess and I re-enter the gallery, Nicola pulls up in the Ferrari. It's parked half on the pavement and slightly over double yellow lines. Brenda held her captive for three weeks. She was only released a couple of days ago. As might have been predicted, Frankie paid the outstanding debt. Nicola carries a laptop and mobile. She's lost a noticeable amount of weight. Her skin is pale. For a while, her forlorn eyes dart about unable to settle. Then, hatred flows in my direction. I've not seen or spoken to Nicola since the Liverpool show. Whatever Brenda put her through, she deserved it. Many of us at Greasby agree.

Jane and Nicola share a brief embrace. Nicola doesn't say hello to the twins and they purposely don't greet her.

'How are you, love?' Jane asks.

'I'm okay now,' Nicola breathes deeply.

'How is your family?' Jane regards her with as much concern as she can muster.

'There's always trouble with Nigel and Annabel,' Nicola groans. 'But Annabel has started Saturday morning drama classes. She's doing really well. Enjoys them.'

'Why not have a break, love?' Jane adopts a motherly tone.

Nicola shakes her head.

'Relax,' Jane continues. 'You look terribly stressed. Talk to a doctor. A therapist. Anybody.'

Nicola's eyes moisten and she wipes away tears.

'Give yourself a few more days to recover. Buy new outfits. Have a facial. A massage. Anything.'

I can't dredge up any sympathy for Nicola. I'm surprised Jane can. The twins look at Nicola with contempt. They only wish misfortune on her. Like everyone else does.

'What are you doing about Y's pictures?' I stab at Nicola. 'They're still at my house.'

'I'm working on it,' she answers without facing me.

'That estate car is parked outside again, Nicola,' Jess states.

Silence.

Jane tries to lift the conversation. 'What a wonderful exhibition you have here, Nicola. These Rowlandson's are gorgeous. They've obviously been kept out of strong sunlight for years. Brilliant. What a fun artist he was. Al has developed a fabulous relationship with Brenda. Worked wonders. I wish I'd connected with her. Have you sold any Rowlandsons yet?'

'No,' I answer, 'but there's a lot of interest.'

I glance at Nicola who's full of jealousy.

Jane declares: 'Being involved with art helps the grief. It shifts the melancholy, doesn't it, Al?'

'Yes.'

'When feeling low,' Jane continues. 'I gaze at a painting and lose myself. I live for the world of art. I admire an artist's choice of colours, the subject matter and most importantly, how the paint is applied. The horrible world is soon forgotten.'

'I couldn't agree more, Jane. I've started painting again.'

'Marvellous. I'd love to see your work.'

'I can show you examples saved on my mobile.'

'Are the paintings figurative?'

I nod.

'What's the subject matter?'

'Skeletons in cemeteries. With sex thrown in. They're surreal.

I've always admired Ensor's skeleton works.'

Jane's eyes light up. 'They're really well executed. You've certainly not lost your talent.'

'Thanks.'

'If you need help selling them, I can put you in touch with the right collectors.'

Nicola is desperate to refocus the attention on herself. 'Look what fucking dyke Brenda did to me,' she pulls down her top. I AM A WHORE is branded in three-inch high letters above her breasts.

Jane winces. 'How awful. Have you been to the police?'

'She wouldn't dare,' I prod.

Hateful looks are hurled at me.

'Are you in pain, love?' Jane touches Nicola's arm.

'Not any more,' she weeps.

'You should pay your debts,' I argue. 'Or, Brenda will take you again.'

'Shut up dickhead. Shut up.'

Jane is shocked. Nicola erupts and aims a punch at me. Jess holds on to her.

'What's going on here?' Jane queries, glancing at both Nicola and myself. Jeddy and Juddy move to their mother's side.

Jane frowns. 'After what happened to my daughters, I abhor violence. You could show more respect, Nicola. I can't believe you and Al aren't working well together.'

The twins watch Nicola with animosity. I've learned they call her the Mad Lass, or Maddy for short.

Avril, a middle-aged woman, has ventured from the upstairs office. Employed as a financial controller, she's been ringing one of the downstairs gallery phones. No one answered.

She walks over to Nicola. 'We're overdrawn at the bank. We can't pay wages.'

'Don't pay the Birmingham staff. We're closing that gallery.'

'The London staff believe they may not be paid and are ready to walk out.'

'Good. They can fuck off. I couldn't give a toss.'

Avril is shocked. 'They're threatening to take paintings with them unless they're paid.'

'That's theft,' Nicola's voice quivers.

I want to scream with laughter, unable to believe the irony in her statement. How long can this company last before there's a police raid or bankruptcy is declared? Has Frankie stashed away enough to keep us afloat? The office staff say it's not much. He overspent when the London galleries were opened.

Nicola instructs Avril: 'Stay down here. We're all going soon.'

Avril agrees.

'Our cash flow problem needs to be addressed properly,' I state.

'Mind your own fucking business,' Nicola answers.

Greasby's financial situation is very worrying. I must contact staff, particularly those at Birmingham and advise them of their rights. Nicola shouldn't ride roughshod over any employee. Frankie is also behaving irresponsibly. When I started, he promised a bonus at the end of every month. Last month, it was two weeks late. Asking for the cash is demeaning. The payment should happen automatically.

Nicola's mobile rings. She cancels the call. Ringing again, she does the same. The third time, she shows annoyance but answers.

'Fuck off, Nigel. Fuck off.'

When the mobile sounds yet again, she hurls it at one of the gallery walls. Jess swiftly takes the laptop from her before that suffers a similar fate. It's occurred in the past.

Everyone is perturbed when a police car halts outside. Two uniformed female officers march into the gallery. Both are slim, short and in their early 30s.

'What do you want?' Nicola fires.

'I'm Sergeant Rollinson,' one of them states. 'This is PC Whaley.'

Is this visit connected with the estate car outside? I'm even more curious about the vehicle now.

'We're looking for Nicola Greasby,' the two officers announce.

'That's me, what's wrong?'

'I'm beginning to wish we'd never come here today, Al,' Jane says quietly. Her two lads are unsure how to react but stand close to their mother.

'Is there an office where we can go?' suggests Rollinson. 'We need to talk seriously.'

'I've nothing to hide. Talk here.'

Because there's little seating in the gallery, we're all standing and feeling uncomfortable. Jane has remained seated.

'We've received complaints,' begins Rollinson, focusing firmly on Nicola. 'You've taken money without consent from customers' credit cards and bank accounts.'

'Not true,' Nicola splutters. 'Our area manager is responsible.' She points at me. 'I've told staff to destroy customers' credit card details once a transaction has been completed. No. I'm not to blame.'

Jane is horrified.

I want to kill Nicola. Yes, even with two police officers present.

'Incorrect, Mrs Greasby.' Rollinson shows annoyance. 'You initiated this fraud. We've spoken to your staff. One of them recorded you giving instructions. Now, perhaps we can talk privately. Or, I'm going to arrest you and discuss the problem at the police station.'

Nicola is quiet for a few seconds until facing me. 'You fucking bastard. I'll get revenge if it's the last thing I do.'

'Are you making violent threats, Mrs Greasby?' Whaley cautions.

'No.'

'Each victim will press charges,' Rollinson continues, 'unless they're repaid immediately. With interest.'

'No problem. I can sort it. Shall we go to my office?' Nicola begins to lead the way.

'How much has been taken?' enquires Jane.

'Fifty grand,' Rollinson replies.

'That's a large amount. Can you pay it back, love?'

'Yes, of course Jane.'

Whaley confronts Nicola. 'Over the last few weeks, there's been trouble at this address. That's besides problems caused by the Greasby family at a seafood restaurant. You filled your Ferrari with petrol and drove away without paying. Are you under stress, Mrs Greasby?'

'Fuck off!' Nicola yells, striding over to the officer.

Jane is embarrassed. 'Look, Nicola, we can have lunch another day.'

The lads stand aggressively with their arms folded and legs slightly apart. They're enjoying watching Nicola squirm.

'No, Jane, wait. Please. I can soon sort this out,' Nicola is desperate. 'I'm taking us out for a nice lunch. Please stay. I need to talk much more about the Dali drawing. We have to make a deal.'

'Can we continue this conversation elsewhere, Mrs Greasby?' Whaley is insistent.

Nicola fumes. 'Fuck off.'

'What is wrong, Mrs Greasby?' Whaley folds her arms.

'Leave me alone.'

Rollinson advances closer to her. 'It's been brought to our attention well-known shoplifters regularly pop in and out of here.'

'You're talking bollocks.' Nicola is flustered and shifts about uneasily.

'Calm down, love,' Jane interjects. 'This will do no good. Go to your office and sort the matter out in a proper way.'

Both officers turn to Jane. 'Thank you, madam.'

'Are you taking drugs, Mrs Greasby?' Whaley probes.

'Fuck off.'

'Or do you have a drink problem?' Rollinson adjoins.

'Go away. Leave me alone.'

Rollinson presses on regardless. 'Is the red sports car yours?'

'Yes.'

'It's illegally parked. We need to breathalyse and drug-test you.'

'What about the estate car on double yellows down the road?' Jess jumps in.

'We're here to question Mrs Greasby,' Rollinson responds.

'Fuck off you pair of dykes. Get out.' Nicola launches herself at them.

'Stop it, love,' Jane springs to her feet. Her lads hover in the background.

Nicola is put on the floor and cuffed.

I've wondered how female officers of their stature cope with marauding football fans, hefty drunks, or people out of control. My curiosity has been answered. They have the necessary skills to cope.

'Are you homophobic, Mrs Greasby?'

'Yes. Proud of it.' She's now crying openly.

'What's wrong, Mrs Greasby?'

'Nothing. Nothing, leave me alone.'

Will she tell the police about the kidnapping and Brenda branding her? No, she daren't. Surely?

'Want me to stay and help, Nicola?' Jess voices genuine concern.

'No.'

The doors to the upstairs offices are slightly ajar. Dick and Paul have been watching and listening. They can't help but enjoy the drama. Nicola arrested and in cuffs. Delight shows on their faces.

'Fuck off upstairs and get on with your work,' Nicola barks on seeing them.

'Is that the way you talk to your staff?' Rollinson scoffs.

'We could tell you lots about this bitch,' Paul volunteers with a broad smile.

'This is becoming very interesting,' Whaley comments. 'What can you add?'

Go on, tell them. Let the cat out of the bag.

'We'll leave that for another day,' Dick remarks.

'We'll be going, Al.'

I give Jane another hug.

'You're in my thoughts every day,' she murmurs. 'Ring if you need to.'

'Thanks,' I respond. 'I'm thinking of you too.'

I wink at her two lads and they raise a hand in acknowledgement. Several visitors enter the gallery. Assessing the situation, they walk out.

The police officers haul Nicola from the floor. She tries to kick me but is restrained.

'Bye, Maddy,' the twins say cockily as they swagger out with Jane.

'We ought to go, Jess,' I urge.

'Do you want me to make any calls?' asks Avril, eyeing Jess first, then me.

'Ring Frankie, immediately,' Jess reacts. 'Tell him what's happened.'

Nicola suddenly springs to life. 'Have a safe journey back, Al.'

The comment disturbs me. 'What do you mean?'

She's silent.

# Chapter 15

At 1.45 pm, Jess and I pull away from the Askworth Gallery in a hire van. A bench seat accommodates the driver and two passengers. Jess is driving and I sit next to the window, leaving a gap between us. The ferry terminal is two hours away, traffic permitting.

No sooner have I buckled up, Jess eagerly asks: 'Will you want a fuck later, Al?' There's a sparkle in her eyes. 'I'm wearing a butt plug. It's Nicola's. I've borrowed it.'

'No,' I answer curtly, never failing to be shocked at the forwardness of some women. Passing the mysterious estate car, there's no sign of life and neither of us comment.

'Surely, Al, you fancy a fuck? It must be ages since you've had one.'

'Why do you want to discuss sex so early in the day?'

'I like to have my fucks planned,' she cackles.

'Are you a sex addict?'

'Of course.'

This is the type of mad conversation I experience with her. Unfortunately, more whacky comments are voiced: 'I've brought a vibrator so I can have fun on my own later. Brenda's orgies are brilliant. She's insatiable. I'm in Ellen's films. I loved the torture scenes.'

I don't comment.

'Did you know Frankie and me went dogging? It was great fun. For both of us. He's so pervy. I've heard the same said about a lot of those ex public school boys.'

This might be a trying and awkward trip.

'Al, do you think you'll ever fuck again?'

'I'm not discussing my sex life.'

'We can do anything you like. What do you prefer? A blow job? Anal? A wank? You can tie me up. Do you want me to fuck you?'

'Jess, I don't want to be rude, but shut up.'

'Is that why you're chummy with Brenda? Sex isn't an obstacle. She's a lesbian. She doesn't fancy you. And you don't fancy her.'

The question floats over my head.

'Are you impotent, Al?'

That's another question I won't answer.

'If you are, I've brought Viagra tablets. One of those will help.'

'Shut up, Jess. You're annoying me.'

She reaches over and puts a hand on my leg. I swiftly knock it away.

'Pull your trousers down. I'll play with your dick while I'm driving. I've done the same with Y.'

It's amazing that a woman can behave like this with a man without fear of recrimination. The opposite wouldn't be true. Women would go screaming to the police. What decision should I make now? Ring the police and claim I've been sexually molested? I bet they'd be really supportive.

'After Nicola got home from Brenda's,' Jess begins, 'she beat up Nigel. It's a wonder he wasn't killed. Two of his ribs were broken. His face and body are a mess. I saw it happen. He contacted a solicitor and the injuries were photographed. Annabel was terrified. She cowered in a corner.'

'I hope she's not affected by these incidents later in life.'

'I take her to drama classes. Nicola can't be bothered. Annabel loves them. She's talented. I'm sure she'll go far. Annabel's tutor has entered her for a big role in a kids' TV drama.'

I divert the conversation back to the fight. 'Didn't Nigel offer any resistance?'

'Not much.'

'Were the police called? Will Nicola be charged?'

'It's up to Nigel. I doubt anything will happen.'

'Did they have sex after the fight? That's what they do normally.'

'No. Nigel wasn't in a fit state. He's having trouble walking right now.'

'Why were they fighting?'

'There's been another cock-up with Nigel's church. The details are boring but Nicola has to pay out more. We need to sell that last batch of Y's pictures. Fast. I've been faking provenance and sending out details to collectors. There's little interest.'

'Word has probably spread that the pictures are nicked. This will tumble down on us.'

'Your link with Brenda is keeping Greasby afloat.'

'I know.'

'Al, you need a wank. Flop your dick out and feel me.' She pulls down her black leggings. 'Go on, have a touch, I'm really wet. We have to enjoy ourselves. Like my frilly knickers? Does sexy underwear get you hard? I'll dress up if that's what you want.'

I put on the radio to drown out her voice until she laughs and switches it off.

'Have a cold shower, Jess, as soon as we board the ship.'

Whenever she reaches over trying to touch me, the van swerves dangerously across the dual carriageway. This inconveniences other drivers when trying to overtake and they make their feelings known.

'Stop it, Jess. Concentrate. Keep your eyes on the road. You could easily cause a nasty accident. We could be killed.'

'Live dangerously, Al. Enjoy the excitement.'

'I'm getting annoyed, Jess.'

Whilst it's a nice day outside, there are thunderstorms in my head.

'Let's have sex, Al,' Jess cajoles. 'I'll reveal details about the big job. The one you keep asking about.'

'Not interested.'

'All can be revealed. I thought you were desperate for information?'

'You've often said there's nothing to tell me.'

'I might know a teeny-weeny bit.' She shapes her left-hand fingers to give emphasis to the words.

This is a nightmare. What will it be like sharing a cabin? I should've booked two separate ones.

Jess lights up a joint. 'I could've done this trip on my own, if you would've preferred.'

'No. Brenda wanted me to go. I promised to make sure the paintings were packed and transported correctly.'

'I've brought plenty of packing material.'

'Good.'

She blows smoke in my direction and I drop down the window.

'Are you carrying drugs?'

'Only a few bits and bobs.'

I show frustration. 'Keep well away from me when we board the ship, and when we step off at the other end.'

Jess smiles. 'Nicola has sold a picture to the woman we're seeing. Brenda's friend, Kirstin. It's in the back. Nicola also gave me documentation for her.'

'I didn't know about the sale. Pictures keep popping up without me knowing. This is the second one today.'

'I thought you knew.'

'What's the picture?'

'A George Grosz watercolour. From the Berlin Period.'

'That's incredibly rare. Is it an original?'

'Yes.'

'How was it sourced?'

'Me and Frankie picked it up a few days ago.'

'How did Nicola know that Kirstin was interested in a George Grosz?'

'Not sure.'

I don't believe any of this.

'Kirstin wanted provenance details. She was obsessive. Nicola has sorted it. A photograph was discovered of an owner posing with the picture.'

Locating a George Grosz watercolour is too good to be true.

'Is Brenda aware of the Grosz?'

'Don't think so.'

'What about Jane's Dali drawing? Why does Nicola want it?'

These questions bounce off Jess without a coherent answer. She has a confidence I've not seen before.

'Aren't you tempted to have a fuck and discover more information? I know everything.'

I'm not tempted in the slightest. There's a lot going on behind my back. It's worrying.

Jess interrupts my thoughts. 'Like me to feel your dick, Al? Are you horny? We can stop and enjoy ourselves.'

Having sex with her isn't even a consideration.

'Pack it in, Jess. I'm not interested.'

Leaning over again, she causes the van to veer to one side. On correcting the movement, we narrowly miss colliding with a passing lorry. The driver blows the horn long and loud. Although I've never struck a woman, it'll be an option if she continues.

'Come on, Al. Bet you want me to feel your dick.'

I raise my hand but quickly put it down.

At first, she looks scared but laughs. 'So that's what you like. Beating women. You can spank or even cane me. I don't mind.'

'Shut up, Jess. Shut up. You're driving me crazy.'

I've brought a sketchbook. Tonight, I can find a quiet corner on the ferry and develop ideas. Jess will want to drink, smoke joints, snort coke or whatever. Art, like Jane said, is a salvation. The lustful quick sexual release has never been of interest. I enjoyed being in love with my wife during the early years of our marriage. We produced a wonderful son. Now, he's dead. So is my libido. I've no craving for unregulated sexual excitement. So often, sex leads men into big trouble. There's no temptation. I feel nothing and shun any stimulants.

'I must talk to the Greasby staff in Birmingham. They can't be made redundant on a whim. Proper procedures haven't been followed. They can claim a Protective Award.'

'Beware of sticking up for them too much,' Jess states

seriously. 'You could be next.'

I'm confused.

'Nicola says you're the highest paid member of staff. By sacking you, a big saving will be made.'

'She wouldn't dare take me on.'

'Don't you want to know about the big job? It's fascinating. Your kind of project.'

'If there are strings attached, then no.'

'Y said he mentioned the big job to you after the meal in the seafood restaurant. You were driving the Rolls. Taking Frankie home.'

'He did, though gave no details. I don't want anything to do with him.'

'Don't you fancy me, Al?'

'That's not even a consideration.'

Should I tell her to drive back home and then make the trip on my own? I've never driven in Europe.

'Relax, Al. Put your hand down my knickers. I waxed last night. I'm really smooth.'

We approach roadworks. A youth is working a Stop-and-Go sign. He flips the sign to Stop and begins talking with a mate nearby. We halt in front of them.

Jess summons the pair over. The sign is dropped to the ground.

'Which one of you two has the biggest dick?'

'Me,' they both answer.

'Okay then, show me, I'll judge.'

They're salivating. Jess opens her door and the lads immediately notice she's half undressed.

'Go on, have a feel if you want.'

Both men jostle each other to take advantage.

Jess lifts her top, leans back and gasps. 'You guys know how to excite a girl.'

With no sign visible, drivers are backing up behind us, wondering what's happening. A cacophony of pipping horns assaults the ears. The two lads laugh. There's a competition to see who can pleasure Jess the most. I make a mental note of their expressions, to use in a skeleton orgy picture. I'll include plenty of humour.

One lad stares at me. 'I bet you'll be fucking her long and hard tonight. Won't you, mate?'

'Too right,' Jess beams. 'He's a virgin. I'm going to kill him.'

'On his first fuck?' One of them is incredulous.

'Yes.'

'Lucky bastard. Pleasant death, mate.'

'Pack it in now, lads,' I comment. 'Time to move on.'

Both of them chuckle, give Jess long kisses and we drive away.

'I didn't think they'd play ball.' Jess readjusts her clothing. 'Often, men don't like it when women make the first move.'

I'm silent.

'Promise to fuck me later. Then, we can discuss the big job.' Jess is buoyant after the brief sexual encounter.

'Concentrate on driving, Jess.'

'I'm disappointed you won't make a promise. I've never been rejected.'

'Is the big job art related?' I probe carefully.

'Maybe it is. Maybe it isn't,' Jess sniggers.

'I'm not playing verbal games.' I peer out of the side window. 'One of the staff will tell me. Sooner or later.'

'When I heard details of the big job, I said to myself, this is sure to fascinate Al. He'll want to be involved.'

There's silence for a few minutes until Jess restarts the dialogue.

'Frankie wants to come out as transgender. Don't you think it's marvellous people can now choose which sex they want to adopt?'

'Yes.'

'Last week, I showed Frankie how to apply make-up. He's going to be called Frances. He feels comfortable wearing my knickers.'

I must create pictures depicting transgender skeletons. A

whole new ball game. Modern attitudes ought to be reflected in my work.

'What do you think about transgenderism, Al?'

'As a trade union officer, I supported a transgender bloke at an industrial tribunal. He worked in the Finance Department. The Council sacked him because he wanted to work in a dress. I won the case.'

'Never tried gay, Al?'

'No. But as an artist I support freedom of expression and a person finding their true identity. That should be the same throughout the world.'

Jess smiles in agreement.

'What's Paulene's reaction to Frankie's decision?'

'Couldn't care less. She's bought Renta Stud. Sucked loads of cash out of Greasby. Frankie and Nicola aren't happy. Paulene wants to open more stud farms. It's what they'll be called. Together, we'll launch a massive advertising campaign. I'll help, as long as I can try out some of the studs.'

I move my head away, not wanting to fully acknowledge the humour.

'Paulene doesn't want Frankie living in the house anymore. He's been staying with me. It's an open relationship. Fucking whoever we want and we're drug buddies.'

This is drivel.

'Frankie and me enjoyed ourselves when we went away.'

'Where did you go?'

'For a short break.'

'Where?'

'No place special.'

'Was it connected with the big job?'

'Are we having a fuck later?'

'No.'

'Well then, I'm not saying,' she answers petulantly.

'I'm the area manager, I should know what's happening.'

'Nicola doesn't want you knowing anything.'

'Surely, Frankie wants me to know?'

'He's not said one way or the other.'

'I'm insulted. This is undermining my position.'

'I could be persuaded to tell you.'

'I'm sure you could.'

Jess lights another joint and, once again, playfully blows smoke at me. Thankfully, her driving is unaffected. She's handling the van well. But, the vehicle is a little noisy and gives an uncomfortable ride.

A police car slows alongside. Jess looks at the male officers and rolls her tongue provocatively down her fingers. One of them blows a kiss before they hurry away with the blues flashing.

'Brenda's made a major discovery,' I begin. 'Know any details?'

'Hasn't she told you anything?'

'I expect she will soon.'

'Whenever I've been with her, she's too interested in sex to mention anything else.'

I'm frustrated but don't react.

'Maybe Nicola knows details after being with her for over three weeks…poor thing. Brenda put her through hell.'

Jess tries to grab my hand again, only I pull it away.

'The big job will be the best thing to happen at Greasby for years.'

'Really?'

'Yes. Pity you don't want to know anything.'

We pull up at a petrol station and I fill the vehicle. The card given to me by Frankie is declined. I phone Alice, the office administrator.

'Frankie shouldn't have given you that one,' she explains. 'He knew there was nothing left on it. We're struggling to pay off his cards.'

'What can we do? Jess and I are on the way to Germany.'

'Use your own card. We'll reimburse you. Keep receipts.'

'Brilliant,' I say sarcastically.

On our arrival at the ferry terminal, about 50 bikers show.

They belong to a group known simply as Bikers and this name is emblazoned on hats, T-shirts and sweat shirts. Motorbike engines rev menacingly.

'I once had great sex with a gang of bikers,' Jess enthuses. 'Fucking all day then all night.'

Once we park on board, the bikers gather behind us. Jess drops down her leggings and knickers. Bending over, she parts her cheeks to reveal the jewelled butt plug.

# Chapter 16

The next to come aboard the ferry is a group of transgender people. They're mainly middle-aged, exquisitely dressed and with fantastic make-up. Many have brightly-painted vehicles. On witnessing Jess's action, two of them in long flower-patterned dresses bend over and show their own butt plugs. Laughing so much, they nearly fall over. One of them, tall and hefty, walks towards us.

'Hi. I'm Bobbi.'

'Hello. I'm Al and this is Jess.'

Bobbi is keen to talk with her. 'Where did you buy that lovely jewelled plug?'

'It's my boss's.'

'Do they want to sell it? I collect them,' Bobbi enthuses. 'I have five hundred.'

'I'll ring her later.'

'Okay. I'd be interested to hear what she has to say.'

We chat a little more and Bobbi reveals the trans group is off to a demonstration in Germany.

As we wait in a queue for passports and tickets to be checked and confirmed, the Bikers and trans people jostle each other. I hope this doesn't veer out of hand as the journey progresses. The office has booked us in a suite. It's luxurious and has two separate comfy beds, as well as an *ensuite* bathroom. Putting Jess in the same cabin was madness. If the harassment for sex continues, I shall pay for one on my own.

After I take a shower – Jess doesn't bother – we hit one of the bars. She has a few drinks. Well, too many. I sip a lemonade.

There was a plan to upgrade and eat in the ship's exclusive

*à la carte* restaurant but, unable to use a company credit card, we'll have to give it a miss. To me, *à la carte* is only marginally better than the standard dining-hall carvery. Although it might not attract the riff-raff in the carvery, the food is much more expensive. We make our way to the dining hall where, I have to admit, there's a fantastic selection of food.

The carvery includes sides of beef, turkey, gammon and pork. Generous cuts are placed on our plates. I've chosen beef, Jess pork, and we select from a fine array of potatoes and vegetables.

People of all ages are greedy. They take more food than is necessary. Both hands grip a plate piled high with food. Most are overjoyed, as if a gold prize has been won.

Amongst the other diners are lads and lasses attending stag and hen parties. A few are in fancy dress. One youth wears a Native American outfit with a full headdress. Others are Robin Hood, Billy the Kid, Dracula and Frankenstein. Some of the girls are French maids, Wonder Woman and Marie Antoinette. A number have even put on a full wedding dress. There's much frivolity and laughter. I overhear a group of lads say they intend to sample the delights of a German superbrothel. Everyone has sex together in one enormous room.

Also eating with healthy appetites are groups of pensioners. Jess and I find a table close to Bobbi and friends. All wash food down with beers and wines.

I must depict a carvery in a cemetery. Skeleton chefs serve food wearing white uniforms and tall hats. Walking away from the serving area, skeletons carry full plates of food back to tombstones. These will be laid out like ordinary tables with chairs round them. More skeletons might be seen already seated and tucking into the grub. I smile to myself at the imagined possibilities. Brilliant.

It's 7.30 pm, and no sooner do we start eating than Nicola calls Jess. They're in conversation for 25 minutes.

Jess eventually provides details: 'Nicola's been charged with homophobic slurs and assaulting police officers. She's been bailed.'

'Brilliant. I hope she goes down.'

Jess frowns.

'She would struggle to survive inside,' I smile.

'They arrested Frankie for coke possession.'

'What?'

'He went to the police station to help Nicola. In front of a sergeant, he accidentally pulled out coke packets. They were confiscated and he received a caution.'

'He was lucky they didn't bully him into revealing more details. Very fortunate.'

'Whilst we're in Germany, Nicola says we must pick up a batch of pictures from Y.'

'Oh no. Definitely not.' I stop eating and move my plate away. I'm suddenly not hungry. 'Greasby is brokering this trip for Brenda. She's paid us plenty and won't approve. It's not happening.'

'A pity, Al. This is the big job. Surely you want to know more?'

Jess snorts coke and several pensioners watch her. 'I'm like Frankie,' she states. 'I need to be off my face every day.'

'Are these pictures nicked?' I try to hold her attention, only it's not possible.

'Can't say.'

'How much are they worth?'

'Millions. Some are priceless.'

'This has been arranged behind my back. I don't want to be involved. Get off the ship, Jess. I'll pick up Brenda's pictures on my own.'

'Too late, Al. We've set sail.'

'You can take the next ferry back. I'll drive to Germany and find the way regardless. I'm not travelling any further with you.'

'Nicola said if you don't do as she says, I'm to take charge.'

This is unbelievable. I'm fuming.

'Failure to obey a reasonable instruction will get you the sack.' Jess's expression bounces between cocky and sneering.

'A reasonable instruction isn't asking someone to pick up a

pile of nicked pictures. That's laughable.'

'We're doing the job whether you like it or not.'

'How are we going to get rid of them? We've not sold the last batch from Y.'

'Nicola has already found buyers. She's discovered a new seam of rich American collectors. Frankie and me are taking them to the States.'

'How are we paying? Money has been incredibly tight.'

'Nicola's robbed cash from everywhere. It's in the van.'

'I'm not getting involved.'

'These pictures shall rescue us, Al.'

'Will Dick and Paul produce a load of fakes?'

'Maybe. I hear they're thinking of retiring. They've had enough of the company.'

'Who might take their places?'

'Frankie could pull out his brushes again,' she laughs.

I ring Frankie but without a response, then try Brenda.

Deb answers. 'Is it important, Al? This isn't convenient for her. I'll see if she wants to take your call. Oh yes, she's indicating she will.'

After a short pause, Brenda comes on the line and I explain about picking up Y's pictures.

'Do whatever is required of you.' She sounds distraught. I've never known anxiety reflected in her voice before. Usually, she's so positive.

'Are you okay, Brenda?'

'No. I've had bad news.'

'What about?'

'The project I mentioned to you in Liverpool. Sorry, Al. I'll reveal more when you get back.'

We end the call.

'Your problem, Al,' begins Jess, 'is that you've never had to make money from art.' She pauses to swig wine. 'You sat comfortably in that Council job for too long. You're out of touch. Those cosy art gallery days are over. Things have changed. I visited your gallery on a school trip. It was boring. Art needs to connect much more with ordinary people. It's too far removed. Too highbrow.'

What a load of nonsense. I can't believe this is spouted from an art historian.

'You've never had to raise money to survive. Nicola is brilliant. She has to generate more and more every single day.'

'I'm surprised she cons people into buying fakes. Nobody questions authenticity.'

'They do,' Jess snaps back. 'But, they're frightened to miss out. Once, I took a picture to a collector in Los Angeles. He was convinced it was a fake. I told Frankie and he said, "Ask the guy to pay your air fare and bring the picture back." The collector kept it. Scared he might be making a bad decision.'

This isn't what I want to hear.

'Nicola is desperate to keep the company afloat. She's a brilliant plan for Jane's fake Dali drawing. The sale of this George Grosz picture will help. Otherwise, we're going under.'

'Show me the George Grosz documentation.'

'It's down my knickers, whenever you're ready.'

I don't take the bait.

Jess is greedily eating the pork. Talking and chewing simultaneously. Annoyingly, strands of meat project from her mouth.

'Not hungry, Al?'

'No.'

'I'm starving. You need to eat and build up your strength for when we're fucking later.'

'Don't start that again.'

She takes my plate and attacks the remaining food.

'You're a fossil, Al. Life's for enjoying. Not mourning. If he was alive today, your son would be shagging, snorting coke and up to all sorts of skulduggery.'

'Stop talking about him.'

'Forget creating skeleton pictures. Produce something more saleable. Paint modern pub scenes or look at the subjects the

Impressionists tackled. Manet's *A Bar at the Folies-Bergère* or *Luncheon of the Boating Party*. Study Seurat's *A Sunday Afternoon on the Island of La Grand Jatte*. These are subjects that could be interpreted in a modern way. And would be piss-easy to sell.'

Her words are spoken with confidence. A drunken confidence.

'I've never been involved with making money from art,' I explain. 'Greasby isn't what I thought it would be.'

'Art cons people. That's what everybody thinks today. Greasby also cons people. We create and sell fakes. Plenty of them.'

Why am I listening to this?

'People are hostile to art. It's for snobby people,' she continues.

'Rubbish.'

'Please, Al. Can we have sex? Then, I'll tell you about the big job. Nicola says I should keep my gob shut. But, I'm willing to make an arrangement with you.'

These comments are pathetic.

Slowly, Jess sucks each finger.

'Want a blowie, Al?'

'No.'

'Never had any complaints about my blowies. Everybody shouts with joy when they...'

'Shut up.'

'Are you a tit man Al?'

I'll have to find a spare cabin. Can't put up with this.

'Have a squeeze of my tits.'

'No.'

'I could settle down with you, Al. You're a good man. This argument is sexy. I'm falling in love with you. We're opposites but might be good for each other.'

'This is nonsense, Jess.'

'You're sacked if we don't fuck. I'm taking charge now.'

'That'll be an easy case for an industrial tribunal. Somebody sacked for not having sex with their boss. Greasby will be taken to the cleaners.'

'Nobody takes any notice of trade unions or tribunals. It's not the 1970s and 80s now. You're sacked, Al. I'm in charge.'

'Why are you so persistent about having sex. What's the reason? There must be one.'

'Despite what men think, a few women, like me, enjoy sex.'

'You're nothing but a jumped-up shag-bag.'

'What are you doing tonight if not fucking?' Jess asks miserably.

'Working up painting ideas and planning an article for *Art Happening Today*. I'm writing a book with Brenda: *Lesbian Art*. I don't want any distractions.'

'Boring,' she sniffs.

I contact Frankie again.

'Hi, Al. How's the trip going?'

'Nicola has put Jess in charge. Jess has sacked me just because I refused sex with her.'

Frankie is amused. 'Nicola and Jess bet the girls in the Askworth office they could fuck you.'

My mobile is switched to loudspeaker.

'The bet was for a grand. If either of them was successful, I promised to add the same amount. Nicola dismissed the idea weeks ago. Now Jess is trying. She has an outstanding debt with a very unsavoury coke dealer. Sounds like the bet is careering out of hand. It started out as a bit of a hoot. I only wanted to cheer you up. Don't worry, you're in charge. No question about that.'

'Okay, fine,' I say.

Having heard Frankie, Jess can hardly contain her annoyance.

'Do you like the Grosz picture, Al?' Frankie effervesces.

'Not seen it yet.'

'It's a gem.'

'An original?'

'Oh yes, a hundred and ten per cent. I've paid out a large sum to buy it. We can make a healthy profit. I'll tell you more when we see each other again.'

'Where are you?'

'In a hotel with young friends having fun. I promise, Al, we'll speak soon.'

'Yes, okay.'

I confront Jess: 'What a horrible person you are. I'm afraid you've lost the bet. Nothing's happening.'

Jess is perspiring and a stink of sweat wafts my way. Her make-up is blotchy.

'You and Nicola see me as a joke figure.'

'Pull the butt plug out, Al. Please.'

'No chance.'

'We can share the cash.'

'Forget it.'

Our voices are raised and people are earwigging. Pensioners express annoyance at the gist of the conversation. Others take no notice, maybe recalling they behaved badly in a long-lost youth.

'Feel my tits,' Jess stands up and pounces at me. 'I'm not losing the bet. I need the cash.'

'Stop it, Jess. Stop it now.'

She tries to grab my hand and a scuffle breaks out.

'Get your hand down my knickers.'

Bobbi has been listening with displeasure, and he attracts Jess's attention.

'Have you asked your boss about the butt plug?'

'She doesn't want to sell it to a weirdo. She hates your kind of people.' Her eyes flit about not settling on him.

'There's no need to be rude. You could have considered your response more carefully.'

Jess rounds on me: 'You need a fuck, Al, to chill you out. I can help.'

Bobbi isn't impressed, looking at her with disdain. 'Leave him alone.People shouldn't foist their sexual hunger on others. You could be arrested for what you're doing.'

Bobbi is made aware of the bet.

'That's appalling.'

Jess is unconcerned. 'I'll make you fuck me, Al, if it's the last thing I do. I'm not losing two grand.'

Forcefully, she tries to unfasten my belt and pull my trousers down. I stand up, though she continues. People look open-mouthed in our direction.

'Fuck me, Al. Fuck me.'

# Chapter 17

The Bikers seen earlier make a bold entry into the dining hall. The majority are male. Most of them stand over six feet tall and weigh 18 stones plus. Their presence is frightening. It'll be interesting to observe the amount of food they pile on their plates. Some of them are pissed. Walking unsteadily, they shout slurred words to each other. Nearly all sport T-shirts, leather waistcoats and camouflage shorts down to their calves.

Motorcycle riders I've met in the past have been courteous and caused no trouble. I know Askworth Motorbike Club members and they're affable. The Bikers I see now could be very different.

One of them, the largest of the bunch, acts like their leader. I've never seen anyone so huge. In his mid-30s, he must be seven feet tall and weigh over 40 stones. He has long brown bushy hair and a wiry beard. Both arms, calves, and even his face, sport tattoos. Piercings are visible in his eyebrows and ears. An enormous beer belly bulges in front of him. A heavy gold chain hangs from his neck.

Noticing the altercation taking place between Jess, myself and Bobbi, he makes an approach with a strong air of menace. A silence spreads across the dining hall.

'Hi. I'm Tez.' He looms over us. 'What's happening?'

'I've bet my mates two grand I could shag my boss, Al.' Jess points at me. 'He's said no and I really fancy him.'

'Is that right, sweetheart?'

'Yes.'

'Al's said no and she should accept his decision,' adjoins Bobbi.

I'm feeling uneasy, being in the middle of a melee. Bikers

blow kisses and make snide comments to the trans people. However, they're responding well. Members of both groups urge others to back off. Live and let live is the overall theme, only I fear the confrontation is ready to escalate.

'Why won't he shag a nice lass like you?' Tez looks hard at me. 'If you don't fancy her mate, you're off your head.'

'He's obsessed with Modern Art,' begins Jess. 'Nothing else.'

'That's a lie,' I protest.

'None of what she says is true,' Bobbi affirms.

'Modern Art is for weirdos. I hate it,' snarls Tez. 'Artists should produce something recognisable.'

'A ridiculous statement.' I feel my hands balling up in frustration.

'I agree,' says Bobbi with authority. 'Art should always be a marriage between the subject and how it's executed.'

'Shut up, dickhead,' yells Tez. 'Have a look at proper art.' He motions for a woman in the group to approach. She could audition for *The Addams Family*. Wearing a long, loose-fitting black dress, she lifts it up to her shoulders. Revealed is a tattoo of Marilyn Monroe extending along one side of her body. Admittedly, the image is accomplished.

'That's real art,' states Tez proudly.

Pausing from eating their meals, then standing up, most diners are stunned at what they see. No Biker has gone to the carvery. They're all grouped round us.

'Brilliant,' exclaims Jess. 'Who did the tattoo?'

'Me,' vaunts Tez, 'I'm a tattoo artist. I went to the Royal College of Art.'

'You have prostituted yourself and your talent,' I stab. 'That's not proper art.'

Tez seethes.

'I need the two grand,' Jess appeals to him. 'I'm desperate to pay a debt. If I don't, a dealer will cut me.'

'What's your name, love?'

'Jess,' is the bold reply.

The Bikers are in disbelief as she pulls down her bottoms and shows the butt plug once again.

'This slapper has tried to rape Al,' submits Bobbi. 'It's criminal. I've seen it myself.'

'Why not fuck me and my mates?' Tez regards Jess lasciviously. 'We'll pay as much as you like.'

'When? And where?'

'Here and now.' Tez and his mates punch the air. 'Yes,' he continues, 'the ship's entertainment tonight is shit. We'll have an orgy.'

'Yes please,' Jess laughs. 'I love orgies with men *and* women. I'll fuck everybody, any way they want.'

'This is ridiculous,' comments Bobbi.

Jess strips off, unzips Tez's trousers and plays with him.

'She's pulled his dick out,' one of the stag lads shouts. 'It's like another limb.' His mates fall about laughing.

Bikers begin fondling Jess. People gawp in amazement. Some have broken off from eating, others pick at their meals.

Overflowing with testosterone, three Bikers shift plates from our table and lift Jess on to it.

One Biker carefully removes the butt plug. Others toss it about amongst themselves. Each tries to hold the plug as a trophy, but is encouraged to keep throwing it about.

Jess works furiously, making every orifice available for pleasure. Her commitment is disturbing. People's standards are so low.

Twenty Bikers form a queue ready to have sex with Jess. People point their mobiles, hustling to record videos and take pictures. Catering staff and chefs look on, riveted by the action. It's a pity the excellent food may go untouched and be wasted.

Raucous laughter sweeps like a wave over the dining hall. Bikers regularly throw twenty-pound notes at Jess and cash is strewn everywhere. Female pensioners are revolted by her.

'Get your knickers back on, you little slut.'

'Everyone's having sex out in the open,' another pensioner remarks. 'It's disgusting. People today have no shame.'

Scenes develop as more people indulge themselves. Female

Bikers strip off, pull down the trousers of Biker boyfriends and perform fellatio. Others in their group clear plates, cutlery and drinks from tables to provide convenient areas for sex. Several Biker women are bent over chairs and penetrated from behind.

Those in the stag and hen parties are not to be left out. They provide surreal episodes. The Native American and one of the brides entertain themselves, Wonder Woman pleasures Robin Hood and Marie Antoinette is with Frankenstein.

Deviant sex can be watched on the Internet day and night. Very few people are able to indulge themselves in what they see and desire. Here, both men and women fulfil what they've craved.

Some of the stag lads closely watch their mates performing. Then throw food, trying to upset their rhythm.

A few of the pensioners make for the exit, passing further examples of fancy-dress frivolities. A woman dressed as Maid Marian is with a man costumed as an executioner. No member of the ship's crew is bothered about bringing any order to the scene. One of the chefs waits for the opportunity to entice Marie Antoinette.

'Stop it, Jess.' I move over and try to intervene. 'Why do you want to be abused?'

There's no reply. I watch on helplessly as she's involved with three blokes at once. When this group finishes another is keen to take over.

Jess is oblivious to everything, screaming with pleasure and pain. The Bikers are making sure she earns the money. Elsewhere, other cries of delight are heard.

'Get off her,' I plead with the Bikers. 'She's drunk and coked-up. She's lost control.'

The Bikers are annoyed with me.

Bobbi and the trans people observe the action and listen intently.

Tez is furious. 'Fuck off. We'll decide when she's had enough.'

'Stop it. This is sickening.' Again, I try to shift the Bikers away. 'You're a bunch of brainless, oversexed animals.'

'You're not spoiling our fun,' Tez responds.

'Leave Jess alone.'

'I've heard enough.' Tez throws me over his shoulder. I'm tightly held in a fireman's lift.

'You're going overboard,' he announces. Bikers cheer loudly.

'Put me down, you gorilla. Put me down.' I flail my arm towards his head.

Bobbi attempts to intervene but is smashed in the face.

The trans people try to thwart Tez, though he fights them off. I suspect he's had martial arts training. Bobbi regains composure but is covered in blood.

'Put him down!' Bobbi screams at Tez.

I'm panicking, feeling terror and confusion. I punch Tez constantly about his face, kick out and try to break free.

'I'm sorry for criticising your tattoo art,' I plead. 'Forgive me.'

There's no reaction.

From Tez's shoulders, there's a bird's-eye view of the restaurant. It's a great angle for an orgy painting. I'm more concerned about survival. Wrenching Tez's rings from his ears and gouging at his eyes, neither has any effect. No. This can't be happening to me. He must let go. I'm fighting for my life. I must never express my opinions on art in public again. People say never discuss politics or religion. Maybe art can be added to that list.

'Man going overboard!' Tez shouts. 'Man going overboard!' For a few seconds he swivels me round.

No one can believe what they're hearing. The trans people are desperate to help.

'He's mad,' Bobbi shouts. 'Stop him. He's a nutcase.'

Tez sweeps the trans people's rescue efforts aside and I'm almost dropped.

'Help!' I yell frantically. 'Please.' I can't believe I've annoyed Tez so much.

'Fuck off, posh bastard,' I hear one Biker shout at me.

'Bye-bye,' scoffs another. 'Hope you're a good swimmer.'

'Dump him in the sea, Tez,' shouts one more. 'Then hurry back for a fuck. Jess looks like she can go all night.'

Bobbi displays amazing tenacity and punches Tez continually as I'm carried towards a deck. The others make valiant attempts to pull me off his shoulder. They stab him with broken bottles. Several have kicked off their high heel stilettos and lost their wigs in the scuffles. Still Tez clings on to me. He forces his way past people in a corridor.

'Out of the fucking way,' he shouts to them. Without hesitation they obey.

'Leave him alone, you monster,' one po-faced woman fires.

Tez spits in her face.

'Put me down.' I scream in desperation. 'Put me down.'

'You're going overboard, pal. I promise you,' he stutters. 'You're going overboard.'

A few trans people produce flick-knives and stab Tez wherever they can.

'Kill him,' Bobbi shouts to them.

Two blades are stuck into Tez. Only minor cries of pain utter from him. He's bleeding badly. Can he ever be beaten?

'Kill him,' Bobbi screeches again. 'He must be stopped. For fuck sake, kill the bastard.'

The sound of the sea is closer. Where are the ship's security people when you need them? Not one is to be seen.

Waves crash fiercely against the side of the ship. Bobbi and the trans people finally manage to down Tez, knifing him repeatedly. I've certainly found friends in Bobbi and his team.

Then, with one colossal effort, they pick up Tez and throw him overboard.

# Chapter 18

During late afternoon the following day, we arrive at Kirstin's detached house. It's deep in southern Germany. We'll stay overnight before heading back. In the past, she's helped with my articles by providing photographs of pictures from her collection. I've never met Kirstin. But numerous telephone calls and emails have passed between us. There's no doubt Kirstin is wealthy. In her late 40s, and single, beyond that I've no other details.

'What a brilliant Art Deco house,' Jess exclaims, getting out her mobile and taking pictures.

The property is set in its own spacious grounds. Gardeners are cutting grass and pruning bushes.

'Wait.' I raise a hand. 'Shouldn't you ask permission first before photographing?'

'No. I don't think so,' she counters, shuffling uneasily.

'What's wrong?'

'My fanny's a bit sore,' she whines. 'I fucked 23 of those Bikers last night and made a grand. Never enjoyed sex so much. Don't worry, Al,' she laughs, 'I'll be okay if you fancy a session later on.'

I show disgust.

'Think I'll have to fuck Kirstin?' she queries brightly.

'Shut up, Jess. You're a nightmare.'

'It's better than being a boring cunt like you. Have a fuck and liven yourself up. I'll give you a quick blowie for starters. Then we can get really serious later.'

A female, 30, slender and tall, greets us. 'I'm Anna. Kirstin's assistant.' With long blonde hair, pulled back in a ponytail, her strong blue eyes convey friendliness. She looks classy, attractive, but has dressed herself down, to avoid becoming the object of male lust. Nonetheless, Jess gives her a suggestive smile. Other staff pass fluidly through the property.

Entering the house, Jess's eyes sweep everywhere, admiring the Art Deco furniture and antiques. She faces Anna. 'Can I take a few pictures? Everything is really impressive.'

My eyes roll with annoyance.

'Yes. I'm sure Kirstin won't mind.' Anna looks a little mystified but I sense she aims to be as helpful as possible.

Jess busily takes photographs, more than I consider necessary. Whilst leading us up to our rooms, Anna explains that Kirstin is having a telephone conversation with Brenda. Jess snaps even more pictures as we climb the stairs.

'When you've freshened up a little, we can join Kirstin,' says Anna, leaving us.

Thankfully, Jess and I are in separate rooms. A sigh of relief is breathed. I've had enough of her already. After 30 minutes, we venture downstairs.

Kirstin's face has exquisite bone structure and she looks a little austere until smiling. That alters her significantly. A head of short brown hair is flecked with highlights. Her small mouth reveals expensive teeth and restrained make-up is applied. With a bell-like form, she's wearing a jacket, matched with a necklace, loose-fitting slacks, and a pair of flat black shoes. Like me, Kirstin is a private person and aims to avoid drawing attention to her appearance. Although seated, she rises to firmly shake my hand. Jess receives a long hug and a peck on the cheek.

Kirstin's living room is undeniably lavish. It contains an impressive collection of René Lalique glass, from his Art Deco Period.

'You look exhausted, Al.' The comment is made with a gentle voice.

Jess offers an explanation: 'Al complained I was driving too fast. He was scared. Especially along stretches of road with deep drops at the side. That's why he's pale. I was okay. I'm fearless and up for anything, or anybody.'

Jess ends with a wide grin. It's obvious she's trying to make a good impression with Kirstin. For whatever reason I wouldn't like to speculate.

Kirstin gestures for us to sit down.

'Would you like a drink, tea, coffee or a glass of wine?'

'Nothing for me,' I reply.

'I'll have a beer. Is there one?' Jess enquires.

'Yes, of course,' Kirstin answers.

Anna walks out of the room, then reappears with cans of cold beer.

Jess takes a long drink from one of them.

'Brenda is very upset,' Kirstin announces dramatically. 'Very upset.'

Jess and I are nonplussed yet remain silent, anticipating more information.

'Has Brenda told you of the collection she discovered recently?' Her eye lids blink rapidly.

'Vaguely,' I respond, furrowing my brow.

'With my help, she contacted the Schmidts, an old German family of art dealers. During the 1930s, they acquired, very cheaply, paintings from rich Jewish collectors before those people fled the country. Pictures were retained long after the war and for decades they've remained unseen. It's been speculated the family held works from the 1930s by a group of noted lesbian artists. Predictably, the Nazis considered these women degenerate. Brenda employed a top German research team to make a thorough investigation. She was tenacious.'

'I mentioned in one of my articles,' I begin, 'that work by German lesbian artists from the pre-war period had gone missing. I understand these women went into hiding or fled abroad. Some of them were Jewish and persecuted.'

'Your article sparked Brenda's interest. There's no doubt about that. I know you're a good friend of hers. She speaks very highly of you, saying your knowledge of art is encyclopaedic. I've read your articles. They're fascinating.'

'Thank you.'

'The researchers confirmed a collection of lesbian art was still with the Schmidts. Brenda negotiated with, Otto, the head of the family, and worked out a deal. Horrendously, the pictures were stolen from the family's house in a vicious armed raid a few nights ago. It was a well-planned, professional job. The thieves may have had inside information. Who knows?'

'Are there any suspects for the robbery?' I ask.

'Rumours have circulated that a Russian gang is robbing art across Europe.'

I swallow deeply. My eyes flit from Kirstin to Jess and from Jess to Kirstin. My brain is overloading.

'The Schmidts were at home during the theft,' Kirstin relates. 'The robbers threatened to chop off their hands if they didn't comply. Everyone was tied up and gagged. All were terrified and suffered severe shock, though no injuries. One of the security staff, a female, was attacked and died in hospital hours later. Guard dogs were shot dead. The police are following up various lines of enquiry. Brenda is devastated someone lost their life. Feeling she's to blame for this tragedy, guilt is overwhelming her.'

'That's terrible.' I'm appalled, my eyes fix on Kirstin.

Jess remains quiet, not displaying the same sense of shock.

'When Brenda came out as a lesbian,' Kirstin explains, 'her father was furious and ridiculed her. Since he died, she's been fiercely independent and championed the lesbian cause. Building a Lesbian Art Museum is to be a monument to her efforts. It's in defiance of her father's vile prejudice. Particularly as she's using his money to establish the building. The robbery has been taken personally. Mentally, I think it could set her back years. She'll be aggressive in searching for the thieves.'

I'm speechless and purposely don't look at Jess for a reaction.

'The pictures were to be an important addition to Brenda's museum,' adds Kirstin. 'She'd already paid the family a ridiculous sum of money.'

'Will it be refunded?'

Kirstin slowly shrugs her shoulders.

'Were the pictures insured?'

Another slow shrug.

'I spoke to Brenda on the ferry,' I reveal. 'She was obviously upset.'

Jess is uncomfortable.

'It would break my heart if anything similar happened to my collection,' Kirstin admits. 'Pictures are like children for me.'

Swallowing uneasily, I note that Jess still remains silent.

'Evidence from the other robberies is being examined to determine whether there's any similar pattern.'

'Good,' I state.

'Two people were seen photographing the house shortly before it was raided.'

'Did they only take the works Brenda had bought.'

'No. Others were taken. A collection of family pictures that had been with the Schmidts for decades, including a Caspar David Friedrich.'

'I hope they capture the thieves and locate the pictures. Swiftly, for Brenda's sake.'

'Yes. Indeed.' Kirstin smiles thinly.

'How many lesbian works from your collection are we taking for Brenda?' Jess pipes up unexpectedly.

'Thirty in total. They're securely packed and ready to go.'

'Brilliant,' Jess adds.

'Anna has much experience with authenticating art,' explains Kirstin. 'Especially works on paper. Her apprenticeship was a long one. She knows the tricks of the trade, how to detect forgeries and make a thorough assessment. I'd like her to examine the Grosz you've brought before finally deciding on the purchase. Anna will take it to her workshop upstairs. If everything is okay, a bank transfer to Nicola shall be made a little later.'

'Yes, fine,' I say uneasily, hoping this Grosz isn't a fake, lashed up by Dick and Paul.

'I'll give you the documentation once Anna has done her

examination,' Jess states.

Before Anna takes away the Grosz, I see it's a typical work from his 1920s period. Depicted is a semi-naked obese woman in a compromising position with an old, overweight German businessman. A simple effective line drawing in ink with minimal colours of wash.

'Whilst Anna examines the Grosz would you like to see my collection of his drawings and watercolours?' invites Kirstin. 'I'm proud that it's a major private collection. I'll have pleasure showing you both. I also possess original John Heartfield photomontages. They're works from his anti-Nazi years. My interest is not really lesbian art but German decadent art of the 1920s and 1930s. My Grosz pictures are from the 1920s – before he fled Germany to America.'

'I'd love to see them,' I respond. 'I never knew you had John Heartfield pieces. His work is brilliant.'

'Yes. I've had those for years. As you're aware, he endured lots of persecution in Germany and a number of other countries. I've great sympathy for him.'

Kirstin's collection is housed in a spacious gallery extending from the rear of the house. She says it measures 150 feet by 75 feet. It's reassuring to see the atmosphere is controlled and constantly monitored by sophisticated apparatus. There's CCTV, and each picture is alarmed. Windows are barred on the inside, with roller shuttering outside. The works are displayed in plain wooden frames that incorporate UV protective, shatter-resistant glass. Very impressive.

The pictures for Brenda are in the gallery and lean against one of the walls.

For a few seconds, I consider producing a painting that shows an art exhibition taking place in a cemetery. A number of skeletons with glasses of wine in their hands would be seen viewing the display. Two or three others might be holding trays and offering nibbles.

Jess faces Kirstin. 'Is it okay if I take pictures?'

'Of course,' is the response. She's trying to smile at every opportunity and make us welcome.

To my surprise, Jess starts photographing general views of the gallery as well as the art works. She's moving a little easier than when we first arrived.

My eyes are overwhelmed at the sight of the Grosz treasures. They're in pristine condition. The colour washes haven't faded.

Pausing, Jess removes her T-shirt. 'Excuse me, I'll have to take off my bra. It's uncomfortable. I can't find one that fits properly these days.'

She slowly kneads her ample breasts whilst firmly looking at Kirstin. 'They've gone numb. I'll bring them back to life.'

Kirstin stares in stunned silence.

Jess then yanks down her leggings. 'I might as well adjust this thong. It's gone up my arse. Does a thong suit me, Kirstin? I hate knickers with an arse in them. Only grannies wear them.'

Anger blazes in my eyes.

Kirstin talks fondly of items in the collection, what she paid for them and the current value. She speaks as a proud parent might about their child's academic or sporting achievements. Without doubt, the Grosz and Heartfield pictures are stunning.

'Looking at Grosz's work,' I begin, 'the viewer instantly recognises German society in the 1920s and 1930s was a huge cesspit.'

'It was a horrible era in our history,' Kirstin agrees. 'Thankfully, these artists reflected what was happening in their work. My pictures are the children I never had.'

Tears fill her eyes.

Jess looks away.

'I spend hours in here enjoying these works. And trying to imagine how they were conceived. What had Grosz seen to inspire him? The torment and anguish he experienced before fleeing to America.'

'Does Anna appreciate your collection?' I enquire.

'Yes. That's why we're good friends.'

'It's priceless. Full credit to you, Kirstin.'

'Thanks, Al.'

I like Kirstin very much. Being in her presence is enjoyable. A good honest woman who's pleasant and easy-going. I'm convinced she does everything possible to help others collect art. We feel the same passion for the subject. She's a kindred spirit. Art is in our blood.

An hour or so passes before Anna finishes her investigations. She requests to speak in private with Kirstin. Both walk out of the room. How will I react if Anna declares the Grosz is a fake? I'm biting my nails and trying to rehearse a response, but nothing is forthcoming. Has Brenda mentioned anything to Kirstin about Greasby's criminal activities? I have to dismiss that from my mind. It's too painful to contemplate.

'I'll kill you and Nicola if this Grosz is a fake.'

'Stop worrying, Al. It's genuine. Do you think Kirstin fancies me?'

'Pack it in, Jess.'

A few minutes later, Kirstin is excited and full of joy. She keenly shakes my hand and cuddles Jess.

'Another beautiful child is joining my ever-growing Grosz family,' she proudly announces. 'Anna has done the necessary tests. It's okay. I'm very pleased. You can both have a little bonus for safely delivering the picture.'

'Not necessary,' I begin, until Jess interrupts: 'Thanks. That's very kind.'

Jess hands Kirstin an envelope containing provenance details. 'Nicola was lucky to find a photograph of one of the picture's former owners.'

Kirstin carefully pulls a tatty creased photograph from the envelope.

'The woman in the photograph owned the picture in the 1960s,' explains Jess, before adding sales talk: 'Now Nicola knows what you collect, she'll be on the look-out for more George Grosz works.'

Kirstin hands over the photograph and I'm horrified. The photograph has been aged and looks like it's been screwed up in someone's pocket for a month. My chest tightens as though a boa constrictor is coiling itself round me.

I loathe this Greasby criminality, which gathers momentum each day. The woman depicted in the photograph is instantly recognisable.

It's Jess's mum.

# Chapter 19

'Brenda tells me you're an artist, Al,' mentions Kirstin while we're viewing the Heartfield works. 'She says you're producing great art.'

A selection of pictures is displayed on the mobile. My hand shakes as I'm still in shock over the photograph.

'They're brilliant, Al. Email a selection to me. I'll download them and make prints. I'd like to have a proper look.'

'Okay. No problem.' Stuttering, I feel tongue-tied.

'What are you working on now?'

'Orgy scenes in cemeteries. A visual contrast between sex and death.'

'I know the perfect place to gather brilliant source material. It's not too far away, in the city centre. Das Sexhaus, or in English, The Sexhouse. We can go tonight. I know the owners. The experience could inspire memorable works.'

'I don't want to participate.'

'Okay,' she answers. 'Anna, myself and Jess may like to have a little fun.'

Jess preens. 'Wow. Yes.'

I feel nauseous.

Kirstin has focused on Jess. I thought she would've possessed a more discerning taste. Anna was ogling at her too. Sex knows no bounds.

'Do you want to freshen-up in your rooms before setting off to Das Sexhaus?'

'Brilliant,' laughs Jess.

My room is high-ceilinged, pleasant and, like every other room in the house, furnished with impressive antique furniture. There's an *ensuite* bathroom. I should shower but can't coax myself into action. Seeing the photograph of Jess's mum was upsetting. I'm unable to decide what to do. Kirstin is a nice person. She must not be stabbed in the back with Nicola's fake provenance. It's a pity that Anna, with all her knowledge, didn't examine the photograph more closely. A massive oversight.

Nicola's treachery knows no bounds. She's ruthless. Frighteningly ruthless. Incapable of remorse. Not a drop. Did she bribe Dick and Paul to create the photograph? What about Jess saying they were considering resigning? How true was that statement? It's difficult to believe anything.

Why can't Nigel kill Nicola when they're in a violent scrap? Or, one day, why doesn't a duped collector storm into the Askworth Gallery and shoot her? Greasby Fine Art, once the envy of the commercial art world, is floundering in the dirt. I could kill Nicola myself. I hate her almost as much as the drunken, coked-up bastard who killed my son.

Gazing at my reflection in a fantastic, ornate full-length mirror, tears fill my eyes. Torn apart with anger and hating myself, I wish the job with Greasby had never started. It's poisoning my mind. Self-loathing is drowning me. Art is brilliant. Being associated with paintings and drawings is exclusive and exhilarating. Yet, every now and then it's shit. Working for the local authority is long past. Sadly, my old beloved art gallery no longer performs its original function. A recent local newspaper report stated the conversion to a glorified store has been completed. There's no going back. My old way of life has gone forever.

In this room, there's a refrigerated drinks cabinet. It's much larger than one found in an average hotel room. The alcoholic drinks are ignored and a bottle of water pulled out. I take a sip, only I'm not thirsty. Lifting my mood feels impossible. I slowly take several deep breaths and walk restlessly about the room. Violence boils within me. This is not, Al, the usually passive, dedicated artist and art historian.

What will Brenda think of me if she discovers the treachery behind the photograph? Any chance of a job will vanish. Should I call her? Can't decide. Yes. I need advice. Maybe she'll volunteer to tell Kirstin about the photograph. What punishment would Brenda have in store for Nicola? I must make contact before Kirstin makes the final payment for the Grosz.

Unfortunately, it's Deb who answers. 'Brenda's in the torture chamber with some teens. She really needs to unwind. I can't disturb her.'

'Okay, I'll call again.'

I ring Frankie and spill the beans.

He's furious. 'Why did Nicola need to do that? It's a genuine Grosz.'

'Kirstin requested as much provenance as possible. Nicola was only too willing to provide it.'

'The work stands on its own merit. Nicola should've told Kirstin to fuck off. Jess was stupid to involve her mother.'

'This could blow up in our faces.'

'Do what's necessary, Al. You have my support.'

'Thanks, Frankie. Are you okay?'

'No. Paulene is bleeding me dry with her Renta Stud ambitions. I've taken out a bank loan with our house as security.'

Ending the call, I lie on the bed for a while. Unable to settle, anger is bubbling up inside me. I burst into Jess's room. Discovering she's naked, I see clothes strewn everywhere. The curtains are open and light floods in. Pleasuring herself with a purple missile of a vibrator, she moans loudly. Other sex toys are visible in an open suitcase. A fan wafts cool air across her. What a disgusting sight.

'Hi, Al. Suck my tits, I'm almost there.'

I'd no idea vibrators could be so noisy.

'Helping me to orgasm may win the bet.'

'Shut up,' I attack, moving over to her.

'I'll give you half my winnings.'

'Pestering for sex nearly got me killed last night.'

She ignores the comment.

'The woman in the photograph is your mother. Was that your idea or Nicola's?'

It's a struggle to restrain my anger.

Jess continues exciting herself. There's not a hint of remorse, or even guilt on her face.

'I think my mum looks convincing, don't you? She was more than happy to play the role. Earned a nice fee and was well pleased. The Grosz is genuine. What's your problem? It's only a bit of fun. Kirstin was a pain, continually pestering Nicola for provenance. Now she's got it.'

'It's fraud. A criminal offence. Stop that contraption. I can't hear myself speak.'

'You're mad, Al. Not having your bollocks emptied for ages has sent you doolally.'

'Shut up.'

'Get your kit off. Want to fall into me?' Her legs are opened in a lewd pose. 'How long is it since you've seen a woman like this?'

'I've told Frankie about the photograph. He's really pissed off with Nicola and you.'

'Fuck off. Nicola should be admired. She's just brilliant. Takes chances. Definitely what's needed today.'

'She's stupid. We'll be arrested and locked up.'

'Kirstin's not lily white,' Jess snarls. 'I've heard some of the Grosz pictures were nicked for her.'

'Who from?'

'One or two people.'

'I'd like to believe you, Jess but you tell lies. Nicola and you are both liars.'

'You're so naïve. That German bitch talked a load of bollocks earlier. You worked for Askworth Council too long. Step into the real world. The *real* world.'

'Stop that contraption. It's annoying.'

'It might be annoying you, but it's exciting me.'

'Get dressed. Tell Kirstin the photograph is fake.'

I throw the discarded clothes on top of her.

'No.'

'Put the clothes on. Do it. Turn that off, will you? Turn it off.'

Jess laughs, her boobs bouncing freely.

I phone Nicola. Unsurprisingly, there's no answer.

'Contact Nicola on your mobile. I want to speak to the bitch.'

Jess obeys. 'Hi, Nicola. Al wants to speak to you.'

The mobile is handed over. I switch to loudspeaker.

'You okay though Al, you okay?'

'You corrupt bitch. That fake photograph is outrageous.'

'Fuck off, wanker,' she volleys. 'Ringing and telling my dad everything. You'll not be working for us much longer.'

'Can I take his place?' Jess shouts.

'Of course.'

'How is Annabel?' Jess sits up.

'Fantastic. Won the first round in that acting competition.'

'Amazing.

'We're really pleased.'

'Al's not fucked me yet. Don't think he's capable.'

'How selfish. Men should always be there for a woman's needs.'

'I agree.'

'Brenda will be hearing about this photograph scam,' I interject. 'Expect a visit from her and the girls very soon.'

'Do what you like. I'm not scared. I'll have her sorted.'

'I wonder what words Brenda will brand on you?'

'Fuck off.'

'We're not picking up Y's pictures. No chance. We're coming straight back in the morning.'

'Do as you're told, Council Prick,' she growls.

'If you want the pictures, pick them up yourself. I'm not getting involved with criminality.'

'I've sacked the Birmingham staff today.'

'They can apply for a Protective Award. You'll not win this one.'

'Do what the fuck you like. Make sure Al has a pleasant trip back, Jess.'

'What do you mean?' I yell.

Nicola has ended the call. I toss the mobile at Jess. Despite the shenanigans, I must not be intimidated. Retirement ought to be seriously considered. My pension is adequate. But there's a need to stay involved with art. I must continue to fight and make Greasby healthy and profitable. Jess isn't having my job. A murder could occur before that happens.

'Tell Kirstin the photograph is fake. This can't go on any longer. Make up a story. Say it was a bit of fun.'

'No.'

I try to grab the vibrator though without any luck. It's like trying to snatch a bone off a snarling dog.

'Turn it off, Jess.'

'No.'

In a struggle, I slump on top of her, though rapidly regain my balance.

'Give it to me.'

'No, Al. I need to be in the mood later for a *ménage à trois* with Kirstin and Anna.'

She leaps to her feet still grasping the vibrator.

'If you won't fuck me, I'll fuck you. That way I could still win the bet.'

Forcefully, she aims the vibrator at my backside. I try unsuccessfully once more to take it from her.

'Shall we have fun, Al? Know what fun is?'

Grabbing her in a headlock, we fall to the floor. Still she holds on to the noisy sex toy.

'Help. Help, someone,' she screams and laughs raucously. 'He's nicking my vibrator.'

We continue to struggle until finally I release the toy from her grip.

'Give it back. A girl needs her vibrator. It's her best friend.'

I fling it against a wall. Finally, silence.

'You bastard, Al. Why did you do that? It's provided me with countless orgasms.'

'You're evil, Jess. One of the most evil bitches I've ever met.'

'Want to fight? I'm like Nicola. I enjoy a scrap, then having a mad fuck after.'

Still on the floor, Jess takes a swing at me. 'Fight and fuck.

Fight and fuck.'

'Shut up.'

Restricting her movements, my hands slip round her neck. Smiling, she continually bangs her crotch against me.

'Yes, Al. Treat me to my favourite sex game. Asphyxiation. It's brilliant. Really love going to the edge.'

I squeeze her throat. She closes her eyes, resembling the female in Edvard Munch's work, *Madonna.*

Gasping slightly, Jess breaks free. 'This is much better than a fuck, Al.'

The words mean nothing.

Long black Goth nails dig into me. 'Harder, harder. I'm coming. I want to come before dying.'

I'm lost. Don't care about anything. Both thumbs press on her wind pipe.

With arms flailing, she throws wild punches and, continually raising her legs, there's a desperate effort to unbalance me. Yet, all attempts to escape are thwarted, until she scratches my face and the hold is broken.

'Stop. Please, stop.' Panting for air, she's endeavouring to crawl away.

Pinning her down, I squeeze again. Desperate to break free, she knocks my hands away. 'Stop, Al. Stop. Enough. I've had enough.'

She deserves to die. I despise her, Nicola and Greasby Fine Art. I want revenge. Faces appear before me. Nicola's and the scumbag who killed my son.

Once more, Jess evades my grip.

'Murder. Murder,' she shrieks at a deafening level. 'Get off me. Please, let go.' Tears stream down her face. Fingernails dig further into me.

'Murder! Murder. Help. Somebody, help.'

I squeeze again. She's fisting harder. Again and again we battle. I feel dominant, powerful, overcoming her and the humiliation suffered recently. Jess is the embodiment of my hatred.

'Help me,' her mouth moves but no sound is heard.

For a few seconds, I'm with my son. We're playing football in a local park. He's wearing the new kit I bought earlier in the day. Some clever moves are shown that were picked up from a Saturday morning football club.

Slowly, Jess's resistance subsides and her body is limp.

Kirstin and Anna rush into the room and push me away.

'Stop, Al. Can't you tell she's had enough?' barks Anna.

'We heard screaming and came at once,' mouths Kirstin, totally bewildered.

Colour has drained from Jess.

'No. No. Please. Not a murder in my house.' Kirstin is frantic. 'I'm praying she's okay.'

Ever practical, Anna goes to work on Jess. Kirstin and I kneel down but allow plenty of space. Sweat pours from me.

'Erotic asphyxiation must be done with a proper technique,' begins Kirstin, eyeing me fleetingly. 'Or, serious injury, even death may occur. I'm shocked you both enjoy this deviation.'

I don't comment.

'Is this what excites her the most, Al?'

'I believe so.'

'Does she always encourage you to be dominant during sex?'

'We've never done this before.'

'What?'

'Never.'

'Poor girl, she looked full of life. Will she be okay, Anna?'

'Don't know yet. She's breathing.'

'Shall we call an ambulance?'

'Not necessary,' Anna responds.

Jess slowly opens her eyes.

'Are you okay?' asks Anna.

Jess nods and gently gets to her feet, heads to the bathroom and heaves.

'This is a massive stroke of luck,' scolds Kirstin. 'You've both been very fortunate.'

I'm numb.

Kirstin stares at me long and hard. 'You need to learn the practice of erotic asphyxiation under the supervision of an experienced master or dominatrix.'

Tears trickle from my eyes.

Jess strides over to Anna and gives her a long hug.

'Thanks, Anna.'

Kirstin beams. 'Are you okay, Jess?'

'Yes.' She's radiant once more. 'It was my fault. Al was naïve.'

Jess tries to embrace me. 'I enjoyed the experience, but you must stop when I say so.'

I duck out of the way.

Poking her nose into a drinks cabinet, she takes out a small vodka and takes a swig.

'Please, do not practice choking games in my house again,' appeals Kirstin.

Still wheezing a little, Jess is unrepentant. 'I love going to the final seconds before death. Been at that point quite often.'

After examining the smashed vibrator and throwing it into her case, Jess reclines on the bed and laughs. '*You'll* have to be my sex toy now, Al.'

It's not lost on Kirstin and Anna that Jess is still naked. Anna's tongue runs over her lips. Kirstin focuses her attention on Jess's waxed lower regions.

'Don't worry about the toy, Jess,' Anna volunteers. 'We've plenty. You can have a replacement.'

'After what's happened, I don't think we should go to Das Sexhaus tonight,' sighs Kirstin.

'Oh no, we must,' Jess responds. 'I'm okay. I'm already looking forwards to it.'

'No, you've had enough for today.' Anna frowns. 'A rest is needed.'

'That's right,' I interject.

'We're going, no question.' Jess avoids my gaze.

'See you both in a while,' smiles Anna as she prepares to leave with Kirstin.

'Wait, Jess has something to say,' I pipe up.

'What is it?' Kirstin responds.

'Nothing,' Jess answers, her breathing now calmed.

'Don't hold us in suspense.' Anna looks at her.

Jess touches Kirstin's arm. 'How did you acquire those Grosz pictures? By fair means or foul?'

'Foul,' Kirstin replies acidly without a hint of hesitation. 'A collector has to seize opportunities wherever they can.'

Jess is triumphant.

'Can you give more details, Kirstin?'

'No need to,' she hits back.

# Chapter 20

Kirstin and Anna decide to drive to Das Sexhaus in Kirstin's two-seater sports car. Jess and I prepare to follow in our van. The two German women are wearing loose-fitting patterned dresses with flat shoes. Jess has a short figure-hugging black dress and heavy boots. Her eyes are outlined in black, the lipstick bright-red.

There's no desire to join them. I've lost interest in gathering pictures for orgy scenes in a cemetery. Resting and spending the evening alone would be preferable. Or, having a second look at Kirstin's collection. I'm stifling yawns after a long day. It's a humid evening but bearable.

Two thick-set female security guards will watch over Kirstin's house whilst we're absent. They have German Shepherds.

Jess takes pictures.

Annoyed, I challenge her: 'What are you photographing now?'

'The dogs. They're beautiful.'

Along the way, our conversation is sparse.

'Are you feeling okay, Jess?' I eventually ask.

She's bright. 'Yes. Never felt better.'

'Good.'

'I want to stay at Das Sexhaus all night and be fucked until I can't stand up.'

I resist commenting.

'Al, before we came out, I checked something with Nicola and the girls back in the office.'

'What are you talking about?'

'Choking me can't win the bet. A fuck is the only way to grab the cash.'

'You've lost the bet.' I avoid looking at her.

Das Sexhaus is located in a four-storey, Brutalist building. Kirstin mentioned earlier that each floor caters for different sexual orientations – gay, straight, lesbian and trans. There are other Sexhaus clubs throughout Germany. Anna and her frequent this one at least once a week. Ample car-parking space is provided in an adjacent area where an impressive selection of luxurious vehicles are seen. Jess parks the van and annoys me straight away. Texting, her fingers move fast and furiously. Kirstin and Anna stand alongside and fold their arms in frustration.

'Can't that wait,' I thunder.

'I won't be long.' Jess doesn't intend arguing. With her back to me, I can't see any of the text's content. 'You three go ahead.'

Walking towards the Sexhaus entrance, Kirstin and Anna stroll hand-in-hand. Both smile. Clearly a contented couple.

Ten minutes pass and Jess isn't with us. I'm angry and jog back to the car park. She's still texting. I grab the mobile. Struggling with me, an unsuccessful bid is made to snatch it back.

'Hurry up, Jess.'

'You're such a pain, Al. Want to strangle me again?'

'Shut up. Get in there and be ready to leave in an hour, no longer. I'm knackered.' The mobile is handed back.

She strides forwards, promiscuity dripping from her.

Access to Das Sexhaus is available to members and their guests. Kirstin and Anna show membership cards at the foyer area kiosk. Jess and I are signed-in as guests. Fees have to be paid for tonight's session and Kirstin obliges by using a credit card. It's explained that besides access to the club, this allows favours from working women and men. They're available to perform sex within any of the floors. I'm told there are beds, couches, chairs, tables and other items for sexual convenience. Everyone is encouraged to participate in one mass orgy. For extra-special services, the working women and men can accept tips from the members and guests. I notice the club's hourly rate is exorbitant. Kirstin pays for three hours.

'Can we stay longer if necessary?' pleads Jess.

'Of course,' answers Kirstin. 'As long as you want.'

'Can't we stay for two hours or even an hour and a half?'

'Fuck off, Al, trying to spoil everyone's enjoyment,' Jess snaps. '*I'd* like to stay longer.'

'I'm really tired,' I protest. Kirstin glances at me sympathetically but doesn't comment.

A pleasant fragrance plays about the foyer. It's busy with people of various ages flashing membership cards and paying their fees. Occasionally, they buy Das Sexhaus merchandise. This ranges from fridge magnets to sweatshirts. The usual kitsch objects. Most items contain the slogan: *I'VE HAD SEX AT DAS SEXHAUS.*

Kirstin knows the club owners, a husband-and-wife team, Stefan and Petra. Stefan has a remarkable physical presence and obviously keeps in shape, despite being in his 50s. Standing six feet tall, he has sparkling white teeth and short blonde hair. He's wearing an open-neck red shirt with sleeves rolled up, plain black trousers and casual shoes. To me, he looks a nasty piece of work.

Petra isn't present as she's having the night off. Stefan exchanges restrained hugs and kisses with Kirstin and Anna. The security team – male and female – appear fearsome. They're dressed in grey shirts, black trousers and black boots.

'Are those people necessary?' I ask Anna, pointing in their direction.

'Yes. Wild and violent activity is normal here.'

Photography in Das Sexhaus is forbidden but Kirstin talks politely to Stefan about my art and obtains permission.

'Everyone will be skeletised,' I clarify.

Although accepting the explanation, he doesn't look pleased, which is off-putting. I can produce at least four cemetery orgies based on the individuals already seen tonight – straight, gay, lesbian, trans.

'Are you here again?' Stefan views Jess aggressively.

'I'm insatiable,' she shoots back, as we observe the situation uncomfortably.

Stefan waves his finger at Jess. 'I want no trouble tonight.'

Jess shrugs with hardly a flicker of surprise. 'What's wrong with you? Big mouth, small dick?'

'We'll be watching you.'

She attempts to rub his crotch. 'Is that a pistol in your pocket or are you just pleased to see me?'

'Don't touch me, fucking shag-bag,' he growls, moving away.

Kirstin, Anna and myself are curious to say the least.

Everywhere, people have broad smiles. I've never seen as many relaxed and content individuals. They're eagerly anticipating sexual release. My cemetery orgies must include happy expressions on skeleton faces.

Five German lads burst into the foyer. Aged between 20 and 25, each one is dressed casually in jeans, open-neck shirts and trainers. Startlingly, they recognise Jess.

One lad, tall, broad-shouldered, and with blonde-hair, moves forwards. 'Jess, will you fuck us all again?'

'The same way as before?' presses another. 'We've talked about you all the time.'

With her enticing figure, Jess preens. They greedily kiss her, roughly grab her generous boobs and stuff their hands up her dress.

'We're meeting some mates here,' the blonde Adonis enthuses. 'Will you fuck them too?'

'How many?' she asks gleefully, her sexual appetite knowing no bounds.

'Twenty or more.'

'No problem,' she answers hungrily.

'We'll tip you plenty.'

'Brilliant.'

'You're a better fuck than any girl working here,' one of them comments.

Jess almost falls over laughing.

I sigh audibly.

Stefan is annoyed and narrows his eyes. 'Would you all move out of the foyer.'

Ignoring him, the lads pull off Jess's dress. She squeals with delight. Adonis and three others lift her off the floor. This allows another to perform cunnilingus with her. With eyes closed, she enjoys her first sexual encounter of the night.

Kirstin and Anna observe the activity with fascination.

'I'll join you girls in a while,' Jess shouts to them.

'Hope so,' responds Kirstin. 'Only have straight sex, Jess. We don't want a repeat of earlier dramas.'

Stefan makes a final demand from the crowded foyer: 'Could everybody please move on to your chosen floors? I wish you success in every sexual adventure.'

A few of the German lads expose themselves, and Jess fondles each one. Then, she kisses three lads passionately with a man-eating mouth.

Four women greet Kirstin and Anna and invite them to the lesbian floor.

'Follow us, Al.' Kirstin tugs at me, temporarily forgetting Jess. 'We'll enjoy ourselves. Start taking pictures whenever you like.'

'I'm a little nervous. Won't people object? Should I ask permission first?'

'No. No. We know most people here. We're regulars. Everything will be fine. You'll get some great material. Your art is brilliant.'

The lesbian floor contains an area where costumes can be hired. Lockers are offered for people to leave their clothes and belongings. Sex toys and bondage equipment are available. Thankfully, the vibrators aren't as noisy as the one Jess was using earlier. Otherwise, it would sound like a motorbike rally. There's a bar at one end of the floor. Though members are more interested in sex than drinking. Everyone is keen to enjoy the night.

Before selecting costumes, Kirstin and Anna fling off their dresses. They stand unabashed. No knickers. No bras. Kirstin slips on a nun's outfit, Anna a ballet tutu. Both are delirious with excitement.

Other women are seen as French maids, policewomen, nurses and schoolgirls. One lady is Wonder Woman, another wears latex. A few help each other to fasten strap-on dildos. Two insert strapless ones into themselves.

For my pictures, I'm unsure about depicting skeletons in uniforms. But concede it might splash character and colour into otherwise drab cemetery scenes, with muddy brown and black tombstones.

Kirstin is involved in a scene with Wonder Woman. Anna decides to entertain a police woman. Kirstin stops in the middle of one activity and encourages me to take pictures. She arranges group scenes and I'm happy to photograph them. This develops into an orgy involving 30 women or more. Some ask if I'll email pictures to them. This is over-the-top decadence. Definitely a playground for the rich and, dare I say it, the perverted. Nonetheless, there's an urgency to gather source material.

One woman dressed in red latex is vocal: 'Oh Kirstin, I wanted to be a nun tonight. Can we swap costumes in a while?'

'Of course,' Kirstin promises.

Later, I move to the straight floor where Jess has settled. Sighing and whimpering, she's having sex with a bunch of virile lads. More queue in a line awaiting their chance. Her well-developed Botticelli Venus figure is a magnet for them. The room is packed with other sex-hungry people.

Yet, the atmosphere is uneasy. The working girls are furious with Jess. Not earning any lucrative tips, they remonstrate loudly. Two of them try to attack her, but are stopped by bouncers.

Jess is unable to express love. There's no foreplay with any of her partners. Lovemaking does not exist. Or, even a consideration. She craves sexual excitement for herself and nobody else. That was evident on the ship when she was with the Bikers. On the pill since eleven, that's when she lost her virginity. Sex has been looked upon in a toxic way. A desire to have children has never been mentioned.

Five women approach me for sex. They're dressed in leather, latex, rubber, besides stockings and suspenders. I'm promised a good time with one or two of them or all five together. It's up to me to choose. I refuse and dart past them.

Before any more pictures can be taken, I'm seized and punched by male and female security staff. They're armed. I blink rapidly, unable to understand what's happening. It's like being across Tez's shoulder once again. I certainly don't belong here. I'm having second thoughts about depicting orgies in my work. The room falls silent as they drag me out.

Staff bundle me along several corridors and into Stefan's sparsely furnished office. Thrown on the floor, I'm scared, my chest is tight.

'Are you a fucking weirdo?' Stefan kneels down and shouts in my face. 'Why do you want to take photographs instead of having sex? Will you look at them later and wank yourself silly?'

'I've no interest in sex.'

'Have you had an erection tonight? Can you still raise a smile?'

'Not tried,' I answer vaguely.

Two of the security staff stand at the door.

'Allow me to go, or I'll call the police.'

'I'm an ex-police inspector,' he sneers. 'Contacting them is no good.'

If not a policeman in an earlier life, Stefan might have been a porno stud.

'What's your relationship with the shag-bag? Are you her partner, husband, dad, uncle?'

'None of those,' I wheeze. 'I'm her boss.'

'What's your job? Tell the truth, or you'll disappear.' His words are venomous.

'I'm Greasby Fine Art's area manager and an artist. The pictures I've taken will be used in my work. I like humour in art. It's time art made people laugh.'

'I need to know if you're telling the truth.'

One of his staff snatches my mobile.

'What do you know about the Schmidt art robbery?'

'Nothing. Kirstin only gave details a few hours ago.'

Stefan is still close. 'I'm an old friend of the Schmidts. Their property isn't far from here. Some weeks ago, two people, fitting the description of shag-bag and an older man, were seen outside the Schmidt's house taking photographs. The man has been a Sexhaus member for a while. Who is he?'

'Frankie Greasby. He's managing director of Greasby Fine Art.'

'They were both here on the night of the Schmidt robbery. Why was he in Germany?'

'What he does is none of my business. He'll only discuss matters when he wants to.'

'He came dressed as a Viking and brought a load of coke. Handed it out freely. That's not allowed. I don't want to be raided and closed down.'

'He's a real coke head.'

'Why was the shag-bag with him?'

Before answering, I try to sit up but I'm forced down again.

'Frankie has split up with his wife. Jess doubles as his sex and drugs partner.'

'Both of them came with a Russian called Yaroslav or Y. I know him. He's the brother of Olga who makes costumes for Das Sexhaus. He fucks like a machine whenever he's here. Women love him.'

'This is news to me.'

'What do you know about Y?' Stefan thrusts his face closer to mine.

'Very little.'

'Are you a stud, like him? Did you intend to perform after taking pictures?'

'No,' I laugh. 'I've been celibate ever since my son was killed in a road accident.' How many more questions will be posed? I want to escape as soon as possible.

'The German police have been watching the Russian closely.

Where is he tonight?'

'No idea.'

'I hate Russians. The female guard, murdered during the Schmidt robbery, was an ex-colleague. I want to find out who killed her and did the robbery. Russian gangs have interested me for years.'

'I'm sure.'

'There's been much talk about the robbery. Other art collectors are eager for the police to have a result. Shag-bag fucked countless blokes last time. Hungrier for sex than any of the girls working here. Fucked one man so much he died of a heart attack. They'd shared lines of potent cocaine. The police closed me down for 24 hours. I didn't expect to see her again, especially with Kirstin. She tried it on with me but I told her to fuck off. I bet she's riddled with disease. All my girls are checked regularly. Why are you both here?' His eyes glow like headlights.

One of the security team confirms my mobile contains Sexhaus images and hands it back.

Then, I explain to Stefan: 'Kirstin has sold pictures to an English collector. I'm here to see they're safely transported back to the UK.'

He gets hold of my shirt. 'Why were the shag-bag and Frankie Greasby here several weeks ago and on the night of the robbery? Is the Russian involved? Give me answers or I'll beat them out of you.'

'I haven't a clue.'

'You're the shag-bag's boss and work for Frankie Greasby. You know something.'

'I'm afraid not.'

'You're a liar. Englishmen always take the piss. Where were you on the night of the robbery?'

Before I can answer, Stefan punches me again. Winded, I want to vomit.

'Leave him alone, Stefan,' Kirstin explodes as she bursts in and ignores the security staff. She's dressed as Wonder Woman, while Anna is Supergirl.

Anna attacks Stefan with deft movements and he's on the floor. One of the female security staff tries to tackle Kirstin but she's downed in one. Unbelievable. I'm impressed.

'This is barbaric behaviour,' shouts Kirstin, bending down to Stefan. 'You're nothing but a bully. When Petra isn't here, you lose control. I'll report your behaviour to the police chief. Al is my guest and would never do anything wrong.'

Stefan is deflated and rubs bruised ribs.

'Quick, Al,' Kirstin instructs. 'We're going to get Jess.'

Anna helps me to stand and Stefan is left in stunned silence. Today, I've seen different sides of Kirstin and Anna. I like them both. But for their intervention, it's anyone's guess how I would've escaped.

Heading to the straight floor, we see Jess entertaining three lads. More wait for an opportunity. Playing with themselves, ribald instructions are directed at Jess and the trio. I tell her we're leaving.

'No. Definitely not.'

'Move, Jess.' Kirstin is impatient.

'I've only been fucked by a few men. These others have been waiting for the last half hour. They can't be left with full bollocks. It wouldn't be fair.'

'We're going,' I insist.

'I'll get a taxi back to Kirstin's house. Cash is being thrown at me.'

Kirstin and Anna shove the three lads away. Anna picks up Jess's mobile and her cash scattered on the floor.

'No. No. I'm not ready yet,' she protests, but there are working women telling her to leave.

Taking Jess in a head-lock, I drag her forwards.

'I'm not coming with you.' She's adamant and tries to break free, until Kirstin and Anna clasp handcuffs on her.

'What's wrong?' each one of the three lads show surprise.

I point at Jess. 'This bitch gave me gonorrhoea last night. I'm experiencing a constant discharge.'

They rush to the Gents, believing they can rid themselves of any infection with a scrub of hot water and soap.

## Chapter 21

I release Jess from the handcuffs and we climb into our van.

'Will you be okay to drive?' I wonder if she's pissed or has snorted too much coke.

'Yes.' She fires the ignition and aggressively floors the accelerator.

Jess is naked as we didn't bother to retrieve her clothes. Still in their Sexhaus costumes, Kirstin and Anna are in front.

It's been a long day and a shower is needed. I'm counting the hours to leaving Germany and sailing for England. My thoughts switch back to the photograph depicting Jess's mum. Brenda shall be informed. I'll ask if a job can be created for me. There are plans to establish a gallery in New York. That would provide a perfect opportunity. I can't take any more of Greasby. My efforts must be increased to produce pictures.

'I had the best sex ever back there,' Jess relates, easing the disappointed look from her face. 'I wanted to enjoy more.'

'Don't you ever close your legs?'

'No. I'll be buried in a Y-shaped coffin.'

'I'm sure.'

'Don't suppose you fancy a fuck later? I'm randy.'

'Are you joking? I'm still upset about that photograph.'

'We were booked into Das Sexhaus for three hours,' Jess reflects. 'We only stayed for an hour. What a waste. Did Kirstin get a refund?'

'No idea.'

'What happened to my cash?'

'Anna has it. Your mobile too.'

'I don't want to go back yet.' Jess is agitated and bites her nails. 'I want more sex.'

'Kirstin's says she'll fix us supper.'

'They've not taken their eyes off me all day. I want to tease them. They want to fuck. I'll have them chomping at the bit.'

'Playing pathetic sex games is tedious.'

'Didn't you fancy a fuck in there, Al? You could've enjoyed whatever fantasy you craved. There were some very pretty girls.'

Roll on tomorrow morning. I want to go home. There's no way I'm picking up Y's pictures.

'Let's stop for food,' Jess proposes. After flashing Kirstin, we pull into a lay-by. The two women stand at the side of the van.

'I've worked up an appetite,' Jess explains. 'I want a steak and a beer.'

'There's plenty of food at home,' answers Kirstin.

'I want a steak.'

'You can't waltz into a restaurant naked,' states Anna.

'Somebody could go inside and order.'

'Don't be ridiculous,' snaps Kirstin 'We're not stopping anywhere.'

'You didn't have your money's worth at the club,' Jess confronts Kirstin. 'We left far too early.'

'Not bothered. I'll sort something out with Stefan. We had to leave. *You* were upsetting people.'

Driving off, Jess is deep in thought. Five minutes later, our headlights flash again and we slip into another lay-by.

'What's wrong?' I probe.

'There's a tyre problem.'

Jumping out of the van, she bends down and examines the driver's-side front tyre.

'Now what's wrong?' Kirstin fumes.

Jess stands up and explains the concern.

'There's a tyre gauge in our car,' says Anna. 'I'll get it and check the pressure.'

On seeing Jess naked, male drivers brake and pip. She waves at them, bends over and parts her arse cheeks. Nicola's butt plug is visible. Other motorists are curious at seeing Anna and

Kirstin in their Sexhaus attire.

One car stops and two handsome blonde youths in their mid-20s emerge. Togged up in open-neck, short-sleeve shirts, shorts and stylish slip-on shoes, they approach with a dick-thrust swagger. A thick haze of testosterone engulfs them. I hate to contemplate what might happen next. Kirstin's face shows anger.

'Hello, gorgeous,' one lad says in a loud, confident voice to Jess. 'You look horny.'

'You're right.'

'I'm Hans and he's Klaus. 'What a beautiful waxed pussy you have.'

'Thank you,' laughs Jess.

'Unwaxed pussies look like a baby mouse caught in a bundle of twigs,' Hans jokes.

'Does your pussy have a name?' laughs Klaus.

'No. It's a fanny not a dog.' Her eyes drop to their lower regions. 'Check out your trouser bulges. That's the first thing I notice about a bloke. A bulge means a thick dick.'

Both lads ceremoniously unzip their trousers and expose themselves. They gaze at Jess's perky breasts.

'I'm wide and dripping already.' Jess flutters her eyelids. 'My favourite song is *Orgasm Addict* by the Buzzcocks.'

Standing a short distance away, I'm longing for the ground to swallow me.

Anna has the tyre pressure gauge in her hand. But Kirstin and her are distracted when two females shout to them from a car. It's slowed down to a snail's pace. 'Do you want to do some scissoring with us?'

They're ignored.

What I'm witnessing with these lads could be inspiration for a painting – male skeletons comparing penis sizes. Perhaps a couple of females can be taking measurements. Although unsure about depicting male skeletons with protrusions, it could be humorous.

'We had to stop and see if you needed help,' Hans and Klaus

chirp. 'We'll do anything.'

Jess drapes her arms round them. 'Thank you. That's very thoughtful.'

She relates the problem to Hans.

Klaus bends down and runs his hand over the tyre. 'I don't think you've picked up a nail.'

Jess ruffles his hair affectionately.

'Where are your clothes? Are you a nudist?' asks Hans.

'Only when I feel like fucking.'

More drivers on this dual carriageway slow down and the road is choked. Motorists on the opposite side also brake.

Kirstin attempts to shield Jess from becoming everyone's focus of attention, without success. Jess continually moves away from her. She waves, blows kisses and showily wobbles her boobs at everyone – male and female.

'Stop this lewd behaviour.' Kirstin remonstrates with her.

'We'll change the wheel,' says Hans.

'Thank you so much.' Jess darts her tongue into his mouth.

'Stop this now.' Kirstin moves forwards to separate them. 'We can solve any problem ourselves. We may be women but we're not totally useless.'

'You're spoiling the fun,' Jess retorts whilst rubbing Hans's crotch.

'There's nothing wrong,' states Anna, having checked the pressure in all four tyres. 'The driver's-side front tyre is lower than the others though no cause for concern.'

'Are you sure?' asks Jess. 'I was having difficulty steering. Positive there was a problem.'

Kirstin and Anna look at each other in desperation.

'We can pump up the tyre. Or change the wheel,' offers Klaus, patting Jess's bum.

'What a good idea,' adjoins Jess, still with an arm round Hans.

Anna stares at both lads. 'It's not necessary.' She appeals to Jess with concern. 'If you feel unsafe, I'll drive the van back to Kirstin's.'

'No, I'll manage.'

Another car stops, occupied by four young studs. It's evident they're friends of the first two. After embracing Jess, they offer help.

Male drivers halt on both sides of the road and zip down their side windows. 'Sit on my face', 'give us a tit wank', 'suck on this', are some of the lewd comments heard in a perfect English tongue.

From this little scene tonight, I sense promiscuous men and women are observed differently. A sexually active man is viewed in a positive light. He's admired. Put on a pedestal. A woman is regarded as a slut. A whore. Ultimately, the male is procreating and firmly believes in keeping the human race alive.

'Drive home, Jess. We've confirmed there's no problem with the tyre.' Kirstin tries to shift the six studs away.

'It's my birthday today,' announces Hans, eyeing Jess. 'We're having a party at my place. Want to join us?'

'I'd love to. I feel like fucking all night.'

'So do I,' agrees Hans.

'Oh no,' I interrupt, advancing forwards. 'We've an early start tomorrow.'

Kirstin and Anna nod in agreement.

'No. I'm fucking a couple of these lads first.'

'We're causing a massive traffic jam,' I protest, overwhelmed by the situation. 'We'll be arrested.'

Jess stamps a foot in frustration. 'I want to enjoy myself.'

If she attempts to move away with the lads, I'm ready to put her in a head-lock again. This is definitely our last trip abroad together.

'Enough, Jess,' demands Anna, boiling with anger. 'You've caused *far* too much trouble tonight.'

'Don't worry,' Jess taunts her, 'I can fuck you and Kirstin before leaving tomorrow.'

Kirstin is outraged.

All is forgotten when a police car pulls alongside.

Anna moans. 'We don't need this.'

The lads rush back to their vehicles.

Two male officers – six feet tall and with short blonde hair – observe Jess's enticing figure and smirk. This is the highlight of their evening, no doubt. My face blushes bright red with embarrassment. I hope they don't ask if Jess is the van driver, then drug test and breathalyse her.

Briskly, Anna fetches her own dress from the car, throws it at Jess and tells her to put it on. Meanwhile, two more police cars arrive.

Officers emerge and aggressively order the stopped cars to drive away. Three officers march over to us. Kirstin explains it was thought the van had a flat tyre but everything is okay. We're told in no uncertain manner to leave.

## Chapter 22

At Kirstin's house, two vans hurtle towards us in the middle of the road. Headlights dazzle on full beam and the horns blare. Kirstin and Anna swerve to avoid them and crash into a wall.

'Watch out,' I yell to Jess.

The vans hurry past, one of them clattering the driver's side and pushing in our wing mirror. With a clever manoeuvre, Jess avoids a serious collision and performs an emergency stop. The men in the cabs were wearing balaclavas and black combat gear. Unfortunately, I was unable to note the number plates or the makes of vehicles.

We leap out to see if Kirstin and Anna are okay. Escaping serious injury, both are dazed. They refuse my suggestion of seeking urgent medical assistance. The sports car is wrecked.

'What's been happening in my house?' Kirstin is hysterical. She rushes forwards with Anna. Jess and I follow.

The scene we find is pitiful. Kirstin's gallery has been savagely looted using a mechanical digger, now abandoned. One end is completely demolished. Horrifically, the two security guards and dogs are dead. No alarms are sounding and the CCTV cameras have been ripped off the walls.

Kirstin's George Grosz and John Heartfield pictures have gone, along with those for Brenda. Anna promptly calls the emergency services. A small consolation is the George Grosz we brought for Kirstin has been left behind in Anna's workshop.

Kirstin throws herself down in the middle of the empty gallery. Wailing, she violently fists the floor.

'A monster has snatched my children. They've gone forever.'

'I've lost a child myself and know how you must feel.' Kneeling down, I try to offer comfort.

Amongst German art collectors, Kirstin is royalty. This is a major incident. A terrible disaster.

Swarms of police cars arrive, disgorging officers. They're joined by paramedics and two ambulances.

Jess is quiet, nervous and reluctant to acknowledge anyone. Anna coaxes Kirstin to rise from the floor and they hug. Moving to another room, both sit down. A group of officers and the paramedic follow. One police woman makes Kirstin, Anna and myself a drink. Jess requests a cold beer. Kirstin shuns the suggestion of transferring her to the hospital.

'I must wait for my children to come home,' she mumbles vaguely.

Anna explains to the female officer in charge there are high-resolution images of both sets of stolen pictures. These are on a computer in her workshop.

'I can put them on a memory stick,' she says.

The officer utters words of gratitude.

Whilst Anna is absent, I sit with Kirstin.

She pulls me near. 'Al, do you think somebody will bring my children back?'

'Yes, I'm sure.'

Jess stands aside from everyone in the room. For her, a serious encounter with the police is deeply disturbing. Continually glancing at her mobile, she receives no calls, yet texts are heard coming through.

Kirstin's face is full of tears. We're concerned for her welfare after suffering a loss of such magnitude.

One detective, in his early 30s, fixes an intense stare on Jess. Stupidly, she starts to flirt with him, usually withering men with her looks. Not on this occasion.

A forensic team goes to work and a police photographer takes pictures of the crime scene. When two insurance men arrive to make an assessment, they only talk to Anna.

Jess and me are separated for police questioning. Before speaking, I'm informed a recording is to be made of the interview. Immediately, the value and importance of Kirstin's collection is emphasised. Pressed if Greasby has ever been involved with a Russian art dealer named Yaroslav, I say buying pictures is not up to me. That's down to Frankie and Nicola Greasby. The recent Schmidt burglary and the other violent art robberies across Europe are mentioned.

Fear envelops me. I must avoid being roped into something. Remaining aloof is paramount. It's evident the police have an idea about those responsible for the robberies, though not saying as much.

They want to know if Greasby has bought any pictures from Europe over the last few weeks. I explain my job mainly involves dealing with Brenda's account and staff matters. Grilled if I've been to Europe recently, my answer is no. I wonder how Jess will reply if the same question is put to her?

Reporting our vehicle was slightly damaged when one of the vans careered past us, I'm told a forensics team will make an assessment.

After an hour or so, the police allow me to go upstairs. I shower and slip into bed.

It's unbelievable that art causes so much mayhem. Murder, robbery, deception. How might George Grosz have reacted to his pictures being stolen in such a violent attack? He wouldn't have been shocked. That's for sure. Depraved human behaviour is the same now as it was in his day. My thoughts are broken by a knock at the door.

'Al, are you awake?'

'What do you want?'

Opening the door wider, with mobile in hand, Jess creeps in.

'Can I cuddle up with you, Al? I'm frightened.'

'Go back to your own room.'

Stripping off Anna's dress, she stands naked.

'I need to be loved.'

'Get out. Conniving bitch. How can you contemplate sex after what's happened?'

'I thought we could comfort each other.' Jess is tearful.

'If you think I'm following ten hunks, you're sadly mistaken.'

Our eyes meet, though I avert my gaze first.

'It was 13 actually.'

Her flippancy is exasperating. 'You knew about this robbery, didn't you?'

I jump out of bed.

'That's ridiculous.' Advancing further into the room, she stands with the door ajar.

'You delayed us arriving back here. A robbery was taking place and you knew.'

'You're mad. Full of paranoia.' She glares at me, desperately trying to convince.

'Have you no thought for the two people who've been murdered. Or even the dogs you photographed earlier. The poor families left behind will grieve forever. What are you getting out of this, Jess? Tell me. Cash? Sex with Y? Coke from Frankie? A quick scissoring with Nicola? I'm sick of the sight of you.'

I'm afraid our voices will be heard throughout the house.

'Bollocks. Kirstin nicked most of those Grosz pictures or paid fuck-all money for them. She's not lily white. Just a con artist and she's conned you. Pathetic drama queen. "Lost her children." What a piss-take.'

'Why were you here in Germany with Frankie?'

'Having kinky sex and doing loads of drugs. You ought to try it.'

When I attempt to drag her out of my room, she resists.

I snatch the mobile. 'Who were you texting before we went into the Sexhaus?'

'Fuck off, nosy bastard.'

She screams at me to hand back the mobile. I manage to read a text received from Y. 'Everything is okay, Jess.'

I thrust the mobile in front of her.

'What does this dickhead's text mean?'

She lunges forwards. 'I'm not answering any questions. Give me the mobile.'

'Did the police ask you about Y?'

'No.'

'Or, about being here recently?'

'Fuck off. Who do you think you are?'

Wrestling, we fall to the floor.

'Al, I want my phone.'

I press call to contact Y.

Someone hurries up the stairs. It's Anna, and she rushes into the room.

Y answers: 'What's wrong Jess? Jess? Are you there?' Not hearing a response, he hangs up.

Anna glares at us. 'This is outrageous. I'm shocked you're behaving like this in Kirstin's house. Have you no respect?'

Ashamed, I'm lost for words.

'She's suffering enough. What's going on? I hope no more sex games. If you can't behave, please leave.'

'Sorry, Anna.' I spring to my feet.

'Jess, I've finally persuaded Kirstin to rest. The police will talk to her again in the morning. She'd like a chat with you. Could you go to her room?'

'I'm really tired. I must sleep. We've a long drive later today.'

Anna is deeply hurt and storms out.

# Chapter 23

I'm alone with my dreams until woken by Anna's screams.

'No! Kirstin. Why? Wake up. Wake up.'

I leap out of bed and venture on to a landing. Kirstin's bedroom door is wide open. Anna is on her mobile, calling an ambulance.

Kirstin lies naked across the bed unconscious. Her face ashen.

'Kirstin's taken an overdose,' Anna announces, showing me an empty bottle. 'Help is on its way.'

I'm frantic with worry. 'Will she be okay?'

'Her heartbeat is slow.' Tears fill Anna's eyes. We move Kirstin on to her side. Then, Anna struggles desperately to make her regain consciousness.

'How far away is the hospital?'

'A couple of miles. Make sure the front door is open.'

I might have guessed Kirstin would attempt suicide after losing her collection. Her children.

Within minutes, an ambulance screeches to a halt outside. Anna shows the crew a label on an empty bottle. The medics go to work.

I wait for a while, then ask some questions. No one offers any information.

'I'm going with her in the ambulance,' Anna announces. 'I'll be in touch on the house phone.'

Despite the commotion, Jess hasn't stirred. I bang on her door.

'Who is it?' she eventually responds.

'Al.'

'What do you want?'

Jess is bleary-eyed and I relate what's happened. Retreating back inside, she flops on to the bed.

'Have you nothing to say?' I yell.

'I wouldn't have tried to save Kirstin,' Jess comments coldly. 'She won't cope without those fucking pictures.'

'You cynical bitch.'

'They were nicked anyway. Y got them for her.'

Trudging downstairs into the lounge, I lie on the sofa and wait patiently for the house phone to ring. I'm disorientated. Why does this have to happen to a nice person like Kirstin? I don't believe what Jess has insinuated. Why can't something nasty happen to Nicola or Y?

Although an atheist, my hands join together and a prayer is said for Kirstin. I hope she pulls through for Anna's sake.

My urge to create is strong. Once on the ferry, I plan to have a quick meal, and develop skeleton ideas. Jess can be left to her own devices. I want to distance myself as far as possible. What a waste of space. I must make a big effort to stage an exhibition. This offers hope. To keep sane. Before dying, an impressive body of work shall be left behind.

My eyes scan the room, admiring the antiques. Then, sleep overwhelms, until an anxiety dream torments. I've experienced this often when feeling restless. My son stands in front me, holding his arms out and crying for help. Always, I wake up startled.

Waiting for news of Kirstin's condition is painful. I don't have a mobile number for Anna. Should I search for it? No. I won't poke and pry in someone else's house.

I expect Brenda to discover details about the robbery. Maybe she or even Deb might call for an update. I can't imagine Brenda's reaction.

Frankie rings my mobile.

'Al. Jess has told me what's happened. Truly, an awful situation.' His voice is warm and friendly.

'This is a nightmare trip, Frankie.'

'I'm sure.'

'Did Y and his murdering gang organise this robbery at

Kirstin's house?' I blurt out.

'I've no idea, Al.'

'I'm not picking up Y's pictures. A few hours ago, the police questioned me. They definitely know about him and the robberies. It's only a matter of time before he's arrested. I don't want to be involved.'

'Al, we should talk calmly.'

'No way. Is the dodgy car still parked outside the Askworth Gallery?'

'Yes, I believe so,' Frankie answers impatiently. 'Al, profits from this new collection will boost our finances enormously.'

'Sorry. Can't help.' Standing up, I pace the room.

'Here's a deal. If the pictures are collected, I'll give you a mouth-watering bonus. You can also have two days a week off to produce pictures.'

'No, Frankie.'

'One favour deserves another, Al. I gave you a job. Through Greasby, you met Brenda. Your artistic spirit was reawakened by me.'

'What you've done is appreciated but I'm not working with Y. Has Nicola sold Jane's Dali picture?'

'It's just a replica, worth dog shit.'

'Won't she sell it as an original?'

'Not sure.'

'I'd like to believe you, only you tell lies.'

'Al, I'm desperately unhappy in my body,' he blubbers. 'I need a sex change. Help me.'

'Can't hear you, Frankie. It's a bad line.' I hang up, sick of listening to him. A few minutes later, the mobile sounds again. It's Nicola.

'You okay though, Al? You okay?'

'What do you want?'

'Pick up those pictures. Or, Jess will do it herself and leave you behind.'

'Don't think so. I have the van keys.'

'Get the fucking pictures,' she shouts.

'Kirstin has tried to kill herself. Aren't you concerned?'

'Couldn't give a shit about a fucking dyke.'

'Brenda will be after you for nicking her pictures. She'll brand you: THIEF AND MURDERER.'

Nicola ends the call. I'm furious, drop down on to the sofa and close my eyes. My head is filled with disjointed thoughts. I must connect Brenda with Stefan. That's if she doesn't already know him. Might she fly over here or send Deb? Perhaps establish her own German team and make a thorough investigation? This is messy. I must be useful to Brenda. The robberies will make a serious dent in her plans for the Lesbian Art Museum.

Ten minutes later, Paulene calls.

'Al, sorry to disturb you. What an ordeal you've suffered.'

'Frankie has just spoken to me .'

'I know.'

'Has he asked you to call?'

'Yes.'

'I thought so.'

'I'm begging you to pick up Y's pictures. Greasby is desperate for cash.'

'Might that finance his sex change and you to splash out on more studs?' I'm losing my cool.

'Yes, all of that. But there's another consideration.'

'What is it?'

'Please do it for Annabel.'

'Annabel?'

'Yes. There's a brilliant future for her as an actress. She needs to attend an exclusive drama school. Be away from Nicola and her dickhead dad, constantly fighting. If Greasby collapses that won't be possible. I'm sure you, of all people, would want the best for a child. Acting can be the making of Annabel. It's brought a focus to her life. So far, she's had an awful upbringing.'

This is a jumbled argument. Reluctantly, I agree to do as requested. Life is a continual struggle to reach a plateau of contentment. Each day, I try and climb to that position. It's difficult to remain resolute, make erudite decisions and do what I want.

'Thanks, Al. I knew you would help. That's made me very happy. You're a true friend. I'll be forever in your debt. Feel free, to take pictures of me and the studs for your skeleton pictures when you want.'

'Thanks, Paulene.'

'Bob in for a chat anytime.'

'Okay.'

Jess struts into the room naked. Without question, she's proud of her physique. Never depressed and always optimistic. A bowl of cereal is being wolfed down.

'I've made coffee if you want some, Al.'

'No, thanks.'

'I had a nosy round Kirstin's bedroom. There are lots of books on erotic asphyxiation. I've taken one. We can read it together tonight on the ferry.' A friendly leer is tossed my way. 'No wonder she gave us a lecture. Must be an expert and there's a pile of sex toys.'

'Put the book back...why aren't you dressed?'

She throws herself into an armchair and provocatively raises a leg over one side.

Both of my comments are ignored.

'I've phoned Anna. Kirstin is okay. Out of danger.'

'You contacted her?' I'm annoyed not to hear the news first.

'There's nothing to worry about. Kirstin should make a full recovery.'

'What a relief. I'm pleased she's okay.'

'Anna told me some great news.'

'What is it?'

'They're getting married. I'll be best woman at the wedding. You're invited as well. I'm going away with them on an exotic honeymoon. All expenses paid. They're a fantastic couple. Don't you agree?'

Shocked, there are questions to pose, only my words won't form. In any case, a pack of lies would be heard.

'You had Anna's mobile number?'

'Nicola texted it. They've been in contact before.'

Jess adds that Anna is due back later. Another meeting with the insurers is arranged. A builder is coming to assess the damage and carry out emergency repairs. Anna says news about the robbery is splashed over the German media. Rewards are being offered for information. A special team of detectives has been established. They'll investigate the murders and robberies. A spokesperson for the Schmidt family has already commented on a news programme. Anna has agreed to be interviewed in a while.

'Shall we set off soon? Y has given instructions about where to meet.'

I grit my teeth. 'Will he be at the meeting?'

She considers her answer carefully. 'Maybe.'

Twirling away, she has a quick preen in a mirror. 'I'll have ten minutes with one of Kirstin's vibrators, shower, dress, have a few lines, then I'm ready. Really looking forwards to meeting Y's men. I'll have to fuck a few of them. You can make sketches. They're animals. All blokes say I'm their best fuck. That's a real turn-on. You don't know what you're missing, Al. Another day and more fucks. Brilliant. I can't wait.'

'Is your suitcase full of condoms, Jess?'

'Yes. They're ribbed, flavoured and ready.'

# Chapter 24

Jess and I climb into our van. It won't start. The battery is flat as the headlights were left on last night. Whilst this is a frustrating beginning to the day, I must not overreact.

Jess contacts Anna and learns there's a charger in the garage. This will delay us a while.

Y rings. 'Have you set off, Al?'

'No.'

'Why?'

'Trouble with the van.'

'I'm sure Jess can sort it.'

The call is ended. I can't speak to him any longer.

Jess reappears from the garage. 'The charger is missing.'

She contacts Anna again. We're told to try and jump-start the van from her car.

'Do you know what you're doing, Jess?'

'Yes, my dad is a mechanic. I'm mad about cars. I was driving at 12.'

Jess ventures into the house but is frustrated. 'I can't find the keys. They're not where Anna said.'

Contact is made with Anna yet again. She calls a breakdown company and they should be here within a couple of hours.

Y phones. 'Al, have you set off yet?'

'No, there's still a problem.'

'But, you will pick up the pictures, won't you?'

'Who knows?'

After three hours, and irate calls from Y, our journey begins. According to Jess, we're heading for an industrial estate. One hour later, we approach the area and it contains ramshackle buildings. Weeds grow out of control.

'This is it,' announces Jess.

We stop and wait. She fizzes, anticipating mad sex. Warehouse double doors open. A dozen men in their early 30s walk outside. All are dressed in black. At least six feet tall and broad shouldered, they stare straight at us.

Inside the building, I notice a van and several cars. Neatly crated pictures are stacked near the entrance. These must be the ones we're transporting back to England. I wasn't expecting such professional packaging. The van looks similar to one of those leaving Kirstin's house last night.

Jess springs from our vehicle and I step out too.

The men are armed. Why did I volunteer to do this? For Annabel's future, I remind myself.

Jess throws off her dress and proudly stands naked except for heavy boots.

Raising her arms, she shouts: 'Okay then, lads, who wants to be first?'

I scan the faces looking for Y. He's not here.

A rat-faced man steps forwards, flanked by one with a Rottweiler appearance. Rat slaps Jess hard. She drops to the ground and Rott kicks her.

'Hand over the cash, fucking slag,' stabs Rat.

Jess is paralysed with fright. 'What's the problem? Don't you want great sex?'

Nobody answers.

Three other men with guns stand in front of me. Rott pulls Jess up by the hair.

'Don't fuck with us.'

'The cash is in the back of our van,' Jess tells the pair.

Rat boots her.

'Why am I being treated like this? I know Y. Really well. Where is he? I'll do anything you want.'

Everyone is quiet.

Our suitcases are thrown out, then two boxes unloaded. I thought these contained packing material but now believe the cash is hidden in them. A group of men carry the boxes into the warehouse. A few more begin loading the pictures into our vehicle. We're not allowed to move. Before long, the van is full and our suitcases put on board.

'What's wrong? Are you all fucking gay,' Jess shouts angrily at the men.

Rat and Rott motion for her to kneel down. She's relieved and ready to give both men blow jobs. Three others point guns at her head.

Rat and Rott, still remaining expressionless, unzip their trousers. Pissing into her face from close range, it's like they've opened valves on two water jets.

'You dirty fucking bastards.' Tears gush from her. 'This isn't my scene.' She tries to duck out of the way but the guns restrict movement.

Disgusted, I remain silent. What a nasty set of bastards.

'Y never treats me like this,' she bawls. 'I want to please you.'

Sneering, the two men move away. She attempts to stand up until shots are fired at either side of her. 'Please stop. Don't kill me.'

Rat and Rott tell us to fuck off. The other men laugh and jeer.

A towel is grabbed from my case and handed to Jess. Burying her face into the soft material, she cries hysterically. I put an arm round her. Slowly she calms down and slips back into the dress.

'Do you want me to drive?' I offer.

'No, I'll be okay.'

Her disorientated look is worrying.

Back on a main road, we begin the long drive to the ferry.

'I shall be glad to get back home. Will you, Jess?'

There's only a vague reaction.

'How much cash did we hand over?'

'You don't want to know.' She attempts to pin a smile back on to her face, only it continually falls away.

I hope there are no drugs concealed in the crates but don't press for information.

Over the next few miles our conversation is sparse. Whatever I say, she answers quietly, yes or no.

Jess insists on having a shower and changing her dress. We pull into a service area. She has lines of coke. Despite my protests, it's argued a pick-me-up is needed. People walk nearby. She's oblivious to them.

I drop into a café and order a coffee.

As we walk back to the van, two youths approach Jess and fondle her boobs.

'Fuck off. What do you think you're doing?' She whacks one of them and kicks the other. They hurry away.

'I'll never give myself so easily again.'

My eyebrows raise. How long will that last?

'Do you want me to drive?' I ask.

There's no reaction.

Half-an-hour later, I'm surprised to see her wiping tears away.

'Do you want to stop again? To have a drink or meal?'

'No.'

I'm at a loss what to do. 'The nightmare is over, Jess. Put it behind you.'

It's a struggle for her to respond.

'The drama is over. It's over,' I repeat.

'It isn't.'

'We'll soon be on the ferry. You can get pissed and snort whatever you want.' Sadness is an aspect of her I've never seen or dealt with before. 'Jess, everything is okay.'

'No, it isn't.'

'What's wrong? Tell me.'

'A van is following.'

I strain to catch a glimpse in the wing mirror.

'It's been with us for the last ten miles. The same van we saw in the warehouse. Three men are inside.'

'Keep driving. Put your foot down.'

'We're coming to that tricky winding road with deep drops on either side.'

'This section was the most frightening.'

'They're trying to overtake.'

I have a plan. 'Wait till we're near the sharp bend up ahead and let them overtake.'

'What?'

'Allow them to overtake.'

'I don't want to die,' she mumbles.

'Neither do I. Slow down when I say.'

The bend approaches rapidly.

'The van is tight up against us.'

'Let them pass.'

Jess slows down. The vehicle overtakes, the occupants stare straight ahead.

'Slow down now. Slow down.'

Their van stops and is positioned across the road. We can't pass.

'They want to take back the pictures and shoot us. Put your foot down now. Run them over the edge.'

'I don't want to kill anyone.' She's trembling.

'It's them or us.'

'I can't do it.'

'Push them over. Make sure we don't go with them.'

Her foot hovers on the accelerator.

'I'll fuck you tonight.'

Jess stares at me in shock.

'I'm a proper stud. I can go all night. Wore my wife out. She was sore most mornings. You'll have super sex and win your bet. Two grand in your hand.'

'It's a deal.'

## Chapter 25

Shortly after Jess and I leave the ship and clear customs, someone rings. It's Y. Although angry, I answer pleasantly: 'Hello, Y. Are you okay?'

'Hi,' he responds warmly. 'Yes, I'm well. Good trip back?'

'Fine. Jess and me had a pleasant meal, then slept soundly.'

'I'm pleased. Maybe we can see each other soon? Work together.'

'Good idea,' I bullshit.

'Call whenever you can.'

'I will.'

'Keep in touch.'

'Okay, have a great day, Y.'

'You too, Al. Give my love to Jess.'

'Gladly.'

Pulling up outside the Askworth Gallery, Jess and I observe two 4x4 vehicles speed down the road. They park awkwardly on the opposite side. Several women surge from them to violently beat a young man. Two more women emerge and join in.

'You fucking arsehole,' shouts one woman, still in bright-pink pyjamas. 'Keep away from our kids.'

I'm stunned and face Jess.

'A perv or a flasher,' she predicts. 'They hang out at the school on the next street. It's a magnet for them. Mothers can't be bothered to phone the police. So, dish out their own punishment. Pervy lesbos hang round too. I've watched them get hammered as well.'

A few schoolkids walk past, busily texting and not even noticing the unfolding drama. The suspicious estate car is still parked nearby. Fury ignites in Jess.

'I'll break into this fucking scrap heap. Let's have a good look inside. I'll bring a screwdriver from the gallery.'

She slips out of the van.

'Stop. Don't cause trouble,' I protest, stepping into the street. I'm ignored.

Smackheads Carl and Di show up, carrying a couple of bulky bin liners. If auditioning for a horror movie, both would be rejected as too scary. Still pregnant, Di seems like she might give birth at any minute. She reminds me of a Blue Meanie from the Beatles' *Yellow Submarine* film. I want to laugh but hold back. Prominent is a black eye.

'What happened to you?' I point to her bruised face.

'A punter beat me up last night. Then robbed my cash. I earned fuck all. Carl usually watches my back. He didn't yesterday. If we see the bloke again, Carl will stab the fucking prick.'

'Too fucking right,' her boyfriend brags.

'We're rattling. Need cash asap,' Di groans.

'We've nicked dresses, tiaras and wigs for Frankie,' Carl announces.

'Is he in the gallery?' asks Di.

'Jess might know. She'll be back in a minute.'

'The dresses are beautiful,' Carl begins. 'We've had to guess his size. Hope they fit.'

'Brilliant,' I comment.

From another bag, Di finds a blonde wig and puts it on. 'Do you think it suits me.'

'Yes,' I fib. In fact, it makes her even scarier.

'There's a couple more wigs, a black and a ginger one,' she enthuses.

It's a struggle not to air an honest opinion.

'Are you after anything?'

'Not today.'

Jogging towards us, Jess tells the druggies: 'Frankie's not here. Never is this early.'

Both kick the car in frustration.

'We need a dig. Can you phone him?' Di grabs Jess's arm.

Frankie doesn't answer.

'For fuck's sake,' Di looks desperately at her partner.

'Any idea when he'll be here or where he is?' Carl probes.

'Haven't a clue,' Jess replies.

'Want a fuck or a blow job, mate?' Di asks desperately. 'I'll do anything. You can piss or shit on me if you like.'

'No thanks.'

Jess tries the estate car's doors. They're locked. She goes to work with the screwdriver but is frustrated.

I'm anxious and hold my breath, watching for anybody observing what's happening.

Carl and Di show interest in the problem.

'I can break in there,' Carl offers.

Jess moves aside.

'Whose car is it?' Di queries.

'No idea.' I grudgingly join the conversation. 'It's been here for days.'

'We'll have it away,' crows Di. 'It might get us a few hundred quid.'

Carl pulls a crowbar from a bag. He probably carries one as regularly as other people have a pen.

As the driver's-side window is smashed, people walking past are alerted. A man pulls out his mobile and records events.

Before there's a chance to glimpse inside, Carl sparks the car into life. He gestures for Di to join him. Smiling, like Lottery winners in a Rolls-Royce, they pull away. Di even blows me a kiss.

# Chapter 26

Jess and I walk into the gallery as Nicola parks her Ferrari. It's a little after 10 am. We're opening for business. Wearing a light-grey trouser suit, Nicola breezes in full of arrogance and self importance. Carrying a large bag, mobile and laptop, she has a split lip and scuffs on her face. Trying unsuccessfully to disguise the marks with make-up, she resembles a heavily powdered 18th century female.

'Everything okay with the collection, Jess?' she asks.

'Yes.'

'Brilliant.'

'How's Annabel?'

'She won the audition for the television series.'

Nicola is shocked to see me and glares at Jess.

'How has *he* got back here?'

Jess twitches her shoulders.

'What happened?' She's eager for an answer, glancing in my direction, then at Jess.

I hold back from reacting.

Nicola throws her mobile, making me duck. The laptop is next to be flung.

Forcefully, I pin her by the throat against a wall. Dick and Paul walk through the door ready to start another day. They spring into action. Dick holds on to me while Paul stands in front of Nicola. Other Greasby staff arrive and hurry past not wanting to be involved. They make their way to the upstairs offices.

'Don't lose your freedom throttling this cow,' Dick says coolly.

'The bitch isn't worth it,' Paul adds. 'Go home for the day,

Al. You must be knackered.'

'You're sacked, Council Prick,' Nicola gasps, desperately trying to recover her composure.

I don't reply.

'Haven't you two any work to do?' She stares at Dick and Paul.

'Plenty. Have you cash to pay us?' they respond.

'Nobody's getting fuck all.'

Scanning the gallery, I notice Jane's Dali drawing is still present and holding a prime position. Outside, a battered car comes to a rest. Paulene emerges with two casually dressed blokes. I recognise them as the studs, Tyrone and Ross. I hear they're working as Paulene's assistants in the Renta Stud business. They troop into the gallery. Paulene wears an unflattering short skirt, jacket and a blouse that plunges far too low. After spending long hours on a sunbed, she and the two studs are over-cooked.

'This looks interesting,' observes Dick.

'More fireworks and it's not even bonfire night,' adds Paul. Both move to a low-level seat, making themselves comfortable. I sit down at a desk.

Tyrone winks at Jess though is ignored. Nicola gestures for Jess to leave and she obeys, racing away in the van.

Paulene gives me a half smile and I respond in the same way.

'Not missing Frankie's cock then, Paulene?' Dick teases.

'Never have done, love.' The response is curt.

'Hello mum,' Nicola ventures sheepishly.

'The fucking Porsche has been repossessed,' Paulene blasts. 'My credit card is blocked. I've no money. Frankie's not answering his mobile. What the fuck is going on? I've been ringing you for days.'

'We're short of cash, mum.'

'Don't fucking lie.'

Walking through the door, financial controller Avril overhears the conversation. 'There's a cash flow problem, Mrs Greasby.'

'Fuck off, snotty cunt. Give me your credit card, Nicola. And your car keys.'

'We're struggling, mum.'

'Fuck off. You and Frankie are fucking useless. Why has he re-mortgaged our house?'

Nicola is lost for words.

'The financial crisis is only temporary,' states Avril. 'We've invested in collections.'

'Where are they from?' snaps Paulene.

'From Y,' states Paul.

'Not the fucking Russian.'

'Yes, from Russia with love,' jokes Dick.

'Soon we'll be okay,' submits Avril. 'Please be patient, Mrs Greasby.'

'Fuck off.'

Both studs stand with folded arms in front of Avril.

Several people enter the gallery. I rise and tell them we're not open, then lock the door.

Paulene moves closer to Nicola. 'When you were a kid, I gave you everything.'

Nicola isn't intimidated. 'Fuck off. My childhood was lousy. Fucking lousy. I didn't graduate. You and dad made me leave. Remember? I wanted to party, get fucked, pissed and drugged-up. Like other students. No, I had to read art books and help run this poxy business.'

'You fucking ungrateful bitch.' Paulene slaps her hard.

Dick and Paul rock with laughter.

'Where's the Greasby cash going?' demands Paulene.

'On Nigel's church.' Dick is happy to stir trouble.

Paulene is furious.

'The exterior is complete,' Paul elaborates. 'I passed by the other day. Must have cost a few million. Contractors are fitting out the interior.'

'Is this true, Nicola?'

She daren't reply.

'I ought to erect a cross outside,' Paulene begins, 'and crucify that dog-collared wanker, Nigel.'

'Have a real biblical scene,' Paul proposes. 'Erect crosses either side of Nigel, and crucify Y and Frankie.'

'What a good idea,' Paulene chuckles.

'Frankie is transferring cash from his offshore account,' Avril re-joins the conversation. 'To help our cash flow.'

The information inflames Paulene. 'Hand over your fucking credit card and car keys, Nicola.'

'No, mum.' Trying to move away, she's seized and both women fall to the floor.

'There's only one winner here,' quips Dick.

'I agree,' adds Paul.

Both of them chant in their best football hooligan voices: 'Paulene. There's only one Paulene. One Paulene. There's only one Paulene.'

It's sad to see two extremely talented men taking pleasure in this pathetic scuffle. They should be upstairs, breathing life back into celebrated artists' oil paintings and watercolours.

'You fight well, Paulene. Ever thought of boxing or wrestling professionally?' Dick jests.

'Twenty quid says Paulene wins,' Paul predicts.

'No contest,' chuckles Dick. 'Pity somebody can't dump a ton of mud in here. There's something erotic about female mud wrestlers.'

Would a mud fight in a cemetery between two female skeletons be a good subject? Yes.

Although Nicola puts up a reasonable defence, Tyrone and Ross intervene. Ross firmly holds her in a head-lock on the gallery floor.

Avril wants to help but daren't intervene. I ask if my expenses can be reimbursed. 'Sorry. No. Call Frankie if you're desperate.'

Paulene punches Nicola. Blood soon drips from her nose on to the trouser suit and gallery floor. The fight is over. Paulene is victorious.

'Why don't you step in and run the company, Paulene?' Dick says enthusiastically. 'We'd love to have you on board.'

The question falls on deaf ears.

'Meetings constantly ending in a punch-up would be lots of fun,' Paul states.

Smiling, Tyrone hands over Nicola's bag to Paulene. Taking out the Ferrari keys, she's pleased to find a credit card and a large bundle of notes.

'How much is here?' Paulene confronts Avril.

'Five grand.'

'Give us some, Paulene.' Dick and Paul stand up, only they're ignored.

'Don't take the cash, mum. It's for Annabel's drama lessons.'

'Fuck off.' Paulene hands the bag to Ross.

'My nose is broken,' Nicola holds a hand up to her face and tries to stop the flow of blood.

'I'll bring you some tissue,' says Avril, who then yells: 'Stand up, Al. Nicola has to sit down.'

Eventually, Avril hands a toilet roll to Nicola.

This is outrageous. Family members ought to pull together and support each other. That should've happened with my wife and I after Alex was killed.

'With a bust nose, Nicola, you might not look so snotty,' laugh Dick and Paul.

'Shut up,' barks Avril. 'Don't be horrible.'

'Women always earn pity no matter how obnoxious they are,' Paul claims.

'Is there money on this fucking card, Nicola?' Paulene roars.

'Yes, a hundred grand,' answers Avril. 'We need it all to pay the bills.'

Paulene stoops down to Nicola. 'If I don't have more cash soon, the Ferrari will go. Ross and Tyrone have already lined up a buyer.'

'No, it's financed.' Avril is shocked. 'That's illegal.'

Paulene slaps her. 'Get real, bitch. This company was built on dodgy deals. If you don't know that by now, fuck off.'

'Stop it mum, please,' begs Nicola with tissue stuck up her nose.

'Fuck off, I'll do what I like.' Paulene underlines her words by thumping Nicola again.

Dick and Paul look on with joy. I'm disgusted.

'All we want now is for Brenda to burst in,' jabs Paul.

'Yes please,' says Dick cheerfully. 'Treat us to more fireworks, Brenda.'

'Greasby cash is not building a fucking church,' Paulene shouts at her daughter.

'Or for Frankie to have his dick chopped off,' Dick howls. 'Hey, Paulene, is it you castrating tranny men?' he's keen to add.

'No. Frankie would have been my first victim.'

'What are you talking about?' I ask.

Dick informs: 'Tranny men have been murdered. Their wedding tackle stuffed in their gob.'

'Hope they seize Frankie,' swipes Paulene, preparing to leave with the studs.

'Murders?' I query.

Nobody replies.

'Any of you lot know where Frankie's pictures are?' Paulene's eyes flit between us. 'He sneaked back into the house and took them away.'

'I've no transport,' Nicola cries.

'Get on a bus.' Dick flicks a two-pound coin at her.

Paulene coils her arms round the studs. 'We're off, lads. Slip your dicks out. Stick it in any hole. I want to be fucked all day. Then, we'll think about work.'

No sooner has the trio left, a middle-aged, suited man enters. His face displays a blank expression. A woman in her 20s tags along. She doesn't have a hint of a smile.

'I think there's more entertainment coming our way,' Dick shuffles with excitement as he and Paul look on from the low-level seat.

'Where is Mrs Greasby?' the man asks.

'She's there.' Dick points excitedly at Nicola still in the chair.

'I'm John Gold.' He speaks well and with authority. 'This is Sophie Simms. We're from Smith & Wallace, a debt-collecting agency. We've a court order awarded to your landlord, Colin

Ford, to collect an unpaid amount for service charges.'

I was surprised to discover this property isn't owned by Frankie, but leased. I've met the landlord, a pleasant, intelligent and reasonable man. He's Irish and gives talks on The Troubles. Frankie often aims nasty racist comments at him.

'We're not paying fucking service charges,' Nicola bawls. 'Rich cunt Ford can pay.'

'I'm afraid that's not an option.' Gold pulls out a mobile. Any confrontation is to be recorded.

Avril pipes up: 'Nicola, I've been telling you and Frankie for weeks this bill needs paying. You tore up the court order last week.'

'We've no money.' Nicola stands and confronts the debt collectors.

'How much is owed?' Dick cheekily asks Gold.

'Twenty grand.'

'Only the cost of a few pews for Nigel's church,' Paul jests.

'We want to be reasonable, Mrs Greasby,' Simms explains. 'We'll give you seven days to clear the debt. If it's not paid within that period, we'll take goods to recover the amount.'

'Fuck off out of here. You're getting fuck all.'

Simms moves over to the Rowlandson watercolours. 'I'm putting stickers on these and noting the value. If the debt isn't paid within seven days, we'll put them into auction.' With her mobile, she begins photographing the pictures.

Although blood is still dripping from her nose, Nicola tries to wrestle Simms away but is thwarted by Avril, Dick and Paul. Simms looks like she's never had a fight in her life. Not even a slap from her parents.

'These works aren't ours. They're on consignment,' I argue, but I'm not heeded.

Frankie's coke dealer, Abe, strolls cockily through the door. He tries to grab someone's attention. 'Is Frankie here?'

'No, he fucking isn't,' bellows Nicola. 'Fuck off out.'

'I've scored some brilliant gear.' He holds up sachets of white powder. 'Only his debt needs settling first.'

'Get in the queue,' Dick and Paul laugh.

Nicola marches over to Abe. 'Fuck off, scum.'

'Okay, clever cunt.' His face rams forwards. 'Pay up or I'll be back to break his legs and yours.'

With the front door unlocked, other people enter the gallery. A middle-aged woman tackles Nicola. 'I'm Mrs Redlands. You sold one of my pictures for thirty thousand. I've not been paid.'

Nicola looks at Avril who signals Mrs Redlands is telling the truth.

'There's no money. No money!' screeches Nicola.

'We'll pay very soon,' interrupts Avril. 'Please be patient.'

'No,' she volleys. 'I'm taking these Rowlandsons until I'm paid.'

What a calamity. Arnold Fitch's collection doesn't deserve to be at the centre of a chaotic feud.

Pulling a small screwdriver from her handbag, Mrs Redlands unfastens one of the works. A scuffle breaks out as Simms tries to stop her. 'We have first call on these pictures. You can't take them.'

A fearsome, hefty man enters and scrutinises the gallery. Remaining silent, he has a screwdriver and prises five Rowlandsons off the walls.

'We're experiencing a cash flow problem,' Avril appeals to him.

Still silent, he brushes her and Simms aside, then makes off with the pictures. I watch him dump them in a vehicle. Bursting back into gallery, he's intent on removing the Dali, until I stand up. 'This picture belongs to me. Go away.'

More people walk in, though I tell them the gallery is closed.

'Call the police,' Gold instructs Avril.

As if on cue, flashing blues reveal a police car is parking outside.

Nicola falls to the floor, completely beaten.

'I'll jump in front of a train if things don't improve.'

Avril attempts to console her.

Brenda's name appears on my mobile screen.

'Hi, how are you?'

'It's Deb. Would you drive over Al, as soon as you can?'

'Yes, of course.'

## Chapter 27

My car is parked at the rear of the gallery. As I slip inside, the mobile rings again. An unfamiliar number is on-screen.

'Hello, Al,' greets a female voice I slightly recognise.

'Who's speaking?'

'Mrs Adams. I live a few doors away.'

'Hello.'

'Hope you don't mind me phoning?'

'No.'

'Seven weeks ago, you sold one of my pictures. I saved your number.'

'How can I help?'

'Our neighbour, Elsie Naylor, says your burglar alarm went off briefly early this morning.'

'Can you be more precise?'

'Three thirty. Another neighbour said your security lights came on. Elsie's not seen your car for a couple of days. She wondered if something was wrong. This is why I'm phoning.'

'I've been abroad. I'm back now and will be home soon.'

'Trixie, who lives opposite, has CCTV. Ask her if anything was recorded.'

'Good idea. Thanks for calling.'

'Hope everything is okay.'

'Yes.'

My burglar alarm has activated before in the middle of the night. It was a few days after Alex was killed. Crazily, my wife became convinced it was a message indicating he was okay. I've never believed in the supernatural. But who knows?

Now, my plan is to speak with Brenda and update her on events. First, I must go home, check nothing is wrong and freshen up. The journey will take half-an-hour. Whilst on the way, Brenda's number flashes again, though I don't answer. She'll have to wait. I'm not risking being caught using my mobile whilst driving.

I ponder on the Greasby financial situation. How serious is it? Are we heading towards insolvency? What about Avril mentioning investment in collections? I know nothing of these and I'm area manager. Being made redundant, if that's a real possibility, isn't a concern, as I've no money worries. Weeks ago, Frankie mentioned the merits of bankruptcy to clear company debts. He said the assets could be bought back for a pittance in a pre-pack arrangement with the liquidator. Of course, Nicola liked the idea of abandoning debts in a dodgy move. I thought it was outrageous. Both she and Frankie never gave a second thought to our creditors or to the harm it could cause. Some might even go bust themselves.

I need to land a job with Brenda. Admittedly, she's weird but has a deep passion for art. That's applaudable. Neither Frankie or Nicola shows the same trait.

At a set of traffic lights, I watch a delivery driver knock on someone's front door. When there's no answer, the package is placed on the doorstep. Moving back, she uses a mobile to take pictures. Then, the item is picked up and the woman jumps into her van. Corrupt bitch. Will this massive online mail-order bubble ever burst? Greedy people shall make it happen.

I'm brought to a halt at a roundabout. A few women are making a protest. Three other cars are in front and nobody can manoeuvre past. I step out to investigate. From the placards held aloft, this is a climate demonstration.

A good idea for a picture might be skeletons protesting outside cemetery gates. About what? Not sure yet. Must give it more thought.

Nearby, men and women of various ages are wearing high visibility orange vests. They're carrying out community service hours, removing graffiti from the side of a building and picking up litter.

A call is heard.

'Hi, Brenda.'

'No, Al, it's Deb. Brenda wants to know how long you'll be?'

'I'm caught in a traffic jam. Tell her not to worry. I'll be there soon.'

Suddenly, the protesting women remove their clothes. Community service males hurl obscene remarks at them. Not phased, the women shout back. Two youths pick up knickers and bras, then prance about wearing them. The activists stand snooty and unaffected. One of them ought to have picked a better time of the month to protest. She stands brazenly, with a mouse's tail hanging down.

Traffic is building up. Two community service supervisors try to bring order to the situation without any luck. An old man on a mobility scooter stops, pulls out a small digital camera and takes close-ups of the nude women's lower regions.

'Fuck off, you pervy bastard,' two of them shout. They can't move, having glued themselves together. Others are stuck to the road.

They kick out at the old perv and the youths. Moving away, the man uses his grab-and-grip picker to steal a pair of knickers. Laughing, one of the community blokes drapes another pair over the perv's head. Unable to see, he crashes and falls off the scooter. Everyone is amused, regardless of whether any injuries have been suffered. A yobo uses the grab-and-grip picker to hurl a lump of dog shit at a protester. Members of the public who've gathered in numbers applaud.

The road is choked with traffic. Some vehicles behind me reverse in a side road and find an alternative route to their destinations. I do the same, only realise a massive detour through countryside is necessary to reach my house.

Progress is restricted on a number of occasions by slow-moving tractors. Perhaps there's a tractor convention somewhere. Approaching a small rural town, I'm surprised to see a bull in the middle of the road and heading towards me. It's escaped from an abattoir nearby. That's happened on a few occasions previously. Behind the animal, police vehicles are in pursuit. I swerve to the opposite side of the road and brake.

A wannabe matador attempts to throw a coat over the bull's head. The beast is unimpressed and tosses him into the air. A police van corners the animal. Springing from one of the vehicles, a firearms officer takes aim. A crowd watches, along with helpless, bemused abattoir staff. Nearby residents peer out of house windows enjoying the excitement. Disobeying police instructions to stand back, individuals shout in protest at the marksman. One of them even tackles him. How can people be so stupid? The wise bull isn't to be outwitted and heads off in another direction. Unfortunately, towards a school.

I breathe deeply and drive away to follow another alternative route home. Every day, I attempt to immerse myself in art. To have it interrupted so much is frustrating.

My street is a mixture of 1930s detached and semi-detached properties. I live in a detached house. The street's residents includes teachers, accountants, solicitors, journalists, a bank manager and an author. Everyone's front gardens are always well-kept. Residents take pride in tending to their shrubs and colourful roses.

The front door to my house is slightly ajar. Cautiously toeing it open, I avoid touching any surfaces. There's also a fear somebody may be inside. Checking each room downstairs, no one is present. To my horror, everywhere is trashed. A knife has slashed my three-piece suite. The dining-room table is tipped over and the surface scratched. Crockery, electrical goods and a laptop have been tossed about.

Racing upstairs, I discover the remaining stolen Swiss pictures being stored here have gone. Clothes in my bedroom are torn to shreds. In a spare-bedroom studio, recently finished paintings are on the floor and tubes of paint squirted on to them. Preliminary sketches are ripped up. Brushes and pencils have been snapped in half.

It doesn't matter. I can produce more paintings. I've lots of ideas. George Grosz must have felt the same way when his works were confiscated by the Nazis. Art must carry on.

In another bedroom, there's a shrine to my dead son. I drop to my knees and weep. The bed was covered with the racing car duvet he liked so much. His favourite toys were in here, as well as lots of framed photographs of him displayed on the walls. A small wardrobe and chest of drawers contained his clothes. I took them from the family home after the divorce. Newspaper cuttings reporting his tragic death and the subsequent trial were pasted in a scrapbook. Everything is destroyed. One moron has even urinated on the bed. Overwhelmed, I can't move for a while.

Life can be so cruel.

I don't really know Trixie whose security camera points towards my house. I've said 'hello' to her on the odd occasion. Although she's called Trixie, in the neighbourhood her nickname is 'Miss Bike' because of frequently entertaining men. I must discover if the burglary has been recorded.

She has a detached house. In the front garden, a collection of garden gnomes greets visitors. They've large protrusions showing in their trousers. I knock on the front door. Inside, I can hear David Rose's *The Stripper* playing loudly.

Trixie is a tall, shapely blonde in her late 20s. I have to concede she's beautiful. She stands in the doorway wearing only a skimpy black *négligée*. The reason for my call is explained and I'm invited inside. Numerous nude male sculptures are displayed in the hallway and front room. In fact, the house could be a shrine to the penis.

'The alarm went off at 3.30 am,' I begin.

'My cameras record images to a hard drive which is in my bedroom,' she responds warmly. 'I can flick back to that time. We can watch everything on the screen up there.'

'Thank you.'

'I'm a stripper,' she announces proudly as we ascend the stairs. 'I've had weirdos follow me home. They knock on the doors and windows in the middle of the night. Cameras are installed front and back.'

'Got plenty of work?'

'Yes. I'm very busy, performing in clubs and at private shows. Men are putty in my hands.'

I don't react.

'I'm a trained dancer and started stripping at university.'

'What did you study?'

'English. I continued stripping after graduating.' She converses easily. 'Friends went into teaching or became smart-arsed journos. Too boring. No excitement or money. I've paid off my student loan, bought my own house and regularly have holidays abroad.'

Although involved in a seedy worthless job, she has confidence and intelligence.

'How do you earn a living?' Moving close, very close, she looks deep into my eyes.

'I'm area manager for Greasby Fine Art.'

'My passion is art. I visit galleries often.'

There's trouble hearing her because of the loud stripper music. Thankfully, the volume is lowered.

Settling on the bed, I watch the screen intently as the footage starts. Men in black approach my house and break in. A few more head to the back. The alarm sounds for a few seconds and the security lights activate. Nobody is disturbed in any neighbouring properties. Minutes later, men bring out the Swiss pictures. Their features aren't distinguishable. The job is undertaken with military precision. Are they Y's men? It's a strange and disturbing experience, watching individuals burgling my house. A van, with the number plates disguised, stops. Men with guns stand alongside, making sure no one disturbs them as the pictures are loaded.

Thoughts pound my head. Would they have burgled my house if I'd been there? Could I have been attacked? Or even murdered? Is this revenge for pushing the van over the cliff? I'm convinced Nicola organised the burglary with Y's help. The entire operation was well-executed.

Trixie hasn't shared my involvement in the playback. She's

gone into another room.

'I'm phoning the police,' I call to her. 'They'll want to see this footage. Can I send them over?'

'Yes, of course. Before you came, I was ready to run through my act with Herbert.'

'Herbert?'

'Yes.' She has a five-foot-long snake on her neck. 'Herbert is a Burmese Python.'

Not being fond of snakes, I'm startled.

'Blokes often say I've a beautiful figure. What do you think, Al?' Her eyes sparkle as she anticipates a complimentary response.

I attempt to show interest. Trixie moves her head, arms and hips enticingly.

'I'd like to strip for you. I can go from mild to wild. You'll be breathless. I can perform the bachelor party special. Otherwise known as the heart attack special. Or, I can do in-your-face style. Up close and personal. Tipping generates a fortune.'

Curiosity makes me ask: 'How many men have fallen under your spell?'

'Two blokes tried to rape me but I beat them to a pulp. I'm a 3rd Dan black belt in taekwondo. Four men kidnapped me a year ago. I fucked them to death. Another night, I woke up and a small guy was sitting on the edge of my bed. He wanted to say my act was so arousing. I easily threw him out. I'm in touch with the police regularly. Often, I strip at their private shows. They're a pervy lot.'

I must leave. She's got verbal diarrhoea.

'You're exactly the person I imagined you'd be, Al,' she waffles. 'Kind, intelligent, not lustful or having sex constantly on the brain like most men.'

Whilst cavorting round the bedroom, her eyes maintain contact with mine. Occasionally, the python's head is angled in my direction. The reptile shares my disinterest. I can't help but wonder whether animal rights activists might object to the exploitation of the snake in her act. But it provides inspiration.

Skeleton strippers performing with snakes in a cemetery. Men wearing flasher raincoats could be leering at them.

'I must go home and contact the police.'

'Stay a while and watch me. Then have lunch. We both live alone and should get together.'

'Yes, another day Trixie.' Hurriedly, I descend the stairs. 'Thanks for your help.'

What an insensitive bitch.

I've often reflected that sex and procreation are massive distractions. I shouldn't have got involved. Attempting to earn a living producing art would have been a better option. Nature's urges have a lot to answer for. I'm pleased my libido is dormant. Professional men have been ruined because a strong sexual appetite has clouded their judgement. They've lost thousands of pounds, their self-esteem and, in a number of cases, their freedom. Society is only too zealous to punish men for sexual misdemeanours. With full bollocks, they can't make rational decisions that adhere to society's laws.

# Chapter 28

Back in my own house, I make a video call to Frankie.

'Hi, Al.'

'Where are you today?'

'London. I'm in a pub.'

The words are slurred. As usual, he's started to drink early. A red wig sits badly on his head. Raised voices are heard.

'Who's shouting?'

'Some yobs. They don't like my clothes.' Moving the mobile down his body, he reveals an orange trouser suit and yellow high heels.

Through tears, I tell him about the Swiss pictures and what I've seen at Trixie's.

'Don't cry. Something can be worked out.'

'The house is a mess. My dead son's possessions are trashed.' Rushing upstairs to Alex's shrine, I pan the mobile inside the bedroom.

'My wife wanted to throw everything away. Said it was morbid to keep things. Now they're gone.'

The stink of the urine on the bed attacks my nostrils. I wipe my eyes, blurred with tears.

'This is heart-breaking, Frankie.'

I show the empty bedroom where the Swiss pictures were stored.

'Easy, Al. Think carefully.'

'The police and my insurers must be contacted.'

'No. Not yet. Don't give any details about the pictures.'

'I won't.'

'Say you had your own collection at home. Then, we can make a sizeable claim.'

'No.'

Proposing a scam was predictable. Before I joined Greasby, Frankie and Nicola took advantage of a roof leak in a gallery storage area. Watercolours of little value were put in there and Nicola threw buckets of water on them. Our insurance company was conned into paying three hundred thousand pounds.

'Al, we can make easy cash.'

'No.'

'I'll back you up,' he reassures. 'We can split the proceeds.'

'Did Y's men burgle my house?'

'No idea, Al. You must make a claim and help me out.'

'Where's the Greasby money gone, Frankie?'

'On the big job. Don't worry. Soon, cash will roll back in. Nicola is more entrepreneurial than you think.'

'What was in the crates Jess and I brought back?'

'Ask Nicola.'

'She'll spout a pack of lies.'

'Make the most of this burglary.'

'I won't be part of a fraud.'

My stomach is rumbling. I've not eaten anything since having breakfast on the ferry.

'You're a criminal yourself, Al. Jess said you sent a van over a cliff.'

'It was them or us. Your scumbag daughter arranged for me to be murdered.'

'You didn't report the incident,' he answers, cockily.

'I've not reported any of Greasby's scams. Do you want me to start now?'

Frankie sits with two muscly lads at a table. One looks to be a Thai. The other is black. They're in their 20s and I've not seen them before. The black lad leans over and gives Frankie an open-mouth kiss. Not to be outdone, the Tai lad snogs him too. People are disgusted at the spectacle and shout abuse.

'Who are your friends, Frankie?'

His mobile moves, affording a better view of the pair.

'I met them whilst cruising.'

He points to the Thai lad. 'This is Robbi and the other boy is Denny. Aren't they truly gorgeous, Al. I'm so lucky. Still not sure whether I prefer men or women. Must try and find a hermaphrodite. Robbi is post-op, Denny is pre-op. Robbi tells me the surgery is extremely painful, but worth it. I don't fear castration. Fuck what Freud said in the past. When I divorce Paulene, these lads will be my husbands.'

Both have a smooth, baby-faced complexion. Robbi has dyed-blonde hair. They both sport sweatshirts with slogans on the front.

One reads: *I TRIED BEING NORMAL ONCE. WORST TWO MINUTES OF MY LIFE.* The other: *DON'T BULLY ME I'LL COME.*

'I support whatever happens to your body, Frankie.' I'm desperately trying to put together the right words. 'But won't be involved in criminality.'

Constant abuse is heard. Frankie and the two lads have stepped into a straight pub. One drinker shouts in Frankie's face: 'Have you still got a dick, mate? Want me to chop it off? You fucking weirdo.' A zombie knife is brandished.

More individuals jostle near Frankie.

'My wig is on fire,' he shouts. Punches are exchanged as Frankie's two friends try to shield him. It's difficult to focus my attention and seconds later the link is lost.

When connected again, Frankie is outside the pub, sitting on a bench weeping. Robbi shields him. Denny has one of the culprits on the ground.

'Are you okay, Frankie?'

There's a vacuum of silence as his thoughts are gathered. 'I've been burned.' He swallows deeply and dabs away tears, smearing the poorly applied mascara.

'Someone has called the police. Those yobs tried to set me alight. The landlord didn't help. He threw us out and it's pissing down.'

The wig is singed and askew on his head.

'I'm determined to be a woman. That's where the power is

today. In female hands. Instead of chasing fanny, I'll have one myself.'

I'm not judgemental in any of this. Just pleased that people in certain parts of the world can chose to do what they like with their bodies.

'I've lived as a man so far in my life,' Frankie frowns. 'Now, I want to be a woman. Nobody is sympathetic.'

His words are thick with emotion.

'Look deep into yourself and find more conviction, Frankie.'

'But there's disappointment. I won't have periods. I was looking forwards to buying sanitary towels.'

'Have you lost interest in Greasby Fine Art?'

'Nicola and Paulene call me a freak. Say I look ridiculous in a wig and dress. Both laughed when I fell over wearing six-inch high heels. Paulene thinks I should be burned. People are so prejudiced towards a man changing sex.'

'That's sad, Frankie. It may take time for people to accept you. Bigotry will be here for a while.'

'After my stroke, I decided to live the rest of my life as a woman. The last visit home was hell. Paulene tried to attack me with an axe. She wanted to chop off my willy. One of the gardeners dialled 999. If the police hadn't intervened, she would have succeeded.'

'Are the police pressing charges?'

'No idea. Few people change their lives dramatically. But, I shall be one of them.'

In the background, more insults are hurled.

'It's not easy, Frankie, when people step outside the norm. You must cope. Be bold.'

'Paulene is furious over the bank loan I took out. Defaulting on the repayments means the house will be seized.'

'Can you afford the repayments?'

'I don't know.' He wrinkles up his face. 'Nicola is nicking cash from the company.'

'Roger in admin said that months ago. You didn't listen to him.'

'I had to support Nicola.'

'Poor Roger. The company's best interests were at heart. Sack Nicola. Give her a gallery. We can function comfortably and still make a good profit.'

In family businesses, members often close ranks and blindly support a relative. This is regardless of whether they're an asset to the company or, in Nicola's case, involved with dodgy dealings. Paulene has always told Frankie that one day, Nicola would hang him. That day looks like it's fast approaching.

'Our finances are drained, Al,' Frankie begins. 'Make an insurance claim. Your neighbour's CCTV footage will confirm pictures were stolen.'

He's right. That puts me in a dilemma. Could I be incriminated in any way? What a mess.

'Help me, please, Al. I'll kill myself if I don't have a sex change.'

There's a desire to support him like I did with other people in the past as a trade union officer. Now, finding the enthusiasm and compassion is difficult. Greasby has made me experience feelings and emotions that previously I never could have imagined.

'Did Nicola tell Y's men to burgle and trash my house?'

'You must be very careful,' he sniffles.

'Why?'

'Y's men have attacked enemies with military-grade nerve agents.'

'What?'

'Your gate, door or other surfaces may have been smeared with a noxious substance.'

The information floors me.

'When did you discover the burglary?'

'Half-an-hour ago.'

'You might be contaminated. Are you feeling ill?' He smirks nastily.

Yobs pour out of the pub ready to attack Frankie and the two others. People on the street stop to watch the drama unfolding.

Fortunately, a police car arrives, though this doesn't stop a violent fracas taking place.

Is Frankie lying, or winding me up? I can't take any chances and have to be proactive. Swiftly ending the call, I shake with fear and struggle to tap in 999.

## Chapter 29

Will I die quickly or in extreme pain?

A simple text is sent to Brenda: 'I've had a terrible shock. Can't make it today.'

Within seconds, Deb replies: 'Brenda is disappointed. You're the only man she trusts. Be here as soon as you can.'

Hurrying downstairs, I wait for the emergency services to arrive. Annoyed that Jess has told Frankie about the van incident, I make video contact with her.

'Hi, Al. I'm knackered. Didn't have much sleep on the ferry last night.'

Her mobile is attached to a small tripod. She's nude.

'Where are you?'

'At home, in my bedroom. I entered a competition and won a waxing kit. Just reading the instructions,' she answers. 'Blokes don't like fucking a deep-pile carpet. Women don't like licking one.'

She bounces over to the screen giving a lewd full-frontal view.

'Do you prefer me smooth Al?'

This is painful. Women waxing away unwanted pubic hair is beyond my understanding. Depicting female or male skeletons waxing pubic hair could be hilarious.

'Feeling a twitch in your trousers?' Her boobs wobble at the screen.

I'm as excited as someone ready to have a root canal filling.

Relaxing on to the bed, she bursts into song.

*I love sex, I love sex.*
*Up my front or my arse.*
*I love sex, I love sex.*

*Up my front or my arse.*

She moves her hands and body rhythmically whilst warbling. This is nauseating.

'Come on Al, you can sing along with me. If you don't want to say the "up my arse" bit, just keep quiet on that section. Join in, Al. Sing after three. One, two, three…'

I remain quiet.

'Oh, you're so boring. Ever enjoy yourself, Al? Haven't you any mates to get pissed with, or go to a massage parlour?'

'I prefer my own company.'

'Want to see my new vibrator, Al?'

'No.'

'There's a voice inside this one. Listen. It's fun.' She holds the sex toy in front of the camera.

Amidst a whirring sound, a male voice shouts: 'Fuck, bitch, fuck.'

'It's so real. Lads often shout that at me. Want to hear some vibrator jokes?'

'No.'

'Heard about the farmer who grew a field of vibrators? Now he has a problem with squatters. Fifteen per cent of women admit to having used vibrators. The remainder said they bought them new.'

The vulgar wisecracking is boring.

'Why did you tell Frankie about the cliff?'

'Who cares?' Her answer carries the habitual nonchalance.

'Have you told anybody else?'

'Only Nicola, but she knew already.'

'What? How?'

'Don't know.'

Jess yawns.

'Don't tell anyone else.'

'I won't.'

'Where did you sneak off to earlier?'

'Took the van to Nicola's house.'

'Where are the crated pictures?'

'Don't know. Nigel said he would take care of things.'

'Nigel?'

'Yes. He phoned for a taxi so I could get home.'

'Did Nigel drive the van?'

'Don't know.'

'Why was Nigel involved?'

She shrugs.

'How is the church progressing?'

'No idea.' She bursts into song once again. '*I love sex. I love…*'

I groan. She has a degree in art but hardly mentions the subject. Regards her job with no more interest than an office worker might do about theirs. People would be thrilled working in an art gallery. Though not with Greasby.

I keep glancing out of the front window anticipating the arrival of emergency vehicles. Nothing is seen. I'm careful not to touch any surface. Continually, I stare into the hallway mirror. Are there any physical changes? No.

Jess continues our conversation: 'Dick and Paul say a car has parked in the same place as the one taken by Carl and Di. It's another old, battered vehicle and has a curtain in the back with a camera peeping though. No traffic warden or police are bothered that it's parked all day on double yellow lines.'

'Did Dick or Paul see anyone with it?'

'No.'

'That's frustrating.'

'Where are you, Al?'

'I've been burgled. The Swiss pictures have gone.'

'Bet you've been wanking yourself silly to relieve the anxiety. One survey revealed seventy eight per cent of adults masturbate. Remember, Al. It's natural. Nothing to be ashamed of.'

'Any ideas who did the burglary?'

'Jeddy and Juddy. They're up for that sort of thing. You mentioned the pictures were at your house when they came with Jane a few days ago.'

'I think Nicola organised the burglary with Y.'

'Why would anyone nick pictures already nicked and sold to us?'

'Have we paid for them?'

'Yes.'

Jess moves in another direction. 'Dick and Paul said that more Rowlandsons have gone.'

'What's happened to the Dali?'

'It's in their studio.'

'Is Frankie staying at your house?'

'On and off. He nicks my clothes, make-up, drugs and anything else he fancies.'

'Is he short of cash?'

'No. Got plenty.'

'Greasby is full of liars.'

'Obviously.'

'Will Frankie change sex?'

Jess smirks. 'It won't happen. Castration is a Freudian nightmare for a man.'

'I'm not so sure.'

'Why would a man want to fuck a man with a fanny? Why not go to a woman? It doesn't make sense.'

There's no point in commenting.

'Want to do a bit of hoovering, Al?'

'Hoovering?'

'I've a pile of coke to snort.'

'No.'

'Or do you fancy a quickie?'

'That will never happen.'

'I want us to enjoy regular sex,' she states with brazen promiscuity.

'Shut up, Jess.'

She grimaces.

I'm annoyed. 'Jess, answer this honestly.'

'What?'

'Have you ever known Y or his men to use a military-grade

nerve agent?'

Falling back on the bed, she laughs wildly. 'Who's suggested that?'

'Frankie.'

Louder peals of laughter are emitted. 'Frankie is mad. Can't you see that?'

I'm flabbergasted.

'We've been using spice,' she declares. 'I thought it was brilliant. Frankie hallucinated. His brain is fried. He'll experiment with any drugs.'

I've made a huge mistake by contacting 999. It's excusable after suffering a massive upset.

My concentration is broken by the sound of sirens. From the front window, I spot a multitude of flashing lights shooting from police cars, ambulances and fire engines. Neighbours appear totally shocked, never witnessing anything like this before in a street known for its tranquility. If there has been a nerve agent attack, I hope none of them are at risk.

# Chapter 30

A major terrorist incident was declared. My street cordoned-off and various agencies went to work. Scotland Yard's counter terrorism officers led the investigation into a possible nerve agent poisoning.

Trixie and her house were examined – even Herbert. Officers took Trixie's hard drive and watched the burglary. Earlier in the day, a postman and a man delivering circulars had visited my house. They too were traced and checked. It was assumed the trashed items in Alex's shrine had been smeared. I don't expect to see anything ever again.

The incident was reported in the local and national press, on radio and television.

*RUSSIAN CHEMICAL ATTACK IN ASKWORTH* was the common headline.

All this occurred whilst I underwent an intense medical examination in a specialist isolation unit. The sight of television news crews on my street was unbelievable. Thankfully, no noxious substances were found on me or anywhere else. I was taken to a safe house by a witness protection officer. When asked about the stolen pictures, I said they were Frankie's, explaining he's going through a bad patch with his wife. He didn't want Paulene selling them behind his back.

Frankie was located and questioned. Seeing the wisdom of falling in with my story, he confirmed the details. The pictures were insured, even away from his house. A massive claim can follow. Frankie told the police nothing was said about nerve agents. Or Russians. This made me look a fool. Fortunately, officers confessed they believe Frankie is deranged.

Questions were posed about who might have trashed my

house and did I upset anyone recently? Nicola's name was suggested as we're sworn enemies. Arrested and held for ten hours before being questioned, she was eventually released. No pictures were found at her house. The accusation caused intense annoyance.

For the police, questions remain unanswered. What was the motive for the robbery? Who were the individuals burgling my house? Why did Frankie mention a chemical attack? What was the reason for denying he knew any Russians?

The incident was a massive drain on police resources, but a strong response was necessary. I applaud their commitment. During the investigation, an attempt was made to grasp how Greasby operated. Predictably, confusion reigned. I sensed a presumption that art is for upper-class people who rarely squabble. Laughable.

Throughout the whole episode, my treatment was respectful. The police were brilliant. They had no hesitation in concluding I played no part in the robbery. I reiterated my job involves dealing with staff and one client, Brenda, not buying art for Greasby. No details were given about Y.

The incident has created a dilemma. Should I tell the police everything or remain silent? Making a decision is difficult. I must not implicate myself. Concern was expressed regarding my security and advice given on planning movements carefully.

A few days after the crisis, I'm allowed to go home. It's a Friday afternoon. Curtains twitch as police officers in a marked car drop me off. Neighbours walk outside and give a friendly wave.

Later, three people from the neighbourhood watch scheme knock at the door. Each one offers help. They can supply furniture, basic electrical goods and crockery. Or, remove trashed items and assist with the redecorating. Once more, it restores my faith in human nature.

Trixie visits with Herbert draped across her shoulders. She says I can stay with her for a few days or pop in whenever for a meal. The offers are appreciated.

Items were removed from the house during the investigation and it's almost empty. Only a few odd pieces of furniture remain. A claim has been registered with my insurance company which promised to respond quickly. Security cameras must be installed front and back, as well as in certain rooms. Over the next few days, quotes shall be sought. I don't want to be visiting Trixie and Herbert too often. Police officers were excited when telling me she'd been interviewed. They've booked her to perform at one of their functions.

I go upstairs to the empty room once housing Alex's shrine. Another large part of him is lost. An impressive arrangement of flowers must be bought and placed on the grave.

My mobile was taken and thoroughly investigated. When it's brought to life, there are texts from people expressing concern and hoping I'm well. Amongst them are Brenda, Jane, Dick and Paul, Kirstin and Anna. This is besides staff at the Greasby galleries. There's nothing from Jess, Nicola or Frankie.

A message from Paulene raises several questions: 'Where has Frankie hidden his pictures? Have they been sold? Did you have anything to do with the sales?'

A reply must firmly state I know nothing.

It's undecided whether the subjects in my destroyed paintings ought to be revisited. Pictures shouldn't be precious. They must be a learning experience. That's what one of my art college tutors said. She's right. After not producing art for years, a lot of experience and confidence was gained from those recent efforts.

Looking in a smashed bathroom mirror, my image is fragmented. But a positive one is thrown back. Despite being a victim of crime and losing my son's items, I feel strong. Ready to continue with life and art. Especially art. I'm aching to climb the ladder of success. I can rise above everything.

In the isolation unit, a few days ago, my thoughts threatened to overwhelm. But counselling by specialist officers helped and I'm ready to accomplish anything. I feel unbreakable.

Swallowing deeply, I think Alex would be proud of me. Although there's a reluctance to accept the existence of an afterlife, I'm sure he's watching. Alex is my inspiration.

I say to myself. *Ars longa, vita brevis*.

Jeff Nuttall's words are in my ears once again: 'Art stands outside society and prods it.' I will prod it hard. When Alex was born, I promised myself he would be the most important person in my life. Even more important than art. Now he's gone, there's only art.

Revenge on Nicola isn't a consideration. I know my feelings are being bottled up. Will they escape again? Like they did when I tried to throttle Jess? Not sure.

A good idea today would be to venture outside and breathe fresh air. I was cooped up for nearly a week in a ward and then a police safe house. Where can I go? Askworth's Victorian cemetery? Yes. A visit there has been planned for weeks. I need to photograph the elaborate tombstones and include them in my work.

It was my intention to erect a large Victorian-style monument to Alex, but presently there's no chance. Everything is burdened with restrictions.

# Chapter 31

Askworth cemetery was opened in 1854. The Victorians called it 'The Garden of Sleep' and the Neo-Gothic entrance was the 'Gateway to Heaven'. There are thousands buried here.

Belgian artist James Ensor mixed death and humour in his work perfectly. I need to do the same – laugh in the face of death.

To encourage ideas, I search graveyard humour on my mobile. These jokes pop up:

*'Last night I was about to take a short cut through the graveyard when two young ladies stopped me.*

*'Can we walk with you?' said one of them. 'Please.'*

*'Sure,' I said, and off we went.*

*'It really freaks us out walking through the graveyard after dark,' explained the other.*

*'No problem,' I said. 'It used to freak me out too, back when I was alive.'*

I laugh at this one.

*A man was taking a 6 am stroll, when he saw someone crouching in a graveyard. Trying to be polite, he tips his hat and says, 'morning.'*

*The man replies, 'nah just taking a shit.'*

Although I'm alone in the cemetery, my mind is alert to potential dangers. Nobody has been buried here for years. A new cemetery was opened in the 1930s on the other side of the city. Alex is there. At his funeral, the youngest person present was dead. Disturbing.

This 1854 cemetery is tended by a group calling themselves the Friends of Old Askworth Cemetery. A website exists to provide details of the area's history, how to carry out research on people interred, and various other matters. I find Victorian death culture fascinating. Properly commemorating the departed was considered an important part of everyday life. I smile when observing tombstone inscriptions. Here's one:

*Remember Me As Thou Pass By. As Thou Art Now. So Once Was I. As I Am Now. So Thou Wilt Be. Prepare Thy Way. To Follow Me.*

A digital camera has been brought as it can act like a sketchbook. Years ago, I did simple sketches of items to be included in pictures. A Polaroid camera was also used. Digital cameras are brilliant. They make recording material so much easier. I approach an elevated part of the cemetery, overlooking a lower section. My imagination is fired. I shall use this to depict skeletons playing on a rope swing. They can have big smiles whilst gliding across the hollow.

The afternoon weather is pleasant, with a steady breeze and clouds overhead. There's an even light everywhere. It's perfect. Strong sunlight and dark shadows aren't helpful. Recording unusual, yet typical features of an old burial ground, is the intention. A start is made by photographing tombstones sinking haphazardly into the soft soil. It's weird that the end of someone's life is marked by a gravestone. How inappropriate. A few angels show damage and I snap details from various angles. Close-ups are taken recording headstone inscriptions, weathered by two centuries of rain, of broken wrought ironwork bordering graves. And of old trees with gnarled trunks and branches. That's besides the abundance of bushes and flowers.

After half-an-hour, I sense another presence. A young teenager holds a skull on a stick. Others of a similar age are dressed in a slovenly mixture of sports and designer gear. Having broken into a vault, they toss skulls to each other as if in a bizarre rugby game.

'Hey, pack it in,' I scold. 'Show respect for the dead.'

The teenager taunts me with the skull. The others gather close and laugh. I don't panic. None pose a real physical threat. They're much smaller and lighter than me.

'What the fuck will you do if we don't?' A girl, looking no more than 12, angles a blade towards me. I want to kick it out of her hand though restrain myself.

'Nothing,' I say, holding my hands up in a surrender-type gesture.

All are amused and we go our separate ways. Nearby, six pensioners jot down tombstone inscriptions. They're from a local history group. We exchange pleasantries. Several state the more impressive tombstones were erected to men not women.

My thoughts disperse when I receive a video call from Dick. Paul is also present.

'Hi, Al. Are you recovering? Thought I'd cheer you up with this.'

Always full of fun and pranks, he shows a drawing of a large vagina that includes arms, legs and Nicola's facial features.

'Recognise her?' Dick laughs proudly.

'You ought to have an exhibition of your Nicola cartoons.'

'Yes. I've done some good ones.'

I'm shown a sketch of a penis incorporating Nigel's head. Then, another of Frankie lifting up a dress. He has no genitals. Holding them aloft in a hand, they're dripping with blood.

Dick and Paul howl with laughter.

The image of Frankie is distasteful. I support his decision to have a sex change and my stance remains the same.

'Frankie is terrified of being murdered,' Dick discloses. 'Another tranny has been found dead with dick and bollocks stuffed in his mouth.'

'Keep the drawing private,' I begin. 'Or, people might think you're involved.'

Paul changes the conversation. 'Are you coming back, Al?'

'Yes.'

'Good. We miss your steadying influence.'

Both question why I'm in a cemetery.

'Taking pictures. The tombstones are brilliant.' I pan my mobile. 'I want to include a selection in my work. The intention is to create a body of work for an exhibition or book. The title for both projects is *The Cemetarians*. All kinds of activity will be portrayed, suggesting there's a great afterlife. Skeletised people are just carrying on everyday activities as if still alive. They are happy and have smiling faces. Eating burgers or ice creams. I've done a picture of a football team called Cemetery United which competes in the Graveyard Cup. Often, scenes featuring a cemetery have dramatic skies and are full of horror clichés. That won't happen in my work. Even a funeral is celebrated. I'm working on a picture titled *Welcoming the New Cemetarian: Johnny Champagne*. Recently, I read that a bar owner called Johnny had died. At his graveside, there was big piss-up with mourners guzzling Champagne.'

Both roll with amusement.

'That sounds brilliant,' says Dick. 'Humour in Art. Not often tackled today. Only boring formal values are pushed forward.'

'Keep painting, Al,' encourages Paul. 'Your work is skilled and unusual.'

'You need a lucky break,' adds Dick. 'It'll happen. Be patient.'

These comments please me as both men are accomplished artists themselves. They promise to offer constructive criticism whenever required.

'You ought to visit other cemeteries like those in Glasgow, Bradford and Highgate in London. Build up a good selection of graveyard pictures.'

'I will Paul...what's been happening at Askworth?'

'We've faked John Heartfield anti-Nazi collages,' he confesses. 'Nicola showed us original work from the 1930s and we had to create convincing forgeries. She handed over old photographs of Hitler and his cronies.'

'Heartfield's works were unfamiliar,' states Dick. 'But, after research, we're impressed.'

Alarm bells ring in my head.

'How did Nicola obtain the Heartfields?'

'Jess brought them back from Germany, along with more pictures,' they both answer.

'When?'

'While you've been absent,' Dick replies.

The sly conniving bitch.

'We tried to interrogate Nicola on how the Heartfields were found,' Paul begins. 'She threw a wobbler and told us to fuck off.'

'Where are the original Heartfields now?'

'Nicola has them,' Dick answers.

'Where?'

Neither has an explanation.

'What about Jane's Dali drawing? Jess mentioned it was in your room.'

Paul smiles. 'Yes, but we put it back on display today.'

'Why?'

'No idea,' he responds.

'What are we hanging on to that for? Has anyone tried to buy it?'

'Plenty,' Dick reveals. 'The bitch won't sell it.'

'Unbelievable. Has she appeared with any George Grosz works, or pictures depicting lesbian scenes?'

Dick is thoughtful. 'Not yet, but they may be amongst those Jess delivered.'

Shocked, I take the conversation in another direction. 'Is Greasby still solvent?'

'Yes,' beams Dick. 'Frankie has poured cash into the company.'

'He told me he didn't have any money.'

'It's from his bank loan,' informs Paul.

Whilst talking, I continue to show them the wonderfully-sculpted angels.

Dick has something else on his mind. 'There's still a car parked outside the Askworth Gallery. Nicola and Frankie are shitting themselves. Both believe they're under surveillance. Nicola suffers from nightmares and takes loads more anti-depressants. Frankie, too, has disturbed slumber.'

'Seen anybody with the vehicle?'

'No,' Paul replies, 'but there's definitely a camera hidden in the back.'

'Annabel is doing well at drama class,' states Dick.

'I'm pleased for her.'

'You must leave Greasby, Al,' asserts Paul. 'It's a waste of your talents. Our redundant Birmingham staff applied for a Protective Award. They were successful and received a payment. Most have new jobs now, but not with art.'

'That's sad.'

'They send thanks to you,' adds Dick.

The two men explain they're busy on a lucrative job, cleaning a large batch of pictures from a country house. I'm alarmed when informed Nicola has sold pictures from the private collections stored in the Askworth basement. Amongst those missing is a Henri Gaudier-Brzeska drawing. It belongs to a billionaire who's away on his yacht. He collects this artist's drawings and sculpture. They're priceless.

Dick mentions Y and Nicola have shared the profits from these purloined pictures. Unscrupulous collectors bought them. I hope this foolish activity is detected, so Nicola can face a long jail sentence.

# Chapter 32

Venturing to another area of the cemetery, I encounter four girls and two lads – in their teens or early 20s. They're grouped near flat-lid tombstones smoking crack. All have sallow complexions and puny bodies. Their brains must be hardwired for self-destruction. Everyone's clothing isn't even charity-shop standard. They, and others, have been here before as the area is strewn with crack bottles and syringes. One girl, with tracksuit bottoms down, injects heroin into the femoral vein. It makes me wince. The scene is a snapshot of life's underbelly.

With Alex's unnecessary death always swamping my mind, I want to dash up to her and scream: 'You pathetic scum. Stop wasting your life. Do something else. Develop a career. Contribute to society instead of shunning it. Get a grip.' Holding back, I consider her behaviour might be the result of abuse, or a childhood spent in foster care.

Another girl approaches me.

'Hi, I'm Daisy.' At a guess, she's 18, her face and arms are badly bruised. She has the appearance of an exhumed corpse.

'What happened to you?' I probe. A stale smell pervades her.

'A punter beat me up last night.'

'What type of men do that?'

'Pathetic pricks. There's no sex at home so they take revenge on us.'

'How can you live with yourself after standing on a street corner? What would your parents, grandparents or anyone else say if they saw you?'

She's indifferent.

I feel sorry for the punters' wives, or partners. After paying these girls for sex, the men go home and pretend nothing has happened. What can women do in this awful situation once they realise what has been happening behind their backs? Leave the man they thought was loyal? Pretend nothing has happened and continue to sleep together? Kick him out and fend for themselves? These are unenviable choices. That's not forgetting the effect on any children.

'Are you a heroin or crack addict?'

'Both,' she admits. 'Want business?'

'No, thank you.'

She sniffs.

'How did you earn cash today?'

'Tony and Jack mugged a pensioner. He might even be dead. We robbed a hundred quid off him.'

Appalled, I shouldn't even be talking to her. 'Do you like heroin?'

'Fuck off. No, I don't.'

'Why take it?'

'To feel normal. I need more and more each day.'

This is confusing. My inner turmoil could never be released through empty sex, booze or drugs.

'Give me cash. Then I won't have to go on the street tonight.'

Girls who stand on a street corner selling themselves to strangers are mentally ill. They court danger unnecessarily.

'Why not go cold turkey?'

Her head moves from side-to-side.

'Or go into rehab?'

There's a sad pause.

Druggies are wimps. I've suffered pancreatitis in the past. For the pain, morphine was given. Afterwards, there was uncomfortable sweating and shivering. This was cold turkey. But it only lasted a couple of days. I didn't risk my life, or demean myself, trying to obtain more.

'What are you doing here?' she probes.

'Photographing tombstones. I'm an artist. I paint skeletons in funny graveyard scenes.'

'Any paintings on your mobile?'

'Yes.'

'Are you famous?'

'Maybe one day.'

By now, the other three girls have gathered near. Lice crawl in their hair, eyes are sunken and the pupils microscopically small. All four are amused on seeing my work.

I explain that orgies in cemeteries will be amongst my next subjects.

'If you pay us,' Daisy enthuses, 'we'll be your models. Me and these lasses will strip off and the lads shag us. You could even photograph us smoking crack.'

These are good ideas. Undressed, I suspect they resemble skeletons. The orgies must be painted on sizeable canvases. In the background will be spectacular angel tombstones. A nice contrast with the deviant sexual activity taking place in front of them.

'Go on, mister. Pay us.'

Daisy licks her dry lips in anticipation of the response.

'I've only one hundred and thirty quid cash.'

'Brilliant,' the girls agree. 'That'll do.'

The lads show reluctance.

'Tony, get your dick out,' Daisy pleads.

'Can't you do lesbian scenes?'

'No,' the girls answer.

'After smoking crack, we'll be limp,' argues Jack.

'Try it, or pretend,' urges Daisy. 'We're earning a hundred and thirty.'

'You can earn more on the street tonight.'

'Fuck off. You go out there and sell your arse instead.'

The cash is handed to Daisy. Removing their rags, countless sores and needle puncture marks are visible. That's besides bruises and stab scars. I'm right, without clothes they are skeletal.

They take up positions. The lads perform half-heartedly, while the girls offer encouragement. Images are caught from various angles.

'Try different positions,' I shout.

An old couple visiting the graves of long-lost relatives react with disgust. So do members of the family history group seen earlier. This is for art and it can't be censored.

A text pings through from Anna. Can she and Kirstin chat to me on a video call?

Yes, I'm pleased to answer.

The two women sit together on a sofa. The video is from a mobile positioned in front of them.

Kirstin is fragile. She's lost weight. By contrast, Anna is healthy and focussed.

'You look well, Al,' Kirstin comments.

'Thanks, I feel okay.'

'Where are you?' Anna asks.

'In a cemetery. Some druggies are posing for me.' I carefully move the mobile to keep the image stable.

Both howl with laughter.

'Very funny, Al,' states Anna. 'They're living skeletons. It's *plein air* with a difference.'

'Decadent sex. Brilliant. Love it, Al,' confesses Kirstin. 'You've put aside that horrible burglary and creating art. Wonderful. Wonderful. This is the first laugh I've had in days. I often muse whether George Grosz drew from imagination or had people pose for him.'

'Thought you couldn't raise a smile, Jack,' yelps Daisy, a short distance away.

'I feel okay,' he answers with self-satisfaction. 'I'm enjoying myself.'

Anna offers a serious look. 'Kirstin has received nasty letters. I'll read one to you: "We have your pictures. One day we'll get you".'

'That's terrifying.'

'We employ minders 24 hours a day,' admits Kirstin.

I have to listen carefully over the druggies' unexpectedly loud cries of pleasure.

Anna extends an arm over her partner's shoulders. 'Kirstin

rarely leaves the house. She's undergoing therapy. It's helping.'

Daisy kneels on top of a tombstone and is entered from behind. My mobile is angled so Anna and Kirstin can view the action. Both move excitedly on the sofa, peering into their screen.

'Are we doing okay, mister?' Daisy is keen to provide value for money.

'Yes,' I answer, continuing to take pictures. They've understood my aims.

All this is very amusing for my German friends.

The girl who injected earlier has collapsed over a tombstone.

'What's wrong with her?' I ask Daisy.

'Gauched from smack. She'll be okay.'

'You wouldn't believe the girls could enjoy sex after what is experienced every night,' states Kirstin.

'Yes, I'm amazed too.'

'Have them fucking together,' instructs Kirstin. 'Then, organise one girl to take both men at once. Have a lesbian scene nearby.'

The instructions are relayed to my models.

'The sex could be more deviant,' submits Anna. 'Tell them to break-off saplings and lash each other.'

Daisy has overheard the conversation. 'We can do anything. Give us more money.'

'Sorry. Nothing left.'

'Make another arrangement with the girls,' recommends Anna. 'Tie them up. Have them suspended from trees. The lads could penetrate every hole and from all angles. Be imaginative.'

'Yes, they're good suggestions.'

'Those track marks and sores are a sorry sight,' observes Kirstin.

'They have lice in their hair,' I comment.

'Photograph the girls combing lice out of each other's pubic hair. It could be a fun painting,' Kirstin suggests. 'Show them injecting heroin. Or, holding up a crack bottle, triumphantly blowing out smoke.'

'There are plenty of ideas to explore,' I answer.

'Once a week, we cheer ourselves up at Das Sexhaus,' Anna relates as smiles stretch across their faces.

'We know about the fake George Grosz provenance,' begins Kirstin. 'Roger, one of your old Greasby colleagues, told Brenda.'

'Don't worry, both of us accept you had nothing to do with the scam,' reassures Anna. 'We know Jess was involved. What a bitch, including her mother in deceit. It's a pity you didn't strangle Jess.'

The druggies put their clothes on. Tony and Jack have climaxed and don't want to be involved in the theatrics any longer. No matter. Enough photographs have been gathered.

Leaving, they wave, happy with the cash to buy more drugs.

'The Grosz picture bought from Nicola,' starts Kirstin, 'is a fake.'

'I made an error,' Anna admits.

Kirstin holds on to her. 'Don't worry. Judgement can be flawed.'

The drawing has been examined by experts in Germany. Despite what Anna concluded, everyone stated it was forged. Sworn statements were submitted to back up the verdict. Although Greasby is well-known for making fakes, I'm puzzled. Dick and Paul have not confessed anything.

'I will be taking legal action,' Kirstin begins. 'Nicola has to refund the money and pay damages.'

'There's been massive coverage of the robberies,' Anna is keen to report. 'Kirstin is to make a television appeal for information.'

'A plan has been worked out with the Schmidts and Brenda,' says Kirstin. 'We want you, Al, to play a major role.'

I reveal my intention to see Brenda over the weekend.

'She's been through a major crisis,' Kirstin informs. 'But, is okay now and looks radiant.'

'Good,' I respond and the conversation is ended.

Walking towards one of the cemetery's exits, Jonty makes

contact. He's a manager at one of Greasby's London galleries. Being my first day back home, it's pleasing people want to talk.

I thank him for enquiring about my ordeal, then sense he's eager to part with information.

'Today, Nicola brought a George Grosz watercolour and a lesbian scene for us to sell. Would any of your contacts be interested?'

I'm stunned. Surely, she's not stupid enough to sell nicked pictures through one of our London galleries? Or are they fakes?

I tell him to photograph them and email copies to me.

Potentially, Greasby could be handling four batches of stolen pictures. There are: the Schmidt's own pictures; Brenda's from the Schmidt collection; Brenda's pictures from Kirstin; and Kirstin's Grosz and Heartfield pictures taken out of her gallery. Are they all with Greasby? If so, where are they being stored? The location of the remaining stolen Swiss pictures remains a mystery.

I can't wait to hear Brenda explain my major role, but this thought is broken by another call. It's Y.

'Al, are you okay? I can't believe what's happened to you.'

My anger is difficult to control. 'Yes, fine. I'm recovering.'

You two-faced slimy bastard. Why are you living and my son dead? You should die the most horrific death imaginable. Will he mention the incident at the cliff? I hope not and settle on one of the cemetery seats.

'Somebody has a grudge against me. Any idea who it might be?'

'No, Al.'

'Who is sick enough to trash my son's shrine?'

'I've no idea.'

The intention is to be friendly and show him respect. Not show anger or antagonism. Russians have a habit of killing people in a nasty way. Think of Trotsky and the ice axe.

'I think Nicola was involved.'

'She's bitter and twisted. Leave Greasby as soon as you can.'

'That's my plan.'

His words are chosen wisely, then carefully laid in sentences. They're held together with syrupy sincerity.

'Travel over and stay with me for a while, Al.'

Is this a revenge-seeking invitation?

Y continues: 'We can discuss working together.'

'I refuse to be involved with criminality.'

'My relationship with Greasby is misunderstood. I want nothing more to do with them. Nicola is out of control. Art absorbs you and I. We need to know each other better. Spend a day fishing. Build up a proper relationship. A partnership.'

'I'll give it some thought,' I lie.

# Chapter 33

After taking more photographs, I leave the cemetery. My head explodes with ideas. I decide to buy artists' materials from a retail park store. In a text, Kirstin states she's happy to commission six pictures depicting orgies in cemeteries. Impressed with my ideas, she thinks they're dark but humorous. Art today, she says, lacks fun and I agree. An indication of costs is required then an advance payment can be transferred. A start must be made as soon as possible. Money. Money. Money. My first real commission.

Art is giving me confidence again. I will emerge from a long, long, mourning period that seemed interminable. Kirstin insists my career must move up a gear. I agree. My aim isn't to be fantastically rich. Only comfortable. I started out as a figurative artist and plan to move forward in that vein. The goal is to be a modern and cheekier version of James Ensor.

The art shop sells all the essentials needed by amateurs, students and professionals. Surprisingly, the business is surviving despite competition from online traders. Aware of the incident at my house, the manager expresses sympathy. He's president of Askworth Art Club, whose members I snub. Their paintings show no spark of originality. He digs into the rumour Greasby might go bust which is rife amongst the local art community. A clear answer is avoided. Everyone, he mentions, is aware Nicola sells fake and stolen paintings. He thought I would've known better than to join the company. Offering no response, I thank him for a generous discount and leave.

I buy a laptop and printer from another store to download and print the images taken earlier. A sensation that I'm being followed troubles me, only nothing is seen. Frightened that Y's men might seek revenge for their chums being pushed over the cliff, I must relax but take care. Trouble shouldn't be met half-way.

Stopping at a Chinese restaurant, a meal is enjoyed in convivial surroundings. The first one eaten with enthusiasm or appetite for several days. I arrive home at 7 pm.

Shock is felt when Nicola's name pops up on my mobile screen. The intrusion annoys me.

'Hi, Al. You okay though, Al? You okay?'

'Yes, fine. Why aren't you calling on a video link? You could have flashed your crotchless knickers.'

The joke is ignored. What's so important for her to make contact? Why hasn't she asked Jess, Frankie or even Nigel to phone? It's out of character.

'Are you and Nigel beating each other up tonight?'

She ignores me again.

'Got any court dates yet to answer your charges?'

'They've been dropped.'

Her good luck is unbelievable.

'Sorry to hear about your son's shrine, Al. I was heartbroken.'

Annabel chirps in: 'Will daddy pull that plug out of your bum again tonight, mummy?'

'Annabel's won a major part in a film,' Nicola reveals. 'Earning thousands. She'll save Greasby. Like I did a few years ago.'

'That assumption isn't shared by anyone.'

'Who are you talking to, mummy? Give me the mobile. Give it to me.'

'Shut up, you little cunt. I'm talking to Al.'

A scuffle is heard as Annabel snatches the mobile.

'Al is a wanker, a wanker, a wanker. Pulls his plonker, pulls his plonker all day long, all day long.'

There's a loud slap and Annabel cries out before Nicola speaks again.

'Do you have either Jeddy or Juddy's mobile number?'

This question throws me and I laugh. 'If they hear your voice, they'll end the call.'

'I need to contact them urgently.'

'Why?'

'Can't say. Do you have Jane's home number? She's not answering her mobile or emails.'

'It might be in an old phone book. If that's still here, and not been bagged up and taken by the police.'

'Can you look now?'

'Why the urgency?'

'A car is outside the Askworth Gallery again. It's been there for days. Can you get rid of it?'

'Are you organising something dodgy?'

'No.'

In the front room, I kick damaged furniture ready to be thrown out. Pity it's not Nicola I'm booting.

'What did Jess bring back from Germany a few days ago?'

'I'll tell you soon. Do you have Carl's number? Can you persuade him to break into the car and drive it away?'

'Why would I have a druggie's number? Ask Jess to move it.'

'She's at a shagging marathon, raising money for a local charity.' Nicola releases a giggle. 'A few rugby teams are involved. Jess said she was looking forwards to the challenge. Isn't she lucky with sex?'

I'm silent.

In the background, Nigel is singing words from the Sensational Alex Harvey Band's *Swampsnake*. Occasionally, he voices the lead guitar fills.

'Shut up, Nigel! Shut up with that fucking drivel. I can't hear myself fucking speak.'

Her attention switches back to me. 'We really should try to work in harmony, Al.'

What an insult. I've been patiently waiting for an opportunity to attack and can't hold back any longer. 'If I ever find out you were involved in wrecking my son's shrine, you're dead.'

She's no longer friendly: 'If it had been, I would've bombed your house with you in it. Fuck you and your dead son.'

I end the call.

The death of a child is deeply traumatic for a parent. Only people who suffer the loss can feel deep emotion. Those who don't want to understand and show compassion are scum.

It's curious why Nicola needs to contact Jeddy and Juddy. I easily find my phone book and ring Jane's house number. Her partner, Ron, answers and pleasantries are exchanged with him. It's a while since we spoke.

'Is Jane there?'

'No, out, and she's left her mobile here.'

'What about Jeddy and Juddy?'

'They've gone for the night.'

'Have you a number for either of them?'

'They don't want to be contacted.'

'Okay. How's business?'

'Al, it could always be better.'

'Give everyone my regards when you see them.'

'Yes. Bye, Al.'

Minutes later, Frankie calls. 'Al, do you have Jeddy or Juddy's mobile number?'

'No. Jane's partner says they can't be contacted. Neither can Jane.'

'Nicola is desperate to speak with any of them.'

'Why the urgency? What's happening?'

'No idea. Thanks, Al.'

'Bye, Frankie.'

'Wait, Al. Know anything about the dodgy car outside the Askworth gallery?'

'No.'

There's a scam afoot here. I shall stand back. My life is moving in another direction. New friends have been found, even patrons.

An hour later, Frankie wants to speak again. 'Al, Nicola no longer needs to contact the twins.'

'Okay, fine.'

'The dodgy car has gone too.'

'Good.'

'Nicola has taken more cash out of Greasby,' Frankie blubbers. 'I can't stop her. Business is poor. Do you think Brenda would buy the company? I want to retire and live my new life.'

'The question can be raised.'

'Thanks, Al. Thanks.'

Settling down finally for a night alone, I heave a sigh of relief. Preliminary drawings are made in a sketchbook bought earlier. The results excite me and I'm pleased. I feel at peace. A stage is being reached that surprises me. Grief is moving aside and I'm producing art.

Before I know it, the clock shows 11 pm. Fatigue is overwhelming me. I bring in a camp bed from the garage to sleep on tonight. The inconvenience doesn't matter. Could've booked in at a B&B and billed the insurance company, only didn't bother. Paulene invited me to stay with her. So did Brenda. Both offers were declined. As soon as the insurance money arrives, the house can be made comfortable again.

My mobile sounds. It's Frankie and he's crying. 'Al, you must be at the Askworth Gallery immediately. There's been a robbery.'

'Is my presence necessary?'

'Yes, of course. You must liaise with the police and the insurers. Hurry, Al.'

'Okay, I'm on my way,' I groan.

# Chapter 34

Within half-an-hour, I reach the gallery and see marked police cars present. To access our car park, I need to drive down a short road at the rear of the building. Two uniformed officers stop me. Explaining who I am, they allow entry. It's a surprise to see the Askworth Mayor's limousine in the car park. Another police car is there with its blues flashing. The Mayor, Eric Dunning, who's also chairman of the Council's Cultural Services Directorate, stands in his shirt and tie, but without any trousers or underpants. Nearby are two female officers, a working girl and the Council chauffeur. Naked from the waist down, the girl wears only a scruffy T-shirt and denim jacket. Clearly, she's not wearing a bra. Her boobs hang down like a couple of tennis balls in a pair of football socks. Clothes belonging to Dunning and the girl are strewn on the ground.

The car park is a noted area where girls bring their clients. Condoms are regularly found. With winks and little gestures, the chauffeur indicates what's been happening. Whether he was a participant is anybody's guess. Maybe just waiting to follow the Mayor.

I've clashed with Dunning in the past. It was under his instructions the city art gallery was transformed into a general store. In his late 50s, he's a caricature of a pathetic kerb crawler – fat, bald, shifty eyes and with greasy skin. An election leaflet always shouts he's a happily married man with two grown-up daughters. Will the press expose him and ruin his career? Doubtful. A police van reverses down to the car park, ready to transport Dunning and his companion to Askworth police station.

'Can't I go? I've done nothing wrong,' cries the girl. 'My

bloke will burn me if I don't earn cash for his habit.' Nasty marks are clearly visible on her legs.

'No. Don't move,' an officer responds.

Dunning shouts at the girl: 'I've not had a jump. I want my money back.'

'Fuck off. A working girl never gives refunds.'

A tussle ensues until the officers drop Dunning to the tarmac. I bend down to him.

'Serves you right, dickhead.'

An acetylene torch has been used to remove the steel door at the back of the gallery. This is Jeddy and Juddy's work. Scenes of Crime Officers are investigating.

On entering the building, I've an uneasy feeling. What's in store next? Unpleasantness, no doubt.

The gallery is shabby. Dust everywhere, and coffee cups left on desks grow mould. The front window screams to be cleaned. Fluorescent tubes need replacing, giving the area an uneven light. Staff not replacing dud tubes was always one of Frankie's pet hates. He doesn't care anymore. Spaces on walls, due to the missing Rowlandsons, are filled with other watercolours. They're inappropriate, not depicting similar subjects or dating from the correct period.

Frankie is crying. He's settled on one of the low-level seats, clearing tears with a handkerchief.

'This is an outrage,' he snivels. 'I've never been burgled. Never. It's so upsetting.'

Wearing a pink wig, short red skirt, white blouse, fishnet tights and black high heels, he has freshly applied make-up – even at this hour. His two mates, Robbi and Denny, comfort him, tightly holding his hands. Their T-shirts display two more slogans: *WARNING: MAY START TALKING ABOUT TRANSGENDER RIGHTS* and *I LIKE MY MEN HOW I LIKE MY WOMEN. THAT'S IT, THAT'S THE JOKE. I'M BISEXUAL.*

I'm pleased they are looking after Frankie. Not for his money but for what he is, or would like to become. How the trio could earn a living is another matter.

Nicola doesn't present a tired and dishevelled end-of-day appearance. Her hair glistens, and the make-up, like Frankie's, looks exquisite. She's in a well-cut blue trouser suit, strong perfume wafting everywhere. I feel untidy. My hair is tousled, I need a shave and the same casual clothes have been worn for the past few days.

'Hi, Al. Thanks for coming,' says Nicola insincerely. 'Sorry for interrupting your night. Were you snorting coke and fucking two working girls?'

Pointing to a cut lip, I jibe: 'Been fighting with Nigel again?'

Not answering, she introduces Detective Inspector Paul Brevitt and Detective Sergeant Sybil Grant. Uniformed constables are also present. Brevitt is a tough-looking giant of a man with an intense stare. In his early 30s, he has a full head of hair and wears a grey suit. Tenacious and committed to discovering the truth, his eyes dart everywhere. I hope Frankie doesn't make a pass at him. Sadly, he does. The DI ignores him.

Shaking my hand firmly, Grant releases a thin smile. She gives the impression her job is done efficiently and without frills or fuss. I expect Nicola to take the leading role in tonight's drama which ought to be titled *The Scam*. This is blatantly obvious.

Nicola continually fidgets. Suggesting the two detectives be seated, they ignore her and remain standing. So do I. Several uniformed officers leave the room to check if anyone is still in the building.

Brevitt's eyes watch every facial and bodily movement of Nicola and Frankie. His colleague does the same. When announcing an original Dali has gone, Nicola tries to maintain eye contact with them. The information slaps my face like a wet mackerel.

'The Dali is beautiful,' Frankie comments tearfully. 'It's from the 1930s. Surrealism's best years.'

Nicola passes a large colour photograph of the drawing to the police. They look at it with mild interest before handing it to me. The work was done by a competent copyist named Jake Greaves. I notice his signature has been erased and Dali's added. Nicola's obsession with scams is pathetic. My attempts to gain respectability for the company, by establishing a working relationship with Brenda, has counted for nothing.

'Al, will you ring our insurance broker, Dennis, and say he's needed urgently?' Nicola requests. Without facing her, I agree and then make contact. Although it's late, he promises to be here shortly.

'The Dali is worth a few million,' Nicola informs. Grant watches her closely.

'Do you want to make everyone a drink, Al?'

Cheeky bitch I'm not skivvying for her.

The police don't respond to her offer of refreshments.

Through the front window, a rowdy Friday night atmosphere is seen amongst young revellers walking past.

Near the T-junction, a short distance away, there's a strong police presence.

'What's happening there?' I draw the scene to the officers' attention.

Brevitt takes the floor: 'It's the end result of our surveillance work. Obviously, not much can be said, but we've been watching a building.'

Being a no-bullshit type of man, he speaks clearly and confidently. 'Criminal activity has been taking place there and we're raiding it. The operation is now complete.'

Hearing that Greasby hasn't been watched, Nicola is ignited and punches the air. 'Yes. Yes. Yes!'

Frankie leaps to his feet and tries to hug Brevitt who scrambles out of the way. A chase ensues until both men spill to the floor. Frankie smothers him with kisses. The DI is horrified, believing he's been snogged by an alien.

'We've never done anything wrong,' Frankie claims vocally. 'Never. Never.'

Father and daughter crazily skip round the gallery holding hands until squeezing each other tightly. Grant indicates to her colleague that his face is smeared with pink lipstick. Swiftly, it's wiped away.

Nicola explains that besides the Dali, a number of pictures from the vault have been stolen. A few artists' names are mentioned, though mean nothing to the police. I hope they're wondering how she's managed to inspect the vault so soon and list the missing items.

Before arriving here, the detectives may have considered an art theft to be a pleasant break from chasing armed robbers, drug dealers or people smugglers. Something out of the ordinary. They're mistaken. Nicola is a criminal the same as the rest. Please, drag her away in handcuffs for further questioning. Greasby ought to be rid of her forever.

When Nicola says a Henri Gaudier-Brzeska drawing has been taken, Frankie sparks to life again.

'The work is superb, the economy of line sumptuous. The artist died in the First World War when only 23. He was a beautiful young man. Ken Russell's film *Savage Messiah* about his life, is sensational. Tears could be shed forever over the talent we lost.'

Nicola moves with confidence and arrogance. She's keen for me to underline the importance and value of the stolen pictures. It's explained I know very little about the Dali or its provenance. I won't be part of this charade. My company role is played down and it's added that I'm only working for Greasby three days a week. This enables me to concentrate on painting. Nicola struggles to contain her anger.

'Have any of those daft Modern Art pictures been taken?' sneers Brevitt. 'Pictures that could be hung upside down and you wouldn't know.'

I hurl a disdainful look in his direction. People with knowledge in their own subject often believe they possess the ability to express opinions on others. Invariably, they talk crap.

Jeddy and Juddy have obviously carried out the burglary and retrieved the fake Dali. I expect the pictures Nicola sold from the vault will be on a list presented to the insurers for compensation. An outrageous sum for the items will be sought. Claiming for the vault pictures is clever. Her best scam to date, providing she's not sussed. I can't help but recall Annabel's earlier comment about the butt plug and struggle to stop myself grinning.

It's disgusting that Jane and her sons are involved with the Dali scam. They've betrayed me. Has Jane been promised a percentage of the insurance cash for the Dali? Maybe. Will she blackmail Nicola for more money? Very likely.

The building's alarm system wasn't activated by the intruders. Nicola is ready with an explanation when questioned.

'Obviously a malfunction. Even if it had gone off, who reacts to burglar alarms these days? People run a mile when they hear one.'

The DI looks at her hard. Avoiding his scrutiny, she's well-rehearsed and prepared. It's nauseating. Annabel should have a great acting career if she performs to the same standard as her mother tonight.

The burglar alarm is connected to a control centre. I'm the named person for contact in the event that the alarm is activated. I state nobody has been in touch.

Nicola is lost for words. I hope the two officers try to establish a relationship between the facts and what she's spouting.

When approaching the building a few minutes earlier, I noticed the exterior security lights and CCTV cameras were switched off. Did they malfunction? No. Nicola worked hand-in-hand with Jeddy and Juddy to engineer this situation. Why did she want to contact them earlier? Observing the surveillance car parked nearby put their planned operation under threat. Its absence gave them the green light.

I feel at odds with myself. Hopefully, our insurers will reject any claim. I'm exhausted and in no mood for Nicola's shenanigans. At the earliest opportunity I'm gone.

Nicola believes Frankie's appearance, along with that of Robbi and Denny, is jarring with the police and undermining her performance. A brazen display of hedonism isn't what they want to see.

'Can't you clear off, dad? You're no use here.'

Frankie ignores her.

'Not so fast.' Brevitt raises a protesting hand. 'We want to question you both, but separately.'

Our attention is interrupted by a group of pissed-up lads outside, swigging from cans of beer. In their teens and 20s, they're heading to a nearby nightclub. Arrogantly, one ducks under the police tape. He holds out a polystyrene takeaway box containing a lump of dog shit.

'Is this Modern Art?' he shouts derisively. 'Want to stick it in your posh gallery window? Only fifty grand.'

Throwing the box at the window, his mates laugh and record the gesture on mobiles. This sums up Joe Public's attitude towards art. Shallow and uneducated.

Amused, Brevitt stands up. The lads unzip their trousers, pleasure themselves and hurl abuse. 'Wankers, wankers, wankers.'

A uniformed officer steps outside. 'On your way, lads. Don't cause any trouble.'

Grant has continually looked over and smiled. There's been mutual gazing between us. She's unimpressed by Nicola's performance and obviously regards Frankie as a weirdo.

'You can go, Mr Cooper,' she begins. 'We know it's your first day back home after your ordeal. It might be necessary to speak with you again over the next few days.'

# Chapter 35

At 11 am the next day, Saturday, a journey to see Brenda begins. I'm curious to hear what major role is planned for me. She lives at Banton Hall, built during the 1860s in an Italianate style by one of her ancestors. Palatial and sumptuous are the only words to describe the property inside and out.

Designed by a well-known architect, Banton Hall is arguably one of his best works. Set in a 30,000-acre estate, the house has two storeys, boasts 35 rooms, is built in limestone and has a tiled roof. Brenda has spent her entire life there. It's well-maintained. This is where I belong, on a country estate, and soaking up the atmosphere will be a privilege.

Driving down a tree-lined avenue, I notice ride-on lawn mowers at work with female drivers astride. More women manicure the formal gardens. Annually, these win awards. The women wave a friendly hello as I head towards the Hall. Placed in the grounds are life-sized white marble statues of attractive young females posing provocatively.

At the front of the Hall, I park alongside two Range Rovers, a Bentley convertible and vans belonging to decorators and carpet-fitters. The smell of freshly cut grass assails my nostrils. So does the fragrance of colourful flowers in seasonal plantings and displays. For a few minutes, I take in the romantic view of the formal gardens. What a beautiful tranquil setting.

Brenda's mates, Deb, Ellen, Jen and Barb rush outside. Alarmingly, they're wearing blue-and-white butcher's aprons and brandishing long knives.

Aware of the recent ordeal, they welcome me with wide grins and loud cheers. They even put down the knives and clap.

'Great to see you, Al,' all chorus. Each one shakes my hand

and gives a hug. Surprisingly, they scoop me up to shoulder height. Punk singer, Jen, leads them in a tribute ditty.

*What a man, what a man, what a man.*
*We are dykes but we love you.*
*What a man, what a man, what a man.*
*We are dykes but we'll fuck you.*
*We are dykes but we'll fuck you.*

Brenda emerges from the Hall and is amused. She's wearing a light-blue silk blouse, black trousers and light-blue high heels. Like the others, she too has a butcher's apron and holds a long knife.

'Put him down,' she scolds. 'Put him down. Show respect. He's the perfect man. Doesn't want to fuck anybody.'

Immediately, I notice she's lost weight and radiates a positive self-image.

'What's going on?' I enquire. 'Why are you all dressed like this?'

'Waiting for a delivery,' Brenda answers. 'And here it is. Are you ready, ladies?'

Two Range Rovers stop. Deb, Ellen and Barb nip into the Hall and come out with video cameras.

'What's happening, Brenda?'

'Ellen is making a video for her website, FEAR. Deb and Barb help her. Fear is part of sexual excitement. Castration is Ellen's subject today. FEAR is a subscription site accessed all over the world. It makes Ellen a fortune.'

My idea of working for Brenda is falling apart.

Emerging from the vehicles are eight burly women, flaunting dyed and cropped haircuts. Devoid of make-up, their attire includes dungarees, denim shorts, leather shorts and combat boots. All sport armbands incorporating the letters WLA. Several swig cans of strong lager. Two wear knuckle-dusters. With cold eyes, they epitomise the word scary. Having arrived at Brenda's, every woman punches the air and give each other high fives.

Two gagged and bound trans men, their dresses torn, are

hauled from the vehicles.

A few women bend down and taunt them. 'You fucking sissies. Sissies. Sissies. Sissies.'

Both men, white with fear, sweat and tremble.

Three cameras move in close to record their expressions and restricted movements. The men are kicked and punched. Their faces show cuts, swollen eyes and bloody noses. One cowers and tumbles over, revealing French knickers, stockings and suspenders. The other is wearing a white dress now splattered with blood. They struggle on the ground like fish out of water. Desperately wanting to take flight, there's no chance.

Jen leaps in front of them clutching a guitar with a plug-in amplifier. She plays loud, choppy guitar riffs, improvising a song in her monotonous Punk style.

*We're gonna cut your dick and balls off.*
*Dick and balls off. Dick and balls off.*
*We're gonna cut your dick and balls off.*
*You'll not like it. You'll not like it.*

'What happens after the men are filmed?' I ask.

No one answers.

Two of the WLA women move uncomfortably close. In their late 30s, they give flat, dead stares. One's head is shaved and a leather collar punctured with spikes circles her neck. Razor blades drip from her ear lobes. The other woman has garish sunglasses and spiky facial piercings. Besides the WLA armbands, they have military stripes.

The first woman has BULLY flashing in neon above her head. Grabbing my throat, she shouts: 'Hello, Mr Wimp. I'm going to enjoy hurting you.'

She has filthy teeth, with a front tooth protruding in an ugly way beyond the other.

'Stop, Sergeant. It's okay.' Brenda steps forwards and shoulder-charges the woman away. Deb restrains the other.

'Al is my best friend,' continues Brenda. 'He's the only man I trust.'

I move back. 'Who are these women, Brenda?'

'The Women's Liberation Army.'

'I'd like to have a quiet chat.'

'So would I. But later.'

The two men are dragged towards the Hall's entrance.

Brenda recognises my concern. 'Trans men love this, Al. They've starred in Ellen's videos. Loads of good reviews are left on the website.'

Brenda angles her long knife at the men's faces and lower regions. Their eyes bulge with terror.

Two of the WLA women strap on dildos, remove the men's gags and ram the protrusions into their mouths.

Laughing, Brenda bends down to one of them. 'Enjoying yourself, sweetie?'

Although given the opportunity to speak, he screams at me instead: 'Help. Please help. They'll kill us. A trans mate was murdered last week.'

Brenda and the others split their sides laughing. They insert the gags back in the mens' mouths.

Springing to mind is the information mentioned by Dick and Paul in the cemetery: '...another tranny has been found dead with dick and bollocks stuffed in his mouth.'

'I loathe trans men,' Brenda barks in her fast talking and intimidating voice. 'We don't want fake women in our ranks.'

'Live and let live,' I offer.

'No,' shoots Brenda. 'In titillating frilly frocks, they portray the wrong image of women. We're enjoying a new identity.'

The Hall's entrance opens to a large, circular reception area. Paintings of explicit lesbian sex, painstakingly executed, adorn the walls. A scene in a large colourful cartoon dates from the late Victorian period. It depicts mermaids performing various crazy sex acts.

Illuminated rotating display cases house lesbian erotica. One example is a blow-up sex-ball with realistic vibrating dildo.

The trans men are pulled inside.

I watch in astonishment as uniformed female servants and cleaners don't react while performing their daily chores.

Adopting a similar disinterest are female carpet-fitters and decorators, busy in two separate rooms leading from the reception area.

Do these people know what's going on?

'Real drama must be injected into your work, Al. Down in the torture chamber, you'll be inspired.'

'I'm not bothered Brenda. Can we arrange another meeting?'

'No. I insist you see what's happening.'

On the walls leading to the chamber are slogans.

*PAIN IS REAL. ENJOY IT.*

*SAY GOODBYE TO YOUR DICK AND BOLLOCKS.*

*YOU WILL NOT LEAVE HERE ALIVE.*

The two men are bumped feet-first down the staircase. Ellen keenly videos every detail and from all conceivable angles.

A cleaner on the stairs wears a skimpy uniform and polishes a brass rail. In her early 20s, she looks Swedish. Her long blonde hair is tied up at the back and hangs down in a pony tail. No reaction is offered as we brush past.

Inside the spacious chamber, huge video screens show scenes inside an abattoir. Pigs, cows and lambs are slaughtered. The pigs screech horrendously. It's deafening. Close-ups show glee splashed across slaughtermen's faces.

The trans men are thrown on separate tables and tightly held down. One bloke's eyeballs almost pop out of his head. The other's flash at me, imploring 'this is not pleasure.'

Gags are removed and genitals exposed. Women sharpen long knives in front of them. A stink reveals both men have shit themselves. Cameras close in for facial reactions.

Deb and Ellen laugh manically.

Jen sings another ditty.

*Now, we've got you.*

*Now we've got you.*

*You'll not like it.*

*You'll not like it.*

Sickened, I don't want to witness what might happen. If these men die, I could be an accessory.

'This isn't for me, Brenda.'

I hurry to the stairs.

She laughs. 'Calm down, Al. Men enjoy fear. For them, it's orgasmic.'

Words fail to form.

'At university, I worked during the evenings as a dominatrix.' Her eyes brighten. 'Men loved it and paid well. Some still contact me, even now.'

Together, we retrace our steps to the ground floor. I gasp for air. Will those trans men be murdered like the others? This can't be happening.

'My dad dragged me down there when I was a teenager,' Brenda confesses. 'He attempted conversion therapy. Butchers came brandishing sharp knives. My clothes were ripped off and I was fastened down with legs wide apart. They cut my tits until I promised to fuck men instead of women.'

She removes the apron, unbuttons the blouse and unfastens a full-cup bra.

I wince in horror. 'Those lacerations weren't visible when you stripped off in the gallery.'

'I use cosmetic scar make-up.'

'How could a parent do that?'

'Mother watched and often yelled: "get a proper trouser snake up you. Not a fucking rubber one".'

'Awful.'

'At school, I was Head Girl and academically brilliant. It counted for nothing with mum and dad. The butchers raped me regularly.' Slowly, the blouse is fastened. 'That lasted until I went to university.'

Her face is tear-streaked.

Feeling distressed, my breathing is irregular.

'I cried and cried while being abused.'

'Brenda, there's no doubt you've had an awful childhood, but I must go.'

'We're visiting the new Lesbian Art Museum. There's lots to discuss. And, I have a confession to make. Before that, I'd like to show you what's been sent in the post.'

Walking into an office, she picks up an effigy resembling her as a dominatrix. It's slashed and covered in red paint.

'Look at these letters.' She holds them in front of me. 'They're vicious death threats. I'm convinced everything is from that Russian cunt, Y.'

'Do you employ a security team?'

'The WLA provide protection day and night.'

# Chapter 36

The Lesbian Art Museum is spectacular and wildly eccentric. It comprises a huge vagina-shaped entrance, and six domes. These resemble breasts and include prominent nipples. Brenda parks her Range Rover near the entrance, alongside vans belonging to contractors and individuals working on the building.

'I thought there was a planning permission problem with the entrance, Brenda?'

'Yes, but I challenged the planning committee chairperson, a Mrs Satterthwaite. I said the building would be devoted to women. That did the trick. She's recently divorced. I also arranged for a heating engineer to sort her out. She likes a good fuck. He's over six feet tall and 18 stones. A monster.'

A bus pulls up nearby and a gaggle of beautiful young girls file out of the vehicle. A few are dressed in basques, stockings and suspenders and uplift bras. There are also the predictable outfits worn by nuns, nurses and French chambermaids.

'It's sex bonus day,' reveals Brenda. 'If we achieve construction targets, one is staged every month. Working girls treat both men and women to sex. Everyone is encouraged to live out their wildest fantasies. I want us to watch the bonus day kicking off to a good start.'

For years, I was involved in trade union activity, regradings, disciplinary hearings and bonus schemes. But a bonus scheme like this. Unimaginable.

Once inside the building, the site boss, Kimmy, affectionately embraces Brenda.

'You look brilliant,' gushes Kimmy.

'I try my best.'

'You're a dynamo, and a way of life.'

Embarrassed, Brenda sneaks a glance at me.

An army of men and women are involved with jobs on both the exterior and interior. The project is progressing rapidly. I'm impressed.

Everyone downs tools as the working girls swarm in. All eagerly discard their clothing. Beds, tables and low-level seating are brought out and the bizarre bonus day begins. Each person glows from anticipation. With the exception of Brenda, I feel like the only sober person in a building full of drunks.

One naked working girl giggles as squirty cream sprays on her. Two electricians greedily attack it with lizard tongues. A female plumber enjoys oral sex. Two women are applauded as they scissor each other. Seven contractors choose a girl for a gang bang, then squabble over the running order.

'Are you joining in the fun, Brenda?' one female electrician asks.

'Not today. I've brought a friend along to discuss business.'

The scenes evolving are staggering.

'In a few minutes, Al, this place will resemble Das Sexhaus.' Brenda shouts to be heard over excited voices.

On a tour of the building, Brenda says the interior is to embrace a number of subjects. Besides the well-equipped and climate-controlled galleries, other areas will feature aspects concerning vaginas and breasts.

'Women have been generous, pouring millions into this project,' she boasts. 'It's been incredible. I've hardly spent any money myself.'

Also shown is a spacious basement, fitted with roller racking, ready to accommodate the reserve collection. Art by females has been donated from across the world.

'If we're overwhelmed with pictures and sculptures, another store can be built.'

We stroll into a room earmarked as the curator's office and stand a few feet apart.

'This is your office, Al. You can be in charge. It's a new and exciting challenge. Of course, your appointment is bound to court controversy. A man running a female venture. Personally, I couldn't give a shit. The job has a generous salary.'

What is happening in the torture chamber? Can I ignore those disturbing scenes and work for Brenda? I feel queasy.

'Don't you want to be the curator, Brenda?'

'No. Other things are on my mind.'

I'm intrigued.

'Another building is planned nearby to house The Brenda Fitch Foundation. To gather and administer funds in support of female aspirations in sport, politics, art and music. Already, breathtaking sums have been promised. I envisage a peaceful revolution. Women deserve more encouragement. Much more. Similar foundations could be established across the world.'

'A great idea.'

'Will you accept the curator's job, Al?'

This is unexpected. 'I'll certainly give it thought. Frankie wants to know if you'll take over Greasby.'

'Yes, of course.'

It's a surprise she's agreed so easily.

'Bring Frankie here. I can have fun with him.'

'Okay.'

'Nicola won't be retained.'

'Agreed.'

Brenda is direct: 'I want to find my stolen pictures, Al. The ones bought from the Schmidts and Kirstin. I want them. Desperately.' She stamps a foot. 'Everyone is convinced Y stole them. They're needed for the building's grand opening. That's going to happen very soon. Kirstin and Anna are helping already.'

'I'll do whatever I can.'

'Help me out, Al. I can arrange exhibitions for you in London, New York and Paris. Or wherever you want. Organise publicity, lectures, whatever is necessary. Finance is no problem.'

'Thanks, Brenda.' I'm buzzing with excitement.

'Have you had any dealings with Y lately?'

'He says we should work together. Hang out with each other.

Go fishing.'

'Perfect. Absolutely perfect. It fits in with my plans. I've discussed them with Kirstin and Anna. Where's he based? Germany? Russia?'

'Haven't a clue.'

'Accept his invitation. The WLA will accompany you. Bring him back here. I need to know what's happened to my pictures.'

'No, Brenda. I'm not risking my life.'

She tuts and clenches her hands into fists.

'Why not beat information out of Nicola?'

'I want Mr Russian Cunt back here.'

Asking me to find and liaise with Y is mind-blowing. I'm an art historian not a sleuth or bounty hunter.

'Why not seize Y yourself?'

'It needs to be you.'

'I could be killed. How can you make such a suggestion? No way, Brenda. Not interested. If that's a condition of my employment, forget it. I'll leave now.'

## Chapter 37

The two-mile journey back to Banton Hall begins in silence. Then, Brenda is made aware of my plan to meet with Askworth police.

'What for?'

'To tell them of Nicola's insurance scam. And the stolen pictures from Y.'

'You could be implicated.'

'Not if I tell the truth.'

'That's madness.'

'I must do things legally. It may lead to finding your pictures.'

'We need to take matters into our own hands,' she declares forcefully. 'The police couldn't give a shit about art. They'll play dirty tricks. Might even pin a charge on you. When reporting my mum and dad's abuse, they laughed. Dismissed me as a lying dyke.'

'I need to distance myself from Greasby's criminality.'

'Have you told the police about Y?'

'No.'

'Keep it like that.'

'The police should know Greasby is part of an international crime syndicate.'

'Keep quiet. We can handle this ourselves.'

Brevitt's stupid Modern Art comment is brought to mind. Admittedly, I have reservations. Police officers aren't culturally aware or sympathetic towards the arts. It's never comfortable to concede, but Jess was right. Art has long since lost touch with the common man and woman.

We pass a marked police car partially concealed in a field entrance. Both male and female officers are outside the vehicle smoking crack.

Brenda points at them. 'The police are corrupt and incompetent. What chance have you, opening your soul to them?'

I feel deflated.

'Sorry, Al. Didn't mean to snap.'

She chews on her thumbnail, then says softly: 'There's a confession to make and I'm not sure how you'll take it.' Uncharacteristically, she's nervous, running sweaty palms on the steering wheel.

'Leave it, Brenda. I must go home.' I can't take another shock.

'It has to be said today.' She fidgets uneasily, adjusting the seat belt.

Back at Banton Hall, a drinks party is underway on a lawn adjacent. Those present include Deb, Jen, Barb and Ellen, plus four of the WLA soldiers. Surprisingly, the two trans men are sipping wine. Two nurses carefully patch up their injuries. The men are participating in an interview with Ellen, whilst Barb videos the conversation. Everyone sits at ornate white garden tables beneath brightly-coloured parasols.

'What's happening now?' I say as we step from the Range Rover. 'Weren't they castrated?'

'Of course not. Trans men contact Ellen and suggest chums who might enjoy a mock castration experience. They pay her thousands. Lots of people are addicted to fear and humiliation.'

'We've great footage, Brenda,' enthuses Ellen. 'Today has been a success.'

'I caught your reaction, Al,' chuckles Ellen, attracting my attention. 'Your terrified look was priceless.'

The trans men laugh heartily.

'I've enjoyed every minute,' one of them admits. 'Took me back to when I was savagely caned at school. I hated it. But enjoyed it too. Fear and sex are inextricably linked. That's definite.'

The men shake hands with Brenda, and warm hugs are

exchanged.

'Sorry, mate, if we alarmed you,' they both confess. 'We thought a weirdo group murdering trans men had caught us.'

It feels like I've been hit by a grenade.

Who is murdering trans men? Is it the WLA?

'Cheer up, Al,' Deb smiles.

The women regard me with compassion before breaking into song once again.

*What a man, what a man, what a man.*
*We are dykes but we love you.*
*What a man, what a man, what a man.*
*We are dykes but we'll fuck you.*
*We are dykes but we'll fuck you.*

Jen accompanies them with lazy guitar chords.

Embarrassed, I want to disappear.

'You must be more open-minded, Al,' charms Jen.

'I'm going home, Brenda.'

Staring at me seriously, her head moves slowly from side-to-side. Holding hands, we enter the Hall and stroll into a spacious high-ceilinged salon. It's painted throughout in a faux marble effect and littered with antiques and furniture. Invading the décor are erotic lesbian paintings and sculptures.

Brenda closes the salon doors, faces away from me and bows her head. Faint laughter from the drinks party outside is discernible. Barely audible too, are the sounds of vacuuming and carpet-fitters at work.

'Brenda. What's wrong?'

She's weeping.

'Brenda?'

No answer.

I don't move. Never seen her like this before. Tears are not Brenda. It's unbelievable. As a trade union officer, I often dealt with men and women sobbing. My reaction, then as now, is to listen and show compassion.

'Brenda. Talk to me.'

Slowly, she turns. Her face is red and blotchy. The eyes

bloodshot and eyelids puffy. We stare at each other for what seems like an age.

'This is so difficult to say, Al.'

'Go on. Tell me what's on your mind.'

'I can't.'

Brenda's confidence has crumpled.

'I'm in love,' her voice cracks. 'I'm in love with you, Al.'

Another shock.

She throws her arms over me. 'I never ever thought I would love a man. But it's happened.'

I'm held tightly.

'It was devastating when your son's shrine was wrecked.' She sniffles and dabs her nose with a handkerchief. 'I wanted to give you another son. Have your baby. You're such a beautiful man. I'll organise fresh flowers to be put on his grave regularly.'

Blushing at her comments, I've never felt such confidence in me from a woman.

Brenda relaxes her grip, eyes wide with enthusiasm. 'I've never been moved in such a good way by a man.' She continues to hold me. 'I'm not sure what kind of love it is, only feel it strongly. It burns fiercely inside.'

Is this a minor breakdown after losing her pictures? I don't think so. My appeal to her is unclear. No attempt is made to kiss me. I don't ponder on whether a lesbian can love a man or not. It's simply an individual showing love for someone else, regardless of sexual preference. That's how it should be.

Mascara trickles down her face. Her heart pounds.

'I'm extremely flattered, Brenda.'

I believe her love is genuine and without an ulterior motive – to ensnare Y.

'How has Deb reacted?'

'We've had a long chat and she's cool about everything. You're a great man, and she wants me to be happy.'

Already, I'm contemplating, can Brenda's love be accepted and reciprocated? I admire her energy. Always have done. She's certainly different from boring museum and art gallery women. But is that enough?

Unnervingly, she continues to cry.

'My father was a monster. I assumed all men were like him. You're everything a man should be.'

'I'm overwhelmed, Brenda.'

'Do you think you could love me, Al? Do you love me already?'

'This is unexpected.'

'I'm not pressing for a physical relationship,' she confesses.

A healthy relationship involves honesty, trust, respect and open communications between partners. All of that is witnessed here.

'I know what you're thinking. Can a dyke change her spots? Yes, she can. Deb and I haven't had sex for weeks. I'm not the first lesbian to love a man. And won't be the last. Don't think you are my substitute dad. You're not.'

Usually, a love confession happens after physical entanglement. This is entirely different.

'Move to Banton, Al. I want to share everything with you.' Her voice is smooth, and not battering everyone's ears as it often does. What a complex woman she is, and yes, I could grow to like her. Even love her.

Our embrace subsides and we gently sink into a comfy, gold upholstered sofa. Slowly, she drapes an arm round me, removes it, then tightly holds my left hand. These movements are timidly repeated.

'There's no need for a silly engagement ring or to get married. I want you as an equal partner.'

I smile affectionately, feeling her love.

'Observing you has encouraged a change of lifestyle. I decided to have a pure interest in art, and a healthy, honest outlook on life.'

Embarrassed, it's difficult to face her.

She presses ahead: 'You've the capability to view the world from different angles. Through the eyes of different people.

That's wonderful.'

Never has a woman declared her love for me first. It's always been the other way. And, that's only happened once before. I thought my wife would be my first and last love. That's turning out not to be the case.

Squeezing my left hand, she's keen to hold my attention.

'I want a new life. I want to spend it with you. For months, I've been hurtling towards a heart attack or another serious illness. A stroke or liver failure. I constantly binged on sex, then ice cream. Addiction is a mood shift. It was a desperate attempt to escape childhood horrors. I've done 12-step programmes. I wanted to complete them before making my confession to you. The female cause and lesbian art still need to be promoted. I'm passionate about both.'

The tears have dried up. Her voice is strong and unbroken. She's ultra-focused.

'There have been multiple addictions but I'm now in control. I have my life back.'

'Well done, Brenda.'

'I've not been stupid and become a religious Jesus freak. I've beaten addictions and standing on my own two feet. I'm very optimistic about us, Al. Everything here can go on as normal. We can have our own life together.'

We hold on to each other. I always thought she was hotheaded with a blow-torch mouth. Now, she's a romantic with a huge heart.

'I'll give you a tour of the Hall. There are rooms and a studio you can use. Move in straightaway, or take a few days to gather your thoughts. I don't mind.'

My dream of living in a country house is becoming a reality. 'I've plenty of ideas, Brenda.'

'Tell me.'

'Besides skeleton pictures, I want to depict heavy goods vehicles transforming into boxers. Fighting in the middle of motorways. Trains metamorphosing into snakes and coiling together.'

'Brilliant.' She now weeps tears of joy.

This is heady stuff. A tidal wave of optimism washes over me.

'I've never felt so happy, Al.'

'Neither have I, Brenda.'

# Chapter 38

Over the weekend, I stay with Brenda at Banton Hall. She's pleased my reaction was favourable to her declaration of love. Prior to the announcement, she'd been a psychological trainwreck.

On Saturday night, we talk for hours on many subjects but especially art. She fully supports my skeleton and other ideas. We order large reproductions of three pictures by James Ensor, *Skeletons Fighting over a Hanged Man*, *Skeletons Fighting over a Pickled Herring,* and *Skeletons Warming Themselves*. Edward Burra's *Dancing Skeletons* is also purchased. They will be framed to hang in my new studio.

On Sunday, we shop and buy plenty of art materials. Brenda treats me to items of clothing. At night, we dine in an exclusive restaurant, then sleep in separate beds. We've a genuine relationship – or perhaps partnership – where the usual troubles arising over the frequency of sex, and money worries, are absent. She's fun, outgoing and supportive.

The running of the Arnold Fitch Corporation has been handed over to Deb, who is the new chairperson. Brenda said the concern embraces a worldwide property portfolio that earns billions. It's how she finances a lavish lifestyle. Deb shall be assisted, where necessary, by Barb and Jen. Each has an important role to play. I'd no idea of the size of the operation. Not a clue.

Brenda wants to step aside from business to encourage my work and be together as a couple. It's flattering. I insist whatever is earned from my art, we must share. I'm lucky to have such a good and sympathetic partner.

The upkeep of the Hall is relentless. An army that includes gardeners, plumbers, heating engineers, electricians and house cleaners is regularly called upon. Brenda follows her father's example. He always kept the Hall well-maintained.

There's no intention of taking advantage of Brenda's kindness. Sensing I'm a little nervous of her generosity, she tells me to 'relax and fall in with life at Banton.' I've even met with the cook to work out a menu for myself.

Early on Monday morning, I leave Banton. My own house needs to be put in order. Speaking with Frankie, he's overjoyed when informed Brenda will buy Greasby.

Today, I want to contact Detective Sergeant Sybil Grant. Brenda and I have discussed this at length. Although still arguing the move is foolish, she says it's ultimately up to me. She remains supportive.

I'm keen to help Brenda find her stolen pictures. Hopefully, meeting the police will be a step in the right direction. Whilst there's little evidence to present, the search needs to be carried out legally. Brenda has shown me commitment. I must do the same for her.

Mid-day, Jane calls. 'Hi, Al. Apologies for missing you on Friday night.'

I tread carefully. 'Sorry to hear about the Dali drawing.'

'What do you mean?'

'I thought it was stolen.'

'No, it's here in front of me. I'm admiring the fantastic imagery now.'

A awkward silence falls for a few seconds.

'Why did the wimp ring, mum?' says one of the twins in the background.

'Quiet, Juddy.'

'Bit of a nosy cunt,' whispers Jeddy.

Jane raises her voice: 'Are you okay, Al, after that awful burglary?'

'I'm coping.'

'Make contact if you feel a chat may be helpful.'

'Thank you.'

'Okay, Al. Have to go. Another call is coming through.'

Details of the Dali scam won't be revealed. I can't implicate Jane and her two sons. Much as I'm hurt by the betrayal and the comments overheard. I contemplated enlisting Jeddy and Juddy to help locate Brenda's pictures. Not now. I would've been upset if Alex had grown up like them. They're yobs. I intend to divulge information to the police about Nicola and Y's activities. That'll be done without a second thought.

It's a surprise that Jonty has not emailed photos of the lesbian picture and George Grosz watercolour that were promised on Friday afternoon.

'Nicola has sold the pictures,' he responds when I telephone. 'A bloke came for them on Sunday afternoon.'

'What did he look like?'

'A typical collector.'

'Was he caught on the security cameras?'

'No, they're not working. Nicola won't pay the monthly charges.'

'Marvellous.'

A police officer needs to listen seriously to my claims about the robberies. Perhaps Sybil Grant is that person. If I'm wrong, I shall reconsider meeting Y. Could I meet him? With the Women's Liberation Army? I can't disappoint Brenda.

I contact Askworth police station and speak to Sybil. Brenda told me to be careful over what is revealed to the police. I agreed.

'Do you have further information about Friday night's robbery?' Sybil prompts.

'No.'

'Why have you called?' The remark is a little off-hand.

'Nicola and Frankie are involved with international art theft.'

'If you're reporting a major crime,' she's quick to point out, 'the proper procedures need to be followed. Detectives from our intelligence unit will ring you.'

'Today?'

'Yes.'

Although disappointed by the cold response, maybe it was predictable.

Two male intelligence officers agree to meet at 6 pm. After busying myself through the afternoon, I drive to an abandoned pub car park. Other vehicles are taking advantage of the free parking. One officer phones to reveal they're in a saloon behind me. An instruction is given to join them and I climb into the back seat, snapping on the seat belt. This is cloak-and-dagger stuff.

In their early 30s, both are well-built, at least six feet tall, and with short hair. Casually dressed, they're in sweatshirts, blue jeans and slip-on shoes. A friendly smile is offered to them. It's not reciprocated. There's stony silence. Shaking my hand firmly, they introduce themselves as detectives Dewhurst and Carmody. Dewhurst has a blob nose and is behind the wheel. His partner has no distinguishing facial features. Nobody takes any notice as we pull away.

I'm apprehensive. Neither officer explains where we're going. Leaning forwards to attempt general chit-chat, there's no response. In the rear-view mirror, Dewhurst's eyes move slowly.

The car noses sluggishly through early evening traffic.

'Do you take drugs?' Dewhurst jabs, catching me unawares.

'No, of course not.'

'If you had a drugs test, would it be positive or negative?' stings Carmody.

'Negative.'

'Ever experimented with drugs?' Dewhurst is antagonistic.

'No.'

'Frankie Greasby has been arrested for possessing coke,' he continues. 'Are you telling the truth?'

'I can give you coke dealers' names.'

'A proper little snitch, aren't you?' Carmody scoffs.

We swerve dramatically and mount the pavement to avoid a head-on collision.

A car hurtles past in a hail of sparks. One of the front tyres is missing. Driving is a kid no more than 14. A liveried police car is in pursuit and the blues are flashing. For a few seconds the monotonous 'woo-woo-woo-woo-woo' sound deafens.

These two don't impress me. They're humourless and the lack of communication is unsettling. Will the robbery details be taken seriously? Could they think my evidence is insignificant? Might something be pinned on me? Good job I'm with Brenda. If anything untoward happens, she will bail me out. Hopefully.

Speak, I'd like to say. I don't want to hear any details of the cases you're investigating. But, what about some friendly banter?

We arrive in Allwood, a dodgy area awash with violent gangs. Dewhurst manoeuvres into the car park at Allwood Farm, a family pub-cum-restaurant. The building is ten years old and situated on the site of a former factory. There are other similar restaurants belonging to the parent company's chain in Askworth. I've never been to this one before. An impressive property, it has spacious living quarters above. Curiously, all the curtains in there are closed.

The car park is half full. A few new cars are spotted, though most are two or three years old. Some even older. There's a sprawling modern housing estate nearby. It contains three- or four-bedroomed detached properties, semi-detached dwellings and a sprinkling of so-called affordable housing.

Two vehicles sit closely in the restaurant's car park. Each has four occupants. From the LED lights hidden in both vehicles' front grilles, they can be identified as unmarked police cars. Walking past, Dewhurst and Carmody acknowledge officers inside.

'Why are they here?' I ask.

Neither answers. Both take note when a well-dressed middle-aged man slips from the restaurant's side entrance adjusting his clothing. He doesn't look at us, hops into a new Mercedes and hurries away.

'Dirty bastard,' jibes Dewhurst.

'I wonder how many slags work here?' Carmody whispers to his mate as they glance upwards.

Inside, the restaurant is packed. There's a good wholesome

family atmosphere. This type of building has replaced the men-only traditional alehouse. They're a breath of fresh air. Customers here today are down-to-earth working class people. Many are employed in Askworth's service industries or at local distribution centres. All eat, drink, chat happily and joke amongst themselves. Men sport shaved heads or silly hair styles. Women have made attempts to reel back the years with dyed hair cut trendily.

Food is ordered at the bar, for the carvery, or chosen from a menu. The carvery offers appetising meat options, turkey, gammon, beef and pork. I notice a good selection of vegetables and potatoes. Piping-hot gravy suits both ordinary and vegetarian tastes.

'Cut the meat thick,' one bloke presses the carvery chef.

'Put another slice on my plate,' a woman demands. The banter is good-natured.

'You'll get me the sack,' the chef retorts, but adheres to both requests.

After a hard day's work, each customer, male or female, is ravenous. They pile food high on plates, eager to have value for money.

The two detectives aren't hungry but order soft drinks for themselves and me. Not having eaten today, I play safe and order gammon and pineapple from the menu. Near the bar is a dessert and ice-cream counter. It's captured the attention of two children. Their mother orders scoops of coloured flavours for them. They're ecstatic. Is there anything better than seeing kids happy?

A lad in his early 20s, wearing a butcher's apron, wheels in large joints of beef on a rickety trolley.

'Deliveries are at the side, son,' says an annoyed restaurant manager. Balding, small and portly, he's fortyish.

'Nobody answered when I knocked, Mr Brunt,' the lad replies.

Inspecting the size of the joints, Brunt can't resist a quip: 'Fucking hell, any bigger and you want to leave the hooves on and drive them in here.'

Brunt's mates laugh raucously, and so does a woman, obviously his wife. The same age as him, she's fashionably dressed, and has thick dark hair with highlights. Her bushy false eyelashes would suit a drag queen.

Continuing to fancy himself as a comedian, Brunt glances at her, then jokes with his chums. 'She's done well for herself. When we first met, she only had elastic in one knicker leg.'

Dewhurst and Carmody fail to be amused. They regard the couple with disdain.

Brunt hasn't ended his performance. He teases another lad, with piercings, approaching the bar. 'I see you're getting a bit of dress sense, Adrian. Only three curtain hooks through your nose today.'

More laughter from Brunt's mates, as their faces display half-pissed ridiculous expressions.

Although there are happy scenes in the restaurant, I sense unease. A spacious room comprises the main dining area. The three of us sit at a table near the centre but to one side. In front, a window gives a panoramic view of the car park. The two unmarked vehicles are still present.

Occupying tables along the window, are Askworth United striker Jamie Burrows, his family and friends. Amongst them, I easily identify his mother, father, elder brother and younger sister. Two friends furtively snort coke. There's a buoyant, noisy atmosphere. Burrows is the centre of attention and bubbling. He's tanned, well-dressed, has a silly haircut and tattoos. Charged with the manslaughter of a known gang leader, he was acquitted recently. A new and lucrative contract with the football club has now been signed. Perhaps this is a party to celebrate. Young people in Askworth United football shirts ask Burrows to pose for selfies. Readily agreeing, he also signs autographs.

I'm perturbed as Carmody pulls out a voice recorder, places the device in front of me, and switches it on.

'Are you an artist?'

'Yes,' I reply uncomfortably.

'Got any pictures to show us?'

Producing my mobile, examples are shown.

'Why are you painting skeletons?' Dewhurst queries. 'Your pictures are morbid. They won't sell. Pity. You obviously have talent.'

'Art is no use to anybody,' digs Carmody. 'What about the Tate Gallery bricks? A complete con. Like all Modern Art.'

'Didn't one artist ride his bike across a canvas?' goads Dewhurst.

Although baited, I won't bite. That's providing they commit to finding Brenda's stolen pictures.

Dewhurst explains that people giving information to the police must be registered as informants. Before this can happen with me, they need to know if I've anything useful.

'What do you want to tell us?'

'Don't hold anything back,' Carmody declares slowly.

I pause from eating. 'Greasby Fine Art is embroiled in art theft. Stolen pictures from Europe arrive in Askworth. The company is a clearing house for stolen art. And pictures are faked and sold as originals.'

'Forgeries should be dealt with by the Council's Consumer Protection Directorate,' Dewhurst eagerly points out.

Before there's an opportunity to continue, Carmody inches closer. 'Who are the main players in these robberies?'

A nervous glance is made towards the voice recorder. 'Frankie Greasby, his daughter Nicola, her assistant Jess Jones and a Russian called Yaroslav. Though he's known as Y.'

I wait for the names register, though the pair admit they've only heard of Frankie.

'How long has this been going on?' queries Dewhurst in a matter-of-fact way.

'A while.'

He's still inquisitive: 'Why report it now?'

'I don't want to be incriminated, nor do any of the Greasby staff. Stolen works of art show up regularly. People in the art world are talking. The staff and me want to know where we stand.'

'How much money is sloshing about?' Carmody joins in.

'Hundreds of thousands.'

'We hear you're fucking a wealthy dyke. Could some cash fall our way?' Dewhurst smirks.

'Frankie's sorted us out in the past,' divulges Carmody. 'That's how he's dodged drugs charges.'

Police corruption wasn't anticipated.

'Are stolen daubs here now,' Carmody skits.

'Maybe.'

'Where?' They both question.

'Hidden, but I don't know where.'

Both officers tut, and lean back in their seats.

'Are these thefts covered by insurance?' Dewhurst questions with sarcasm.

'Yes.'

'Where's the problem?' Carmody glares at me. 'Nobody is losing anything, except insurance companies.'

'One collector in Germany believes she's lost her children.'

Both groan.

'Pictures mean a lot to some people.'

They repeatedly peer out of the window.

All eight occupants of the police cars are now outside and talking amongst themselves, until slowly easing back inside.

'So, it's only rich collectors losing pictures but claiming heavily on their insurance?' taunts Dewhurst.

These responses are disappointing. I intended telling them about Nicola's thefts from the basement store, but can't be bothered. The information would be met with the same indifference. Brenda's earlier comment has proved correct: 'The police are not interested in art robberies.' I'm not daunted. My priority remains fixed. Locate the pictures. I shall not let her down.

Five waitresses serve food to Burrows and his party. The appetizing aroma of sizzling steak hits my nostrils. The footballer tucks in ravenously.

Carmody stirs: 'Do you hold a grudge against the Greasbys?'

'No.' I try not to feel flustered though it's a struggle.

'Are you on medication following your burglary?' Dewhurst stabs.

'No.'

'Can you describe this Russian?' he continues.

I hesitate, reluctant to divulge information. Who knows where it may lead?

'To me, there's only one way forward,' says Dewhurst with confidence. 'If this man, Z...'

'Y,' I correct him.

'If Y arrives in Askworth delivering stolen pictures, contact us. Immediately. Then, we can react.' He hands over a number to ring.

Outside, a people carrier surges past the window. Within seconds, two young women, shabby and bedraggled, jump out and burst inside.

'Help us!' one yells.

'Please,' shouts the other. 'Please.'

Their eyes reflect fear and desperation.

The entire restaurant falls silent.

Two scruffy men in their 30s dash from the vehicle to grab the women.

Brunt looks worried, so does his wife.

Dewhurst and Carmody rise to their feet.

Rushing to help the women, Dewhurst is stabbed by one of the men.

Women scream, scream, scream, as they drag their children to the floor. Two kids won't abandon their ice creams and remain seated. Brunt's wife attempts to stop the two females escaping, but to no avail. They run away. Brunt sneaks out of view.

People attack the scruffy pair. Bowls of hot gravy are thrown over them. A chef follows through with his long knife.

My attention flits outside. Three males with pistols leap from a car. They're wearing pig masks. Burrows shouts a warning to his entourage. Too late. Each bullet finds a target. Bodies twist in ugly shapes. Both gunmen try to escape, only the unmarked cars hem them in. All eight officers jump out. Further shots are fired and four police are hit.

Emitting ear-piercing shrieks, customers rush to the exits.

Hurrying over to Dewhurst, I'm shivering with shock. Carmody sobs. He's saturated with Dewhurst's blood. We both stare at each other.

'Fuck off, pathetic dickhead. Art is shit.'

# Chapter 39

Newspapers – local and national – plastered front pages with sensational headlines about the restaurant massacre and sex traffickers. Both stories provided easy work for journalists to sink their teeth into. Newspaper front pages are like graffiti shouting from grubby walls.

A massive funeral took place for footballer Jamie Burrows and his family. Thousands of Askworth United fans paid their respects. The Allwood Farm restaurant is closed. A sea of flowers and wreaths swamp the exterior.

Traumatised, I'm slowly recovering. Brenda has helped enormously. We both aid each other. She's shown amazing courage to walk away from her Olympian drug-and-sex excesses. I'm proud of her and support will be offered if she relapses. Cocaine and sex are taboo words, now rarely mentioned. Brenda's hair and appearance are always immaculate. Regular visitors to Banton include nutritionists, hairdressers, beauticians and personal trainers. A gym is installed at the Hall and we both use it.

On an overcast day, we're travelling to Alex's grave. The visit is long overdue. Brenda is driving her Range Rover. Following behind in a similar vehicle is Sergeant and her partner who I call Corporal. Deb, Ellen, Barb and Jen are involved with work at the Arnold Fitch Corporation, the Lesbian Art Museum, organising important Banton estate tasks and overseeing my house renovation.

Sergeant and Corporal once entered the selection process for the SAS and only failed by a small margin. A commendable achievement nonetheless. They formerly held jobs at a security firm, until establishing the WLA. Along with other WLA soldiers, they camp in huts at Banton Hall. All wash themselves, naked and unashamedly, every morning in the open air, then fry bacon and eggs. The aromas waft up to my bedroom.

Having a twisted sense of humour, Sergeant and Corporal often kick each other up the arse or playfully tweak each other's nipples. Both regularly undertake rigorous daily workouts, including running half-marathons over a portion of the Banton estate. They put other WLA soldiers through similar tough training routines on the Hall's lawns.

I've watched Sergeant and Corporal emerge victorious from bare-knuckle fights with local men. They're tough with a capital T. Sergeant is okay with me, only I don't trust her. She reminds me of an Alsatian I frequently encountered years ago when delivering newspapers to a local pub. The landlord often assured his dog was harmless. But I saw a man after being savaged by it. He was a mess. I keep on the right side of Sergeant, sensing she's unpredictable like the Alsatian. Not my kind of person. However, it's acknowledged she and Corporal are necessary for the estate's security. I'd sooner have them on my side than not.

Although capable of handling herself, Brenda has WLA soldiers – mainly Sergeant and Corporal – always present. The day after the restaurant tragedies, a chopped-up effigy of Brenda soaked in blood was received. Attached to it was another vicious homophobic note. Despite being unnerved, she didn't inform the police. The WLA are making their own investigations.

Later today, Frankie is expected at Banton Hall to discuss the sale of Greasby Fine Art. Nicola isn't invited. Whether she knows anything about the impending transaction is unknown. I've insisted Paulene must be part of the negotiations and receive a substantial payment from any settlement.

Both Range Rovers stop outside the cemetery. Brenda wears a black trouser suit and blouse. Both of us have bullet-proof vests beneath our clothing. An imminent attack on one or both of us is feared. I hope that's wrong. Besides wearing similar vests, Sergeant and Corporal have combat jackets, khaki shirts, shorts and berets. Both carry guns. They've established a firing range in a Hall barn. A few weapons are licensed at Banton, but to Brenda, not these two. Carefully scanning the area for snipers, Sergeant and Corporal see nothing. Nevertheless, I'm apprehensive.

The cemetery is under local authority control. Access is gained through an impressive ornamental central entrance. Inside, roads lead to the west and east. The burial ground stretches up an incline, then drops down the other side. A road on the west extends to the apex, where it cuts eastwards and meets a chapel, crematorium and administrative offices. In the middle of this west to east road, there's a group of people. Cemetery officials and staff are present, with an excavator nearby.

Both burials and cremations take place at this site. A hearse and other vehicles are parked near the crematorium. From there, a road drops to an eastern exit.

Compared with the older Askworth cemetery, this new one reveals a noticeable absence of spectacular monuments. There are boring upright gravestones, no more than three or four feet in height, as well as flat tablets, desk tablets, ledger slabs and kerb memorials in granite or marble. Inscriptions are simple with no thought provoking sentiments expressed. Vegetation across the area is minimal though tall trees grow here and there. Bright bursts of colour emanate from flowers left on graves.

Dark clouds sweep overhead and rain starts to fall. It doesn't daunt Brenda and I. We take two umbrellas from the Range Rover's boot. They're with the bouquets of flowers bought along the way. These include white carnations, tulips and irises.

Sergeant and Corporal show no concern about the impending downpour. Moving away in high spirits, they leap-frog over gravestones before rejoining us. Corporal offers to carry the flowers. Bird cheeps and warbles are heard, while squirrels scamper about.

My ex-wife never visits Alex's grave. We almost came to blows about the funeral arrangements. She wanted him cremated. I insisted on a burial and won.

The four of us walk along a central pathway towards Alex's

grave, which is near where people are congregated.

Sergeant looks at tombstones, then hits Brenda with a question: 'Have you seen any inscriptions mentioning a woman and her wife or a woman and her female husband?' She always speaks in a loud voice. This is in contrast to Corporal who talks softly and utters few words.

'Not yet, though I hope we will,' Brenda responds.

'Paint lesbian or gay skeletons in a cemetery scene, Al,' suggests Sergeant.

'How would you tell whether the skeletons are male or female?' I ask.

'Show they still have tits or dicks,' laughs Sergeant, her eyes brightening.

After a short pause, Brenda smiles. 'Are you inspired, Al? Any subjects coming to mind?'

'Yes. I see skeletons exercising. Leap-frogging over tombstones, working on parallel bars, skipping or doing press-ups. As well as involving themselves with boxing, wrestling, playing snooker and darts.'

'Brilliant. You'll have plenty of work for an exhibition.'

It's good that she's easily fallen into my appreciation of James Ensor's jokey skeleton paintings. I want a place in British satirical art alongside Hogarth, Rowlandson, Gillray and Gerald Scarfe – even newspaper cartoonist Giles.

'There's an idea in my head for a night scene showing skeletons relaxing on folding sun loungers,' I reveal to Brenda. 'Wearing shades, they sip drinks and eat crisps. A strong moon pierces the sky. The title is: "Moonbathers".'

More and more, I'm convinced Brenda is good for me. It's relaxing in her company and art ideas flow easily. Never before have I been in such a good relationship with a woman.

Brenda is warned that I always plan to avoid bursting into tears when here in the cemetery. On each visit, I fail miserably. My hand is squeezed in a show of support. 'Do whatever you feel is necessary, Al. Don't be afraid to show emotions. I'm here for you.'

'My ex wife frequently demanded I step away from grief.'

Brenda is tactful: 'She's coping in her own way with the loss. You must do the same and not feel bullied or intimidated.'

A lanky, skinny, middle-aged man suddenly springs from behind a tree and exposes himself.

'Does this interest any of you?' His limp willy is waggled vigorously.

Sergeant is livid and responds with alacrity. 'You fucking weirdo.' Kicking and punching him mercilessly, she then pulls out a flick-knife. 'Fuck off or I'll remove your pathetic little dick. And stuff it in your gob.'

Brenda intervenes. 'Stop, Sergeant, don't attract attention.'

My mobile sounds.

Brenda is shown Y's name illuminated on the screen.

'Don't answer,' she tugs at my arm.

'I've decided to meet him.'

'No.' Snatching the mobile, she mischievously runs off. I chase her.

'I must find the pictures. They're needed for the Museum opening.'

'No, Al. It's too dangerous.'

'We can sort that bastard out,' crows Sergeant.

Brenda ignores the comment, draping her arms across me. 'I don't want to lose you, Al.'

There's almost a kiss.

'We're really good for each other,' she confesses.

I want to respond with words of devotion though feel tongue-tied.

'If it keeps you alive, we should open without the pictures,' pronounces Brenda.

'The launch must be spectacular.'

'Other pictures can be acquired.'

I bask in her warmth.

Y has left a voicemail. Retrieving the message, I switch to loudspeaker and the four of us listen. He expresses concern over the carvery restaurant fiasco. How he knows about that is curious. I'm invited once more to work with him and urged to make contact when convenient.

Sergeant is quick to respond: 'You must, Al. Me and Corporal will go with you.'

Brenda dismisses the idea.

A little way off and up the incline to the right, there's a man who I've often seen before at his wife's grave. In his late 70s, with slicked-back white hair, he's overdressed in a dinner jacket, white wing collar and black bow tie. She died suddenly nine years ago whilst they were dining in an exclusive restaurant. Often, he arrives with a small table, two chairs, a candelabra, food and a bottle of Champagne. Fresh flowers are placed in an urn. Romantic music is played at low volume from a device he's brought along. Opposite him sits an effigy of his wife wearing an evening gown. Eating contentedly, he wants to complete the meal so sadly interrupted. The ritual is carried out regularly.

On the road to the left, a SOCO van and police cars with the blues flashing, head towards the group of people in the centre. The rain is heavy now.

Sergeant sprints up to the grieving old man. 'You fucking weirdo. Want me to wank you off?'

Locked in past memories, oblivious to everything, he ignores her. It makes me realise I'm not the only one who can't put aside the loss of a departed loved one.

Fumbling in the man's trousers, Sergeant attempts to excite him. With shorts dropped, Corporal fondles herself whilst giving a flirty grin.

'What a pathetic bastard,' announces Sergeant. 'His dick and brain are disconnected.'

Interacting with him has blown us off course from Alex's grave. The chapel and crematorium are ahead. My attention focuses on a group of mourners emerging into view. An elderly overweight woman has defied convention and is resplendent in a bright-yellow trouser suit and blouse. A wide-brimmed hat of the same colour sits on top of dyed-blonde shoulder-length hair. By contrast, the other mourners, both male and female, are attired in traditional black suits or dresses, white shirts or blouses. All the men have black ties. Many act awkwardly as though it's the first chance they've had to wear best clothes. Some cry or sniffle and others talk in low voices.

Mrs Yellow remonstrates with the hearse driver who's having trouble starting the vehicle. It's spotlessly clean with gleaming chrome but blocking in the other sleek grey funeral cars and a few mourners' vehicles.

'What the fuck is going on?' she shouts, amidst tears, at the undertaker John Finbow. Wearing a top hat and tails, he's the head of Finbow & Sons, a long-established Askworth family of funeral directors.

'I don't know what's wrong,' he answers. 'I'm an undertaker not a mechanic.' For him, this is embarrassment of the highest order.

'I've lost my husband,' she yells, her face contorted in anger. 'This funeral cost a fortune. I can't deal with a fuck-up.'

'Our mechanic has been called. He won't be long.'

'You fucking idiot.' She slaps Finbow's face, her jewellery glittering. 'I want a refund.'

'We can work something out.'

Mourners' kids are bored and run in between the stranded vehicles playing tiggy.

'You could depict a skeleton mechanic attending to a broken-down hearse,' Brenda hints.

'Two female mourners could be feeling each other's tits,' adds Sergeant obliquely.

'Mourners can be leaning over a cemetery wall and talking to skeletons who've popped their heads out of tombs,' Brenda imagines. 'You might show the corpse sitting up in the hearse and wondering what's going on.'

The police cars have stopped. Emerging are two SOCOs and five officers. Two stretch police tape round a grave. A female detective is in charge. I inhale deeply as an awful chill washes over me.

Putting aside the transport problem, Mrs Yellow and about

20 mourners rush to discover why the police are present. Rain pours down.

The female cemetery superintendent, Joan Bletchworth, recognises me. She's with cemetery staff. I've spoken to them in the past. Joan is 40, thin, with pointed features in a waxen complexion, framed by short highlighted brown hair. Wearing a black trouser suit, she bustles forwards. 'I'm sorry, Mr Cooper,' she announces in a strident voice, 'there's been an outrage on Alex's grave.'

Earth from the grave is dumped randomly in untidy heaps. The headstone with the inscription 'Alex Cooper. Lost but not forgotten' is smashed to pieces. So too is a sculpture I commissioned. Special permission had to be obtained to display it on the grave.

Brenda holds on to me while Sergeant and Corporal investigate.

'No!' I shriek, my body trembling. I want to vomit and run away. The same feelings overwhelmed me when the police said Alex was dead.

'It's the most serious act of desecration anyone is ever likely to see,' exclaims Joan. 'A grave should be undisturbed for eternity. Someone must really want to upset you. It's frightening.'

I sink to my knees.

'We've no history of vandalism in this cemetery,' adds Joan. 'It's an isolated incident. Other graves are intact. It happened last night. The excavator was taken from one of our storage buildings.'

My thoughts are in disarray.

'Don't go near the grave, Al. Please. It'll be too upsetting.' Brenda hugs me.

There's no desire to see what's happened. I'd never function again. After Alex was run over, it was me alone who identified his mangled body. The experience constantly haunts my mind.

'Nicola has done this. I'll kill her. I can't take much more, Brenda, I can't.' The shock of his death is relived every day.

I scream loudly: 'ALEX! ALEX! ALEX!'

'Any idea who could have done this?' Joan asks, first looking at me, then Brenda.

Words won't form.

One of the young male police officers openly weeps, shocked at what he's witnessed. A colleague comforts him.

Scared and with hands cupped, I cover my face. This could happen again and again. Has there been a police leak? Does Nicola know I informed the officers about the robberies? Did she hire local thugs to wreck Alex's grave? Is Jess involved? Would she betray me? I contemplate murdering Nicola and Y.

'We need to crack heads,' asserts Sergeant. Corporal gestures in agreement.

'Answers may be prised from Frankie later on,' suggests Brenda.

I slump on to one of the cemetery's benches. Working for Greasby has put a curse on me. Should I contact my ex-wife and tell her what has occurred? No. She'll only reiterate Alex ought to have been cremated. An attempt to wipe rain and tears from my eyes proves futile.

'Security cameras must be installed here. I'll pay for them,' promises Brenda, seeing my eyes melt with grief. 'We don't want this happening again.'

'Why can't Nicola leave Alex alone?' I mumble. 'Has Y got a team over here, Brenda? Can you see any snipers? Are they waiting to shoot us?' Eagerly, I look about.

Joan squeezes my hands tightly then glances at Brenda. 'Mr Cooper is in shock. Urgent attention is required.'

'He'll receive whatever help necessary,' Brenda assures her. 'We must find out who did this. I'll offer a huge reward.' She pulls me into her arms. 'I can help you cope, Al. Trust me.' Her warm soothing breath fans my face.

'There's a little kiddie down there,' Mrs Yellow hollers, standing over the grave. 'He's wearing a football shirt. Who did he support?' An answer is sought from anybody who might take notice. 'Was it a local team?'

Pictures are taken using her mobile. 'I'll make a fortune

selling these to newspapers. I can see a headline: "Ghouls at work".'

'No. Please. Stop,' I urge, clearing my throat. 'This is despicable.' What a sick world when somebody wants to sell pictures of a child's desecrated grave.

Despite strong pleas from the police, Mrs Yellow's pals also take snaps, flashes bouncing everywhere.

I ponder on the relevance of burials. Are they outdated? People who've gawped into the grave relate what they've seen to others.

'It's horrible,' comments a woman. 'I bet I won't sleep tonight.'

Heads pop up and down, eager to see what's happening. One police officer tries to tug Mrs Yellow away from the grave. Both tussle and slip into the gaping hole.

Sergeant and Corporal drag Mrs Yellow out and pin her down. They're all caked in mud. Grabbing Mrs Yellow's mobile, Sergeant hurls it away, then tightly grasps her hair.

'Tell your mates to delete the photographs or I'll carve GHOUL on your fucking forehead.' Sergeant pulls out her flick-knife, eager for blood. Corporal easily thwarts Mrs Yellow's escape attempt.

I pose myself a question: Can I ever depict anything humorous in a cemetery again? Instead, skeletons ought to be depicted torturing vandals who've smashed tombstones.

'Get off her, you fucking dykes,' women yell at Sergeant and Corporal. Political correctness hasn't touched them in the slightest.

'Don't knock it until you've tried it,' retorts Sergeant.

'Everyone, delete the photographs,' Mrs Yellow appeals.

None of them makes a move. Sergeant cuts the G on her forehead.

'Okay, stop, we'll do it,' is the communal cry.

'I like it when people rightfully dish out their own justice,' comments an officer. 'It saves us a job.'

Brenda leaves me briefly, making sure people do as requested.

She's accompanied by two police officers. One mourner tries to flee though Brenda stops him.

'We shall put everything back in order, Mr Cooper,' promises Joan, giving me a hug and holding a brolly over my head.

'Very kind of you, sweetheart,' Sergeant smiles at Joan who doesn't respond to the lascivious pass. People never waste a chance to engineer a sexual opportunity.

SOCOs carefully examine the excavator, take photographs and carry out other duties. The sledge hammer used to smash up the grave is placed inside an evidence bag and put in a vehicle.

'We'll find out who did this,' promises a female officer who announces herself as Detective Inspector Jenny Allsopp. Tall and hefty with blonde hair tied back, she's in her mid-40s. A round face reflects the sorrow I'm feeling.

'Don't hold your tears back, allow them to flow,' she soothes, placing a consoling hand on my shoulder.

'It was Nicola Greasby,' I blurt out. The desire for revenge is overwhelming.

'I'd like to hear more,' says Allsopp calmly and with sympathy. Her attitude is in marked contrast to that of the two male detectives met at Allwood.

'We can make Nicola confess,' brag Sergeant and Corporal.

'I'll do it myself.' My eyelids flicker rapidly.

'No need to dirty your hands, Al. We'll bury her alive.' Both are wickedness personified.

'Nicola's involvement is speculation,' states Brenda.

'Of course she was,' I retort. 'The bitch is jealous of my success at Greasby.'

'All can be explained,' says Brenda to Allsopp who's listening intently. 'Call at Banton Hall whenever convenient.'

'The body must be exhumed,' informs the DI.

'No! Don't touch him,' I screech. 'Fill the grave in now.'

I spring to my feet with life and energy. The bouquets we've brought are hurled into the hole. Looking down is avoided. My head is ready to cave in. I want to live and create. The relationship with Brenda is brilliant. That was helping to numb the horror of Alex's death. Now, it's back to square one. I squat on my haunches in a pool of water.

Allsopp gazes at me then speaks seriously to Brenda: 'I've phoned for an ambulance. Your partner is ill.'

A vicar steps out of the crematorium, wondering what's happening with the funerals he was ready to conduct. Walking towards us, he assesses the situation.

I shout at him: 'How can there be a God when this happens?' I gesture towards Alex's disturbed grave. Sobs shake my whole body.

'That's such a complex question,' he responds.

'Give him a straight answer, you fucking wanker,' snarls Sergeant. Corporal voices agreement. Removing their clothes, except for heavy boots, both stand shameless. They wash mud from themselves in the heavy rain. Both have lost the berets somewhere.

It's surprising I can cry so much and plenty of tears have been shed in the past.

Allsopp offers comfort: 'This is terrible. I feel for you. I really do.'

Glancing up, I see Sergeant and Corporal flicking each other's nipples.

'We need to exhume the body,' insists Allsopp.

'Fuck off. It's not happening,' Brenda states forcefully.

'I'll organise for the grave to be put back in order,' reiterates Joan. 'Don't worry, Mr Cooper, the Council will pay.'

Should Alex be taken out of the grave, then cremated? This could happen again and again. No. No. No.

Brenda moves towards the vicar. 'Will you say a few words?' There's a favourable response.

'I love you, Al,' Brenda murmurs, leaning closely. She strokes my hair as if I was the little boy she never had.

'Sorry, Brenda. I'm failing you. I'll meet Y. Your pictures must be found. I don't care if I'm killed. Can't stand this much longer.'

'Nonsense. Stop worrying,' she says gently. 'Everything will be hunky-dory. You're not going to see Y. I'm sorry it was ever mentioned.'

'I don't care what happens. Can't go on.'

'You need a doctor. The best. And a psychologist.' She stares into my troubled face. 'You shall survive this. It'll make you stronger. Cry and cry as much as you like. I can do anything to help.'

The police aren't permitting entry to any vehicle, so four funerals back up, spilling out on the main road. A police car blocks the east side exit. But officers allow a Finbow & Sons' mechanic access. He's in a breakdown truck and moves over to the company's stranded hearse.

Mrs Yellow approaches, blood trickling down her face. 'Devil worshippers have done this.' She points to Alex's grave. 'They want burning at the stake. Always wearing black. Nobody wears bright colours any more. Me and my husband were hippies and always dressed brightly.'

The words don't register. My hands shake and I want to strangle her.

Mrs Yellow's fellow mourners offer apologies for taking pictures. Make-up runs down the women's faces. Their hair bedraggled by the rain.

'I'll kill Nicola Greasby,' I say feebly to everyone.

A mourner pulls out a hip flask and offers a sip of brandy. It's refused.

A press photographer and journalist bustle forwards, though Brenda soon shoos them away.

One woman – in her late 30s and with a deeply troubled face – reveals her young twins were kidnapped by a paedophile group.

'At least you can mourn at a grave,' she sobs. 'My kids' bodies have never been found.'

'We're not in a grief competition.' I speak in a croak.

Despite the rain, inquisitive mourners leave the queuing funeral cars to discover what's causing the delay. Only a few umbrellas are visible and several people huddle under each one.

Police car blues still pulsate. Temporarily, my focus switches to a young couple. The bloke feels his girlfriend's arse though she fists him in the goolies. Funerals, I conclude, are only a short display of grief.

Brenda holds me tightly throughout the vicar's short eulogy. Conversation ceases and the only sound is rain. Women and men weep openly. At last, a calm respect is shown.

# Chapter 40

After the cemetery ordeal, Brenda summoned a top private doctor. I was sedated. Then, stayed in bed almost a month at Banton Hall. Unable to speak properly for a while, my voice was a mere whisper. Confidence drained away completely.

My bedroom is beautiful, with a view over the grounds, maintained to perfection. I sleep in a fantastic ornate Victorian brass bed. Unfortunately, my nights are still disturbed. In a new recurring dream, I'm looking down into a grave. Alex pleads to help him out. Nicola is nearby in an excavator with a bucket bucket full of earth. She laughs and shouts 'wanker'. Annabel is at the graveside too and spits into the hole.

Apart from the shocks and dreams, I'm content. Banton Hall is brilliant and Brenda can't do enough. I'm ready, more than ready, for a new way of life.

Brenda understands my grief and knows Alex dominates my thoughts every day. Although we're partners, there's no talk of marriage. Neither of us mentions the subject. My feelings for her are deepening. When contemplating our relationship, there's serenity. Constantly watching, without being intrusive, she encourages discussion on any disturbing thoughts. I'm urged to exercise regularly and eat sensibly.

I've not seen Brenda snort cocaine or suspect she's still in a physical relationship with Deb or anybody else. It wouldn't bother me if she was. I've not looked for any evidence. Never been one for checking on a woman's behaviour when in a relationship.

Walking on the Banton estate is enjoyable, often with Brenda and, occasionally without. Birdwatching and observing other aspects of nature is uplifting. Yet, I could never paint traditional landscapes. My work has to involve fantasy and surreal or humorous elements.

A top psychologist, Amelia Jacobs, is visiting me regularly for the foreseeable future. It's helping and Brenda is often by my side. Amelia has recommended cognitive therapy as part of my recovery. Throughout the day, I write down negative thoughts. Then, attempt to disentangle them. But, it's unsettling, not knowing what could happen next.

Frequently, a plan is devised to kill Nicola. I'm convinced she was behind the vandalising of Alex's grave. Amelia understands that assumption. She's using her considerable experience to diffuse the time bomb ticking within me. Amelia and Brenda are concerned about this pent-up anger and where it might lead.

A private doctor has prescribed the necessary medication for my condition. Brenda feels the burglary and grave sacrilege might tip me over the edge mentally. She fears I'll make a suicide attempt. That possibility hasn't even entered my head. She's reassured and pleased with that confession.

Sergeant and Corporal said they'd kill Nicola. No problem. I want to do it myself. Would murdering Nicola rid me of the anger? Brenda and Amelia said no. It would only cause more problems. If I murdered Nicola, could extreme provocation be claimed? They thought not. I would be imprisoned for years, maybe life. Especially as I'd murdered a woman with a child. The dilemma of what to do about Nicola often threatens to engulf me.

I want Nicola to die. Though wishing somebody dead is uncharacteristic, when something evil happens to a family member, it can be mind-altering. A lid must be kept on my anger. I often remind myself of that throughout the day.

A conclusion has been reached about why I was the victim of a burglary and my son's grave was desecrated. It's jealousy. Jealousy with a capital J. People are envious of others' achievements. Nicola is bitter from my success as an individual and with sales at Greasby. She wants to hurt me and in a way that's obvious. Valiant efforts must be made to control myself and not lose what Brenda provides. It would be selfish and ungrateful. Above all, I cherish our friendship and her encouragement.

I believe Brenda is resigned to opening the Lesbian Art Museum without the stolen pictures. While she's in regular contact with the Schmidt family and Kirstin, nothing new has been discovered. Meanwhile, work feverishly continues at the Museum building. Curators from different parts of the country have visited to observe the latest developments and installations.

The WLA patrols the Hall and grounds day and night. A security office, full of sophisticated equipment, has been established. Drones watch over the Banton estate, eager to detect any security breaches.

Everything that's happened to me was reported, against my wishes, in the press. For a while, journalists camped at the Banton Hall main entrance. Pestering to know why I was the victim of these attacks. Scum. Press photographers with long lenses arrived, almost as if they were at a Premiership football match. Climbing trees and hiding in bushes, they attempted to capture glimpses of me in the Hall. Pathetic. Sensationalist. Unnecessary.

No interviews were given and Brenda has kept the media at bay. This did not thwart the printing of outlandish dramatic headlines. My ex-wife was interviewed. Journalists asked her to recall any physical or mental abuse by me. Had I been cruel to our son? Were there any extramarital affairs? Was I a pervert or junkie? The usual tittle-tattle they try to extract from people and blow out of proportion. I'm sure she was paid well. The press was told she'd wanted Alex cremated and pleaded for that to happen.

Journalists even found and interviewed the motorist who killed Alex. Shocking what's done to extract news. No sympathy was shown to me. I hate the attention, it's like living in a goldfish bowl and is extremely uncomfortable.

Other parents who've lost a child read about the cemetery incident. They corresponded expressing sympathy and support.

An invite came to talk about my grief on morning television. It was ignored. Brenda says I ought to have been bold and attended. It would have provided an opportunity to show my art and indicate how grief is being managed. I said it may be considered later.

Sergeant, Corporal and other WLA soldiers went to interrogate Nicola about the grave desecration. They were surprised to meet a bunch of Russian men at her house. There was a scuffle, though this did not present a problem for the pair and the WLA. Amidst the fracas, Sergeant and Corporal attempted to kidnap Nicola and bring her back to Banton Hall.

Annabel threatened them with a loaded pistol. 'Leave my mum alone,' she yelled, 'or I'll blast your tits off. Fucking fat dykes.' Shots were fired, so all the WLA made a hasty retreat.

Later, Sergeant and Corporal kept a watch on Nicola's house and discovered the Russians are working on Nigel's church. Some were accommodated at a local B&B. Sergeant even persuaded a bunch of WLA soldiers to seduce them, though nothing further was discovered. Everyone just enjoyed the unbridled sex.

Over the last few weeks, Brenda has been organising a series of exhibitions for my work in London, Berlin, Paris and New York. They're planned to start in six months. Linked to them are lectures at universities and in art galleries. This exerts a nice pressure. Brenda insists that humour must be kept in my work. I've assured her it will. Deb and Brenda found more emaciated heroin addicts and they were brought to the Hall. I photographed them naked to look like skeletons in various poses.

My commitment to art is soaring to another level. Never before did I believe there would be sufficient funds to paint every day. Being immersed in creativity helps to relieve the traumas. I've lots of ideas. They include depicting skeletons playing one-armed bandits, dealing cards, and golfing.

Brenda has suggested we tour amusement arcades seeking inspiration. It would be a good idea to portray skeletons playing bingo at a cemetery. I can place large signs announcing the amounts of cash that might be won. A funny and surreal image could present a fairground pitched in a cemetery. Skeletons will be participating in lots of entertainment.

Brenda said I ought to consider a set of pictures showing a party of skeletons on a seaside day out. Depict them sitting in deck chairs, eating candyfloss, or fish and chips and wearing *KISS ME QUICK* hats. Even paddling in the sea. We held each other and laughed. Humour always releases tension in me.

Brenda is thinner, much thinner, than when we first met. Both of us stand the same height and fit well into each other's arms.

Photographs of my pictures have been emailed to Dick and Paul. Useful comments were made about the compositions and they suggested different angles that may be employed. Both added my drawing ability and colour choices were developing well. After hearing what they had to say, Brenda proposed we hire a cherry-picker and take it to the old Askworth cemetery. From an elevated position, I might capture exciting compositions to consider.

Deb has no animosity over my relationship with Brenda. She's kind to me and wants to please Brenda. Not upset us with petty jealousies. Ellen continues to create her own sado-masochistic lesbian pictures at the Hall. It's beneficial to live alongside another artist. We talk often for hours about art. This kind of rapport hasn't been enjoyed since art college. Deb and Barb are busy in various activities. Jen is away on a small tour with her Punk band.

Alex's grave has been put back in order and a new headstone erected. Brenda is paying for a replacement sculpture, an even more elaborate one. Via video calls, Joan, the cemetery superintendent, showed the progress being made. Cameras are placed in the cemetery and one is installed near Alex's grave. A new lockup compound for the excavator has been established. Pop-up bollards function nightly at the access points. To sort all this out, Deb met with Joan and the Council's cemetery committee.

Y has phoned, though I've not answered. He leaves messages for me to make contact and arrange a meeting. Eager to discuss a working relationship. That causes more stress.

Kirstin has texted, offering sympathy over the cemetery incident. She told me to immerse myself in art and looked forwards to seeing the commissioned paintings. Anna and her are due in the UK shortly. A meeting is arranged at the London offices of Kirstin's prominent law firm to discuss compensation for the fake Grosz and its provenance. Nicola and Frankie are invited to attend with legal representation. Nicola intends bringing along a female Grosz expert who will argue the picture's authenticity. Only a refund and damages are sought. Kirstin won't entertain discussions on whether the drawing is real or fake. My presence is required, though I might kill Nicola on sight.

Thankfully, I've found a listening ear to offload details about the art thefts and fakes. DI Jenny Allsopp has visited Brenda and myself. After experiencing police corruption with Dewhurst and Carmody, I was initially wary of Jenny. So was Brenda. Making investigations, Sergeant said Jenny was okay. The DI was shocked to hear Carmody and Dewhurst had accepted bribes from Frankie. She apologised for their behaviour. I mentioned that Nicola might attempt to bribe her, though was assured that wouldn't happen.

Jenny is intense and committed. There was a desire to know every minute detail about the robberies. She questioned the motive for Nicola producing fakes and being involved with other criminality. I suggested that Nicola wants to outdo Frankie and be richer. Earning lots of cash is what individuals believe necessary to make themselves feel good. Face life and the next day.

After listening intently to details of Greasby's activities, Jenny couldn't understand why Nicola hadn't been arrested, or slain and dumped in a ditch.

Jenny interviewed the Russians working on Nigel's church. She found their passports in order and no further enquiries were necessary. I suggested she might view the footage of my burglary to see if the same men were involved. As yet, no details have been revealed.

Disappointingly, Jenny said no evidence had been gathered off the sledgehammer or excavator at the cemetery. She's requested details of the stolen Grosz works from Kirstin. Jenny has also contacted the Schmidt family to discuss their robbery.

Brenda showed Jenny the effigies she'd received along with the homophobic notes. The DI promised to interview Nicola. Jenny, along with Brenda's lawyer, told me not to voice in public any unsubstantiated statements about Nicola. Brenda wasn't impressed with the DI. She wants action and quickly. That, I explained, isn't how the police work.

Today, Sergeant and Corporal are bringing Frankie to Banton Hall to seal the Greasby sale. Brenda's solicitors have discovered no evidence to prove Nicola has any legal rights at the company. The deal can't be frustrated. Our intention is to buy the debts and only keep the Askworth operation and one gallery in London. A third gallery is to be established in New York.

There's been no contact with Jess. She'll be involving herself in Nicola's dirty work. It would be beneficial to have her on board at Banton and with the Lesbian Art Museum. I've suggested we ought to employ her. The decision is left to me. Although sex mad, Jess is very competent at a number of tasks. Curator of the Lesbian Art Museum is a tailor-made job for her. This needs to happen so I can fully concentrate on my art. By employing Jess, we may hear where all the stolen pictures are hidden. A considered approach shall be made to Jess with a job offer.

Presently, I'm in my Banton Hall studio, sitting at an easel amidst brushes, tubes of paint and made-to-measure canvases. A competent carpenter and framer is on hand to satisfy my needs. The Ensor reproductions have arrived. All are framed and I'm admiring them now as inspiration.

Brenda sits alongside and I'm showing her my latest sketch

to be developed into a painting. A skeletised bride and groom pose outside an old church. In full wedding attire, the bride is six months pregnant. A burglar can be seen climbing out of a church window with a bag marked swag. Brenda finds this hilarious.

'Is that symbolic of the bride's virginity being stolen?'

A cheeky smile creeps across my face.

Brenda always wanted to be an artist herself, though claims she didn't have the commitment.

Paulene arrives outside the Hall in a Range Rover. She's with the studs Tyrone and Ross. Desperately wanting to be part of the discussions about the company sale, she insists on benefitting from any settlement. I spoke with her yesterday. She still receives payments from Greasby via Nicola. If they're delayed, which is a regular occurrence, she threatens to flatten Nigel's church with an excavator. This always prompts Nicola to pay up. Will Paulene ever feel it necessary to destroy the church? It'll be interesting to watch, wait and see. Although her Renta Stud business is flourishing, she's keen to have the bank overdraft removed from the house. Cash to invest in the business is also required. It's her intention to convert the property into a stud farm.

Paulene is surprised that plenty of women, of all ages, readily pay to hire one or two of her studs.

'Men have always told me that women, after having kids, aren't interested in sex. What a load of shit. They need a good hard dick more than ever.'

Paulene provides female studs for women and occasionally men. 'It's a crazy world, isn't it,' she rambled. 'I'm amazed at my success. Never thought it possible.' But her last words yesterday expressed anxiety: 'I need cash, Al. Or, the bank will evict me. Frankie won't keep up with the loan payments. Please help.'

Brenda and I hurry downstairs to greet her. Brenda is costumed in a red trouser suit, red high heels and has minimal make-up. She looks great.

Climbing out of the vehicle, wearing a dominatrix outfit and a large strap-on dildo, Paulene is vocal: 'I want to give you multi-orgasms Brenda. If you're doing a favour, I'll do the same for you.' She's giddy and strokes the dildo. 'You'll scream long and loud. I'll make sure of that.'

Brenda is unmoved.

'We've brought you a batch of Columbia's finest,' Paulene announces as Tyrone holds aloft a bag of coke.

Men and women belonging to a window-cleaning gang, at work on the Hall, observe Paulene, and nearly fall off their ladders in shock. A group of gardeners, pruning roses and weeding flowerbeds, watch with similar amusement. All are making the building and estate look immaculate. The tranquil existence doesn't deserve to be spoiled by Paulene's vulgar intrusion.

'Are you waxed, Brenda?' Paulene chuckles. 'I fuck women as well as men.'

Typically, Paulene is wearing too much make-up; her acrylic fingernails are brightly-coloured.

'Great to see you looking well, Al, after the dramas.'

'Thanks.'

We exchange a brief hug.

'Where's Frankie?'

'Two people have gone to fetch him,' I reply.

Paulene switches attention to Tyrone and Ross. 'These lads can join us Brenda, if you want a bit of straight thrown in.' She strokes their crotches. 'Both are hung like donkeys. Call out, lads: Hee haw. Hee haw.'

Both unzip their trousers, arouse themselves and stick out their tongues, pretending to lick imaginary orifices.

In black stilettos, Paulene clatters towards Brenda, her boobs wobbling noticeably.

'Are you ready, Brenda?' Paulene fondles the dildo then bounces it up and down.

Annoyed, Brenda doesn't show the slightest interest. 'Stop,' she shouts. 'I'm sorry to disappoint you, Paulene. I know you mean well, only my life has changed. Al and I have a special relationship. We're devoted to art.'

With a grin on her face, Brenda backs away. I move to her side. Paulene is taken aback. I feel sorry for her. Always have done. Yesterday, information wasn't divulged about Brenda and me.

'Sorry, Paulene,' I want to say, not anticipating she'd be over-the-top with her expectations. I wish Paulene well in the Renta Stud business and it's pleasing she has developed her own ideas. More importantly, she's not involved with criminality like Frankie and Nicola. Paulene won't be left out of any settlement and everything will be done to help. I wouldn't like to see her charged for wrecking Nigel's church.

'I'm pleased for you, Al. You deserve a good woman. You both look trim. Fucked the weight off each other?'

Removing the dildo, Paulene hurls it away. 'I feel like an extra in a porno film.' There's despair in her voice. The possibility of eviction and the business floundering are nightmare scenarios. All because of a dickhead like Frankie. He's bound to default on the bank loan.

My mobile sounds. It's Nicola.

'If you grass me up to the police again,' she rages, 'me and Nigel will bomb Banton Hall. Keep your mouth shut, wanker. Keep it shut.'

Annabel is heard singing her horrible ditty: 'Wanker. Wanker. Al is a wanker. Pulls his plonker all day long. All day long.'

'Did you wreck my son's grave?'

'Yes. Yes. Yes, I did. Enjoyed it,' she brags. 'Watch out. We're going to bomb you and your dyke girlfriend. Boom. Boom. BOOM.'

Paulene and the studs stand amazed.

'I'll kill you, Nicola! I'll kill you,' I scream, almost losing my voice.

Brenda wrenches away the mobile and ends the conversation.

'What do they know about bombs?' She scowls at Paulene.

'Nigel was in the Army's Bomb Disposal Unit. After being

discharged, he took a theology degree.'

'Oh, no, not more aggro.' I need to sit or lie down.

Although clearly shocked, Brenda's attention is interrupted by a call from Sergeant. Walking away, she's absent for a few minutes. Then, she reveals Frankie isn't at Jess's. His whereabouts are unknown. As usual, his mobile is switched off. Sergeant said when Corporal and herself emerged from Jess's house, their vehicle was engulfed in flames.

# Chapter 41

Nicola's bomb threat has thrown a dark shadow over life at Banton Hall. Brenda is deeply worried and upset. She took advice from a number of police and Army experts and ordered extra security. Bulletproof glass is installed everywhere. The WLA, with their fierce dogs, patrol the perimeters. Tradespeople are vetted at the main entrance. Everything is planned, then put into place with military precision. Brenda is desperate to protect the Hall.

Deb, Sergeant and Corporal organise most of the manoeuvres. My house is offered for rent. I won't stay there ever again. Brenda hopes that, before long, Nicola is arrested. But, nothing is being left to chance. Hopefully, this intense activity will only be for a short period.

Often, Brenda is quiet. Whilst handling the security arrangements, she's told me to press on with the artworks and trust in her to look after everything else. Whenever circumstances have permitted, we enjoy each other's company.

Anxiety over what Nicola or Y might do next has gone up several notches. Personally, I'm very worried about Brenda. Could the pressure tip her back into addiction? I sincerely hope not. She's spoken of the inner turmoil to Amelia.

A number of questions worry both of us. How would Nicola bomb Banton? A suicide bomb? A rocket launched explosive? It's too frightening to contemplate. Might Y be involved? Could it be a poison attack – for real this time?

When Nicola made the bomb threat, Brenda rang the police immediately. Paulene was unsupportive, saying she wouldn't give evidence against Nicola. Brenda told her and the studs to fuck off. Paulene attacked her, though without success.

When the studs attempted to assist, they were thwarted by two patrolling WLA soldiers who sprang into action.

'Ask your daughter for cash,' Brenda yelled at Paulene. 'See how she treats you. Nicola ought to be put away for good.'

I thought Paulene might have been supportive but as the pathetic statement says, blood is thicker than water. She wouldn't want to look after Annabel if Nicola went down for making violent threats.

Nicola was interviewed by Jenny who said without support from Paulene we couldn't make any charges stick. It was three of them against two of us. Or five against two if Nicola and Nigel joined with the three others. How convenient. Jenny advised us to take necessary precautions.

Brenda still undertakes her daily routines, by seeing personal trainers and other people. Encouragement is offered whenever it's required. She always radiates confidence and says assuringly: 'I'm okay, Al. Don't worry.'

Y has stopped phoning. Maybe he's accepted I don't want to work with him or have any discussions.

It's late afternoon and the temperature hovers slightly below 20 degrees. Sergeant and Corporal pull up in a Range Rover, parking a short distance from the Hall front. Both look feral. After their vehicle was burnt out, another was hastily acquired. Frankie is with them. He's been picked up from Jess's house and is alone – Robbi and Denny aren't in tow. Frankie wears a blonde wig, pink floral dress and red high heels. His face is garishly made-up, but white stubble breaks through. Swaying unsteadily, he's pissed. Or, to use a modern expression, zoned out.

The man before me is completely unrecognisable to the one I first met. Often, I've seen him lecture on art, wearing a pinstripe suit, white shirt and gold tie. Always a gold tie. Imparting a wealth of interesting and well-researched information, his talks were captivating. Deviant sex is a great destroyer of reputations. Sex, drugs and alcohol have destroyed Frankie. My respect for him is dead.

We walk out to greet him. Brenda looks smart, wearing a blue trouser suit, light-blue silk blouse, sensible black shoes, and her hair nicely brushed. Yet, she's not communicated much today.

Sergeant and Corporal stand in the usual attire of khaki shorts and T-shirts. Their heads are shaved. Frankie is hauled out of the vehicle and the doors left wide open. Wearing highly-polished steel-toe-cap boots that crunch on the gravel, the pair begin kicking him in the groin. Ellen and the other women aren't videoing the action this time.

'He enjoys ballbusting,' announces Sergeant with a chuckle and looking in Brenda's direction.

'Yes, I do. The pain is lovely. The cock-and-ball-torture website is often accessed on my mobile.'

Ballbusting. What a pathetic sexual activity, but it'll provide another graveyard skeleton subject.

'Paulene booted me regularly,' Frankie gasps collapsing to the ground. 'It relieved her anger.'

The solidly-built women attack him with a frightening passion.

'Watching a man writhing in pain is what we like best,' confesses Sergeant. 'Any day of the week.'

Corporal agrees.

Needle puncture marks are visible on Frankie's puny arms. He's lost weight. Pathetic.

'You look ill, Frankie,' I comment.

'No, I'm heroin chic.'

'Have you brought any company accounts?' Brenda probes.

'Yes, they're in the car. I can fetch them in a minute.'

Sergeant and Corporal continue kicking him.

'Oh, that hurt a tiny bit,' he tells Sergeant.

'Didn't feel anything with that one,' he admits to Corporal.

Watching this is uncomfortable. 'Stop. He'll suffer permanent injury.'

'It's wonderful, Al. Wonderful.'

'Ballbusting carries significant risks,' I argue.

'How the fuck would you know, Al?' snarls Sergeant.

'I've heard you and Brenda are an item, Al,' Frankie begins. 'A dyke reformed and a self-proclaimed celibate man. How do you excite each other? I'm interested to hear which one of you is the stoker.'

'I've often asked myself the same questions,' scoffs Sergeant.

Brenda is livid. 'Mind your own fucking business. Both of you.'

'Are you wearing perfume, Brenda?' Corporal pushes her nose forwards.

'Yes. Any objection?'

'None.' Corporal steps back.

Brenda moves closer to Frankie. 'You're pissed. I'm insulted. How dare you bowl up to a business meeting in this state? You're not fit to discuss the Greasby sale. Nicola might contest whatever we agree.'

Whilst Frankie looks confused, he's still inquisitive. 'Is Brenda a good fuck, Al? Does everything you desire?'

'Shut up,' Brenda fumes and shifts the conversation in another direction. 'Where are my fucking pictures? I'm not buying your poxy company unless you say.'

'Is funding my sex change still part of our deal?' Frankie and Brenda have previously discussed this aspect in detail.

'Only when you reveal where the pictures are hidden. If not, I'll do the operation myself.'

Frankie shows no fear. 'Oh, you are a tease, Brenda. I've got a stiffy on. I need to pull it off. I'm so excited.'

With Sergeant and Corporal, Brenda viciously rips the dress off him. Then, the black stockings, suspenders and the same colour frilly satin knickers.

'He's got a Prince Albert piercing.' Sergeant is tickled. 'It's like one of my mum's curtain rings. Men are totally pathetic.'

'Definitely,' echoes Corporal.

'I'll be sad to lose my gentleman,' Frankie admits.

'Did Nicola wreck Alex's grave?' I grill him. 'Did she? Were you or Y involved?'

Any sympathy for Frankie has gone. He provided a job when an escape from deep mourning was desperately needed. The Friday night car ride convinced me to paint again. But, I want to know for definite who trashed my son's grave. There's a pain in my chest. It's often experienced when someone doesn't give Alex proper respect.

'Be quiet, Al. I want to know about the pictures.' Brenda looks frostily at me. That's never happened before. Never. If this is the Brenda of old, my life will crumble.

I confront her: 'That's not what he came here for.' She pulls Frankie to his feet.

'Finding the culprit who wrecked Alex's grave is more important than stolen pictures.'

I'm ignored. This is betrayal. Brenda wondered why I've shunned relationships since my divorce. It's because betrayal is abhorrent. Brenda always promised to be supportive with my grief. Now she's not. I'm deeply hurt. Is Brenda craving her old life? Coordinating thoughts is a struggle. They're jumbled.

'Go to your cosy studio, Al.' Sergeant drops her shorts and underwear, and lunges forwards. 'Paint a picture of my fanny.'

'He might as easily depict a dead rat,' jokes Frankie.

'Paint my tits,' jibes Corporal, lifting her T-shirt.

'No, do my arse,' urges Sergeant, twisting round and bending over. Both women split their sides laughing. That's all I need. These two humiliating me.

'Are you ready to discuss the Greasby sale, Frankie?' I want him to state that's what he came here for, not to be interrogated about missing pictures. The question is ignored.

Two electricians have been investigating why the Hall's power often trips out. Emerging from the building, they head towards a van. Both are casually dressed in jeans, sweatshirts and trainers. Tool belts circle their waists. They're unshaven and epitomise the Grunge look. Both are in their 40s. One is barrel-chested, the other is gangly.

Brenda grasps Frankie's hair and forces an arm up his back. Both men show alarm. I guess they believe this is another example of the landed gentry's bizarre behaviours. I hope the police aren't called.

Sergeant approaches them. 'Hello, sparkies.' Touching Barrel Chest, she pretends to receive an electric shock and drops on the ground. Their expressions show confusion. It's clear both don't appreciate her familiarity. Or want to play along with the prank.

I'm frustrated. Maybe Brenda and I should take a break for a week or two. Recharge our batteries before returning to Banton Hall clear-headed.

'Is the electrical problem sorted?' Brenda asks.

They're quick to dispel any doubts. A job at a country house is a good earner for them. A bill far exceeding the normal rate for the work will be charged. I can smell that. Both glance over with disdain, wondering what part I'm playing in the drama unfolding.

'Give us a buzz if there are any further problems,' states Barrel Chest.

'Does the place need rewiring?' Brenda questions, tightly holding Frankie and restricting his movements.

'We can give you a quote,' offers Gangly.

'Yes, do that.'

Noticing Frankie's piercing, Barrel Chest can't help himself. 'That looks painful, mate. Couldn't have it done myself. Each to his own, though.'

'Are you two happily married to your wrists?' Sergeant confronts them. 'Or, are you both going home to fuck your wives?'

'Or, somebody else's wife,' laughs Corporal.

'We're off to a new massage parlour to fuck our brains out,' confesses Barrel Chest.

'Good lads,' smirks Sergeant. 'Off you go then.'

Noisily, the van wheelspins and they drive off.

Have they really solved the electrical problem? I'm suspicious. They look like a couple of cowboys on the make.

Brenda swings Frankie round. 'Where are my pictures? You

must know. Your daughter stole them.' Her eyes blaze.

Feeling the effects of the kicking, he doubles-up in pain and doesn't reply.

'Concentrate on the Greasby sale, Brenda.' Trying to hold her attention, I must intervene here, take control and devise a plan.

'Be quiet, Al, for once.'

Was I a fool to take on Brenda? A self-confessed coke head and sex addict. Can addicts ever recover? No idea. It's beyond my knowledge. Is her love waning? This is our first argument. I thought the picture theft wasn't troubling her too much. Witnessing the change is upsetting. I felt Brenda was a soul mate, to use a meaningless expression. It was assumed she lived and breathed art like me.

Will Brenda constantly fluctuate from her new self back to the old one? Am I overreacting? Can I risk losing everything that's been planned? No. I can't shun the promotional and marketing campaign Brenda has envisaged for my work. It's essential. My skeletons could feature everywhere. On posters, postcards, mugs or perhaps tea towels and duvet covers. That's what an energetic marketing campaign may achieve. I might be extremely successful overnight. Even attain Royal Academician status. Brenda would offer bribes along the way. I must try to keep quiet, though it'll be difficult. I'm determined to press Frankie about the nerve agent incident and the attack on the grave.

'Are Nicola and Nigel planning to bomb this Hall?' Brenda continues to face Frankie.

Stepping back and falling over, Frankie answers: 'The pair of them aren't capable of anything. They can't stop arguing for two minutes.'

'Stand up. Stand up,' orders Sergeant slapping his penis. She's very much at home when intimidating men.

This makes me squirm uncomfortably.

Once on his feet, Frankie is pressed forwards by Brenda. Sergeant and Corporal aim more kicks at him. This is veering out of control.

Nicola's threat of bombing Banton must be tipping Brenda over the edge. She's lost it today. Definitely. Although there's a desire to help her, I'm unsure whether it's possible or that I can. Do I want to?

Arnold Fitch predicted his daughter would never be capable of looking after the Hall, the vast estate and the Corporation. He's still very much in her head, continually taunting. Admitting the burden of continuity is ever-present, Brenda's proved him wrong on many points. Though, it's unlikely she's ever considered the Hall could be blown up.

'You're going to tell me where the stolen pictures are hidden,' insists Brenda.

'What pictures do you mean?' Frankie replies feebly.

'Discuss the sale first, Brenda,' I plead once more. 'These questions can wait.'

She doesn't respond.

'I know nothing of stolen pictures.' Frankie now shows alarm.

What if he doesn't know anything? What then? Ellen isn't here filming this event, which disturbs me. I can't see it developing into a joke like before. It's uncertain whether Frankie will be proudly going home with a DVD of his experience. How far is Brenda prepared to go forcing a confession out of him?

Brenda stops and grabs Frankie's throat. 'I need the pictures back for the opening of my Lesbian Art Museum.'

Frankie is more confused. Is he playing ignorant?

'Where are they?' Brenda yells. 'Where are they? You know. Tell me. Don't bullshit.'

Sergeant grins as Corporal fondles her.

'Later,' dismisses Sergeant. 'I'm enjoying Brenda's performance.'

'Are we discussing the sale of my company?' Frankie strains to break free. 'I've brought a draft contract. It's in the car.'

'Not yet,' snaps Brenda.

Frankie is disappointed. 'I'd love a glass of wine. Have you laid on nice food? I'm starving.'

'Fuck off. Where are the pictures? What do you know? Tell

me. For fuck's sake, tell me.' Brenda is hysterical.

Frankie remains evasive. 'I'm not aware you'd lost any pictures.'

'Liar. You fucking liar.'

'I realise you've experienced trouble in the past, but Nicola tells me nothing.'

I move forwards to Frankie. 'Who wrecked my son's grave. It was desecrated. What do you know?'

'Later, Al. Leave that until later. Please,' Brenda screams.

My future as an artist is crashing down. Brenda has drastically changed. Her confession of love was unexpected but very flattering. A massive change in my life. Does she now regret her admission? Maybe this is only a minor blip. I hope so. We've both been under pressure lately.

Sergeant and Corporal roughly take charge of Frankie.

'Bring him downstairs,' Brenda instructs. 'I'll do the sex change operation myself. When you wake up as a woman, Frankie, we can negotiate the Greasby sale.'

I must intervene, though don't know how.

'Take him downstairs,' Brenda repeats and kicks Frankie.

'Talk about the Greasby sale.'

'That can wait, Al.'

'You're strayed back to your old self.'

Sweat is visible on her brow.

'Stop, Brenda. I'll support you just like you've supported me.'

There's no answer. I'm concerned about what might happen. This overwhelms my urge to question Frankie about the grave incident. The Hall isn't a friendly place anymore.

'Don't do anything horrible to him. Brenda. Please. He doesn't deserve any of this.'

What might Jenny say on learning about this drama? Would I be arrested? I've seen far too much of the police lately.

Crazily, another potential picture springs to mind. Skeletons undertaking a slimming operation, carving flesh off a fat man or woman. Gruesome? Gratuitous? Maybe.

'What fun this is,' remarks Frankie. 'I'm excited to know where I'm going.'

'Stick close, wimp,' Corporal snatches at me. 'Watch surgeon Brenda at work.'

Why do they know what's happening and I don't? Questions shower down on my brain.

'I'm going home. This is way out of hand.'

'Boo hoo hoo,' mocks Sergeant twisting towards me. 'Boo hoo hoo. I'm leaving and going home to mummy. You're like a little boy, Al.'

'Going home to mummy,' echoes Corporal. 'Dab your tears, Al, with a white frilly handkerchief.'

'Say goodbye to your dick and balls,' Sergeant taunts Frankie as we approach the Hall's entrance. 'They're coming off tonight.'

Corporal sings:

*We're gonna chop your dick and balls off.*
*Dick and balls off. Dick and balls off.*
*You'll not like it. You'll not like it.*

'I'll have a vagina instead, wont I?'

Passing through the reception area, Frankie is fascinated by the dildos in the illuminated rotating display cases.

'Stop,' Frankie says. 'Let me view these wonderful exhibits. What fun. What fun. I'd like to borrow one or two items, if I may? They look fulfilling in more ways than one.'

Showing no fear, only arousal, he surprises Sergeant and Corporal: 'Can I have sex with you two later? I swallowed a Viagra an hour ago. I'm looking forwards to excitement. It has to be said though, the pair of you stink. Use more deodorant.'

Not replying, they bundle him down to the torture chamber. Their boots clomp on the steps. Frankie is unsure how to react. Fragrance from a lavender air freshener attempts to combat a stale musty odour. The atmosphere in the windowless room is intense and threatening. Two of the walls have shackles attached. Ropes, canes, paddles, whips and other BDSM paraphernalia are strewn haphazardly. Weirdo latex and leather uniforms are posed on mannequins. Other items visible include a sex machine and cattle prods. Ellen's computer and editing equipment swamp a desk in one corner. Cameras point down on both torture tables. DVDs are piled on the floor.

'Have some coke, Brenda.' Sergeant pulls out a small packet. 'We need to be off our faces.'

'Greetings Mr Greasby. Happy to see you at our BDSM club,' mocks Corporal. 'Are you familiar with Ellen's website FEAR?' Her tongue rolls lecherously.

'Well. Well. Yes, I've seen and heard everything about the club. Never knew it was based here,' Frankie slurs. 'This is wonderfully unexpected. A real treat. I've longed for the experience. Thanks everybody. Is a film being made? Will I receive a DVD later?'

Nobody comments. Without a struggle, he's tightly fastened to one of the torture tables. A strong light source over the table floods everywhere.

Brenda is to the right of Frankie. I'm at the foot of the table. Sergeant and Corporal are to the left and flop Frankie's penis from side-to-side. Corporal has a good look at the Prince Albert piercing as though it's a unique archaeological find.

Bursting into life, the wall screens display a title: *Male-to-Female Surgery: A Guide*.

Frankie's attention flashes from screen to screen.

'Shall I follow this tutorial, Frankie?' sniggers Brenda.

With a remote, she moves the video on a little.

'Is this the operation you want? It's quite gory.'

'Brenda, end this silly joke.'

Frankie sobers up and screams in panic: 'Stop! I want to be a man. Stop!'

My heart pounds madly. The other women ought to be here. Deb would surely put a stop to this.

Brenda strips off to her bra and knickers. Corporal helps her into a light-blue surgeon's gown and mask. Then, she slowly pulls on rubber gloves. It's warm down here. No one has flicked on the air conditioning. Brenda perspires and Corporal mops her brow with a tissue.

This can't be serious. 'I'm going, Brenda. Goodbye.'

Sergeant and Corporal block my exit. 'Move out of the way, you pair of playground bullies.'

'Don't leave, Al. Help me,' begs Frankie.

'Slice his dick off, Brenda. Slice his dick off, Brenda' urges Sergeant in a sing-song voice. 'You can do the operation. You're smart.'

'Come on Brenda. Come on Brenda,' Corporal chants performing a jig. 'Chop Al's dick off as well. If he's got one.'

'Stop, Brenda. You've no intention of doing the operation yourself. This is madness.'

'I want my pictures. Frankie's going to say where they are. Or, his dick *will* be chopped off.'

'Does Jess know about the pictures?' I ask. 'She must be aware of everything Nicola does.'

'Torture Jess until she talks,' suggests Corporal.

'No,' snubs Sergeant. 'She likes pain too much.'

I bend towards Brenda. 'We need Jess to work for us.'

She doesn't reply.

'Jess is busy,' Frankie reveals. 'She's involved in a fantastic new project.'

Not listening to him, I watch Brenda make cuts with a scalpel at the top of Frankie's legs.

He almost faints on spotting the trickle of blood.

'I'm ringing Jenny,' I state forcefully. 'She must be told what's happening. Do you hear, Brenda?'

'Nip upstairs and bring the saw,' Sergeant instructs Corporal.

'What saw?' Please, can somebody admit this is a big joke? The focus must be shifted in another direction.

Images on the screens jump about then freeze. Electrical devices are so temperamental and calling companies to honour a warranty is such a pain. Pathetic excuses are invented.

Brenda steps away from the table and fiddles with a remote control. Nothing happens.

'I thought you were organising my exhibition programme.' I stare at my so-called partner. 'You've wasted energy researching and watching this video. Are you still on drugs, Brenda? Are you?'

'Want me to sort out your dickhead boyfriend, Brenda?' Sergeant stares hatefully.

'Come to your senses, Brenda.'

I'm on edge wondering where this is going.

'I've lost my pictures.'

Corporal descends the stairs with a chainsaw. Grinning, she angles the power tool out in front of herself.

'Brum-brum-brum-brum-brrrrrrrrrrrrrrrr,' is voiced loudly. 'Brum-brum-brum-brum-brrrrrrrrrrrrrrrr.'

The saw is hovered frighteningly close to Frankie's lower regions. Corporal easily pulls the tool to life. The noise is deafening. The stink of petrol everywhere. Nausea threatens to overwhelm. I need to leave. Live frugally off my pension and paint. Never will I go back to Greasby. There's no need for a job. I must struggle by and battle aggressively for recognition of my art.

'Tell Brenda where the pictures are,' yells Corporal at Frankie, angrily contorting her face.

'Shut up, you stupid bitch,' I snap, though keep my distance. 'Tell her to back off, Brenda. This is out of hand. Stop. For goodness sake. Stop.'

'Where are the pictures?' Sergeant barks at Frankie, now visibly quivering with fear.

'Yes. Tell me,' Brenda swipes. 'I'm ready to operate. I've no experience but shall follow this DVD.'

'What about anaesthetic?' Frankie frowns.

'Only this,' Sergeant holds aloft a large mallet.

'Your dick is coming off unless you start talking,' promises Brenda.

Sergeant laughs: 'Will he be another bloke found with his dick and balls cut off and stuffed in his mouth?'

Brenda doesn't react. I sincerely hope she hasn't been

involved with the trans murders.

Corporal breaks into song again.

*We're gonna cut your dick and balls off.*
*Dick and balls off. Dick and balls off.*
*You'll not like it. You'll not like it.*

With Jen absent to offer a musical accompaniment, Sergeant plays air guitar and jerks up and down.

Brenda waves the scalpel in front of Frankie's nose, then makes more incisions.

'Have my pictures been altered?' She leans close to his face. 'Have you made fakes from them?'

'End the joke, Brenda. End it. Please. I have an idea. It's a great idea. Listen to me.'

'We must move fast, Al. Anything could be happening to the pictures.'

'Dick and Paul have said nothing.'

'They'll take Nicola's cash and keep quiet.'

'That's speculation.'

'Greasby needs to talk. Start now, dickhead. Speak.' Brenda bristles with fury.

'Help, Al, please. I reawakened your artistic spirit.'

'Stop, Brenda. It's a joke gone too far.' She moves about as I try to attract her attention. 'Get a grip.'

'I know nothing.' Frankie struggles to break free. 'Tell her to release me, Al. I know nothing.'

'Liar. You and Nicola are compulsive liars.' Brenda plays with the scalpel under his nose. 'Was it Nicola who organised the burglaries?'

'I don't know. I don't know. I swear. Please, let me go.'

'You were in Germany when the Schmidts were robbed.'

'I'm a Das Sexhaus member. I've enjoyed myself there for years.'

'Nicola delivered a George Grosz watercolour and a lesbian scene to one of your London galleries. Jonty told Al. Where are they now?'

'I'm unaware that occurred.'

'You're full of shit. Confess. You know everything. Every little detail.'

An attempt is made to coax Brenda away from him. She resists. 'Leave me alone, Al. I'll prise a confession out of him if it's the last thing I do.'

'Where's Y based?'

'He regularly moves all over Europe.'

'Did Y's men rob Kirstin's house?'

'I don't know that lady.'

'Liar,' spits Brenda. 'Fucking liar.'

Sergeant moves to Frankie's side, pulling hard on the Prince Albert ring. 'Chop. Chop. Chop. Do it, Brenda, chop off his nasty man toy.'

Frankie cries in pain.

Sergeant continues to pull the ring.

'I loathe men,' she sneers.

'Steady on,' Frankie is distraught. 'I haven't a clue where the pictures are. Ask Nicola. Or, Jess. I don't know.'

'Chop it off now, Brenda. Chop. Chop. Chop.'

'Chop. Chop. Chop,' echoes Corporal, peering down at Frankie, while still holding the noisy saw.

'No. Stop! Don't hurt my gentleman. We've been good friends for years. Stop. Please leave him alone.'

Sergeant takes no notice, pulling the ring in all directions.

'I don't want a sex change. I'll stay as a man. You can have Greasby, Brenda. No charge. Just unfasten me. Tell her, Al. I don't want the company.'

He struggles to release himself from the leather straps fastening his arms and legs.

'This is theatre, Brenda. Bad theatre.'

More cuts are made on Frankie. Sergeant and Corporal watch excitedly. 'Come on Brenda. Come on Brenda. Come on Brenda,' they both sing.

Have they seen her do this before? Were the murders done here? Is Brenda guilty? I puzzle how to encourage Frankie to talk. Does he know anything? It's doubtful. Panic hammers at me.

'Where are the pictures?' Brenda persists. 'I want them back.'

'There's a secret place over here,' Frankie pants.

'Where is it?'

'Don't know. I swear, I don't know.'

'He's a liar, Brenda,' Sergeant shouts. 'Kill him.'

'You can have my company, Brenda. It's yours. I'll sign anything. I don't want a sex change.'

Suddenly we're in darkness. The electricity supply has tripped out.

I'm incensed. 'Those two electricians have ripped you off, Brenda. Emptying their bollocks was the priority. Have them back to do a proper job.'

Fumbling for my mobile, the torch is activated. Corporal and the chainsaw are a safe distance away. Thankfully, she's killed the power.

Frankie relaxes. 'This is hilarious. If you were trying to terrify me, Brenda, it worked. Fear is wonderfully exciting. I'm sure dying in erotic pain would've been a pleasant death. My gentleman is stiffer than ever. Remove these straps. I want to pull one off. Or can I have sex with Sergeant? I'd love to. You had me slightly worried for a while, Brenda.'

I sprint upstairs to a room housing electrical fuse boxes and central heating boilers. It's located off the entrance hall. With only my mobile for illumination, I search for the relevant fuse box to restore power. Those so-called electricians never undertook any repair work earlier. I was suspicious of them as soon as they arrived. I'm really angry.

Sergeant has followed and attacks: 'It was brilliant here before you conned your way in, sweeping Brenda off her feet with your fancy art talk. We had orgies and coke parties every night. Brenda needs to be back to her old self. Doing sex and drugs. That's what makes her happy. She's wasting her life with you. When you're asleep, Brenda snorts coke, then fucks me and Corporal up hill and down dale.'

There's always been a layer of frost on our relationship and it's obvious this venomous bitch has waited for an opportunity to spout these allegations.

'I'd like to believe you, Sergeant, but you tell lies. Big lies. Lots of them. Why don't you and Corporal stop playing at soldiers and focus your energies in a better way?'

I hate this seriously ugly stinking woman and her equally foul mate. I'll take them on, whatever the consequences.

She stares hard at me. 'When you're walking over the estate be careful a stray bullet doesn't find you.'

The comment doesn't deserve a response.

Back in the torture chamber, Brenda is found collapsed on the floor. Her wrists are slashed.

I poke 999 into my mobile.

'Ambulance, please. Banton Hall.'

From my First Aid knowledge, acquired years ago, I believe Brenda has cut veins rather than arteries, though blood is everywhere. Emergency procedures are carried out.

'I'm sorry, Al. Don't leave,' Brenda gasps, almost losing consciousness. 'Please. I love you more than anything.'

Tears flow down her cheeks.

'Don't worry.' I kneel down to offer comfort. 'I'm staying. We both need each other. *Ars longa, vita brevis.*'

She sobs wildly. Blood seeps through the makeshift bandages I've applied.

'Everything is okay, Brenda. I have an idea.'

'What is it?' She gazes intently.

'It may help us find the pictures.'

'Tell me. Tell me.' Her face is lined with anxiety, the make-up a mess.

'Later. We'll talk later.'

'Unfasten me, Al,' Frankie begs.

I take no notice.

Sergeant and Corporal move away in disgust. Ascending the stairs, their arms stretched round each other.

'You two want to grow up,' smacks Sergeant, glancing back at us.

'Get your fanny out,' Corporal says to her partner. 'Those two lovebirds have put me in the mood. I'll lick you dry.'

# Chapter 42

Thankfully, over the past week, Brenda has recovered. I've forgiven her. If indeed there was anything to apologise for. The Frankie incident is now looked upon as a piece of theatre. Silly theatre, brought on by anxiety over the stolen pictures. Brenda was taken to hospital, though discharged herself the next day. Whilst both wrists are still bandaged, she looks much healthier. The colour is back in her cheeks.

We didn't kiss and make up. There's still no intimate physical contact between us. It's difficult to imagine that happening. Brenda has said little about her actions. She did make a promise – no more displays of irrational behaviour. I smiled affectionately and didn't comment. My reaction can't be predicted if there's a reoccurrence of the antics. Any doubts about our relationship have been jettisoned from my mind by drawing and painting.

Brenda gave an assurance that no drugs were taken prior to the Frankie incident. This, of course, is contrary to what shit-stirring Sergeant had alleged. Brenda says there's no urge or desire to use coke ever again. Or take any of the anti-depressants prescribed by her personal doctor, preferring to ride white-knuckle through abstinence. Brenda continues to work with Amelia on all aspects of her recovery.

My plan for locating the stolen pictures has yet to be announced. Brenda has often questioned what it is, though I've kept quiet.

My own sanity suffered a little after the Frankie incident. I've experienced nightmares. Brenda is seen either self-harming or snorting coke with Sergeant and Corporal, then torturing trans men. The nightmares add to the ones I already endure about Nicola wrecking Alex's grave again. No matter. I manage to grab some undisturbed sleep.

Frankie didn't make any complaints about his ordeal, or even want compensation. Before leaving, he took a few of my clothes. Dresses aren't for him any longer. Walking towards a taxi, he surprised Sergeant by kicking her up the arse. Contented, Frankie waved to me as he went away, obviously pleased about keeping his gentleman.

Frankie was overjoyed cameras had recorded his ordeal in the torture chamber. Ellen edited the footage and sent a batch of DVDs for him to pick up at Jess's.

Brenda has bought Greasby and contracts have been signed. Nicola is no longer part of the company. Any payment owed to her is Frankie's responsibility. The same is true for Paulene. Nicola intends to run a new business from home with Jess's help. Greasby has been slimmed down to the Askworth Gallery and one London gallery. Those in Knutsford and Birmingham have closed.

I was interested to learn how Frankie might occupy himself in future.

'Not a clue,' he replied. 'I might even paint myself.'

Following the minor breakdown, Brenda has immersed herself in work, particularly at the new building. Our days begin at 7 am and don't end until late evening. Brenda handles most of the publicity herself, talking to international art magazines. This is the only occasion a collection of female art has been assembled on such a large scale. People are amazed at the size of the project and the building itself. Television crews plan to produce documentaries about Brenda and the scheme. It's given her confidence and helped restore her sanity.

The title of the building is no longer the Lesbian Art Museum. Brenda doesn't feel that Lesbian in the title is appropriate. It's now the Brenda Fitch Gallery with the subtitle A Celebration of Women in Art. Pictures and sculptures for the permanent collection arrive every week. Eventually, we hope enough works can be assembled to tour venues at home and abroad.

For a while, I'll oversee running the remaining Greasby

galleries and Brenda's new one. Ideally, Jess should be appointed to help out and gradually take over my role. The intention is to concentrate fully on my work. Frankie didn't give any further details about Jess's new project before he left.

Sophisticated drones and high-resolution cameras continue to keep watch over the Banton Hall estate. Brenda confessed she'd cracked up because of the constant threat of a bomb attack. She's spent hours in the surveillance office watching for any sign of that happening.

'Staff are doing their best,' I said. 'Have trust.'

'Easier said than done, Al.'

When walking over the estate, a keen watch has been kept for Sergeant and Corporal. I'm mindful of what Sergeant said about a stray bullet and don't leave the Hall without a bulletproof vest. After all, they both carry handguns and rifles when on patrol. Whenever we meet, their fingers shape like a gun and take aim at me.

Every time, the response is the same: 'Stop threatening me. I don't scare easily.'

They drop trousers or shorts and flash. On countless occasions, Brenda has told them to behave. Always, it falls on deaf ears.

To my horror, they often fire at birds flying over the estate. Rare species have been killed.

Sergeant and Corporal argue that shooting practice is necessary in case a drone carrying a bomb has to be downed.

# Chapter 43

Early evening, mid-week, I'm ready to put a job proposal to Jess. This has occupied my mind throughout the day. She must see the folly of working for Nicola – a disaster waiting to happen. It's long overdue and inevitable.

I'm convinced Jess has information about the pictures stolen from Brenda, Kirstin and the Schmidt family. Not knowing what's happened is at the root of Brenda's anxiety, I'm sure.

It's a gamble Jess will divulge information and be disloyal to Nicola.

I video call Jess.

'Brilliant, Al,' she answers enthusiastically. 'Just in time to watch the start of a sexathlon.'

'Where are you?'

'In a hired school gym. It's a short distance away from the main building. For a few hours one night every week, I'm running Jess's Sexhaus. A sex, drugs and booze club. A gym standing empty every night is a waste. The club is six weeks old. Soon, I'm opening two nights a week.'

This is a bad mistake. I should've texted beforehand.

'I'll hand you over to Kai, my new boyfriend,' Jess says. 'He used to be Head Boy at this school. Then, I can explain about the club.'

Kai is a towering, broad-shouldered man in his mid-20s.

'Look at him, Al, he's beautifully hung. We have an open relationship, fucking who we want, together or apart.'

With a cheeky grin, she looks comfortable and confident. Her hair is dyed bright-red. Beneath a flimsy, black see-through gown is only a thong. Heavy black boots encase her feet. Long, red acrylic nails extend from her finger-tips.

'I'll guide you round the gym, Al.'

'Perhaps another night.'

'Follow me, Kai.'

As the mobile tracks across the room, naked and semi-naked teenagers are everywhere. Girls wear gymslips, stockings, suspenders and high heels. Lads have short trousers and school caps. Desperate to be different, a few sport severe 'footballer' haircuts. Some have attempted to grow beards though many are no more than bumfluff. Well-drawn imaginative tattoos are visible. On leaving art college now, would I have become a tattoo artist? Opening a studio on the High Street, alongside the hairdressers and nail salons replacing traditional businesses? Maybe.

A man in his 50s wears only underpants, while a woman of the same age tries to be sexy with a powder-blue basque. Their involvement is curious.

Also present is Jess's mum, Philomena, known better as Mena. A bubbling, little woman with a podgy face, she's the only one still fully dressed. Mena's made no attempt to look sexy or even attractive. Out of place in an orgy, she supports Jess regardless.

The students enjoy sex in various positions on mats or a number of hobby horses set at a low height. There's a bed in the middle of the room occupied by cavorting couples. Nobody is bashful. Having sex in a communal atmosphere isn't a problem.

Floor-to-ceiling windows surround two sides of the regulation-size school gym. It's 85 feet by 50 feet. Heavy blue curtains are drawn across them, shutting out light and peeping eyes.

'I wanted to put a proposition to you, Jess. Let's speak again in a couple of days.'

'No, wait. We can talk soon.'

'Hello, Al,' Mena shouts.

'Hi,' I answer.

The mobile switches back to show Jess.

'How old are these kids?' I press.

'Over 16. Their IDs are checked.'

Students snort coke from trestle tables. A bar provides alcoholic drinks. Mobiles record all the action. People today can't be deprived of these devices. Their life will drain away without them.

'Lads and lasses from two of the city's schools attend each week and compete,' Jess explains, nodding knowingly at students. 'I stage inter-schools shagging competitions. The response is brilliant. It beats boring school sports' days run by bossy teachers full of shit.'

The two teams present are identified by students wearing their school's name on vests. One shouts: *ST MICHAEL'S SEX TEAM*, the other *ASKWORTH SHAGGING ACADEMY – NOBODY BEATS US.*

'Students from other cities are making bookings,' Jess continues. 'Between 30 and 50 attend every week, though more and more want to join in. Sixty are here tonight. I'm booked up for the next few weeks. Everyone adores these sessions. My Sexhaus members pay a club fee of fifty quid, then twenty quid each time they come. Oops, sorry, that's a daft play on words, isn't it?'

My pulse races.

With her face filling the mobile screen, Jess stares at me unflinchingly. 'Don't look so shocked and miserable, Al. We're enjoying ourselves. A BDSM club wants me to organise a night for them once a month. I'm thinking about it. They've offered loads of cash. Stupid money really.'

I don't comment.

'Students bring their own coke by the way. Plenty of kids deal in schools.'

'How legal is this?' My screen is held close, so everything from Jess's mobile can be seen.

'Deirdre, the chairperson of this school's governors, helps me out,' Jess admits. 'She's a coke head and runs a string of massage parlours in the city. Deirdre's a councillor too, and sits on the local police committee. That's her wearing the basque.

The lads often gangbang her. She'll be in a gobbleathon later. It's a contest to judge how many lads she can service over ten minutes. Whatever's achieved, I shall try and beat. Last week, Diedre did 20 lads in ten minutes. Terrific!'

The mobile switches to Deirdre. A lazy hand lifts to give a silly wave. I recognise her from my Council days and never thought she'd be in a scenario like this one.

'Club members are very competitive,' Jess gushes, weaving through the various activities. 'Everyone stretches their sexual boundaries to the limit. People are insatiable. Don't you think so, Al?'

Her hands raise to emphasise a point, or an arm affectionately slips round a student. A gaggle of lads wave their protrusions at me. Lasses blow kisses or expose themselves explicitly.

'Are parents aware of your club?'

'Yes. Yes. They want me to open a Sexhaus in Askworth city centre. Similar to the one in Germany. Financial backing isn't a problem. I'm taking a large group of parents on a trip there in two weeks. A few have already been.'

It's no use trying to persuade Jess to work for us. More effort must be put into perfecting my plan for locating the stolen pictures.

'Keep watching, Al. Lexi, one of the female students, is ready to compete in a sexathlon circuit,' Jess announces. 'The challenge is open to lads and lasses. There's shagging, drinking and snorting coke. Amazing timings are achieved. Ten lasses are involved tonight, one after the other. A lesbian sexathlon is later. You must stay and watch. It's really sexy.'

Focusing my attention on any one event is difficult.

'You'll like what you see, Al. Even inspired.'

I muse that a sexathlon in a cemetery with men and women might be a great subject.

'Take pictures here one night or make sketches. Join in if you want. No problem. Sex is fun. Fun is sex. That's how it should be. Get into position, Lexi. We're ready to begin.'

There's a happy atmosphere. Joy is evident on most faces.

Several girls are lost in themselves, moving up and down like machines on lads laid across the floor.

'Who is the older man, Jess?'

'School caretaker, Tom Dealey. Don't know what I'd do without him. Lives in a house nearby. Sets everything out each club night. Stores the bed in his garage. And provides towels for the showers at the end of a session. It's fabulous. We shower together.'

Dealey is a caricature of a pervert, with stubble on his face and filthy teeth, reminiscent of a burnt fence. He has a full head of badly dyed hair. It looks as if he's wearing a dead ferret.

'What's in it for him?' I chew on my bottom lip.

'He's treated to a wank, fuck or a blow job by me or one of the lasses,' Jess answers easily.

'What about his wife?'

'She's only too pleased we can help out,' Jess laughs. 'You know what wives are like after 20 years of marriage. They hate fucking, and men find mistresses or sex workers. Tom's dick is like a baby's arm. If requested, he spanks people. Lads and lasses. He's only just started snorting coke. Loves it.'

Competitor Lexi is naked. Strikingly good looking, her hair has highlights and is fashionably tied back. Earlobes sparkle with gold studs. Mena arranges lines of coke that rapidly vanish into a nostril. Then, Lexi straddles a lad lying on his back. Naked chums shout encouragement.

Finishing that, Lexi downs a pint of beer before moving on to have oral sex with four lads. Mena follows with a stop watch. Completing that stage, Lexi scissors two girls. Grunts, groans and cries of pleasure reverberate in the room. I'm shown disgusting close ups. Students watch and cheer. Peals of laughter are frequently heard.

Deidre leads a few blindfolded lads into the gym.

'What's happening there, Jess?'

She keeps walking up to the mobile so her face is caught full-frame in mine. 'These lads are participating in the quickest hard on competition. Once the blindfolds are removed, lasses will excite them. Deirdre judges who stands to attention first. That's followed by a wanking contest.'

'What's happening behind you, Jess?'

'It's the lasses' Orgasm Corner. With weirdly-shaped vibrators they'll see who comes first. Tom is the judge. As you can hear, once the vibrators are switched on it's noisy.'

Jess's mobile shows close-ups of the girls' faces. Two of them wink and smile at me. Kai then scans Jess's device over the room. I roll my eyes, convinced these students are sex robots. Programmed for pleasure, they occasionally pause and chuckle to one another.

'Any problems with gatecrashers, Jess?'

'Two huge men are employed for security. They're outside now. What did you want to talk about?'

Announcing the job proposal, Jess isn't impressed. In fact, she's annoyed.

'Name your price. Brenda promises to pay well for running the Gallery.'

'I'm not leaving Nicola. No way. Or, jacking in running this club. Nicola's my mate as well as my boss. I can run Jess's Sexhaus and work for her. She wants to get involved one night. My life is great. I'm enjoying every minute and endlessly orgasmic.'

Her response was predictable, but worth a try. Brenda is going to be annoyed at Jess's decision.

'How are things with Nicola?'

'Same as always. Struggling for cash but we can survive. What's it like living at Banton?'

'Brilliant.'

'Are you shagging Brenda?'

'Mind your own business.'

'Or, is she shagging you?'

'Part of the job offer would be helping to promote my work,' I state.

The joy on Jess's face flips to anger. She's sensed I strongly disapprove of this club and want to haul her back to the straight and narrow.

'Your paintings are pathetic,' she fires. 'Too safe. Don't challenge anything. Not exciting. Only cartoons. No more than that. Nicola and me laughed at the ones you emailed recently.'

'I don't care what Nicola thinks.'

'They're poor Ensor copies. No. I don't want to promote your art. I think it's shit. So does Nicola.' She moves about, unable to stay still for a second.

The comments are disappointing. My arm aches from holding the mobile. I can't sustain the pose much longer nor watch the activities. Why am I even observing them? All are sickening. The video link must be severed.

'I feel so sorry for you, Al,' Jess babbles. 'Brenda and the others must torture you every night. Is that what you like?'

'Kirstin is taking legal action over the forged provenance.'

'Don't care. Nicola can hire a top barrister. Everything will be sorted.'

'Not if the barrister demands an up-front payment.'

A commotion is heard. Detective Inspector Jenny Allsopp, in a charcoal-grey trouser suit, barges into view. She's accompanied by a group of ten uniformed officers, eight men and two women. Their expressions are intense. This was predictable. I fear for Jess. Could she serve a long sentence for involving teenagers in sex and drugs? Not to mention misuse of Council premises. She might even enjoy a stretch inside. Shut up, I scold myself. That's an awful thought.

Unmoved by the intrusion, students carry on competing. Many believe the police to be part of the activities. Girls throw their arms at male officers. One girl jumps forwards on to a WPC, smothering her with kisses. Three girls pull relentlessly at one PC's trousers, trying to remove them. All tumble to the floor. Colleagues attempt a rescue as more girls snatch at his trousers. A battery of mobiles captures the action. Male officers are unsure where to place their hands on naked bodies. Maybe they fear recriminations later. Half a dozen lads surround DI Jenny and provocatively thrust and wave their manhood.

Handcuffs and pepper spray appear.

'Who are you?' Mena confronts Jenny. 'Are you in a competition?'

Tom is scared, wanting a place to hide, though can't see one. Perhaps he's familiar to the police. It wouldn't surprise.

Jess shows frustration, angry the evening's thrills are disrupted. A few students try to hide the drugs.

'I'm a police officer,' Jenny yells, escaping from the male group. Striding up to Jess, she presents identification. 'Jessica Jones, I'm arresting you for handling stolen works of art. You do not have to say anything…'

'Fuck off, stupid bitch,' Mena interjects, shoulder-charging Jenny away from Jess. 'Arrest fucking Nicola Greasby. My daughter has done fuck all. Go away. You're spoiling the fun. Go fuck yourself.'

Ugly confrontations ensue and the connection with Kai is lost.

# Chapter 44

I'm pleased to wake up in a morning. Thrilled to be alive and happy when I see Brenda thriving too. We still sleep separately. It doesn't bother us. Apart from a few aches and pains, I'm physically fit. Although, if I sit too long painting and drawing, my back hurts. No matter. A small price to pay for creativity throughout the day and occasionally during the night.

Mentally, it's a struggle first thing in a morning. I have to go through a number of routines set by Amelia, who visits me every fortnight. Brenda sees her weekly. I walk or cycle over the estate. The Hall's gym is often used. There's also a sauna. A healthy breakfast, prepared by the cook, is eaten in the kitchen. Alcohol is rejected and my caffeine intake limited. Frequently, cognitive therapy is employed to interrogate my negative thoughts. Anti-depressants have been left alone. It's a challenge. There's strong evidence mood disorders, such as depression and bipolarism, are more prevalent among artists and writers. Aiming to disprove the theories, a great amount of concentration and commitment is required.

Anti-depressants took the edge off my creative urge. Raw emotions must be felt. It's the only way motivation can be achieved to create. Once I've gone through the early morning routines, there's tranquility. I always make sure my clothes are smart yet comfortable. Out loud, a phrase is repeated: 'I'm happy. I'm happy. I'm happy.' That's before work begins in the studio. I'm in there now. My art involves humour. I love to laugh.

The only regret is I didn't find solace in art sooner. When starting art college, a tutor offered advice: 'Whatever you do, don't waste your time.' In future, I don't intend to.

Brenda puts no pressure on me about anything. I love living with her at the Hall. Besides providing plenty of support and motivation, she constantly occupies herself with a multitude of tasks: the running of the Hall, overseeing security arrangements, and organising work at the new gallery. We've received invitations to visit galleries across the world and intend accepting them in due course. Brenda is also working hard on my forthcoming exhibition programme. I'm trying to complete enough pictures.

It's late morning. Sunlight pours through the studio window. Brenda bursts in clutching her mobile.

'Jess is at the main entrance. Sergeant says she's sobbing and desperate to see you.'

'Good. Hope she's okay.'

Brenda and I smile together. Is this the answer to everything? Can Jess reveal the whereabouts of the pictures? Hopefully, they've not been sold. A small sigh of relief is released.

Using the mobile, Brenda instructs Sergeant to bring Jess to the Hall. I'm pleased she's here. Surely, we can coax her into working for us. Brenda is thinking along the same lines, but expresses a serious concern: 'Before giving Jess clearance, Sergeant must check whether she's wearing a suicide vest. Or, if her car has a bomb.'

A few minutes later, I peer out of the studio window and see Jess driving towards the Hall. With the passenger- and driver's-side doors wide open, she's with Sergeant and Corporal who stand either side on the vehicle's sills. Gun-toting, the pair occasionally fire into the air. A WLA drone hovers overhead, recording their arrival.

Over the last few days, attempts were made to contact Jess, only without success. I was desperate to learn more details about her brush with the law. Jenny wasn't forthcoming with any information when contacted. She's spoken once again to Kirstin and the Schmidts, gathering more details. Dick and Paul gave particulars about the fakes. Jenny contacted the collectors with pictures missing from the Askworth basement. Each one had them insured so were reluctant to make any statements. Yet more people have returned fakes and further legal demands are pending. Whether these remain relevant now Greasby has changed hands is another matter.

Brenda and I rush out to meet Jess.

Sergeant and Corporal forcibly drag her from the car and on to the gravel. A dozen WLA soldiers of various shapes and sizes sprint forwards. They wear camouflage short-sleeve shirts, shorts and heavy boots. Their body equipment is similar to that of crack police officers patrolling airports. Several have machine guns. Like a pack of hungry wolves, they circle Jess. A few fire weapons skywards.

She's still in the see-through black gown and thong from the other night. The dyed red hair is matted to her head. Make-up, usually so prominent, non-existent.

Excited, Sergeant and Corporal pull at the thong.

WLA soldiers shout ribald comments. A lot glance disdainfully at Brenda, who's stylish in a knee-length Tweed skirt, jacket and black high heels.

Covering almost every inch of WLA skin are many colourful and elaborate tattoos. There must be millionaire tattooists in Askworth. A few owning Rolls-Royces.

A group of Hall staff, weeding, pruning and cutting grass, stop work, gather a short distance away. All eager to discover what's happening. A wave from Brenda is enough for them to disperse.

Will Sergeant and Corporal torture and kill Jess? They know she's Nicola's pal. Brenda and I must intervene to get information.

Aroused by Jess's half-naked body, the WLA elbow each other, attempting to fondle her. With arms and legs held down, Jess is terrified and screams. Everyone shouts at once, creating more mayhem. They tweak her boobs and fight to stuff fingers inside her.

'Lick this, bitch,' one soldier barks. I know her only as Big Ada. Thirty five years old, she weighs in at 18 stones. One half of her head is shaved, the other closely cropped and dyed blonde. With a large chiselled face and square jaw, she's humourless and I sense psychotic. Occasionally, we've met on the estate, though no words passed between us. Her concentration is always elsewhere. Now, she's frighteningly animated and sexually charged.

Discarding a machine gun like an unnecessary piece of clothing, she drops her shorts and underwear, then squats on Jess's face.

'Me next, Ada. Me next,' her comrades shout, each one eager to explore new flesh.

'I can't breathe,' gasps Jess. 'Help, Al.'

'Enjoy, bitch. Enjoy,' shouts Big Ada.

'Lick it, bitch. Lick it,' everyone chants as they swarm Jess.

I struggle to find a way through them. 'Leave her alone,' I yell, tugging at Big Ada. It's like trying to move a block of concrete.

'My go, Ada. My go,' the jostling mob cry.

The stink of sweat overwhelms.

Trying once again to shift the large woman away, I'm knocked over by a flailing arm. Sergeant and Corporal kick me whilst I'm down.

Jess will be crushed and suffocate. She must have some knowledge of the stolen items' whereabouts. A widely-publicised substantial reward offered for information drew a blank. Nobody came forwards. Nothing has been revealed for the police to work on. Brenda must take control.

WLA soldier Nicky the Knife pulls out a blade, slashing Jess's gown to ribbons. The thong is easily cut away, giving eager hands every opportunity to make further rough explorations. Nicky cuts chunks off Jess's hair.

I dash about wondering what to do. She must not suffocate. Not now.

Big Ada's eyes are shut tight. Her head rolls about in pleasure. Having difficulty breathing, Jess fights furiously to break free. Several women drop their shorts ready to be next in line.

Jess has got to survive.

'Stop this, Brenda. We must hear what Jess has to say.'

'Enough. Everyone move back,' orders Brenda calmly.

Jess attempts a swing at Big Ada though misses. The heavier woman laughs.

'Hurry, Ada. Me next,' begs Corporal.

'Back off!' yells Brenda. 'Back off.'

Why can't people make more from their lives, create and achieve a goal? Instead of seeking split-second relief through sex.

Brenda fights a way through the mass of bodies. Big Ada grips Jess's hair, dragging the younger woman into her lower regions.

'Let us have the bitch, Ada,' Sergeant and Corporal appeal. They close in, exciting themselves. Others do the same.

Communal masturbation in a cemetery. Is this another subject to tackle? Maybe.

'That's enough, Ada!' Brenda easily shifts bodies aside. 'Get off her.'

Eyes flit from one WLA soldier to another, eager to discover what might happen next. Standing half-naked, they jog up and down.

'Hold her legs back,' shouts Sergeant. 'She's waxed. I'll go down on her.'

'Move away!' Brenda yells.

'We all want to fuck the young cunt,' swipes Corporal. 'Everyone's excited. It's only natural.'

'Pack it in,' Brenda repeats.

'You go next with the bitch.' Sergeant stands in front of Brenda, though is forcefully knocked away.

'You're soft in the head, Brenda,' spits Sergeant, looking aggressively in my direction.

Brenda headbutts Sergeant. Nasty expressions spray other faces.

Watching Brenda rule with a rod of iron is always entertaining. Sergeant often tries to upstage her though without success.

It invariably ends with a violent confrontation. And only one winner.

Brenda punches Big Ada hard in the side of the face. Before dragging herself away, the large woman bends down to Jess. 'See you later, Honey Bee.'

Jess doesn't reply, her eyes stream with tears. The soldiers fix their eyes on her breasts, unconcerned by the rape she's endured.

Corporal steps forwards hoping to replace Big Ada. A scowl from Brenda is enough to make her think twice.

Jess's arms encircle me. 'Help, Al. Please. I don't want to be locked up. I'll never work for Nicola again. She set me up.'

The WLA women stare at her with hatred.

'Drag her down to the torture chamber,' commands Sergeant, wiping blood from her face. 'We want some fun.'

Corporal looks at Jess and licks her lips.

'Are you okay, love?' Brenda moves to protect Jess. 'What's happened?'

She unfurls herself from me. 'I've been arrested. Charged with conspiracy to burgle and handling stolen art. Bastard coppers locked me up in a piss-ridden cell for three days…' She pauses and pants, '…with smackhead working girls throwing-up and begging for a fix. Had to gobble two male detectives before they brought a drink. Two female detectives fingered me.'

'Take it easy, Jess,' I urge. 'Have a breather. Speak when comfortable.'

'Mum picked me up from the police station. I went home for my car and came straight here.'

'Why not make contact earlier?' Brenda is curious. 'We could've helped.'

'The police took my mobile and wouldn't let me have a phone call.'

'What did they say about your sex club?' I question.

'They found a load of coke. I might be charged with possession, even intent to supply. Please help, both of you. I don't want to be locked up.'

'I'll help you, Jess,' promises Brenda. 'But where are my pictures?'

Jess is at rock bottom. A marked contrast to a few days ago. Her energy and confidence have both drained away. Nicola's betrayal hurts.

Frustrated at not reaching a climax earlier, Big Ada lies down. Two WLA soldiers hold her legs back. Then, she's violently fisted.

Jess grips Brenda. 'Help me. I'll fuck each one of you. Do anything. Please help. I've no money.'

'What's Nicola done with the pictures?' insists Brenda. 'You can stay here. Have a job. Just tell me.'

'For fuck's sake. To the torture chamber,' growls Sergeant. 'Torture. Pain. Torture. Pain.' She slams her face within half an inch of Jess's nose. 'I've got the perfect dildo for you. When it goes up your arse, you'll think it's a broken bottle.'

Her WLA chums cheer and punch the air. Many still jog on the spot.

'Stop!' I scream. 'We need to talk.'

'Dump this jerk, Brenda, and have fun with us,' Sergeant sneers.

'Where are Brenda's pictures?' screeches Corporal.

The words slap Jess in the face. 'I've no idea. I'm sorry. Truly, I've no idea.'

'We need to know,' I state. 'We want them for the gallery opening. They're the icing on the cake.'

'Have you no idea?' probes Brenda aggressively.

'I'm sorry,' Jess whimpers.

Brenda's head drops. She was desperate for news. Details of my plan have still not been revealed. I keep mulling them over.

'She's bullshitting,' insists Sergeant. 'Me and Corporal will make her confess.' Brenda thwarts an attempt to seize Jess.

'For God's sake, Jess,' I shout. 'Tell us where the pictures are.'

Nervously, she blinks at Sergeant and Corporal. 'I don't

know anything.'

Nobody responds.

'You're putting too much energy into finding the pictures,' Jess states forcefully. 'Nicola might have sold them.'

'Have you sent out details to collectors?'

'No, Al. Nothing.'

Brenda struggles to believe her.

'Are you sure, Jess?' I challenge.

'Positive.'

An appealing look hits us.

'The bitch is a traitor,' swipes Sergeant.

'Yes, I helped in the robberies. I put my hands up to that. But I don't know what happened to the pictures afterwards.'

'Are they still in the UK?' I ask.

'Don't know.'

Everyone present ignores Big Ada's scene and hangs on to Jess's words.

'Sorry I trashed your work, Al. Honestly.' Jess reaches out to hold one of my hands. With large innocent-looking eyes, she continues: 'And for what I said the other night. You know me, always spouting bollocks.'

Kneeling on the floor, looking up, Jess shifts her gaze between Brenda and me.

'She's no use, Brenda.' Sergeant is agitated. 'Hand her over.'

Jess appeals to my partner: 'I want to work for you, Brenda.' Her eyes switch to me. 'I'll help promote your work, Al. Please, take me on.'

'Frankie says the pictures are stored in a secret place,' Brenda submits. 'What does he mean? Have you any idea where it is?'

'No. I don't.'

Brenda groans.

'Fist me, Fist me,' cries Big Ada. 'Faster. Faster. Harder. Harder, you useless pair of bitches. Give it to me.'

'Torture. Torture,' the WLA soldiers repeat ominously. Surrounding Jess, they grasp her arms and legs. 'Down to the Torture chamber. Now,' all of them yell. They carry her fighting frantically towards the Hall's entrance

'Put her down,' Brenda shouts. 'Put her down, now. You fucking animals.'

'Help me, Al. Brenda.' Jess rushes back to us and drops to her knees. 'The police want to arrest Nicola, Frankie and Y. I'll testify against them. I might get a lighter sentence if they're convicted.'

Despite all Jess's unruly, weird and crazy behaviour in the past, I can't help but regard her with a little compassion.

'I'm scared. Really scared. The police are corrupt bastards. If they tell Nicola I'm helping them, I'm dead. Please let me stay here. Please.'

'That has a price,' grins Sergeant, wiping more blood from her face.

Jess continually sheds tears. Brenda kneels down to her. They hug.

'The police know I was involved in bringing the pictures to the UK,' Jess garbles, trying to string coherent sentences together. 'I don't know where they are now. I swear.'

She constantly pauses to cry, her body trembling.

Initially, the WLA soldiers listened intently to the discussion, though have lost interest. Wildly, they chase each other about, tweaking boobs and bumping crotches.

Brenda is restless, trying to assess the situation and reach a decision. Running a hand through her hair, she stands with hands on hips or arms folded.

I'm worried. If Nicola learns Jess is here, an attack could be imminent. From Brenda's anxious expression, I sense she's thinking the same.

'I'll give evidence at Kirstin's hearing,' Jess announces. 'Mum will admit the Grosz provenance was faked. We'll do anything.'

This lights a bulb in Brenda.

'Why should the slag be trusted?' snarls Sergeant.

Brenda doesn't answer.

'We don't want her here, Brenda. She's too much of a risk,'

Sergeant adds.

'Fuck off. It's your job to sort out security,' Brenda rages.

'This bitch is a bomb magnet. Nicola has said she'd blow up Banton.' Sergeant stands close to Jess. 'Do you know anything?'

'No, I swear. No. The police hoped I knew where the pictures were, then explain how they were stolen and who was involved.'

In the background, Big Ada moans loudly.

'Nicola told the police she never knew what I was doing. Denied any knowledge of the robberies and blamed me.'

'Don't listen to her, Brenda,' Sergeant persists. 'She's a liability.'

'Please let me stay, Brenda. Please. Don't let them lock me up. I could get years.'

'She must know where the pictures are.' Sergeant faces Brenda. 'Must know.'

'Only Nicola knows what's happened to them,' Jess argues. 'I always thought she had buyers for pictures before they were robbed.'

'Let's capture Nicola,' offers Sergeant. 'And kill the Russians protecting her.'

'Too risky,' Brenda snaps.

'Nicola is pure evil,' Jess blurts out. 'She's betrayed me, her best friend.'

Brenda is happy Jess wants to support Kirstin. It's second best. A step in the right direction. Let's see where it takes us. I'm pleased that Brenda has resisted the torture option.

'Help, Brenda. Nicola has shit on me.'

'Have a bite to eat,' Brenda invites. 'A bath. I'll organise help. I'm happy for you to work for us.'

'I promise to pay you back. I'll do anything. You can torture me. I'll shag all of you. In any way you want.'

'Not necessary. Kirstin should be very pleased having you onboard. You may have to fuck her and Anna.'

'No problem. With pleasure.'

An ear-splitting shriek is enough for everyone to realise Big Ada has reached her destination. The soldiers who've helped are exhausted.

'At long last, Ada,' Sergeant swivels to comment. 'You're taking longer and longer. Only bizarre sex makes you come now.'

Corporal agrees.

Before we enter the Hall, Jess moves forwards to give a tight hug. 'I love you, Al.'

She can help run the galleries. Presently, Deb assists with everything. Besides opening a gallery in New York, we want to set one up in Los Angeles. Deb is busy making the arrangements. These are exciting times.

'Al says he has a plan to unearth the pictures,' Brenda reveals to Jess.

'I'm not ready to divulge details yet,' I hastily add.

'Al always has a solution to a problem,' Jess submits.

Inquisitive, I pose a question: 'What are the Russians doing at Nigel's church?'

'They're painters, carvers and sculptors. Nigel wants the church to reflect a particular style. That's what I've been told. Don't know much more.'

'Are the men competent?'

Jess shrugs.

'Have you ever been inside the church to admire their work?'

'Nobody else is allowed inside.'

Brenda and myself exchange puzzled looks.

'Religious art is awful,' Jess continues confidently. 'It's old-fashioned. Art needs to be totally free from church influence.'

That's a sentiment close to my heart.

'Nigel is involved with the stolen pictures,' Jess pipes up.

'How?' asks Brenda.

'Whenever I brought pictures from Europe, they were delivered to him. Nicola was never present. A taxi always took me home. Usually, I offered to fuck him or give a gobble to save Nicola a job. He refused. Always eager to get rid of me.'

This information will need assessing and passed on for Jenny to investigate. Nigel is such a pathetic figure. A churchman not wanting sex with a nymphomaniac like Jess, yet is only aroused after a thumping from his criminal wife. Incredible.

Fully dressed again and beaming, Big Ada approaches Jess. 'I didn't mean any harm, Honey Bee. I want us to have good sex and for you to be mine.'

Brenda frowns at her, ready to land another punch.

'Fuck off, Ada.' Sergeant stands between her and Jess. 'Get back on duty.'

Obeying, she moves off, machine gun clasped close to her chest.

With a fierce expression, Brenda summons Sergeant forwards and holds her forcefully by the throat.

'Everyone must be vigilant and on full alert. No fucking about. No having a quick finger or fuck with your mate or anyone else.'

Sergeant does not attempt to struggle free. Blood still drips from her nose.

Brenda's relationship with the WLA is far from orthodox. Sergeant is viewed with murderous intent. 'If you fuck up, I'll personally tie you and Corporal down on the torture tables and set your horrible hairy fannies on fire. Ellen will make a video, reminding you pair of cunts to never fuck up.'

Sergeant remains silent.

'Are you smooth like a billiard ball, Brenda?' Corporal grins. 'Can you confirm that, Al?'

Brenda is incensed. 'You cheeky bitch. Mind your own fucking business.'

Corporal feels a backhander across the face.

'Don't laugh, bitch, unless I say so.'

'Sorry Brenda.'

'Expect the unexpected,' Brenda continues, facing Sergeant. 'Shoot down anything. Anything. Practice on fucking ducks or geese flying over the fucking estate. Don't come telling me some namby-pamby twitcher, with his finger up his arse, has complained dozens of protected species have been killed. I couldn't give a fuck. Remember, "bomb Banton, bomb Banton" is the mantra cunt Nicola constantly repeats to herself. Given the chance, I'll stuff a bomb up her fanny. Me, Al, this Hall and estate, have got to survive.'

She headbutts Sergeant's again. 'Understand?'

'Yes, Brenda. Understood,' Sergeant cries.

# Chapter 45

Brenda, Jess and I make our way into the Hall's kitchen wing. With walls painted magnolia, the main room is lofty and light pours in through two tall windows. The middle floor area is dominated by a large pine table. Amongst other features are pine cupboards, Formica work surfaces and a cream-coloured AGA. Light brown and well-worn flagstones cover the floor. The entire room is always spotlessly clean. Always. Certain items from the original Victorian kitchen have lingered here, giving character to the place. These include copper utensils.

The kitchen is the coveted domain of Miss Joanne Beal, Banton's cook. A tall portly woman in her 50s, she has natural blonde hair cut to her shoulders, light make-up, a cheery smile and friendly disposition. At Banton since her teens, she's never married. Joanne lives alone in a flat above the kitchen. Occasionally, I've noticed female friends visiting her. Never any males. She owns a short-haired mongrel dog, called Mickey. My nickname for him is Shagger, as he always tries to hump one of my legs.

Joanne is a private person, rarely going out and keeps herself to herself. Providing a menu for breakfast and dinner each day, she caters for a number of Hall residents. Often, this is a dozen people. Meals are taken in an adjacent dining room.

Constantly, there's a tantalising waft of cooking aromas flowing out of the kitchen. Today, it's from home-made steak-and-kidney pies – my favourite. Fourteen of them sit on the pine table. A big pan of onion gravy simmers on the AGA. Mashed potatoes and a nutritious group of vegetables are regularly served with meals. Strong percolated coffee is available at all times. Wearing a white apron and cap, Joanne – not liking the formal Miss Beal – is a caricature of a cook.

Observing Jess's gown in tatters, Joanne's gaze drops to her naked lower regions. It lingers there for a while. Longer than comfortable for the casual observer.

'Oh, you poor mite. What's happened?' Joanne steps forwards.

'Big Ada raped her,' I volunteer.

Jess blinks away tears.

'How awful,' Joanne's face creases in concern. 'I'll see to that bitch later. Are you staying for dinner?'

Jess affectionately recognises Joanne's friendly looks.

Brenda interrupts: 'Yes. Jess could be here for a while.'

'I'll nip to the kitchen garden and pick a few things,' announces Joanne. 'I'll be back in a jiffy. We can have a chat later, Jess, if you like.'

'That would be lovely.'

'Do you want to have a bath or shower, Jess?' suggests Brenda.

'I need to masturbate. Is that okay?'

'Yes, of course.'

'That fat ugly twat nearly suffocated me but it was exciting. Pain and pleasure are special. I'm an orgasm addict. Once sexually aroused, I must come. I'd like to stage an exhibition depicting female masturbation in art. Gustave Courbet's painting, *Le Sommeil*, is fantastic. Gets me really wet. I'll appeal for similar pictures and see if there's a good response. It could be very, very exciting.'

Brenda regards her sympathetically.

'Make yourself comfy, Jess. I must find clothes for you to wear. Al will pour you a coffee and find a packet of chocolate biscuits.'

Before leaving us, Brenda gives Jess a squeeze, treating her like a wayward daughter coming home after a weekend spat.

'Bath me later if you want Brenda. I'll be your baby.'

Brenda blushes.

Moving the pies to the edge of the table, Jess finds room

to recline and raise her legs. 'Pass the rolling pin, Al. That'll pleasure me nicely.'

'Isn't it too thick?'

'No, just right.'

'Squirt liquid soap on. Push it in and out, Al.'

'No.'

'Don't you ever feel anything in your bollocks?'

'Sex leads to a family. That's what I don't want. Why is everybody obsessed with sex? It ruins everything. I'm pleased to be out of a family situation. Most artists I admire functioned better without a family. I remember watching an L.S. Lowry documentary, where he was asked: "when you see a family scene with husband, wife and kids, what is your reaction?" He answered casually: "I'm well out of that". To create great art, there needs to be complete detachment from family life. James Ensor and Edward Burra never had a family, nor did René Magritte. These are my heroes. Artists can't be associated with domesticity. It's distracting.'

Jess stares as though I've landed from another planet.

'You talk bollocks, Al. You're the only artist I know who doesn't enjoy a fuck.'

'That's irrelevant.'

'Why not paint a suite of pictures featuring me. Jess fucking rugby players. Jess fucking barristers. Jess fucking schoolboys. A whole series. It'd be hilarious. Much more fun than skeletons.'

'Don't think so.'

'I'm tense. I want an orgasm. Excite me.'

'You need treatment. There must be other ways of relieving stress.'

'You're always talking shit.'

This attitude is disappointing. Brenda rescued her from the WLA, offered a job and place to stay. That's besides Brenda promising a lawyer to fight any police charges. Much wants more.

'Milk or sugar in your coffee?' I search for cups.

'Fuck coffee. Is there coke anywhere?'

'I've none.'

'Has Brenda?'

'Don't think so.'

'I'll score later. A coke head here must have a stash. Is there a beer in the fridge?'

A can is handed over. She takes a swig, then manipulates the rolling pin.

Unable to understand her antics, I pour a coffee.

'Suck my tits, Al,' Jess giggles. 'Look. My nipples are erect. Lick them. Feel how firm they are.'

Typical. Jess constantly tries to embarrass me. 'Have control. Self-respect. Pride.'

'Fuck off.'

Holding out a hand, she beckons. 'Get me in the mood, Al. Rub down there. I'm really wet. We can enjoy ourselves. How do you excite Brenda? You can say. We're old mates.'

'Arouse yourself.'

'Join in, Al. I need relief from the shit I've suffered.'

'Stop it, Jess.'

'Get your dick out and have a wank. You need an orgasm once in a while. Do you jerk off regularly? What porn do you watch?'

The questions are ignored. I've never felt sexually frustrated. That's an honest confession.

'Have you actually shagged Brenda? When we came back on the ferry, you paid me not to have sex. You're weird, Al. What's the matter with you? Climb on top and I'll put it in for you. Can you remember what to do?'

I don't move.

'After an orgasm, I always feel good, Al. You might too. Then, my role can be discussed. I'm eager to work with Deb.'

'You can meet everyone later.'

'Orgasms focus me. Totally.'

I make no comment.

'Are you and Brenda tying the knot?'

'She says she loves me.'

'Brenda in love?' Jess cracks out laughing. 'Are you kidding?'
I don't respond.

'Do you love her?'

'She's someone I admire.'

'You're a sponger.'

'That's an insult.'

'Aren't you bothered what people might say?'

'How to deal successfully with criticism was picked up at art college. If it isn't constructive and helps with my work, I don't listen.'

'Me and Brenda get along great,' she states with confidence. 'If you're not fucking her, it can be my job.'

'That won't happen.'

'We've fucked before. I don't mind.'

Will Jess be a liability? That's what I'm thinking. Brenda letting her stay here was unexpected. Could Jess get too cocky and out of control? We can deal with that if it happens. Even sack her. Obviously, she doesn't know where the pictures are. My plan must be announced very soon. It has to be foolproof.

Giving up on involving me in sex, Jess moans and shifts on the table pleasuring herself. Two scruffy old maintenance employees, Jim and Bob, pop their heads round the door. Watching Jess with fascination, both fumble in their trouser pockets.

Full of expectation, Joanne bounces in with Shagger. One of the WLA soldiers took him for a walk over the estate. He's still overflowing with energy. Joanne shoos away the two men, while the dog jumps up at the table, sniffs at Jess, then yaps excitedly. Joanne's eyes are bright. A broad smile sits comfortably on her face.

'I've never been shagged by a dog,' Jess smirks.

'Don't knock it until you've tried it,' Joanne laughs.

'Or any other animal, when I think of it,' Jess continues. 'Have you?'

'Not telling,' teases Joanne.

'I've shagged a few mongrel blokes though,' Jess wisecracks.

Kissing Jess softly, Joanne takes control of the rolling pin. 'Don't masturbate, love. That's what men do to each other in filthy Gents' lavatories. We can have plenty of clean fun together.'

Swiftly discarding the white cap and apron, Joanne then removes her skirt, blouse and bra. Kicking off her flat shoes, she wiggles provocatively out of a leopard-skin patterned thong. Her boobs are firm, not spoiled by breast feeding. But, ruining her figure are rolls of belly fat and chunky thighs.

'Look what I've borrowed from Alice, one of the gardeners. These might be arousing.'

From a plastic bag, Joanne proudly conjures a batch of sex toys. 'Which one do you want to try first?'

Jess considers carefully, then examines a purple, double-ended, bendy dildo. After further deliberation they decide on what the packaging describes as a 'Vibrating Double-Ended Strap-On Dildo'.

'There are different vibration speeds,' announces Joanne sincerely. 'Alice said it's easy to use and the toy is very good quality. She gave it eight out of ten, knocking two points off because it's a bit noisy.'

'I've often found vibrators aren't very secure and move about a lot.' Jess is serious.

'Alice says this one is great and enjoys using it. I've brought lubricant too. I'll squirt plenty on.'

'Marvellous. I nearly came seconds ago. I'd love to start again.'

'Shall we join as one, Jess?'

'Why not?'

This is a side of Joanne definitely not seen previously. Climbing clumsily on to the table, she knocks three pies to the floor. Shagger is immediately on them. I try to move him away. Instead, he growls before humping my leg. Panting and salivating, his tail wags furiously before a kick sends him away.

'You're spoiling dinner, Joanne, for sex.'

'Don't worry, Al. Pie making is easy.'

The world is sex mad.

Within seconds, the two women link together.

'Oh, Jess, I knew we could have fun.'

'I'll be your baby,' sighs Jess, easily switching her attention to Joanne.

'Call me mama. I've always wanted a baby. I'll bath you tonight. And every night.' Her voice is syrupy smooth.

'Mama.'

'Baby.'

They pause. The vibrating dildo sounds like a malfunctioning circular saw. Shagger's continual yelping is also annoying. Switching to the double-ended bendy dildo, they continue.

The dog attacks more pies.

'Pack it in, Jess,' I plead. 'Brenda is due back any minute. You're distracting staff from their work.'

'Fuck off, Al. Join in. Rub our tits. Make yourself useful.'

It looks as if Shagger might successfully mount the table until Joanne thumps his nose. Unconcerned, the mongrel switches to devouring another pie from a foil dish as it slides across the floor.

With my mobile, details are recorded for a female orgy scene in a cemetery. What a subject, skeletal couples performing on tombstone tops. Vendors will be selling pies, burgers, ice-cream, candyfloss and cans of pop.

'I adore older women,' confesses Jess. 'They're so inventive.'

'You're a good fuck, Jess. I'm looking forwards to you staying here.'

The pair are at ease in each other's company.

Snatching one of the pies from the table, I begin eating. As usual, they're delicious. I've a feeling dinner may be delayed.

Constant monotonous groaning mixed with Shagger yelping, brings Jim and Bob back into the room. Dropping their trousers, they excite themselves. This is bedlam. Can we expect any more staff to show up? What will Brenda make of this? Should I exert more authority? Surely, she can't be away for much longer? I ought to stop her coming back in here.

Biting Jim, Shagger thinks the two men are competing with him for action with Jess and Joanne.

A siren gets louder and louder. Is this a fire drill? Brenda never said anything. We've had a few since I've been here. Everyone has to assemble on a lawn a short distance from the Hall front.

'Fire drill,' I announce. 'Everybody out. Quick.'

My thoughts are broken on hearing deafening explosions. Window glass showers everywhere.

Jess's screams of pleasure escalate.

'Come on, Jess, you can do it,' Joanne urges, as genuine as any mother might encourage her daughter in a school sports day competition.

'Push, Joanne, push.'

'Is it nice, love?'

'Oh yes. Yes. Please. More. More!' Jess bites her lip with eyes closed and head tilted back. Both women hold each other tightly. Jess's painted nails dig deep into Joanne's arms.

'Down, everybody,' I appeal.

Jim and Bob shuffle closer to the table, eagerly watching and soaking up the stimulation. Both must have seen plenty of sex at the Hall in the past, though perhaps not from a ringside seat like now.

The siren deafens.

Nicola has launched an attack.

'Yes. Yes,' screams Jess in delight. 'Oh God. Yes!'

'Are you there, love?'

Panting, Jess uncouples herself.

'Everyone down,' I yell.

Shagger barks wildly and snaps at me.

'Sort us out, Jess,' begs Bob. 'We're nearly there too.'

Brushing both men aside, Jess sprints outside. I follow. Big Ada is there. One side of her face is still swollen from Brenda's punch. Scanning the sky, there are two drones in the distance heading towards the Hall. Brenda must still be inside. No. No! How have they broken through?

Options were considered and lots of cash spent by the WLA choosing the correct systems for thwarting this kind of raid. Meetings were held. I attended most, listening intently to the detailed proposals and arguments. Various people and representatives were consulted. It's all counted for nothing. Incredible. WLA soldiers are obsessed by sex. It fogs their brains.

'Jess, Honey Bee, I love you. Let's die together.' Big Ada gawps starry-eyed at Jess.

'Fuck off, fat cunt.'

Jess punches Big Ada, grabs her machine gun and opens fire at the bomb-carrying drones. Exploding mid-air, they bowl us over. Smoke billows everywhere.

Coming round with Big Ada's heavy weight on top of me, I struggle free.

Jess jumps up, unscathed.

'Always feel much better after an orgasm,' she loudly confesses. 'Helps me concentrate. Try it, Al. An orgasm saved your life. It's saved everyone.'

# Chapter 46

The purpose of the meeting at the London office of Kirstin's lawyer is twofold. Firstly, to demand reimbursement for the Grosz picture, now deemed a fake. Secondly, make a significant compensation claim for the phoney provenance. Might Nicola bring strong legal representation to contest the claims? Unsure.

As a trade union officer, I was often successful in confrontational meetings with councillors. Hopefully, I can contribute significantly now. There's a genuine desire to help Kirstin and Anna.

The law firm's office is located on the fifth floor of an ornate Victorian building. It's situated at the corner of a T-junction. The edifice is impressive with balconies and wrought ironwork. I travelled from Askworth alone. Kirstin, Anna and me have arranged to meet inside the building. Jess stayed overnight at Mena's house and they're travelling here together.

When I enter the office's plush reception area, a staff member says Kirstin and Anna have already arrived. I'm led through to a spacious room where the meeting will take place. It's airy and has three sash windows. The walls, with period coving and dado rails, are painted a pale blue. A deep-pile plain blue carpet smothers the floor. Tropical plants, placed here and there, give a false air of sophistication. Sadly, the group of pictures on display clash horribly with the building's age. Those responsible for choosing the interior décor missed an opportunity. It would've been more appropriate to have a group of Honoré Daumier's legal satire prints, professionally mounted and in gold frames. Instead, modern prints, featuring simple, bright, geometric shapes, assault the eye.

Kirstin and Anna are settled on one side of a long table. They rise at once and greet me with affectionate hugs and kisses. Both are sad, nervous and anxious. I'm fearful too, my palms are sticky.

'We're pleased to see you're alive and healthy, Al,' declares Kirstin, 'after those horrifying experiences.' Holding my hand, she is full of compassion.

A smile sweeps across my face.

'How is Brenda? Is she okay?'

A whispered 'Yes' encourages her to release my hand.

'You're living under enormous stress. These ordeals are never-ending.'

'Brenda has stepped up our security. More sophisticated military hardware is being installed. To be truthful, it's frightening.'

Both women frown with concern. I'm apprehensive about how they'll react seeing Nicola face-to-face. They've never met her, only communicated by mobile and email.

Kirstin's lawyer, Emily Broome-Goodfellow, is seated at one end of the table. In her early 30s, with short black hair and considered make-up, she wears a dark-grey trouser suit. Her teeth are capped. No expense spared. She's married, as proved by both engagement and wedding rings. We exchange firm handshakes.

Emily's prestigious clients include film and pop stars. She's used to high-powered complicated wrangles and wins regularly. Emily is one of five lawyers in this office. When Kirstin disclosed their hourly rates, I nearly fainted. Why can't artists charge similar amounts?

The door to the balcony is open, letting a gentle breeze filter through. Outside, it's slightly overcast, the temperature just comfortable at 15 degrees.

Anna reiterates they're not interested in listening to any submissions about the Grosz being genuine. If necessary, written testimonies from two experts, as well as a scientific report, will be presented to kill any claims of authenticity. Having seen everything, I was impressed. The research was convincing. Jess must testify the photograph included in the provenance was staged. A confession from Mena will back up the statement.

One of the female administrative assistants brings in fancy biscuits. A coffee percolator is already gurgling on the table, alongside cups and saucers. To break the monotony, we take advantage of the refreshments.

The meeting was scheduled for 11.00 am. It's now 11.45 am, though neither Nicola nor Jess and Mena are here.

Both German women are tense. Their eyes frequently settle on the door, anticipating Nicola's arrival. We chat generally, but I feel restless and stand up. Phoning Jess, only her voicemail is heard. I resist leaving a message.

Emily sighs. 'We need Jess and Mena to be here. A statement confessing their part in creating the false provenance has not been signed. It's a weakness.'

Frustrated, I walk over to the open balcony door and step gingerly outside. It's a long way down to the pavement. I experience vertigo.

A multi-storey car park is a short distance away. I spot Nicola with a woman, presumably her lawyer, leaving the exit and heading this way. There's no sign of Jess or Mena.

'I've heard Nicola is a nasty piece of work,' announces Emily when I step back into the room. She acknowledges Nicola has links to various criminal and violent activities. However, today she wants our focus to be firmly on Kirstin's claim against Nicola. Nothing else.

'We must not be intimidated.' Emily looks serious, lingering on each one of us. 'From past experience, Nicola's lawyer, Helen Brickdale-Smith, is a formidable opponent. Remaining calm and professional throughout the meeting is essential.'

The three of us agree.

Whether Emily has ever met anyone as volatile or unpredictable as Nicola is another matter.

'I've told the staff to call the police straight away if Nicola loses control,' Emily states.

Nicola breezes in as if she owns the building. With hair

looking silky smooth, she's smartly dressed in a cream silk blouse, and brown pinstripe jacket. A skirt hovers just above the knee and six inch high heels are on her feet. Her make-up is heavy. Slutty. Having sprayed herself generously with perfume, it makes my nose twitch.

In her 50s, Helen Brickdale-Smith has a snub nose and is five feet tall. A light-blue silk blouse shows beneath a dark-blue trouser suit and they match with flat black shoes. She has cold piercing eyes, small scruffy teeth and her hair is dyed chestnut brown. Carrying a briefcase, she's comfortable, confident and solemn. The wedding finger is bare. Emily said there's no interest in men or women. Brickdale-Smith is sure to have done her homework on this case. We need to be on our toes. I'm convinced she is well-prepared for a fight. It could be a dirty one.

By contrast, Nicola has nothing with her. Not even a handbag. Brickdale-Smith introduces herself and shakes everyone's hand.

Nicola is relaxed in Brickdale-Smith's company. As though she's pulling along a howitzer, ready to shoot down any claims against her. Obviously, she's convinced that walking out of this confrontation with head held high is a certainty.

Nicola bounds forwards, blinking false eyelashes. 'Hello, Council Prick.'

'Could we keep the language respectable, please?' says Emily.

Untroubled, I ask Nicola: 'How's Frankie? Enjoying retirement?'

'Fuck off.' She grabs a handful of biscuits and chomps noisily.

Brickdale-Smith is uncomfortable and decides to remain standing.

'With your weirdo mates, Al?' Nicola leans close to Kirstin and Anna.

'Hello, sweethearts. Which one of you two is the stoker?'

There's a gasp of shock.

Nicola holds Kirstin's attention. 'I bet it's not you.'

The hatred between Kirstin, Anna and Nicola is almost

tangible. I'm appalled. Why did I ever decide to work for Greasby Fine Art?

Kirstin rises angrily. 'Don't be so rude. Where are the pictures you've stolen? They're my children.'

Nicola laughs and calmy shrugs her shoulders.

'Where are everyone's pictures?' Kirstin continues.

'You organised the robberies with that Russian murderer,' states Anna, locking eyes with Nicola.

There's stunned silence.

'You're making unfounded accusations,' states Brickdale-Smith. 'Have you evidence to support them?'

Anna is silent and scowls.

Emily listens open-mouthed.

Nicola giggles then rolls her tongue at the German women.

'Can we begin the meeting?' suggests Emily, encouraging Brickdale-Smith to take the lead.

Before starting, the older woman accepts a cup of coffee but declines the biscuits.

'Let's have this fiasco over quickly, shall we?' starts Nicola, biscuit crumbs dropping from her mouth. 'Then I can do proper work.'

'The picture is a real George Grosz. There's no doubt. We have evidence and reports from a number of experts,' Brickdale-Smith argues.

'We're not discussing authenticity,' swipes Anna. 'We want a repayment plan.'

Brickdale-Smith shows alarm. 'You both sit there as art experts and don't want to hear the findings of erudite research. That's incredible.'

'Most likely, it's been concocted,' I attack. 'Nicola is a scammer. A well-known one.'

'Who did the fake?' Anna presses Nicola.

'It's genuine,' she responds easily.

'Was it Dick or Paul?' I ask.

'The paper and paint are right for the period.'

'Bullshit,' I retort.

'We don't care,' Kirstin and Anna state together. 'We want a repayment plan.'

Emily remains quiet, letting her two clients take the lead.

'We want a repayment plan.' They both repeat.

'It's a real George Grosz.' Nicola stands up with a document in her hand.

'Read it,' she shouts. 'Read it, you fucking bitches.'

'No,' states Kirstin.

Nicola aims the document at the pair and it flutters to the floor.

Brickdale-Smith says any demands for repayment should be made to the new owner of Greasby – Brenda Fitch. As Nicola is no longer connected with the company, she's not responsible for any claims. Brushing that aside, Anna submits Nicola personally invoiced Kirstin. The payment was transferred to Nicola's private account. She's solely responsible. No question.

Emily is content to let Anna fire the bullets.

Brickdale-Smith is alarmed. Anger tightens her face. 'Have you evidence to support this?'

'Of course,' replies Anna, confidently handing over papers. 'We sent copies of these to Nicola three weeks ago.'

The lawyer runs a hand through her hair and scans the documents thoroughly, then castigates Nicola: 'Why haven't I seen these before?'

'Never received them.'

'Not true,' attacks Kirstin. 'We received a response from you telling us to "Fuck off".'

Brickdale-Smith sways with annoyance, glaring at Nicola. A large pin has pricked her over-inflated ego.

Where's Jess? It's incredible she isn't here.

'I sent everything to you,' Nicola snarls, ignoring her earlier lie.

'How was it sent?'

'By email.'

'I told you from the outset, service via email is *not* acceptable. Everything must be sent hard copy.'

'We want a repayment plan,' underlines Kirstin.

'You fucking dykes,' screams Nicola.

Emily confronts Brickdale-Smith. 'Please control your client. We need to have a meaningful discussion. Kirstin is extremely upset about what's happened and requires closure.'

'Calm down,' Brickdale-Smith urges Nicola.

'This meeting must not veer out of hand,' adjoins Emily.

Police intervention looks likely and the fake photograph still has to be mentioned. Where are you Jess and Mena? Hurry up. Don't let us down.

'I'll give you a fucking repayment plan,' Nicola announces. Removing her jacket, blouse and unclipping her bra, she flings everything across the room. 'This is the repayment plan.' She prances provocatively, then forces her boobs into Kirstin's face. 'This is the only compensation on offer. Suck these.'

Emily and Brickdale-Smith are lost for words.

Anna stands up, pushing Nicola away.

Undeterred, Nicola drops her skirt, swiftly takes off her tights and knickers before sprawling across the table open-legged. 'This is the repayment plan. Help yourselves. There's no cash. I'm all yours. Do what you want.'

No hint of arousal is displayed by the German women.

Brickdale-Smith and Emily are shocked. I'm not. Nicola's bizarre antics have been seen again and again.

Jumping up, both lawyers struggle to pull Nicola off the table.

'Get dressed, please. This is outrageous behaviour.' Brickdale-Smith hands Nicola her skimpy pink knickers.

She's ignored.

'You fucking bitch, Nicola,' yells Mena, as she flings open the door and strides into our room with Jess.

Thank goodness they're here.

'You grassed up my daughter.' Despite having only a short reach, Mena punches Nicola as hard as she can. 'Grassing. Grassing bitch,' she repeats venomously.

Mena and Nicola crash into the table, knocking over the percolator, biscuits and crockery. Coffee spills on the floor.

Kirstin and Anna stand up, at a loss how to react.

Nicola fights dirty, attempting to claw at Mena's face. 'Fuck off, little fat cunt.'

'What's happening? Who are these two?' Brickdale-Smith asks.

'Why are you here, Jess?' Nicola is shocked. She tries to dodge Mena's slaps, punches and kicks.

'Giving evidence against you,' hisses Jess. Their eyes meet in a mutual exchange of bitterness.

'This is a stitch up,' claims Nicola.

'I'll fucking kill you. My Jess was arrested and locked up.' Mena is irate.

'Who are these women?' Brickdale-Smith questions me.

'Mena is the woman in the photograph. Nicola claims she once owned the Grosz watercolour.'

'What photograph?' the lawyer quizes.

Boiling with anger, Mena has Nicola in a head-lock and, wrestling, they fall over.

'Nicola took a Polaroid of my mum with the Grosz,' explains Jess. 'It's false provenance and fraud.'

Brickdale-Smith challenges Nicola: 'Is this true?'

Office staff from other rooms get involved, wanting to know if help is required.

Jess drags her mother off Nicola. Mena has brought the clothes she wore when photographed. Picking the items off the carpet, she throws them on the table. Anna hands Brickdale-Smith an enlarged copy of the polaroid.

'The woman in the picture is me,' states Mena. 'I wrote a fake letter saying it was bought from one of the artist's relatives.'

Anna happily hands over a copy of the letter.

'Is this true?' Brickdale-Smith confronts Nicola.

Her client blubbers. The false eyelashes hang loose.

'This is totally unexpected.' Brickdale-Smith is exasperated.

She hasn't been properly briefed and is clearly unaware of the fraudulent activities.

'You pestered for provenance,' Nicola mumbles with swollen eyes and a cut lip. 'It was a joke. A joke. I thought you weirdos would find it funny. I intended admitting the photograph was bogus. Nobody gave me the chance.'

'Liar,' I state.

'It's true, isn't it, Jess? Mena?' appeals Nicola.

'Fuck off. That was never the plan,' fires Jess.

'This is scandalous, Nicola,' Brickdale-Smith fumes.

'Fuck off then, short-arsed bitch. You're useless.'

Fastening her briefcase, the lawyer marches towards the door.

'Don't go, Helen,' begs Emily. 'Everyone must calm down. These problems can be surmounted.'

Brickdale-Smith is indifferent, brushing snootily past staff on her way out.

'You've betrayed me,' Nicola screams at Jess.

'You betrayed me first.'

'I can't cope with this. I'll kill myself.' Nicola hurries towards the open balcony door.

We all follow.

'Oh no. What now?' groans Anna.

Sitting naked on the balcony's wrought iron railing, Nicola dangles her legs over the edge.

'Stop, Nicola. This is ridiculous,' I plead.

She twists round. 'Drop your claims, Kirstin. Or I'll jump.'

Kirstin holds her head despairingly. 'Why did I ever buy from this woman?'

'Don't come closer. Any of you.'

Tears trickle down Anna's cheeks.

'Drop your claims, German cunts. Or, I'll jump.'

Insensitive shouts can be heard from below as the incident grabs attention. Traffic is brought to a halt and car horns sound.

Kirstin grasps hold of me. 'Do something, Al. Please.'

Emily displays deep concern, unsure how to intervene. 'I'm calling the emergency services,' she eventually states, prodding her mobile screen.

The vile comments from the street continue.

'Jump, bitch, jump!'

'Want a last fuck before you die?'

'You're holding up the fucking traffic.'

'She can jump for me,' asserts Mena, showing only minor abrasions from the scrap.

'Me too,' adds Jess.

'No. She has a child,' I remind everyone.

'She neglects Annabel,' Jess declares.

Although Nicola isn't hefty, her light weight moves the railing in its mounting. Will it collapse before she decides to jump and send her plummeting?

Nobody wants to venture anywhere near the balcony, fearing Nicola might take them with her. It's a possibility in her delicate mental state. Only I move forwards. I'm uneasy. Sweat gathers under my arms. The last thing I want, five storeys up, is to cope with both a suicide attempt and vertigo.

From below, the horrible yells rise in torrents.

Nicola is crying.

I'm waiting for an opportunity to seize her, though one isn't presenting itself.

Kirstin and Anna tell Nicola they can drop the claims if she comes back into the room.

'Fuck off. I'm a failure. I'm going to jump. Don't try and stop me.'

'Why are you a failure?' I question.

'I need to be better than everybody else.'

'Nonsense.'

'Fuck off, Council Prick. I'm no good.'

'Consider Annabel.'

'She doesn't need me. She's better than me. Already. Everybody is better.'

'When Annabel's performing, you must be in the audience. Giving support.'

'Annabel doesn't need me.'

'Yes, she does. Always.'

'I wanted to outdo Frankie. Earn more cash. I've failed. He's snatched everything.'

'End this, Nicola. Care for Annabel.' My arms are held out

warmly.

'You look after her. When I've gone, tell Nigel you're taking her. He loathes his daughter.'

'That's not the answer. She needs a mother.'

'Nobody wants me. I'm a failure. I've no friends. Everybody hates me. I'm going to jump.'

'No.'

Sirens can be heard in the distance as emergency vehicles approach.

'Re-channel your energies, Nicola. Start afresh.'

'Fuck off.'

'What have you done with the stolen pictures? Unburden yourself.'

Her attention flashes from me to the street below.

'Give up criminality, fakes and everything else.'

'Fuck off, Council Prick. You're pissing me off.'

'Is someone threatening you?'

'Fuck off. Go away. I'm saying nothing.'

Mena is the closest behind me. Jess is further back. I fear Mena is ready to give Nicola a helping hand off the balcony.

Comments from the street are hurled at Nicola every few seconds.

Emily talks to office staff, still present in numbers. Kirstin and Anna move forwards beyond Mena. Kirstin appeals to Nicola in a calm voice: 'Stay with us in Germany. We want to help and protect you. Work together. Change your life. It's not too late.'

Anna gives Nicola a warm smile.

Offering her an olive branch is a great idea.

'Fuck off, dyke bitches. You're not ramming an outsize dildo up my twat every night.'

Both German women gasp. They're baffled and at a loss what to suggest next.

Two men force their way into the room. One has a camera and Nicola sees them: 'Take a picture before I jump.'

Her arms stretch out in an idiotic pose.

'We work for the nationals,' announces the photographer.

'Who is the woman threatening to jump? This is the fourth suicide attempt we've covered today. Two were successful.'

Until now, Emily has controlled her emotions, though loses her cool: 'Fuck off, gutter press. This is outrageous. Fuck off.'

Both men hurry away, as Emily raises a hand to them.

Bloody journalists. Always after a scoop from people's misery. Typical.

Nicola is intent on making a spectacular plunge from the balcony. She stands on the railing.

'Jump bitch, jump,' shouts Mena.

I hold my breath.

The railing collapses, sending ironwork and rubble down below. I catch Nicola as she falls back. We're only inches away from the drop and I drag her inside.

'Fuck off, Council Prick. I want to kill myself. Next time I'll take you all with me.'

Punching me, she dashes away still naked. It was heartening when Kirstin and Anna offered to befriend her. That was a golden opportunity to gather information and locate the pictures. It's gone. I must introduce my plan. There's no other alternative.

# Chapter 47

I pick up my mobile and locate the name. It's under a solitary letter.

'Is that you, Y?'

'Yes. Hi, Al. This is a surprise.'

Apprehensive about how he'd react to me making contact, I'm pleased his voice is warm, welcoming and clear.

'Sorry for not being in touch. I know you've phoned in the past.'

'That's okay. How are you, Al?'

'Unhappy.' I breath out heavily.

'Tell me more.'

'I've had a massive fall out with my partner, Brenda.'

'Bet you had fun with those dykes. Did they perform for you every night? I love a lesbian show. Can't watch enough of them. I'm wanking just thinking about it.'

'They raped me.'

Y is silent.

'I wouldn't have sex with Brenda. She put up with it for so long. Then, she and the other women raped me. Violently raped me. There's a torture chamber in the Hall's basement. I was dragged down there and humiliated. Now I know what every poor woman experiences when they're attacked. Dreadful.'

'I wouldn't mind being raped by butch ugly women. The more butch the better,' he comments in a half-joking, pathetic way.

'I'm not into sex.'

'That's a surprise.'

'I've moved out of Banton Hall. Never going back.'

'Are the police involved?'

'No.'

'Have you told anybody else about the rape?'

'No.' I release a few sobs. I'm performing well, not realising my acting capabilities.

'I'd like to meet Brenda again,' Y states seriously. 'She robbed and humiliated me.'

'I have a plan. A big plan. I want revenge on her.'

'Stay with me for a while.'

'My passport has run out. It'll take a while to renew. Why don't we get together in Askworth?'

'Give me brief details of your plan.'

'Brenda has gathered a massive collection of work by female artists for the new gallery. People have also sent art, worth millions, to be sold for generating extra funds. She's received lots of support. Prominent artists are represented. Many paintings would sit comfortably in the British National Gallery. Or, other galleries across the world.'

A pause is made to ensure he's listening and for any possible reaction.

'Keep going,' he fires back.

'I know where everything is stored, along with the security details. We must rob her. I don't want any reward. Revenge is enough.'

'This is exciting,' Y chuckles. 'The kind of job I like. Really like.'

I'm pleased. He's ensnared. Without any problems. Don't know what I would've done if he'd rejected the plan.

'Are you in touch with private collectors who buy pictures without awkward questions?'

'Yes, of course.'

'Good.'

'Stop, Al. You never know who's listening. I must fly over soon. Tomorrow or the day after. I'll enjoy working with you.'

'You can stay at my house. That's where I am now. It's small but cosy.'

'I'm sure.'

'We can visit the seafood restaurant again.'

'Aren't we banned?'

'Not unless we take Frankie or Annabel.'

Y finds this funny. 'I don't know who's the worst, Frankie or that lousy kid.'

'There's nothing to choose between them.'

'Have you heard anything from Nicola or Frankie?'

I pause before answering: 'No. Have you?'

Y says he's heard about Nicola's suicide attempt but hasn't been in touch with her or Frankie recently. I wonder whether Nicola's threat to jump was a scam. To force Kirstin to drop the claims. Dick and Paul said they would have gladly seen her fall from the balcony. So did many of the other staff. What Nicola might do next is a real worry. She's tenacious. No doubt she'll interrupt my life again, sooner or later. Her last words in the lawyer's office are recalled with apprehension: 'Next time I'll take you all with me.'

'Now the House of Greasby has fallen, who's in control of the galleries?'

'Brenda.'

'You deserve a reward, Al, for offering this opportunity.'

'Not necessary. I can survive on my pension or by selling my art.'

'I'll be in touch again to let you know the flight details. Pick me up from the airport.'

We end the conversation. Luring a person into a trap to be tortured for information is treacherous behaviour. Don't care. Never liked Y from that night we first met.

After a few minutes, Brenda treads nervously into my Banton studio. It's early afternoon.

'I've made contact.'

'It won't work, Al.'

'He welcomed my idea of robbing you. Loved it. Wanted to be involved.'

'I'm suspicious.'

'Y easily agreed to fly over here, still recalling his humiliation in the Askworth gallery. He wants revenge.'

'Let's see if the Russian cunt dares to show his face.'

'He will, for sure. Sergeant and the others must capture him.'

'It's fraught with danger.'

Her arms rest on me.

'Don't do this, Al. I love you. We're a good couple. Everything is fine between us. Don't spoil it. I'm used to you being here and can't stand the thought of losing you.'

She nestles into my arms, burying her face into my neck. Tears splash my shirt. Brenda is worn down with the constant threats. Another attack on the Hall is feared and perhaps one on the new gallery. That's been discussed often.

Regularly, Brenda fights with Sergeant and Corporal when discussing the ongoing security arrangements. I must be bold and make a significant contribution.

'We need the pictures for the gallery opening. Y must reveal where they are and can be tortured until he does.'

This plan is putting me at great risk. But, I won't stop helping people. There's a desire to be of use to Brenda, Kirstin and the Schmidts. I assisted many people when a trade union officer. Those years were wasted. Art should've been created instead. Maybe the plan ought to be forgotten? I can't do that. Is it a weakness in my character? Uncertain.

I hold Brenda tightly.

'How do you know Y was behind the robberies?' She asks softly. Lately, her naturally loud, commanding voice has dropped down a few notches.

'Of course it was him. Who else could it be? He's scum.'

'How can you be sure of a confession?'

'Sergeant and Corporal will persuade him. I've no doubt.'

'Why not torture Nicola?'

'She's crazy. Y is the main man.'

Brenda strokes my arms lovingly.

'I'll start packing. Deb must tell the estate agent to take my house off their letting list.'

'Please, Al. Don't do this. Phone the Russian bastard and tell him you've had second thoughts.'

'No.'

Brenda breaks down. 'You're all I have, Al. A beautiful person. The best.'

'I'm going ahead with the plan.'

'How can you trust Y? Let Sergeant and Corporal meet him. Keep away.'

'No.'

Brenda grips me. Kissing my neck, she sobs. The affection is overwhelming.

'Let Sergeant and Corporal get him.'

I stare into her warm face. 'We don't even know where he lives.'

Our hold tightens.

'I'm frightened. You don't know what you're taking on. This needs to be discussed further. Perhaps talk to DI Allsopp.'

I wouldn't dream of discussing anything like this with the police. Even though Jenny has been relentless in trying to solve the robberies and find the pictures.

'The police are useless. They've unearthed nothing about the drone attack.'

'You don't know that for sure. Jenny won't reveal details of her inquiries. You might frustrate the investigation or get in the way.'

Rejecting the argument, I recall brief details from the conversation with Y, mentioning his pervy desire to be raped by lesbians.

'He may live to regret that comment.'

'I appreciate your concern, Brenda. Of course I do. The plan shall be carried out.'

'Will he arrive on his own?'

'If not, Sergeant and Corporal must decide what to do.'

'I would hate to lose you.' She hugs me.

Her addictions have switched from sex and drugs to being obsessed with gaining self-confidence through me. Perhaps she ought to talk to Amelia about people addiction.

There's a knock on the studio door. Brenda wipes away tears.

'Who is it?' I call.

It's a surprise that Sergeant, Corporal, Joanne and Big Ada stand in the doorway. They edge slowly into the room. Big Ada's bulk instantly makes it feel claustrophobic. She's carrying a machine gun.

All four women weep, their faces ashen. Brenda and I don't know how to react.

Brenda speaks first: 'What's wrong?'

'It's Jess,' utters Sergeant, breathing heavily.

We stare at them.

Their heads bow.

'Wasn't she due back today?' I question.

Nobody answers. Joanne wipes her eyes with a large handkerchief.

'She was bringing Mena to have a tour of the Hall.'

Big Ada wails.

'What's happened? Tell us,' Brenda and I both state with concern.

'Jess isn't coming,' responds Joanne. With flour on her hands and apron, she's been making pies today.

'What?' I probe further.

'Not coming,' Sergeant repeats, her chin trembling.

'What about Mena?' asks Brenda.

'She's not coming either.' Sergeant glances from Brenda to me.

'Has something happened?' I murmur.

'Ambushed on the way here. Both shot dead,' Sergeant solemnly announces.

Brenda is unable to believe the news. All five women sob. The outpouring of grief is loud.

My heart beats furiously. I'm unable to digest the information and feel unsteady, struggling not to collapse. I want to throw-up, only calm myself. Nicola has organised these murders. Revenge for Jess and Mena making a fool of her in the lawyer's office. I was expecting tragedy to befall Jess. It was inevitable, considering how she lived. A terrible shock, nonetheless.

There's an intense display of emotion. Everyone hugs each other. I'm nearly crushed when Big Ada clutches me.

'Jess was my baby,' weeps Joanne, deep creases showing in her face. 'I was her mama. I've lost my baby. I'll never have another. Not like her.'

Whether Jess had siblings is unknown. Family details were sparse. Mena was a rock. She'd go to the ends of the earth for Jess. It's upsetting that Mena was murdered too.

'Jess would've been a great asset to the new gallery,' comments Brenda.

Everyone blinks away tears.

Big Ada's head is still half shaved, and I'm itching to ask: 'Do you really believe that hairstyle improves your appearance?' I keep quiet. Sobbing, she struggles to hold the machine gun.

'Put the weapon down, Ada,' instructs Sergeant. 'Or you might riddle us with bullets.'

'I bathed Jess,' Joanne recalls quietly, lost in the memory. 'I kissed her milky skin. Every crevice. It was beautiful. Heavenly. I was her mama.'

'She was my Honey Bee,' cries Big Ada. 'I'm sorry for raping her.'

Overflowing with hatred, Joanne punches Big Ada. With shoulders like a hod carrier, the larger woman stumbles, knocking over my easel and a picture almost finished. It depicts a group of skeletons ready to board a bus for a day at the seaside.

Joanne's eyes narrow in fury. Shoving her face at Big Ada, there's an eruption: 'Your wild overgrown bush nearly choked Jess.'

'I'm sorry,' blubbers Big Ada, attempting to avoid Joanne's kicks and punches. 'I'm truly sorry. I have to rape or pay people for sex. Nobody knows what it's like being big and ugly.' Craving forgiveness, fat tears drop from swollen eyes.

Unimpressed, Joanne continues the assault. Big Ada grabs her gun.

Brenda, Sergeant and Corporal react swiftly to diffuse the situation.

'You've murdered and raped people in the past, Ada. God knows how you've got away with it. You're a monster.' Joanne is close to hysteria and desperate for a release.

'Let's calm down,' Brenda advises, sighing loudly. 'We all loved Jess and will have fond memories of her for ever.'

A lack of fresh air stifles the room. I open a window. Outside, there's normality. Staff mow lawns while contract workers clean out gutters.

Brenda promises to organise Jess and Mena's funerals. They shall have a grand send off. Kirstin and Anna will be invited. All four women hug Brenda like she's their mother. Having the ability to take control of a situation, she puts people at ease. The women weep buckets.

I inhale steadily, allowing the nausea inside to dwindle. Jess was fun-and-sex personified. Are there any regrets about not having a relationship with her – or even sex? No. To have sex – or make love as I would prefer to call it – I need to be in love with someone. A lot of people have these lines blurred, though for me they're clearly defined. At present there's no urge to make love to any woman. I was fond of Jess though didn't love her. I love Brenda, though don't want to make love to her. That sounds confusing, but I'm happy.

Brenda ushers Joanne and Big Ada out of the studio. Both walk away without talking, but jostle one another.

Brenda and I sit down. Sergeant and Corporal remain standing.

'You can't move out now, Al,' Brenda sniffs. 'Events are way out of control. We could be gunned down next.'

Explaining my plan to Sergeant and Corporal, they're shocked.

'Who the fuck do you think you are, James Bond?' Sergeant stabs.

'You can't see him alone,' Corporal fires. 'You're mad to even try.'

'Have you two ever met him?'

'That's for us to know and you to find out,' answers Sergeant smugly.

'I feel confident doing this on my own.'

Sergeant dismisses my idea as nothing more than a hair-brained scheme. Both she and Corporal say I'm risking my life and should forget it. Yes, I'm scared, that can't be denied. I've never had a physical fight. The way Sergeant always looks at me, I think she's guessed as much. Despite the dangers, there's no backing out of meeting Y.

# Chapter 48

I arrive home, having picked up an Indian meal along the way. That'll do for my tea. It's early evening. The front garden has been flagged. A few tubs, filled with colourful shrubs, are dotted here and there. Very neat and impressive. Deb has organised the work.

Neighbours greet me and offer best wishes for the future. Aware of past incidents, they hope my bad luck is over. I thank them for showing concern. Many of the neighbours are honest, decent people.

Deb has added a sophisticated alarm system and CCTV to the house. Recalling her instructions, I easily deactivate the alarm. Strong locks are evident on every window and door. It doesn't feel like home any more. The furnishing is minimal. There's a three-piece suite in the front room, a table and four chairs in the dining room. The soft pastel colours chosen for the walls and ceilings aren't to my taste. A little too feminine. But everything is adequate for someone renting the property. The house insurance money was transferred to Deb and she's spent it wisely. There's pristine tidiness everywhere. Like Deb herself. Evidently, she couldn't resist placing plants in several rooms. A touch of homeliness. It's lifted an otherwise bland appearance.

From Banton, I've brought two suitcases of clothes, an easel and art materials. That's besides bedding and a few toiletries. My shrine to Alex has gone forever. Upsetting, it will take a while to accept and adjust my feelings. Tears sting my eyes.

Jess will be missed by many. She was a woman of today. A selection of the times we spent together is replayed in my head. Happy. Outrageous. Anxious. Sad.

Wiping away tears, I want revenge for the murders. This isn't an emotion I've felt very often. It's desperately wanted now. Only then concentration can be fully applied to continue painting. *Ars longa, vita brevis*. I'm risking the future mapped out for me as an artist by Brenda and Deb, only I don't care.

There's a loud knock on the front door. It's Trixie and Herbert. Wearing a bright-red basque, black fishnet stockings and five-inch black high heels, she also has rings glittering from every finger. Her plastic nails are long and decorated. Heavily made-up, she displays a jovial smile. Trixie is predatory, forever seeking an opportunity for sex. I sense that's not changed since we last spoke and don't invite her inside.

'Great to see you again, Al. A lovely surprise. I thought you'd gone for good. Lots of work has been going on. Are you moving back?'

'Only for a while.'

'I hear you're living in a country house with a millionairess.'

'Yes.'

'How much is she worth?' Her false eyelashes flutter.

'No idea.'

'You must be incredibly rich, Al? Bet you'll not work ever again.'

'Hope not.'

Why are people so rude? Poking and prying into someone's financial affairs.

'Thought I'd pop over and say hello.' Tossing her blonde hair, it half covers Herbert.

I look her up and down. 'Are you working tonight?' It's an attempt to be friendly even though I'm tired.

'Yes. At a police training college. About 200 will be there. My fee is okay but not brilliant. Four of my mates are coming for a live sex show. Men will be invited on stage. Most think they're studs. Though when sex is offered on a plate, they can't raise a smile.' She sniggers like a silly teenager. 'Join us. The others will be here soon. I'll make sure you come on stage.'

The last thing on my mind is sordid sex with a gaggle of low-life hookers.

'Thanks, but I'm having an early night.'

Men having sex in public on a stage, then creeping into bed with their wives, partners or girlfriends is appalling.

'Are you marrying this millionairess?'

I shrug.

'You need an agreement so that if she divorces you, there's a massive settlement. I'd want that in place before moving in with anybody.'

Holding herself well with a straight back, she asks how my art work is progressing. I mention the exhibitions and lectures planned for London, Europe and America.

'It would be brilliant if we could talk about art. I want to paint pictures. Perhaps you could give a few lessons. I'd love that very much. Herbert could watch.'

A car hurries towards us. Recognising Trixie, the driver slows down. Teenage lads are inside. Windows are lowered and ribald comments hurled.

'Hey, Miss Snake. Drop your knickers.'

Trixie pulls down a thong, giving a full-frontal flash.

'Brilliant. Brilliant. We love you, Miss Snake,' all yell.

'Lovely lads. Each one of them,' Trixie laughs. 'And regulars at my shows. When I'm in the street, they always shout.'

Trying to maintain friendliness is difficult.

Herbert wriggles on her shoulders. She adjusts his position to talk more comfortably.

Strippers performing in a cemetery is definitely a subject to tackle.

'I like earning pots of cash to have plenty of holidays,' Trixie waffles.

I'm desperate to end the conversation and close the door without being rude.

'I've only had four holidays over the last eight months. I need to get away more regularly. We ought to go together, Al, as friends. Visit art galleries. I need to earn loads and go away again soon. Lying naked in the sun is fantastic. Bet you're rolling in cash, Al.'

'I'm comfortable.'

'My friends are staying tonight. If you're still up when we get back, I'll bring them over for a cosy chat, and who knows what else.'

'I won't be up late.'

'You look sad, Al.'

'Two of my friends were murdered today.' I drop my head holding back tears.

'Oh no. How awful. Were you having sex with one of them, or both?'

'No, nothing like that.'

'I'll definitely look to see if there's a light on when we return. Me and the girls shall cheer you up. No problem.'

A neighbour, Mrs Dobney, approaches. She's an old woman, standing a little over five feet, with pointed features. Always exuding snottiness, I've found her to be okay.

'Is that snake poisonous, love?' she confronts Trixie.

'Do you think I'd have it wrapped round my neck if it was?'

'My old man is shit scared of snakes. Some blokes are.'

'I hope none of them come to my show tonight.'

Mrs Dobney strokes Herbert. 'It's not what I expected, love. Not slimy. I prefer a snake when it springs from a bloke's trousers.'

'Doesn't every girl,' avows Trixie.

Mrs Dobney walks away.

Trixie kisses a finger and presses it to my lips.

'See you later, Al.'

Over the next few hours, sketches are made, though nothing impressive. After taking a bath, I slip into bed. It's near midnight.

Jess appears in front of me, dressed as a nun, and in all-white garb. She's even wearing white lipstick and make-up.

'Shag me, Al,' she pleads, removing her clothes, though retains the head gear. 'I can have one final fuck before vanishing into eternity.'

She excites herself.

An erection rises like I've never experienced. It's embarrassing.

'Okay,' I answer. 'This is my last favour to you.'

We're in a house, a bedroom, though the location is unfamiliar.

'Fucking hell, Al. Is that really the size of your dick? Let's measure it. Wow. Can't believe it. A foot long and growing. That won't go up me. We can try, but it'll be a struggle. Never knew you were so well endowed. Never.'

We're both amused.

'What a beautiful dick, Al. Beautiful. Does Brenda ride it every night?'

No words form.

'It's like another limb. Try and ease it up. This will be my last fuck. I've got a wide on. I can't believe it, Al. Wide as the Mersey Tunnel. But, I want to take your purple-headed monster. Your purple-headed monster. You've a lovely purple-headed monster...'

'Wake up, dickhead. Wake up.'

The voice is recognisable, yet coordinating my thoughts is difficult. I feel groggy, switching from dreamed sex to an intrusion in the bedroom.

Opening my eyes, I see Y with six others. In their mid- to late 20s, they're six feet tall, and wearing black polo-neck tops, black ski pants and shoes. Two have cropped hair, the others shaved heads. All are slim weighing 11 stones. Pumping iron is obviously undertaken regularly.

'Did you phone?' I mumble. 'I didn't hear the call.'

The bedroom light is on, making me squint. A glance at my watch reveals it's 1.30 am.

Guns point at my head.

'Fuck off, weirdo,' Y jabs. 'I'm always here.'

'How did you get in?'

'We don't need keys to get in a house.'

'The burglar alarm was put on before I came to bed.'

Y has no reaction.

Shocked, I dreaded something like this happening. Dragged

out of bed, my trousers and shirt are quickly put on. From their brief chatter, it's easy to detect Y's men are Russian. Were they responsible for murdering Jess and Mena? Maybe.

Grabbing hold of me, Y is cocky. 'I want every password and code you know for Banton Hall and this new gallery. Write them down and draw diagrams. You're an artist. It should be easy. Get used to being with us. Until we have that posh dyke's pictures, you're not going anywhere.'

Forcefully moved out of the bedroom, I manage to steady myself descending the stairs.

The front door is ajar. All the lights are on downstairs. I've been outwitted. Naïve. How could I underestimate, Y? The keen judgement, once my asset as a trade union officer, has gone. Now, international criminals are being confronted, not awkward councillors and personnel staff. Although a life-long pacifist, I will put up a good fight. Survival is uppermost in my mind.

At the dining-room table, a pencil and paper are thrust in front of me. Y and his gang circle threateningly. Although boasting earlier of knowing the Hall and new gallery's security details, it's untrue.

Voices are heard at the front door.

'Saw your lights on, Al, so thought we'd pop over.' Trixie and four of her mates, bustle into the house. In their mid-20s, they're stunning. All have long flowing blonde manes, striking blue eyes, blood-red sensual lips, perfect boobs, Panda eyes and false eyelashes. Their black silk stockings and suspenders are a fetishist's dream. Perfume permeates everywhere. I expected them to reek of sweat after a night spent stripping and with lots of sex. Not so.

Trixie has brought Herbert. Another woman also has a snake – Alfie. It's like being in a scene from *The Jungle Book*.

Y's men gawp open-mouthed, following every contour of the women's curvaceous bodies.

'Got your mates here, Al?' Trixie's eyes are bright. Alert. 'We'll do anything you want. Fuck everyone senseless, as long as we're paid well.'

After plenty of sex earlier, they're comfortable being paid for more. Incredible.

Y's men throw off their clothes. Guns are cast aside.

Droping to his knees, Y bursts into tears, holding both hands across his face. 'I'm terrified of snakes. Get them away.'

'Fuck off, wimp,' snaps Trixie. 'Flop your own snake out. Let's get started.'

Hastily bolting into the kitchen, Y slams the door.

Using their own music device, Trixie and a mate cavort sexily in the crowded downstairs rooms. Watching them, two men masturbate.

One girl lays expectantly across the dining room table and two men perform with her. An orgy is quickly in progress. Bleary-eyed, I stand up out of the way. Cries of pleasure are heard from both males and females.

These are rare occasions where women feel comfortable with men using them for sexual gratification. Also, men are at ease releasing their animal instincts and fear no accusations of impropriety. A satisfactory business transaction is agreed between both parties.

My dream involving Jess has dispersed. Was it an anxiety or potential wet dream? Who knows? Regularly experiencing anxiety dreams, they tend to have a debilitating effect the next day. I don't have nocturnal sexual fantasies. The one with Jess was a surprise.

A commotion is heard at both the front and back of the house. Sergeant and Corporal burst in with 20 WLA soldiers. These women are giants. The tallest and heftiest I've ever seen. Their faces are obscured. Each one is uniformed in camouflage clothing and heavy boots. A few have pistols with noise suppressors.

Y's men are easily overwhelmed. Furniture is knocked over in the tussle.

WLA soldiers gag them, then, without breaking sweat, easily fasten their hands and feet using cable ties. Three soldiers produce syringes and inject Y's chums into oblivion.

A mixture of emotions fights within. What have I witnessed? Murder? Don't care. I'm relieved. Calm.

'Fuck. What's going on, Al?' asks Trixie, mortified.

'Not sure.'

Trixie confronts Sergeant: 'Who are you? You're spoiling the fun. There was a chance of earning good money here.'

'We're Al's friends,' Sergeant speaks with a flirty leer. 'From Banton Hall. We can take you all back with us. Cash isn't a problem. We've enough dildos to stock two sex shops. And there's plenty of booze, coke and weed.'

'Are they okay, Al?'

'Yes, fine.'

'Good. I'm bisexual. We all are.' Trixie is elated.

Soldiers slaver as they look Trixie and the others up and down in the same way Y and his men had done, minutes earlier. Trixie's girls play with themselves intimately, teasing the soldiers who can't believe their luck.

'Are you joining in, Al? You're welcome. Me and a couple of girls can fuck you.'

'No, Trixie. I'll follow you all to Banton, though won't participate.'

'You look awful,' Sergeant confronts me. 'Stop trying to be a hero. It's not necessary. Brenda isn't impressed. Leave the fighting to us.'

I'm humbled.

'Why is the Russian bastard in the kitchen?' Sergeant is nonplussed.

'Frightened of snakes.'

Her eyes roll.

'I'm pleased to see you. Thanks.'

A haughty smile creases her face.

'Brenda told us to watch your back. Good job we did. Your plan was shit.'

In the past, I've dismissed Sergeant as a sex-crazed, wannabe soldier, yet she's made a crucial intervention here and redeemed herself. Never again will I stupidly think someone like Y can be tackled. My concentration must stay focused in the world of art. It's the most comfortable.

Sergeant starts a lecture: 'You say the WLA is playing soldiers. Now you'll take us seriously. My dream is to command a women's army. Recruit members from across the world. Put right the bollocks men have dropped. Then, we might see *real* progress in the world.'

Taking Herbert from Trixie, Sergeant moves sprightly into the kitchen. Y is on the floor cowering at the side of the washing machine. A few of us crowd in the doorway.

'No. No. No,' Y whinges. 'Take it away. Please.'

'Where are the pictures you've nicked?' Sergeant presses him, holding the bemused reptile close to his face.

'Get ready, Russian cunt. More pain is coming your way.'

Y gulps audibly.

'Where the fuck are they? Kiss this nice snake, you cissy.'

He passes out.

Clearly, Sergeant, Corporal and the WLA have been watching Y. But they've not discovered what's happened to the collections.

Retrieving Herbert, Trixie and her mates are ushered from the house by a pack of WLA soldiers. Outside, it's deathly quiet. Nobody has been disturbed by the collection of vehicles littering the street.

Sergeant and Corporal order Y's men to be removed.

'Put dresses on them. Stockings and suspenders. Frilly satin knickers. Piles of makeup. False eyelashes. Chop off their dicks and bollocks,' Corporal instructs. 'The usual routine. Dump the bodies over a wide area. Keep the fucking police guessing. Stoke up their belief there's a serial killer loose. Fucking dickheads.'

The soldiers move with alacrity.

Big Ada enters briskly through the front door. She's naked and with a large pink dildo strapped tightly to her. A chilling sight.

'Where's the Russian cunt?' booms Big Ada.

Four soldiers haul Y from the kitchen, yank his trousers and underpants down and hold him across a chair.

On regaining consciousness, terror contorts his face.

'This is revenge for women you've abused in the past,' Corporal hisses.

'No. No. Please,' Y's voice quivers. 'I've never abused women. Always treated them respectfully. I love my wife. We've been married 23 years.'

'Lying Russian bastard. You told Al, you wouldn't mind being raped by butch, ugly women,' Sergeant snickers. 'Ada will now oblige.'

# Chapter 49

I drive back to Banton Hall following Sergeant and the soldiers. Y is with them. Overjoyed to see me, tears fill Brenda's eyes. We hold on to each other like never before. I'm pleased to have survived unscathed. I felt uncomfortable in my old house and it's great to be back at the Hall. There's a good atmosphere about the place.

Brenda feels the threat of an attack has diminished. The main person suspected of orchestrating savage killings and countless art robberies is bound and gagged in the torture chamber awaiting interrogation. Can I watch this? Yes. I'm convinced Y was responsible for Jess's murder and the one attempted on me.

Brenda can't be thanked enough for instructing Sergeant and the others to follow, then intervene when necessary. She's brilliant. I've never had a woman who cared as much.

Brenda met Trixie and her friends on arrival at the Hall. She's paying all their expenses. An orgy, taking place in the Hall's salon, provides much-needed relief for Sergeant, Corporal and a select group of soldiers. Joanne was invited to join in.

Even though it's the middle of the night, Brenda telephones Kirstin and Anna with news of Y's capture. She also intends to contact Otto, the head of the Schmidt family. I argue that making the interrogation a bizarre theatrical event is way over-the-top. My comment is dismissed.

The two German women are overjoyed to hear the news. Kirstin will charter a plane for them to arrive with Otto later today.

Brenda has her mobile switched to loudspeaker so I can join in the conversation.

'Let Sergeant interrogate him, then assess what he reveals,' I submit.

Kirstin suggests Brenda, Anna and herself, along with Otto, have turns in torturing Y. This is to glean specific information about their own stolen pictures.

Kirstin mentions she's struggled to locate other George Grosz and John Heartfield works to begin a new collection.

'Are my children coming back, Al?' She is tearful. 'My lovely children. Does the Russian bastard know where they are?'

It's hoped we can achieve closure later today. This search has gone on far too long. Personally, I doubt Y will reveal anything significant. What then? Mindboggling. I thought everyone concerned accepted the pictures would never be found. Not so, judging by the eagerness of the Germans to fly over here at short notice.

Y's mouth was examined to discover if a tooth concealed cyanide. Incredible, I thought that only occurred in spy movies or novels. Nothing was discovered.

Brenda mentions that if her pictures are located, we may have to put back the gallery opening date. I agree, as any damage has to be evaluated and repairs undertaken. She regularly contacts soldiers on duty in the torture chamber, checking Y hasn't escaped. I tell her to let them do their jobs. Everything is working out fine.

Brenda invites me to sleep in her bed. I accept. I once read: 'For a man not to be in a relationship and feel needed is slow death'. I've not been involved with anyone for years, but never felt uncomfortable or unable to function. We feel each other's warmth, encouragement and affection. Hopefully, Jess won't barge into my dreams again, seeking a final sex session.

It would be great to have children with Brenda – if that's possible given her age. Alternatively, adoption is a consideration. Might we relish the opportunity of raising a child, encouraging them to be involved with art, the theatre or music? Yes. Brenda would love to give a child a warm family life. Something she never had.

I'm comfortable with being a father again. Didn't think that possible, but I am now. Even though the memory of Alex still lingers.

Joanne is more than happy to provide brunch for the soldiers and strippers in the Hall's kitchen. After the death of Jess, Trixie and Herbert are to be her new babies.

Sergeant and Corporal are heard quietly conversing.

'Thanks for letting me go first with Trixie and her snake,' titters Corporal.

'No problem. How was it?'

'Bril.'

'Nothing better than a good orgasm,' Sergeant comments. 'Did Trixie put the snake's head up you?'

'Yes.'

'Like it?'

Both giggle.

'Different?' Corporal responds.

'Definitely.'

'Wiggle it up easily?'

Corporal smiles.

'You whore.'

A weird pair for sure.

Mid-afternoon, the strippers are taken home. The Germans arrive shortly afterwards. WLA soldiers collected them from the airport. Brenda and I are pleased they've arrived safely. We hug and shake hands outside the Hall, chatting for a while. I was inquisitive how people might dress for an interrogation and one that is bound to end in murder. Similar to Brenda and myself, all three have donned casual clothes. This includes open-neck shirts, jackets, jeans and trainers. Each one has brought a suitcase. Maybe they they will look smarter for the anticipated celebrations later on. Wealthy collectors appear strange wearing casual clothes, especially trainers. I've only ever seen them in formal attire. Kirstin has perfectly dyed hair with no unsightly roots bursting through. Anna's natural blonde hair is tied back.

The trio is expected to stay at Banton, at least for tonight, and longer if necessary. In the past, Otto and myself have conversed on the phone, though we've never met. Lofty and slim with thinning grey hair, he's in his 50s.

All exude an uncomfortable air. They're more familiar with strolling leisurely in art galleries, listening to art lectures, and undertaking intense research for academic publications. Each one is highly qualified.

Kirstin has aged from when I last saw her, which was only a few weeks ago. Lines are deeper round the eyes and mouth. Nonetheless, there's a gentility about her. The same is true of Anna.

Kirstin is the most talkative as we enter the Hall. Although a small woman, she usually has a strident voice. It's muffled today and nervous. Without focussing on anyone, she recollects details of the flight, experiencing a bad landing, and a long wait passing through immigration.

Blinking away tears, Kirstin is fragile. Anna puts an arm on her and speaks matter-of-factly: 'Stay calm. The children are coming back soon.'

Swallowing uneasily, Kirstin then wipes her eyes. I hope she's not disappointed later on. The skeleton orgy pictures she commissioned are completed and I intend showing them to her.

The Germans are offered refreshments, tea, coffee, a glass of wine, only refuse the options.

Kirstin is made aware that torturing Y will be disturbing and end with murder. This doesn't trouble her. With an evil look, she promises to kill him if the opportunity arises. There's no holding her back. Indescribable pain has been endured since the awful burglary.

'I'm pleased you two have found love,' Kirstin congratulates Brenda and myself. Anna and Otto share the sentiment.

'We're trying for a family,' Brenda reddens.

The visitors are introduced to Sergeant and Corporal. Otto views the pair with alarm, though Kirstin offers thanks for capturing Y.

The two soldiers acknowledge they're happy to help in any way possible. However, I sense they aren't convinced Y can provide the required information.

What do they know already? They're so sneaky. Are WLA soldiers watching Nicola? Who can guess?

Kirstin, Anna and Otto are impressed with the Hall, heaping praise on Brenda for continuing its upkeep. Kirstin's melancholy lifts significantly when she observes the jokey collection of dildos in the reception area cases. It's pleasing to see her laugh. The guests are led to their rooms and allowed to freshen up before the imminent interrogation.

Brenda has put many bottles of Champagne on ice. Although a non-drinker myself, let's hope the corks are popped later and there's plenty to celebrate.

Castration is a man's greatest fear. Down in the torture chamber, horrific videos of the procedure have been shown to Y throughout the day. This is besides playing tapes about Freud's writings on the subject. Jen also performed at his side.

*We're gonna cut your dick and balls off.*
*Dick and balls off. Dick and balls off.*
*You'll not like it. You'll not like it.*

Strapped tightly to the torture table, Y is naked. He's muscly, but was no match for the WLA soldiers who bundled him down here. Stinking, he's pissed and shit himself. Nobody has considered wearing a mask to avoid the stench. We're not bothered. Gleaning a confession from him is the overriding aim. Throughout the night, two armed soldiers guarded him. Others have been on red-alert across the Banton estate. Curiously, no attempt has been made to rescue him.

The three Germans and Brenda gather close to the table. Sergeant, Corporal and ten soldiers are present.

Sergeant removes Y's gag. Corporal sharpens a long butcher's knife with a honing steel. Pulling at his penis, she threatens to slice it off, then makes gashes at the top of his legs.

Kirstin, Anna, Otto, Brenda and myself have drawn lots for who is to begin the interrogation. I won and plan to extract the required information without violence. Let's hope my negotiating skills can be of use. Brenda has opted not to be involved. Sergeant and Corporal can substitute for her.

Y may prove a hard nut to crack. His ophidiophobia was amazing. I thought he was fearless. The Russian looks deathly as I lean over his prostrate body. There's a palpable hatred in the room for him.

Everyone agrees this is our last opportunity to glean information. It must be played right. I don't want anyone suddenly attacking and killing him before we hear anything. This is a gamble.

'Do you want to live?' I speak slowly. 'Your men are dead. Where are the pictures?'

There's a short pause, before my face is splattered with phlegm.

'You're all dead.'

Kirstin can't contain herself and dashes forwards to viciously fist his face and torso. He attempts to double up in pain though to no avail.

Kirstin's eyes narrow. 'Where are my children? What have you done to them?'

She has trouble breathing. Anna calms her down and says: 'We must keep him alive.'

'Speak Y, put Otto, Brenda and Kirstin out of their misery.' I lean closer. 'Or you'll die.'

There's no reason for this murdering, thieving dickhead to stay alive. Consistently, I've been against the eye for an eye, a tooth for a tooth philosophy. Often spoken out against the reintroduction of the death penalty. Lately, my attitude has changed. There's no reason for a guilty murderer to continue living.

'Tell us, bastard,' Anna shouts in his face.

Kirstin fists Y again. 'Tell us, Russian cunt. Tell us.'

He spits at her.

'Confess,' Kirstin and Anna shriek at him.

Otto takes a small phial from his pocket and slowly pours the contents on Y's stomach. He screams in pain as acid cooks the skin. Satisfaction shows on many faces.

'I'm saying nothing. Nothing. Never.'

A communal gasp of disappointment fills the chamber.

'Can I chop off his dick and bollocks?' Corporal excitedly

anticipates an answer from Sergeant.

After reflecting for several seconds, Sergeant nods, though Corporal holds back as my mobile rings. It's sounded three times over the last few minutes. On each occasion, Frankie's name has illuminated on the screen. I've ignored him. Brenda is insistent I switch off the device or take the call.

'I'm busy Frankie, can I contact you later?'

'There's something very important to say. Very important. I must tell you immediately.'

'What is it?'

Everyone stares at me. Y howls in agony.

'Paulene is on her way to demolish Nigel's church,' Frankie blurts out. 'Stop her. All the stolen pictures are hidden in there. Brenda's, Kirstin's and the Schmidt family's. None has been sold. Go at once.'

Switching to loudspeaker, I beseech him to repeat the information.

Everyone jumps for joy. Kirstin and Anna punch the air. Her children are alive. We must rescue them without delay. Brenda and Otto are jubilant.

Further details are extracted from Frankie. Paulene telephoned him a couple of hours ago for cash. He refused. Paulene was incensed. The house has been repossessed and is boarded up. She's homeless. Nicola isn't answering her mobile. Frankie hasn't spoken to his daughter for a while and doesn't know where she is. Gone AWOL. Perhaps with Nigel and Annabel. He believes Nicola is seriously ill. She ought to be in a mental institution.

Paulene is waiting for mechanical diggers to be delivered at the church site. Demolition is fixed in her mind. She doesn't know priceless pictures are inside.

'Surely, Paulene can't operate a digger,' I comment.

'Her studs can,' Frankie answers.

Fear creeps across our faces.

While, I'm talking to Frankie, Y spits at me through broken teeth.

'Say hi to Brenda,' laughs Frankie. 'I'm glad we worked out a deal for Greasby.'

'Kirstin, Anna and Otto are with us at Banton Hall.'

Brenda urges for the call to be ended. We must move. She doesn't want to hear him babbling.

'I hope everyone rescues their pictures,' Frankie continues. 'I'm glad the House of Greasby has fallen. Business caused too much stress. Threw me in the wrong directions. I'm enjoying myself and it's refreshing to be without drink, drugs, or sex. What a waste of money. I want to embark on a Grand Tour, pretending I'm a rich, eighteenth-century gentleman. Hurry to the church. Valuable art must not be destroyed. Be careful. Y's men may be there. Keep in touch, Al. We should meet soon. Toodle-pip for now.'

Everyone has listened in total silence.

'We need to go,' Brenda shouts, then instructs Sergeant: 'Take all available soldiers. Move.'

There's a mad rush up the stairs, a number of people stumbling.

I phone Paulene, wanting to explain that Brenda can help her. The line is dead.

'How far away is this fucking church?' yells Kirstin.

'A thirty-minute drive,' I reply.

'Hope we avoid a disaster,' Anna responds. Kirstin fists Y once more, then dashes up the stairs, desperate to see her children.

'Is Paulene a reasonable person?' asks Anna.

'No,' answers Brenda, 'she's a fucking nutcase.'

Corporal lingers behind, gladly taking the opportunity to remove Y's genitals. She couldn't resist.

Punching the air with a clenched fist, she yells: 'It's my hundredth castration.'

# Chapter 50

WLA soldiers are ordered to block both ends of the tree-lined country lane which leads to Nigel's church. It's situated in a quaint affluent area. Nobody must witness what is to happen. So far, no vehicles have approached. I gaze in awe at the huge church. Without doubt, it's beautiful. That's not a statement often made by me about a new building. Constructed in brick, it has a Neo-Gothic feel, with a tall spire and pointed-arch, stained-glass windows.

Paulene and her two studs, Tyrone and Ross, are already here. We pull up in Range Rovers and people carriers.

Paulene and the studs are dressed in white boilersuits. Ross climbs into one of two mechanical diggers present. Tyrone and Paulene are in the other. Looking comfortable in the driver's seat, she takes instructions from Tyrone. The machine jerks forward as Paulene attempts to familiarise herself with the controls.

WLA soldiers wearing body armour encircle the diggers and point machine guns at Paulene, Tyrone and Ross.

The loaders are outstretched ready to attack the church. Engines growl loudly.

'Move two people carriers in front of the diggers,' shouts Brenda. 'They must not attack the church.'

'Stop them,' implores Kirstin. 'My poor children are inside.'

The soldiers are ready for action.

Standing in front of Paulene's digger, I beg her to stop.

'Fuck off. I'm wrecking this monstrosity. Out of the way, Al.'

'Please, Paulene, stop.'

Revving the digger frantically, she takes no notice. Diesel fumes fill the air. The buckets smash into the people carriers.

In a rush, I climb on to Paulene's machine and plead with her.

'Stop interfering, Al. They've wasted my Greasby money building this pile of shit. I've got fuck all. Why? Why?'

'Please, Paulene. Stop.'

'Frankie won't give me anything. Nicola has disappeared. All I had left went on hiring these fucking diggers. It'll be money well spent.'

'Brenda can help you, Paulene.'

I'm shouting, competing with the digger engine.

'Fuck off, Al.'

'Brenda will pay your debts, Paulene.'

She isn't listening.

The armed soldiers prepare for action.

I jump from the digger.

Both machines manoeuvre past the wrecked people carriers.

Tyrone screams instructions to Paulene. Concentrating hard, she prepares to smash the loader into the church. Ross does the same.

'Shoot them,' Brenda yells at Sergeant.

'Yes. Shoot,' adjoins Otto.

Panicking, Kirstin and Anna hold each other fearfully.

'Kill them,' Brenda screams. 'For fuck's sake, kill them.'

Soldiers open fire.

Paulene was a friend. I slump to my knees distraught. Why did this have to happen? So many tragic events in life can be avoided.

Brenda puts a consoling hand on my shoulder.

A few soldiers climb on to the vehicles, dump the bodies to the ground and kill the engines. Thankfully, the church is unscathed.

Grinning, Big Ada wastes no time in tossing Paulene over her shoulder and strides away.

'She's dead. What can you do with a corpse?' Corporal shouts after her in disbelief.

Big Ada is silent.

Otto can't resist airing his thoughts in perfect English: 'I can accept women liking women. But necrophilia, I can't…' His voice trails off as he walks away.

Armed soldiers smash down the church door, eventually indicating it's safe to enter the building. Nobody is inside. Y's men are absent. I'm pleased Frankie warned us to be vigilant. Kirstin can't stand still for a second. Tensely wringing her hands, she's eager to discover what's concealed within the four walls.

Whilst the vaulted roof is impressive, the interior is empty – no pews or a pulpit. Nothing. Except four groups of pictures leaning against the walls. Most are crated, others are bubble-wrapped. Soldiers unpack a few. They belong to Brenda, Kirstin and Otto. We saved them from destruction with only seconds to spare. Incredible. Was this building ever going to serve its intended purpose as a church? I'm annoyed. Why wasn't this thoroughly searched before? Sergeant, Corporal and the police have ignored the possibility of pictures being stashed here. Many people would assume nothing criminal takes place in the confines of a church. Nicola and Y have taken advantage of that supposition. I'm convinced the pictures have been here ever since the burglaries. It's a perfect storage area.

Sleeping bags and fold-away beds with mattresses are in one of the rooms to the rear of the church. Food supplies, cooking equipment and laundry facilities can be seen. Y's men have made themselves comfortable. Are there any more of them in the UK? If so, where?

Kirstin's eyes glisten with tears of joy. 'I've found my children. Oh, you lovely, lovely, children. You're with mama once again.'

'It's okay, love,' Anna states cupping her partner's face in affectionate hands. 'It's over. The children are coming back with us.'

All three collectors display relief, happiness overwhelming them.

Kirstin affectionately hugs and kisses each one of her George Grosz and John Heartfield works. I've never seen anyone as euphoric.

'Oh Anna, do you remember when I bought this one?' She voices tales of how and when each work was acquired.

Brenda is emotional and regards me affectionately. 'I'm delighted, Al. We've found them at last.'

Sergeant organises transport for the pictures to be removed to Banton Hall as a temporary measure. Kirstin insists on staying in the church until the vehicles arrive.

Soldiers have gone to Nicola's house. They phone to report it's empty. Neighbours claim they haven't seen Nicola, Nigel and Annabel for a while.

An uneasy feeling causes discomfort. Once again, I recall Nicola's last words after her suicide attempt: 'Next time I'll take you all with me.'

On the way back to Banton with Brenda and Otto, I insist orders are given to discover where Nicola is hiding.

Otto is on his mobile, talking excitedly in German to other members of the Schmidt family. This is the most vocal and animated he's been since arriving here.

'There's going to be an extravagant party at the Hall tonight,' announces Brenda. 'I'm so happy, Al. We love each other. I have the pictures. Now the new gallery can open in a blaze of glory.'

'What more could anyone ask,' I comment.

'We could have a child. Start a family.'

'Let's hope so.'

# Chapter 51

Several months after recovering the pictures, Brenda is weeping. It's just after lunch, and we're in Banton Hall's salon.

'I'm sorry, Al.'

'Don't worry.'

She's lost for words.

'It's not the end of the world. There's much to enjoy. Together.'

Our arms entwine and her head snuggles on my shoulder.

Brenda saw a consultant gynaecologist this morning. Over the last two months, she's undergone a number of fertility tests. It's unlikely we can have a child. Further advice is to be sought from eminent consultants in Europe and America.

'We could give a child a beautiful, warm, stable upbringing,' she sniffs.

'Don't lose hope. It may still happen.'

Life is always full of disappointments though can have compensations. Whatever happens, she has my support. The strength of our relationship can't be compromised. It's strong. Very strong.

'Let's get married,' Brenda effervesces.

'Are you asking?'

'Yes.'

Theatrically, she drops down on one knee. 'Will you marry me, Al Cooper?'

'Stand up. Yes, of course.'

'Our wedding must be lavish, Al. We'll make a big splash.'

'I'm sure.'

Who could be my best man or give Brenda away? Maybe those traditions can be skipped.

The new Brenda Fitch Gallery is set to open in a blaze of

publicity tonight. Already, it's attracted much interest in the press, television and the internet – worldwide. Celebrating women's contribution to art, it's loudly praised as a great idea and long overdue. Representatives from women's groups across the world have been invited. Many art curators are to attend. Arguably, this is the arts event of the year. I'm certain the gallery will scoop many awards. Kirstin, Anna and Otto arrived earlier. They're staying with us at Banton. Kirstin's pictures are now back in place at her gallery – with even tighter security than previously.

Gold-edged invites have been sent out to activists in countries where womens' lives are brutally repressed. It's hoped we'll see many of them tonight.

Askworth's Mayor, Eric Dunning, and his wife will attend. I can't believe he's still in office after being caught with a working girl behind the Askworth Gallery. Other civic dignitaries, from local and nearby authorities, are expected.

The gallery's vagina-shaped entrance is spectacularly illuminated. How Brenda manoeuvred that design through the local planning committee was nothing short of a miracle. The city's tourism industry is bound to benefit from the building's opening. Already, Brenda is erecting a hotel near the site.

I've often thought of Jess. Thankfully, she's not disturbed my sleep again. Pity she wasn't here to help with the publicity and other arrangements. Though, Deb and the other women have coped well.

WLA soldiers have regularly visited Nicola's house and made enquiries, though to no avail. The family has not been there for weeks. I don't feel the WLA has given the search serious commitment. With Y gone, I suppose it's considered irrelevant.

Where is Nicola? Her absence is a mystery. Maybe she's in hospital or gone away. I'll ask Frankie if he's been in touch with her. He's coming tonight. It'll be good to see him again.

Detective Inspector Jenny Allsopp questioned how the pictures had been found in the church.

'An act of God,' Sergeant suggested, with more than a hint

of mischief.

Shortly before 6 pm, Brenda and I are ready to make the trip to the gallery. Brenda looks great, wearing an elaborately embroidered red dress designed and made for the occasion. Her hair is coloured blonde and swept up to fall in ringlets at the back. Pointed black high heels give her elevation and a rightful sense of importance.

I'm surprised to receive a call from an unfamiliar number.

'Hello.'

'Is that Al Cooper?' asks a confident female voice.

'Yes. Who are you?'

The mobile is switched to loudspeaker.

'It's Yvonne Carter. Annabel Greasby's drama teacher. Can you collect her now?'

'Why me?'

'Someone rang to say you'd pick her up when the class finished.'

'Who?'

'Not sure. The class started late. The usual tutor went home ill. I've stepped in at the last minute to avoid cancellation and disappointing the group. There are no other details than contact you to pick up Annabel.'

I wait to hear the little nuisance sing: 'Al is a wanker. Wanker. Wanker. Pulls his plonker, all day long. All day long.'

Nothing. Thank goodness.

'Who dropped her off at the class?' Brenda and myself are shocked and listen intently.

'I've no idea, Mr Cooper.'

'What about her parents?'

'There's been a tragedy.'

We're silent.

'Annabel's father, Nigel, has been murdered. He was shot.'

'Where's Nicola?'

'The caller said you were a close friend of the family.'

'Did Nicola shoot him?'

'Can't help. Could you pick up Annabel as soon as possible?

She's close to tears.'

'Do you think Annabel knows about Nigel or has seen something?'

'Not sure. She's more subdued than usual. Though acting has certainly taken the edge off the unruly behaviour she once displayed.'

'Will you tell her details of the shooting?'

'No. We're leaving that to you.'

I end the call.

'Poor kid,' Brenda begins. 'You must collect her. She can't be neglected. Bring her to the gallery opening.'

'She'll cause chaos.'

'A child must not be abandoned. I know only too well what it's like being in a dysfunctional family.'

Brenda is right. I don't want to aggravate the traumas Annabel may be experiencing. A happy childhood is the key to a good, healthy life later on.

I face Brenda. 'Do we tell her Nigel is dead? How will she react? Might she need medical attention?'

'Bring Annabel to the gallery. I'll make sure there are burgers and ice cream for her.'

'She might not want to eat.'

'We must see how she is first.'

It's an effort to coordinate my thoughts and actions.

'Do you want anyone to go with you, Al? Could this be a trap?'

'No.'

Before leaving, a call is made to Nicola.

Number not in use.

Where is she?

I call Frankie.

No response.

This development is taking the edge off what promised to be a memorable night. It's another occasion where I wish Jess was here. She could've picked up Annabel.

The drama school, on the outskirts of Askworth city centre,

is about half-an-hour's drive away. Taking one of the Range Rovers, I find the school easily. There's ample parking space. Housed in a large former synagogue, built in the Art Deco-style during the 1930s, the school has a great reputation. It's recognised nationally. Young actors and actresses from there have regularly achieved great successes in films and on television.

What can be done to stop Annabel calling me Council Prick and singing her little ditty? Careful thought is required.

Annabel stands with Yvonne Carter. I prepare for her to lash out with a kick. Surprisingly, she doesn't. Moving forwards sheepishly, she hugs me and smiles. This is a first.

'Hi, Al,' she murmurs. I sense she's ready to weep. Looking grubby, with lank hair and dishevelled clothes, a sweaty odour swirls about her.

Yvonne greets me with a handshake. A cheerful 30-year-old woman, she's dowdily dressed in sweatshirt, jeans and trainers. Her hair is swept into a bun.

'I came as soon as possible,' I blurt out.

Yvonne smiles. 'Annabel is our shining star. A great actress already.' She bends down and gives Annabel a hug. 'This young girl has a brilliant future in front of her. She's a natural and knows instinctively what is necessary for a performance.'

I'm unsure what to say. Annabel is a kid from hell, but I must be tolerant. No matter how long she may be at Banton with us. Nigel's murder isn't mentioned. Clearly, Yvonne believes drama exists on stage, not in real life.

Yvonne gives a short account of the drama school. The financial struggles, their achievements and hopes for the future. Throughout, Annabel occasionally grins when Yvonne makes a witty remark.

Then, Yvonne excuses herself. Clearly, she wants to leave and avoid any discussion about Annabel's welfare.

As I steer away from the drama school, Annabel is quiet. Not calling me Council Prick every two minutes or singing her horrible song.

'Did you enjoy your class tonight?'

She nods.

'Were you rehearsing?'

'Yes.'

'For a play?'

'No. A musical. I sing and dance all the way through.'

'Are you tired?'

'No.'

A pause.

'I'm in another film soon,' she announces.

'Good. Do you want to be an actress when you leave school?'

'I've left school. Got a private teacher.'

Noticeably, she speaks in a loud confident voice and the words are pronounced perfectly. Elocution lessons obviously form an essential part of her training.

'Where's your mum?'

'Don't know.'

A long silence.

'My mum's a nun.'

'How do you know that?'

'She wears nun's clothes.'

In a daze making my way to the gallery, I hope everything is progressing smoothly. Guests should be arriving in droves by now. Brenda must cope on her own for the opening speeches and ceremony.

Leaving Banton in a rush, I didn't change into my new tailored blue velvet suit. This cost a fortune and was made especially for tonight. I will look out of place in my present attire of corduroy trousers and open neck shirt, but it can't be helped.

A caterer has been contracted to provide an extravagant array of food and drinks. As expected, WLA soldiers are taking care of security.

The traffic on the road is light.

'Where are we going?' Annabel glances outside.

'To an art gallery opening.'

'Art galleries are nice. I liked granddad's art galleries.'

It's a relief she's okay about attending the function. I thought she might throw a tantrum. Then, I'd be pondering how to keep her occupied and out of trouble.

'I can draw and paint pictures, Annabel.'

'So can I.' After careful thought she asks: 'What do you draw, Al?'

'Skeletons.'

'Can I see them?'

'Yes.'

'I like skeletons. When it's Halloween, mum buys skeleton costumes to wear. I knock at neighbours' doors and scare them.' She laughs heartily and it pleases me.

'What do you draw or paint Annabel?'

'Monsters with big pricks.'

I'm not shocked.

'Came top in my class last year.'

'Do you like acting better than drawing?'

'Both the same.'

Pleased she's behaving well, there's excitement bubbling in me once more about the gallery opening and celebrations. Fingers crossed, Annabel will behave.

The Mayor's limousine is parked at the front entrance. Taking hold of Annabel's hand, we head forwards. I acknowledge Big Ada standing proudly outside. She forms one of the WLA security teams on duty.

'Hello, love. You're a pretty little girl.' Big Ada's bulk creases towards Annabel.

Shrinking away, Annabel ignores her.

'Is she your daughter, Al?'

The question is left unanswered.

Brenda is at the far end of the long, main downstairs gallery conversing with Kirstin and Anna. Frankie is near them dressed in a smart suit, set off with a gold dickie bow. Guests mingle, chat and laugh.

Painted sky blue, the walls show off the gilt-framed pictures nicely. The lighting and temperature are just right. They should be. Everything's digitally controlled.

There's a good attendance and everyone has dressed well for the occasion. A television crew is filming. Journalists are present and the Mayor is being interviewed. Press photographers eagerly point their cameras. Beautiful skimpily-dressed young girls and handsome smartly-dressed lads hand glasses of Champagne to grateful outstretched hands.

I'm overjoyed for Brenda. This gallery has taken an enormous amount of energy to bring to life. Deb, Ellen, Barb and Jen are present. They've helped Brenda tremendously throughout its development. Ellen is busy filming all aspects of tonight's event. An official DVD will be released celebrating the project. Barb is handling much of the PR. Deb and Jen work hard to ensure guests are comfortable. Sergeant and Corporal prowl like grumpy bulldogs. WLA soldiers patrol the galleries.

A nun is wandering on her own. Sergeant and Corporal watch closely and lick their lips.

Suddenly, the nun whips a gun from her robes and opens fire in ear-splitting flashes.

A safe distance is kept. Annabel's hands cover her ears. I hold her tightly. She must not witness the unfolding drama.

Guests are white with fear.

Brenda falls to the floor along with Kirstin, Anna and Frankie.

'This gallery's dyke owner is dead. Now I'll blow it up,' announces the nun. It's Nicola. A surreal combination. Nobody is at home in her head. She's gone. Completely.

'The bitch is wearing a suicide vest,' Sergeant shouts.

'That's right,' brags Nicola, activating the bomb.

There's a malfunction. No anticipated explosion.

'Nigel, you fucking useless, useless bastard.'

Everyone is open-mouthed. A few sob, dropping to their knees. Praying.

Nicola puts the gun to her head. Without hesitation, she fires.

'I can hear mum,' splutters Annabel. 'Is she here, Al? Don't want to see her. Take me away. I hate her. She's horrible.'

Nicola is dead. No more fakes. No more organised art robberies. *Ars longa, vita brevis.*

Brenda, Kirstin and Anna leap to their feet.

Panic is everywhere.

'Get out everyone,' Brenda orders. There's a mad stampede to the exits.

Fortunately, Kirstin, Anna and herself are wearing bullet-proof vests. They're unharmed. Frankie is still down in a pool of blood.

Annabel trembles. Her eyes scared.

Sergeant talks to Brenda as we hurry out: 'I was suspicious of the nun from the minute she walked in. Didn't behave like the nuns we've fucked in the past.'

'Not at all,' agrees Corporal

'We need our bomb squad here,' says Sergeant.

Tears course down Annabel's face. She tightly holds my hand. With both parents gone, I feel an overwhelming sadness for her.

High heels clatter as women begin an exodus in front of men. Some tumble. A few are trampled on. Outside, people vomit. Others sprint as far away as possible, anticipating a huge explosion. WLA soldiers hurriedly escort the Mayor and Lady Mayoress to the Council limousine.

Sirens are heard from approaching emergency service vehicles. There's a massive traffic jam as vehicles attempt to leave the floodlit car park. Horns sound and engines rev in frustration. People are desperate to flee.

A short distance from the building, I hug Brenda, Kirstin and Anna. We're unable to believe death has been cheated. Each one of us embraces Annabel. A pleasant night breeze cools our flushed faces.

Biting hard on her bottom lip, Annabel slowly looks up. 'Can I live with you, Al? I saw mum kill dad. Will you be my new dad?'

'Of course, he will,' states Brenda warmly. 'I want to be your new mum. We love you, Annabel.'

## The End